The
REMARKABLE
CAUSE

Advance Praise for *The Remarkable Cause*

"I enjoyed the characters and historical accuracy of the story. You've made the events 'come alive' through your excellent writing. Through the descriptive language, I could see, hear, and feel the excitement and tension of the era."

—Beverly Ann Chin, Ph. D., Past President, National Council of Teachers of English, Chair, Department of English, the University of Montana

"The Remarkable Cause: A Novel of James Lovell and the Crucible of the Revolution by Jean O'Connor is a highly readable account of Boston Latin School alumnus and teacher James Lovell. O'Connor captures the world of James Lovell, including the political turmoil; young readers will effectively experience the challenging times in which he lived."

—Malcolm Flynn, Historian, Assistant Head Master Emeritus, Boston Latin School

"A splendid book that truly brings to life our rich heritage of liberty—all the more poignant as we commemorate these historic events year-by-year on the way to celebrating the 2026 formal Semiquincentennial of these United States of America."

—Jane Lee Hamman, Montana State DAR Regent 2016-2019, sponsor of a revolutionary ancestor on Pathway of the Patriots

"The Remarkable Cause: A Novel of James Lovell and the Crucible of the American Revolution has all the makings of a classic that can stand with *Johnny Tremain*

and *The Fifth of March.* Jean C. O'Connor's dramatic chronicle of the events leading to the Revolution in Boston not only shows how each event impacted the colonial society, but also demonstrates the fact that the American Revolution was very much a civil war. Sometimes families were torn apart by the events taking place around them. The story of James Lovell will entertain and inform readers of all ages. Students and teachers will also benefit from the accompanying website that contains curricular materials to delve into the history of James Lovell's world."

—Timothy Symington, Professor at Mount Wachusett Community College in Gardner, MA and contributing writer for the *Journal of the American Revolution.*

"In her novel, *The Remarkable Cause,* Jean C. O'Connor uses Boston and a true historical character (James Lovell) to explore the many layers of America's revolutionary experience. Through sympathetic, memorable characters, the book illuminates the painful conflicts among American loyalists and patriots that tore apart many families and neighbors, along with the intrigue, fighting, idealism, and suffering that comes with the well-known curse of living in 'interesting times.'"

—David O. Stewart, author of *George Washington: The Political Rise of America's Founding Father* (nonfiction), *and The Wars and Wives of the Hessian Sergeant, a forthcoming novel of 18th-century New England*

"In *The Remarkable Cause,* Jean O'Connor brings to life the story of James Lovell in the tumult of revolutionary Boston. But this is more than the story of virtuous patriots confronting malevolent stories, as O'Connor shows us the nuanced and conflicted relationships among family members on different sides of the conflict. James Lovell and his father, both teachers at Boston Latin, the nation's oldest public school, both left their home town with the British Evacuation on March 17, 1776—the father as an exile, James, the son, as a prisoner of war. We meet other members of the family—sister Elizabeth, who flirts with a British officer to secure an appointment for brother Benjamin, who orders the wrong sized cannon balls, and see how this remarkable cause strained family ties in the creation of a new nation. This is a well-known story told through the fresh eyes of men and women who lived through and helped to shape it."

—Robert J. Allison, Professor of History,
Suffolk University, author of *The American
Revolution, a Concise History*

"In descriptive, fast-paced chapters, O'Connor successfully takes readers on a journey back to colonial Boston, exploring the celebrated revolutionary events that ultimately led to American Independence, while vividly highlighting the often less remembered harrowing realities...the Siege of Boston, prisoners of war, and how the Cause divided families on both sides of the political divide."

—Christian Di Spigna, author of *Founding
Martyr: Life and Death of Dr. Joseph Warren,
the American Revolution's Lost Hero*

"Brimming with rich historical details, and pulsing with the spirit of the Revolution, Jean O'Connor's *The Remarkable Cause* does justice to a forgotten American hero, while deftly portraying the years leading up to the Revolution, including tensions between loyalists and patriots, conflicts between citizens and British troops, and anxieties within families, as the path to war became inevitable. A hugely enjoyable novel."

—Nina Sankovitch, author of *American Rebels: How the Hancock, Adams, and Quincy Families Fanned the Flames of Revolution*

The
REMARKABLE
CAUSE

A Novel *of* James Lovell
and the Crucible *of the* Revolution

Jean C. O'Connor

KNOX PRESS
An Imprint of Permuted Press
ISBN: 978-1-68261-947-6
ISBN (eBook): 978-1-68261-948-3

The Remarkable Cause:
A Novel of James Lovell and the Crucible of the Revolution
© 2021 by Jean C. O'Connor
All Rights Reserved

Cover art by Cody Corcoran

Permuted Press, LLC
New York • Nashville
permutedpress.com

Published in the United States of America
1 2 3 4 5 6 7 8 9 10

For my family, who save stories, pictures, and letters.

Table of Contents

FIRST SCHOOL HOUSE ON SOUTH SIDE OF SCHOOL STREET.
1748 - 1810.

"First School House on South Side of School Street."
Catalog of the Boston Public Latin School

Chapter 1

The Boston Latin School

AUGUST 4, 1752

"James, would you split some wood for the fire?" Abigail's voice sounded shrill and weary as she called from the kitchen.

"Right away, Mother," James answered in exasperation. He set down the thick stack of books by the heavy wooden trunk that had been his father's and looked about the clutter in the bedroom he shared with two of his brothers, a deep frown on his usually smooth features. Here he was, packing to go off to Harvard in just a couple of weeks. Though he was a recipient of a Hollis Scholarship to Harvard, a graduate of the Boston Latin School with honors, still here he was, expected to do chores at home.

How many things has Mother asked me to do lately? James thought as he glanced down at the pine chest, layered with his best woolen coat, velveteen jacket, breeches, and white linen shirts. He had so little time to pack. Weeding the garden, dipping candles, tending to his younger brothers and sisters—all had kept him busy for weeks. If he could only get his trunk in order, it would be like a bridge to freedom, a channel to better days ahead. *Now the wood,* he thought. With a sigh, he admitted to himself that the more he kept busy, the faster the days would fly before he'd be stepping up into the old carriage and departing for the ivy-clad brick walls of Harvard College. He considered his stack of books, selected one, and put it back on his desk, then turned to go down the staircase.

A whiff of spicy apples simmering caught James's attention as he stepped out the back door. *Baking day,* he thought, his frown relaxing.

Across the cobbled paving stones of School Street, in front of his house, he glimpsed the brick school that stood just opposite the schoolmaster's white house. This orderly, serene, and respectable place had been his home for all of his fifteen years. At the moment, though, all he could feel was excitement about leaving.

A gruff "Hello, my boy," came from his father's study, window open to the mild air. James turned around to see Master John Lovell's expectant, serious face peering through the window at him. "Have you reviewed the information I noted for you regarding course selection yet?" His father gave an anxious tug on the soft smoking cap he regularly wore.

"Not yet, Father, but I will soon enough." James nodded and walked towards the woodpile.

"See to it that you do," Master Lovell said, his voice irritated, turning back inside.

Why must he always want more of me? James wondered, reaching the woodpile and looking about for the axe. James knew his father felt proud of him. His last recitation at the end of the school year had earned the approval of the visiting professor from Harvard and helped him win the coveted Hollis Scholarship. His father, the master of the Boston Latin School, had beamed with pleasure at the professor's dry "Well done," winking at James in delight before turning to clasp the professor's hand.

Certainly, under his father's teaching James had had plenty of practice in speaking. His father always drilled his students in recitations, which were really short orations. Every year the Boston selectmen paid the school a visit, their faces solemn, their manner grave. To prepare for these visits, the boys practiced speeches they had memorized in Latin. No matter how much they practiced, the schoolmaster's face would puff with anger when there were mistakes. He'd brandish his ferule, a stubby stick gray with age, and sometimes even smack the offender on an open palm. James himself had never felt the ferule's sting, though he knew many of his classmates had cringed at the sharp slap.

James crossed the yard to the woodpile and selected a length of pine. As he raised his axe, out of the corner of his eye he saw his older brother John entering the back gate.

"Your turn, John," James called. He held the axe up towards his brother. John worked several hours each day as a novice clerk with a merchant, a position that he felt entitled him to look down on James, even though John had not finished the Boston Latin School and would never attend Harvard College.

"I'm not your servant," John retorted. He brushed past James as he thrust something into his pocket.

James caught the spicy scent of cinnamon. "What's that you've got?" he demanded.

"I've chased off the starlings from Widow Wilson's plum tree for now, and happens it was baking day," John responded with a grin. He stamped dust from his boots and entered the back door.

Likely John's skill with his slingshot had earned him a muffin, then. Or maybe spice bread. James sighed and lifted the axe. Sweat wetting his brow, he stepped back from his orderly stack and passed an arm over his forehead. The August sun shone hot in the late afternoon and the air hung still and sultry. *Just a few more days and I'll be gone*, he thought.

He cracked into a fat log with his sharp axe, spattering the yard with fresh pine. *John always gets away with so much*, he reflected. Once, at school, his father had asked James to go home and fetch him his lunch. Stepping through the garden on the way to the house, he saw John and some of the older boys near the Stone Jail, behind the school. "What are you doing?" James asked. John laughed carelessly.

"See this?" From behind his back he produced a dead squirrel. James noticed a slingshot dangling from his pocket. A classmate standing nearby snickered and swung a limp bird by the head in an arc. "We're going to break up the boredom for those prisoners in there." He motioned to the small barred windows near the roof of the jail. "But don't tell Father. We'll get his beets hoed soon enough." John glared at James threateningly.

It was a privilege for the better students to tend the garden or to press apples for his father's cider. That privilege did not extend to tormenting prisoners, James knew. Master Lovell, who always seemed to defend John's actions, would probably just say John was high-spirited. However, if James had been caught flinging dead rodents into the jail window, he was pretty sure the punishment would be harsh. It seemed his father always treated him more severely than the others.

Yet he was a better reader than John, so it meant his father enjoyed spending time with him, talking about stories, myths, history, and philosophy. *Always books,* James thought. Sometimes he wondered why his father never talked about happenings in Boston.

For instance, once when James was young, he had glimpsed a crowd of angry workers by the docks, shouting and waving sticks, as uniformed British sailors thrust men up the plank to their ship. That was the press, workers taken by the British against their will, unlucky enough to be near the wharves when a ship needing sailors was in port. The press always caused a disturbance. He asked his father about it, but Master Lovell just sighed and looked over his spectacles at James. "The press is legal, though most unpopular. If His Majesty's ships need sailors—well...." He shrugged in resignation and changed the subject.

After that, James noticed more angry mobs. The Knowles impressment riot was one. James was about ten at the time, in his third year at the Boston Latin School. An enraged crowd filed past the school holding high a stuffed effigy of Commander Knowles, a tattered blue coat pinned over its chest, a black tri-corner cockade cap flopping loosely from side to side. The commander had not applied for the proper permit to impress sailors from the provincial governor, earning the anger of the mob when he forced some onto his ship. Master Lovell kept all the boys inside the school until it was safe to walk the streets again. Yet he said little to the boys or to his own family about the alarming episode. James thought forcing people to work on a ship surely should be wrong, even though it was legal.

Once a mob seized one of their neighbors, a customs official, and beat him because the official had been collecting unpopular taxes charged by the British on shipments. True, it was the law, but many in the town were disturbed at being taxed. James remembered shouts, men running past his home brandishing fiery brands, the clang of horses' hooves setting sparks in the night. The whole uproar frightened him. But when he asked, his father calmly remarked that people should not interfere with the lawful collection of taxes.

It puzzled him that there were issues his father would not discuss. Maybe at college there would be others who would want to talk about questions of law, taxation, right and wrong. It was exciting to think that soon he would be around individuals with different opinions. Perhaps he would be able to talk with them about the difficulties he saw in the town of Boston.

He hefted the stack of firewood and strode to the back door, whistling. John might get a slice of spice bread from the Widow Wilson, but James was pretty sure Mother would give him an extra piece of apple pie for splitting the wood. And soon enough these tedious duties would be over, he thought, and he would be on his way.

Chapter 2

At Harvard

October 10, 1757

"Wake up, James!"

James rubbed his eyes and sat up. The intense blue morning sky of early October gleamed in the tall windows of his room.

"It's early—but you asked me to wake you." The shrill voice of Mrs. Harding, the plump, matronly housemother of his hall on Massachusetts Avenue, echoed up the winding staircase.

"Much obliged, I'm sure," James called back.

He sat up, groaning slightly, and reached for his clothes. His stiff arms tensed like the muscles of the arm wrestlers in the tavern last night. *Too much cider*, he thought, pulling his shoes out from under the bed.

Since coming to Harvard five years ago, James had enjoyed visiting with friends and associates. Their conversations would turn to their studies, books, teachers, the issues of the day. Whether at a tavern, where he would meet others for a pint, or at the room of Edmund Quincy, where he gathered with the Katascopic Club, a social organization, James relished the friendly exchange of ideas.

Learning came easily to him, James realized. He felt proud that his Hollis scholarship had allowed him to attend Harvard. His father could never have afforded to pay tuition for college on his teaching salary. Moving to Cambridge had been the most exciting thing he had ever done. The four years of undergraduate study at Harvard flew by. Rhetoric, mathematics, religion, and science fascinated him. Greek, Latin, and even some Hebrew, he relished. Words were his stock-in-trade. Now, in graduate school, he felt confident his studies would earn him a better position.

How different he was from his brother John. John stuck with his position as a clerk with a merchant. His father seemed to approve, telling John, "I always did think you had a wonderful head for figures." James suspected his father was disappointed that John had not shown an ability to read well and become a scholar. Yet the schoolmaster would never admit it.

Last night James had been delighted to join a group visiting with Tutor Henry Flynt in the warmth of the nearby tavern, since the respected Tutor was now retired and rarely appeared at student gatherings. A spindly, kind-eyed fellow, Tutor Flynt had guided students at Harvard for over forty years. Those at the tavern last night enjoyed the discussion with Tutor Flynt as much as James had. His observations were based on a wealth of insight and experience and added to his reputation as a knowledgeable and reliable academic figure. *Besides,* James thought, *Tutor Flynt truly cares about students.*

James buttoned his waistcoat and shrugged on his jacket. *Saturday,* he thought. He would not need to report to his position at the Cambridge Latin School until Monday. Tedious as working with the small scholars was, it paid his rent and tuition, which was particularly important now that he was pursuing graduate studies. Heavens knew he could not ask his father for help. Master Lovell's teaching salary was stretched as it was, what with the needs of his household and James's eleven younger brothers and sisters.

He shut the door to Massachusetts 25 and headed down the walk to the library, the October wind whisking leaves about his feet. A few students trudged across the common, their heads down against the wind, satchels of books slung over their arms.

His stomach growled, and he nearly bumped into a woman with dark, luxuriant hair as he fumbled in his pocket, hoping to find a biscuit. She knitted her arched brows together in disapproval and turned from him with a swirl of skirts. James bowed, watched her pacing down the walkway, and turned to go up the steps of the library.

Hours later, he pushed aside the stack of books he'd been reading, stretched, and rubbed his aching shoulders. He stood to go. The librarian's assistant, a slim-waisted young lady with auburn locks tumbling from her cap like a bouquet spilling from a bride's hand, caught his eye and he found himself staring. Why did young ladies so captivate his attention these days? He could no longer look anywhere without finding some attractive, smiling lass tripping by. The librarian's assistant glanced quickly at him with reproof. He turned from her mocking gray eyes and headed purposefully out the door and down the granite steps of the library. The sun's last rays fell orange on flaming leaves of maple and elm.

Across the common, he reached the homestead of Jonathan Hastings, the prosperous tanner whose wife served the evening meals he so enjoyed.

"Come in," Jonathan said, opening the stout door to his spacious home. "We're about to break bread."

James followed him to the dining room and found a seat at one of the two long oaken tables near the other students. Candles sparkled on the mantel and a bright fire crackled on the hearth. The students were discussing the latest speech by Edward Holyoke, the portly president of Harvard.

Little Mrs. Hastings, nearly as wide as she was tall, entered the dining room, deftly balancing a tray of sliced beef and gravy, while her much heavier daughter Susanna, an Amazon in dark green muslin, followed, bearing tureens of mashed turnips and carrots.

James stole a glance at Susanna. A few years older than he, she was not blessed with a comely appearance, but her strong, fleshy face and thick brown hair were surprisingly pleasing to him. Susanna bent to offer him a tray of warm rolls, fresh from the oven. Her sleeves, rolled to the elbow, revealed clear, softly dimpled skin and sturdy forearms.

"Thank you," James said, as she placed a pat of butter near the roll. Lavender and lanolin, clean and fresh, clung to her ample skirts.

"You are welcome," Susanna breathed, revealing a broken front tooth. Her brown eyes sparkled with warmth, and a mischievous expression caught his glance.

James stopped staring at her and quickly averted his eyes.

"I do appreciate the food—it has been a long, tedious day. My shoulders ache from hunching over books."

"Perhaps later if you return I could apply a poultice—cinnamon and cloves is said to draw out the ache of sore muscles," Susanna said knowingly.

"I may do that. Thank you kindly for the suggestion," James said, reaching for his bread and knife. A flush of emotion reddened his cheek.

Susanna glided away like an enormous ship under sail, but the rest of the evening—as she bore pitchers of water, fetched more vegetables, and carried in mince pie, spicy and fragrant—he kept glancing at her. For all of her size and sturdy appearance, she seemed to him most comely.

◯◢◢◢◖

The evening at the tavern was, as always, long and enjoyable. James enjoyed nothing better than getting together with acquaintances. Cider, fresh from the fall's pressing, and roast chestnuts made for agreeable complements to the lively conversation. James also tipped several glasses of spiced wine, sweet and strong. Tutor Henry Flynt was not in attendance, but the old man's remarks from the night before were discussed and considered by the group of friends clustered by the fireplace. James forgot that the morrow would be Sunday and he'd be expected in church. The talk went on, exciting and fascinating. James was just finishing his last glass of spiced wine when the clock struck ten. To his surprise, the evening had reached the curfew hour. When he finally left the tavern shortly afterwards, his head was spinning, his tongue thick.

The night watch had ceased his round, and the common was dark and quiet. James walked past the tanner's house, skirting the spreading maple with its rustling orange leaves. The window of the back door glowed with candlelight. He paused at the brick walk, uncertain. The door opened and there stood Susanna Hastings, her thick white night dress flowing to the ground, a candle in her hand. *She certainly is large,* James thought, *but friendly and thoughtful.*

"Come in," she said softly. "I've been waiting for you. I can rub the ache out of your shoulders."

James nodded gratefully and stepped into the small entryway. His head groggy with drink and weariness, he gripped her hand, accepting its tender strength as he followed her up the narrow stairs.

Chapter 3

Wedding Plans

JULY 9, 1760

In May of 1760 James concluded his studies at Harvard and accepted a position as his father's usher in the Boston South Latin School. His graduate degree completed, it was time for him to move on and assume a more prominent position than he'd held at the Cambridge Latin School. As usher at the Boston South Latin School, he would be a teacher alongside his father, an assistant responsible for some of the teaching duties. True, he would be paid only sixty pounds a year, but he could look forward to that sum improving in time. He would be in charge of teaching the younger classes, known at the Boston South Latin School as forms. James whistled as he packed his boxes to leave Cambridge.

When Tutor Henry Flynt died in the winter of 1760, James gave the oration at his funeral. Remembering the old man with fondness, he penned the speech carefully in his precise, flowing handwriting. Eloquently, he thought, it began, "At length happy old man, composed in pleasing peace, you have left this mortal state, having finished the labors of life, and fully enjoyed your wishes; you leave us mourning for the loss of you, and go to receive the rewards of a faithful servant." James knew he would truly miss the friendly old tutor.

"A Funeral Oration."
Courtesy Harvard Houghton Archives

Back in Boston, James moved in with his parents to the house on School Street. One Sunday he decided to visit the more formal Trinity Church with some friends. He had been attending the liberal First Church of Cambridge while at Harvard. Usually his parents went to the church at Brattle Square in Boston, a Congregational church. Trinity, an Episcopal church, was an Anglican church aligned with the Church of England. The minister generally offered shorter sermons than those in the Puritan churches to which James was accustomed. He thought the large wooden building plain in appearance, but once inside, he looked appreciatively at the lovely paintings glowing on the walls.

The minister, in his black robes, shook James's hand at the door. "It is good to meet you this fine morning. I hope you enjoy our service." James took his hat off and bowed, then felt his hat bump something behind him. He turned to see a laughing young lady, red curls bouncing on her flushed cheeks, her blue eyes sparkling with amusement.

"Hello," said James, stepping back for a better look at the charming sight. "I hope I did not disturb you."

"You did not," she said, smiling through even, white teeth, "but I accept your apology."

"I am James Lovell," he said impetuously. "I am looking forward to the morning's talk. And you are?" he asked.

"I am Mary Middleton. And these," she quickly pointed to a gray-haired matron clutching a muff and a sturdy, thick-set gentleman looking anxiously at her, "are my parents—David Flick, and my mother, Anne Middleton Flick."

"I am pleased to meet you," David said, bowing solemnly. Anne curtsied politely but said nothing.

Mary turned with a flip of her red curls to go into the church, and James found himself wanting to follow her. He breathed a sigh of relief when David Flick said, "It would be an honor if you'd sit in our pew with us."

"Oh, I would be most pleased to accompany you," James said. He followed the family in and found, to his delight, that he was seated right next to Mary. Most of the service he could hardly concentrate for considering her cheerful red curls, her soft dimples and quick smile, and the heady fragrance of her perfume. Since the name of her parents, Flick, was different from her own surname of Middleton, James thought that David must be her stepfather. Perhaps her own father had died. It was a mystery about Mary that he knew he would clear up, by and by.

James returned to Trinity the next week and the weeks after that to meet Mary and her parents. After a few weeks, David Flick asked if he would like to join them at their home for Sunday dinner. James answered with enthusiasm that he was more than happy to come. He had been hoping for such an invitation. Soon he became a regular visitor to their home on Sundays.

Mary's company became an increasing delight to James. She had a quick wit and offered lively thoughts on so many topics he had never thought about, such as music, gardening, and marketing. When he complimented the family on the tasty fried codfish balls served one Sunday, Anne Middleton Flick nodded to Mary, who explained, smiling, how she had prepared them from dried salted cod. After dinner, Mary played popular songs on the harpsichord that James had never heard, while he watched the rainbow light from fine cut glass candleholders sparkling on the carpet and tried not to notice her slim waist and flushed rosy cheeks.

In fact, it was becoming more and more difficult for James not to realize he was quite attracted to Mary, appreciating her pleasant nature and thoughtfulness while wondering if he would ever touch her bouncing red curls or kiss her scented cheek.

One Wednesday evening in late summer, James came to the Flicks' home. He wore his best linen shirt and brushed his brown hair back, tying it with a black ribbon. The mirror at home had assured him he looked his best, but he still felt nervous when he rapped on their white door.

"David, I have something I would like to talk with you about," he said, when Mary's stepfather opened the door.

"Certainly. Come in with me to the parlor. Mary is in the garden." David motioned James in.

James cleared his throat. "I wish to ask you for Mary's hand in marriage," he said. He glanced anxiously at the older gentleman. He felt his every fortune turned on what David would say. "I find her delightful in all ways. Will you consider it?"

"You have my permission and my blessing," David responded, shaking James's hand. "I know how fond you are of Mary, and I believe she, as well, is fond of you." He shook James's hand with a powerful grasp. "Come, I will take you to her." David led James to the back door and opened it to the garden.

"Look who's come to see you, my dear," said David, calling to Mary. "I will leave you two young people alone for a time," he added. "Enjoy the beautiful evening."

James shook David's hand. "Thank you, sir." Across the garden, Mary set down the basket of vegetables she had been picking and walked over to him. David smiled and went inside.

"Why, hello, James. It is a pleasure to see you—and it's not even Sunday!" Mary said. She stood before him, brushing grains of dirt from her hands.

James laughed. "I have something to talk with you about. Thank you for taking time from your gardening for me."

Mary smiled. "I always have time for you. I can pick lettuce any time." She motioned for him to have a seat beside her on the iron settee under the arbor. A bush bearing fragrant roses climbed over the arbor and sheltered the two from the sun's bright rays.

James sat down and kissed Mary's cheek. She blushed prettily and moved an inch closer to him. The scent of crimson roses perfumed the air; puffy clouds sailed through the deep summer sky. "My dear, I have enjoyed being with you and learning about you more than I can state. I want you to be in my life. Will you marry me?"

There, he'd done it. He looked at her anxiously. But the words were no sooner out of his mouth than Mary smiled hugely and clapped her hands.

"James, I was beginning to think you never would ask me. Of course I will!" Her face glowed with happiness.

"I am so glad!" James answered. He rose to his feet in excitement. "You know I love you."

James sat down next to Mary and wrapped her in a warm embrace. Then he kissed her, a moment he felt he had waited for an eternity. All was quiet, as each thought of the exciting prospect to come.

Clearing his throat, James gave Mary a look of assurance. "We will marry this fall, November, I think, after I have settled in to my position as usher, teaching alongside my father."

"That will be delightful," Mary said, smiling back.

"I am so looking forward to our wedding!" James said. He pictured Mary in a white silk dress, a bouquet in her hand. "I shall learn all about your customs and those of your family."

"I look forward to it as well, my dear," Mary said, her cheeks flushed. More seriously, she went on. "You should know I was still young when my father Alexander—who brought us from Scotland—died. My mother, Ann Todd Middleton, remarried David Flick, who you know works as foreman in Mr. James Smith's sugar refinery on Brattle Street. He has been my father for much of my life.

"My mother, however, tells me of the Scottish customs she learned from my father, so you will learn of those. I can sing to you 'Auld Lang Syne' and make you a plate of fish and chips so tasty you'll want more." She laughed.

"I've always loved fish and chips," James said.

"Just think how beautiful Trinity Church will look, with garlands of flowers and candles in November," said Mary. She sighed and leaned back on the iron settee, giving James a long look.

"It is a beautiful church, but no more beautiful than you," James said gallantly, and planted another kiss on her springy red hair.

He paused and his face grew serious. "There is something I must tell you, my dear," he said. James took Mary's soft hand in his. This moment would be hard, but he must be clear.

Mary's blue eyes opened wide. *What could be the problem?* She said nothing, but watched James intently.

"More than two years ago—while at my internship—I met an older lady, a daughter of Jonathan Hastings, the tanner, with whom I took my meals. We struck up an acquaintance and I kept her company for an evening, maybe two. But no more, in truth."

James cleared his throat and went on. "I realized I wanted no more to do with her, and did not return to the house to take my meals."

He looked anxiously at Mary, then resumed. "When I finished my graduate studies, I moved back here to accept my teaching job."

James looked awkwardly up at the sky, and Mary sensed his discomfort. She glanced down at the thick grass, patiently waiting.

"Imagine my surprise when her father sent word to me two summers ago that he needed to speak to me. I travelled to his home, and there I was admitted. Jonathan took me into the parlor and told me that Susanna had had a child, and died giving birth. I sat in shock for some time. At length I asked how the child was doing. Jonathan answered that he was a sturdy little boy, and that the family were fortunate to have found a nurse. Then he looked right at me and his eyes grew very dark. 'We have named the baby James,' he said.

"I did not know what to say to this. My mind was reeling. Jonathan then said they asked Susanna again and again who the father was, and she refused to say until the very end. Just when the baby was coming she told him, but by then she was worn and weary, at the point of exhaustion."

Mary gasped and took her hand away from James. Her face grew troubled.

"Not knowing what to say, I then told him that I must take my leave and wished him well. He replied, 'How can you think of leaving? You know that child is yours.' I replied I did not know, and indeed I was so distraught I could scarcely think. So I left. Scarcely a day went by I did not think of the child, for though I did not know of the passing of the mother, I wished to do well for the child, since it did seem possible it was mine.

"A year later I was walking on the common and I chanced upon Jonathan the tanner. He stopped me near his home. He told me James was a year old now, and doing very well. He insisted on my coming to his house to see him. And so I did. James is a beautiful little boy. I saw traces of myself in his complexion and eyes."

James stopped and coughed hollowly. He hoped with all his heart that Mary would forgive him, but he must go on. Then he resumed.

"My heart softened towards the little fellow. I knelt to him and took his hands. Jonathan relaxed at this and smiled, for he could see I was beginning to accept the child. I told Jonathan I would come back and send some money each month. And I have kept my word."

Mary said nothing, only looked across the green lawn at the blooming rosebushes with a somber expression. James feared he was casting off all possibility of their relationship. Yet he had to continue.

"Before long I told Jonathan I would make a public confession of my responsibility at the church. This I have done at the First Church of Cambridge and I have received full pardon. Jonathan's family continues to care for him, but when I am married, he will become part of my house— perhaps when he is a bit older—if you will have him."

James looked at Mary uncertainly. So many of his feelings were open and revealed that it was hard for him to remain steady.

She looked up and met his eyes. Her lips trembled, but her blue eyes looked firmly at his. "He is a part of you, and of course I shall love him. I am sure he will be part of our family."

James sighed deeply and took Mary's hand in his own again. A tremendous feeling of relief flooded over him.

"Mary, you are so good. It is for reasons such as this that I love you. I should tell you these things while we have time before our wedding, but, my dear, you have made me very happy."

Mary's blue eyes, like the color of cornflowers, James thought, looked longingly at him. "I am more than happy to be his mother and to be your wife. Do not worry. We will be together and that is what matters."

He kissed her again on the cheek. "James is a good little fellow and you will love him. My position at the Boston South Latin School as usher for my father, the school master, allows me to teach the boys and will permit us to live well if we are frugal."

"All good Scots know how to be frugal," Mary said willingly. "I know how to bake and brew, how to spin and weave. We will do very well."

"I shall be so happy when our wedding time comes. In the meanwhile I am saving money so that we may furnish our home. My dearest, I will call on you soon," James said, pulling Mary to her feet. He took her arm in his and walked her to her door. The sun lingered in the west, touching silver clouds with bronze, and the warmth of the day cooled in a soft breeze. A lark's warble carried from the trees nearby. "Thank you, my dear. I love you," he said, his heart overflowing with happiness.

"I love you as well," Mary responded. She gave him a kiss on the cheek and he walked her to her door, his hand light on her shoulder, enjoying her radiant smile.

There goes a fine woman, James thought, as she softly shut the door. *I am the most fortunate human being on earth to find her. My salary is just 60 pounds a year*, he thought, as he turned to walk home, *but I can take in extra students to tutor, and so make a little more. We will do well, and I am so looking forward to the day we are settled.*

Chapter 4

Protest Against the Sugar Act

NOVEMBER 18, 1764

James carried little James Smith as he walked home from market in the early evening twilight. Jemmy, as Mary and he called the two-year-old, was Mary and James's pride and joy, their first son, and it was their continued happiness to welcome their second, whom they named John Middleton, a year later. Jemmy walked all the way to the market with his father, his little steps struggling to keep pace with his father's long legs. Finally, tired, he begged, "Pick me up, Father." James reached down and picked up the boy, balancing him on one side and the flour, sugar, and spices on the other. Mary was waiting at home with baby Johnny for the flour. She planned to make some bread for their supper. James Jr., James' older child, now six years old, still lived with his grandparents Hastings, as they were very fond of the little fellow.

Night crept up, the sudden early dark of late fall. Candlelight shone from windows and from lamps hanging at street corners. With a rush, hoofbeats ringing on stone split the night. Around the corner dashed a horseman, the horse's hooves clattering on the cobblestones. In his hand the man flourished a brand aloft, fire shooting into the sky. A crowd gathered, cheering, laughing, many obviously drinking from the bottles clutched in their hands.

The horseman circled the crowd and then, before James and his son could leave the corner, leaned over. With a touch, a pile of hay crackled into flame leaping skyward. Above the hungry flames a stuffed figure hung from a pole. The effigy began to burn, twisting and spinning as if it were alive. Little Jemmy looked at the writhing figure, his eyes wide with amazement. The straw man didn't jerk or scream, he just spiraled in silent agony, flaking into craters of smoldering ash.

"Down with the customs collector! Off with his head!" yelled the crowd. Others cheered and whistled. Above the flaming man, a high, white-curtained window in a tall brick home across the street glowed with a light, then turned dark.

James and the two-year-old stared for a few minutes at the licking flames. "Hold on tightly to me," James said to his son. "We must hurry and be on our way. Though I must walk quickly now, hold on tight, do you understand?"

"Yes, Father," Jemmy said, his arms wrapping around his father's neck. "You know I can."

The streets echoed with cries and running feet as James strode as quickly as he could to their home at Chapman Place. He reached the alley just across from School Street and the Boston Latin School and turned in. Behind him, the shouts and calls of the crowd grew fainter.

"That was a sight, Jemmy," James said, opening the heavy oak door to their house and sighing with relief. "I am glad to be home, my boy," he added, setting the two-year-old down. Jemmy looked up at his father, his eyes big. He held out his arms for help removing his coat.

"What did you see?" asked Mary, coming to take the food from James, baby Johnny balanced on her hip.

"The mob is burning a customs collector in effigy down near the market," James said, removing Jemmy's coat from him. "The trouble with that is that violence of that kind only breeds more violence. That's what the law is for, to help people overcome problems. Yet I understand people feel wronged by the Sugar Act. They feel justified in pursuing extreme measures to make their point of view known."

"I hope no one is hurt," he added, pulling Jemmy's coat off from him and hanging it on a hook. "You did very well, my boy, and I am proud of you," he said to the child, who stared up with round eyes at his father, then sat in his own small chair by the fire. "We will have supper shortly. Am I right, Mary?"

"Now that I have the flour, I can make some quick bread. The beans are nearly ready. Give us a few minutes and we'll have our supper. Here, James, take Johnny." She handed the sleepy baby to his father. James sank into his chair by the table and sat down, cradling little Johnny on his lap.

"Explain to me again why the customs collector is so unpopular," Mary said. She sifted flour into a bowl already filled with other ingredients. She stirred, then popped the loaf into a pan and slid it into the brick oven by the side of the fireplace. James watched her movements with admiration. He was so proud of his wife. She was capable, willing, and kind to all. Sometimes he could hardly believe his happiness.

Jemmy looked up at James in dismay from his chair and said, "Poppa, I'm hungry."

"Here you are, son," James said, handing the toddler a couple of crackers. Jemmy took the crackers and went to the front room to find his blocks, where a crash soon reported that his block tower had met its doom.

"King George's Prime Minister, George Grenville, wishes to raise money for the Crown. After all, it's expensive maintaining troops here and abroad. The merchants, for years, have been making a good living in the rum trade. Molasses from the West Indies is shipped here, where our New England merchants make it into rum. Selling rum shipped to England or Europe makes fortunes for many. Often those same ships return with slaves from Africa, who are placed on the plantations of the West Indies."

James continued, his voice warming to its subject and its tone rising in criticism. Mary looked up from setting the table, a question on her lips. "Molasses has been taxed for years, but merchants just smuggle to get around it. Grenville's Sugar Act, passed just last year, makes smuggling a crime tried in vice-admiralty courts without juries. But a British citizen's right is always to have a trial by a jury of his peers!" As James raised his voice, Johnny woke up and began to cry.

"It's all right, Johnny," said Mary, placing the pitcher of honey and some butter on the table. "Your father is just talking."

"Sorry, but some public affairs have me worried." James jiggled Johnny, whose cries stopped.

"You'll note I choose to serve honey, James," Mary said, "not that I don't like molasses, but lately it has been costly. So the Sugar Act affects us, does it not?"

"Surely, as it is taxed," James said. "Another unpopular part of the Sugar Act is that certain goods produced here in America, especially lumber, can be sold only in England. Imagine—the best and broadest boards from the finest trees may be sold only to one customer, the country of England. The English merchants will pay just barely what it costs to ship the boards over to those shores. What kind of business could prosper if it could not advocate for the healthy sale of its products?" Johnny began crying again. James rubbed the baby's gums gently with his finger and Johnny's cries turned to whimpers.

"Teething again, I expect."

"Certainly he is," Mary said. "Now," she added, "I think the bread is done. She pulled the bread out of the brick oven and tapped the loaf lightly. "Firm and ready. Come, Jemmy—your supper is here," she called.

"For years our merchants have been making a living evading the older Molasses Act," James continued, as Mary held Jemmy's chair for him, then took Johnny on her lap. "Now they are faced with stiffer penalties under the Sugar Act. The customs officials can turn merchants over to the vice-admiralty courts. There they are tried without a jury. No wonder the customs officials are unpopular." James poured a bit of honey on a slice of bread and handed it to Jemmy, who bit into it with energy, his eyes fixed on the brown, crusty loaf. Johnny picked up one bean at a time, eyeing each before chewing it carefully.

"Protest must be expected, Mary. The solution is fairer treatment on the part of the British, yet judging from the actions of Grenville, we have a good way to go to achieve that." James helped himself to a big bite of beans with bread, chewing hungrily. Even as he admired Mary's cooking, his thoughts flew far away, to a customs collector likely cowering in his home, and farther to a rich king with his court and Prime Minister, determined to make what wealth they could from the colonies.

"John Lovell (1710-1778)."
Harvard University Portrait Collections

Chapter 5

The Argument Heats Up

AUGUST 10, 1765

His father's graying eyebrows arched like drawn bows as he regarded James. Master Lovell leaned back in his big leather chair. James had stopped at his parents' house to bring them a jar of Mary's strawberry jam.

"So, some have concern that we are being asked to pay a tax on certain items—legal documents, newspapers, marriage licenses, and so on. Why should that trouble us when we have the protection of the best army in the world? Didn't the British just wage the French and Indian War to keep the country from being handed over to the French?" His father set down the newspaper on his desk, folded his arms across his chest, and sighed as if the matter were already ended.

James settled himself in the armchair, its cushions decorated with his mother's needlework. He picked up the newspaper and pretended to scan it, composing his thoughts. His father never tried to see his point of view nor that of any who disputed the actions of Parliament. Teaching in the same building as his father, alongside of him, often caused James to reflect that though he loved his father, he did not always agree with him. James looked up from the paper.

"The Stamp Act enacted by Parliament in March will be very unpopular, since we did not vote for the tax but we have to pay it in order to participate in normal business." There, that statement surely should not offend him, James thought.

"Defiance towards an act of Parliament will solve nothing," John responded emphatically. "We must petition Parliament to make changes. The Virginia Resolves, a poorly thought-out piece of legislation, state that only the legislative body of Virginia has the right to impose taxes on that colony. Yet Parliament surely has that right as well, since we are English citizens." His father looked sternly at James over the thin-wired spectacles he often wore.

"I'm glad you refer to the Resolves," said James. "They state that the General Assembly of Virginia has the right to impose taxes on that people, a right granted by the Charter when the colony was settled. So naturally when a different body imposes taxes, they are resented."

"A different body? We are English, and Parliament still is the legislative body of England, the last I heard." John cleared his throat in disapproval.

James searched for words. *Oh, my father,* he thought. *Why is it we cannot talk about events without great disagreement?* Once again, his father's mind was made up. How could he exchange ideas with someone who refused to see another side of the story? What could he say?

John looked about his study, the bookcases, the paintings, the apple tree heavy with fruit outside the window. Order and balance reigned here, truly. His voice was calm when he spoke. "The Glorious Revolution was an example of rightful protest," he said, choosing his words carefully. "In 1688, when our countrymen overthrew the tyrant King James II, they exercised violence only when no other recourse would do. They were pushed to extremity. Likewise, we must be careful to err on the side of caution in dealing with our civil authorities. As our noted Boston minister Jonathan Mayhew has said, 'Obedience to the civil magistrate is a Christian duty.'" He leaned forward and arranged the pens, books, and candlesticks on his desk with precision, then looked up at James.

James exhaled slowly. *I must not be upset,* he thought. Things were never as clear or black and white as his father would like to think. His father had not had the last word, yet. "Yes, Father, but our English ancestors were sorely tried by the abuses of James II, and were it not for their realization that revolution was necessary they might never have freed themselves from his tyrannical chains. Jonathan Mayhew also reminds us that when the Glorious Revolution occurred there was 'no rational hope of redress in any other way' than revolution. Revolution was necessary 'to preserve the nation from slavery, misery, and ruin,' in his words."

John did not answer right away but looked down, lost in thought. James took advantage of his silence to press his point. "How can we recognize the unfairness of taxation by an unfeeling government an ocean away if we do not insist on our rights?" James glanced directly at his father. The older man stirred uncomfortably in his chair, searching for words. *Yet I really don't want to directly confront him*, James thought. He looked away, down at his newspaper.

Choosing his words carefully, John said with great deliberateness, "Shouting crowds accosting innocent shopkeepers, pelting them with refuse just for following the king's law, betray the trust we establish with our government. We are to be content with our rulers and peaceful in our daily lives." He pursed his lips and placed his hands together, fingers touching softly. No hint of anger showed in his face, yet James knew his father was deeply upset by this conversation. *How can I make it any easier?* James thought. *I must be honest.*

"Yet the Romans realized that no course short of violence would save them from Caesar's tyranny, so they chose to assassinate the dictator," James countered. "What is the point at which we must realize our rights are at stake and must not be trampled upon? As citizens we have the right to fair and lawful treatment, even if this means recourse to violence."

"The mob certainly thinks as you do, James, and behaves oft-times in ways gross and bestial," John answered. He looked at his son as if he wished this argument were over, his eyes softening in reflection. But he went on. "Yet we must choose the course of restraint, not the thrill of forcible resistance to government by unenlightened elements of society who would act without wisdom and foresight. Burning tax collectors in effigy and besmearing signs of shops with foul matter are actions of common people, but we should be better than that. We have studied the law and history, and we agree to taxes in order to affirm our commitment to the strength and goodness of our royal government, as a whole." He finished with a louder voice, feeling his argument build.

When James said nothing, John went on. "John Locke says our private judgment is suspect. Should we rely on it, all politics would become unhinged. Rather than government and order, we would have anarchy and confusion."

"That is not Locke's whole point," James said. John Locke, who stated government's duty to be the guardian of individual rights, was one of his favorite philosophers. It was somewhat surprising to hear his father quoting from Locke.

He got up from his chair and walked to the window. The green leaves of the apple tree brushed against the ripening fruit. "John Locke also says that resisting public abuses before they threaten the structure of the state is necessary to avoid revolution. Men must not watch submissively while their liberties are affected, otherwise they are no more than slaves."

James continued. "We have the right and the duty to protest measures such as the collection of taxes imposed by this Stamp Act—the people should protest, be they cobbler, bricklayer, or vastly underpaid teacher." James coughed and glanced at John, whose gaze flickered to him briefly in disgust, then turned away. "Without action, those treated unfairly are nothing more than pawns and puppets of a greedy and despotic ruler."

"We must stand up for ourselves—and our rights," James added. "The Rev. Jonathan Mayhew also says that resistance was necessary in the Glorious Revolution of 1688—and I believe is necessary again, especially against taxes which we did not approve."

"You are too hot-headed," his father said, an edge of bitterness growing in his words. "Find some measure of peace to accept those actions by government that you do not understand—lest your discordant thoughts cause you to become a cast-off of society, a pariah, a leper repugnant to all."

"I do not fear that choice, Father," James said lightly, almost happily. He spun around from the window and faced his father, arms folded on his chest. "I welcome the opportunity to resist unnecessary acts of government which threaten our well-being as free men. Yes, caution must be taken, and resistance must be circumspect, wise in its choices. Yet inaction is worse than an irresolute course. The mob is governed by principles that—though crude and desperate—are, in fact, bred in the same sense of confidence in individual rights as the confidence of the lawyer at the bar. The law respects our rights as citizens, or it is no law."

Outside a peaceful twilight deepened as the evening moon rose over the rustling apple tree. James drew the brocade curtains shut. He picked up the candle, lit another, and placed it on Master Lovell's desk.

The gray-haired schoolteacher looked at his son with a calm stare. "You do not understand," John said finally. "Our government is the finest, the best in the world. It has given you the ability to enjoy your rights. Our king himself is subject to the same responsibilities as you and must act in right and just ways. In *Cato's Letters*, Thomas Gordon praises our English system of government, where king, nobles, and people are balanced in mutual respect, and where 'the malice of men in power has less scope.' Surely it is worth a little submission to taxes to uphold the rights we enjoy."

"No, Father, I would say we are bound to resist. Those same rights to which we think we are entitled impel us to speak, act, and think as those who are truly free—and this means refusing to be slaves, pawns, and puppets to selfish tyranny."

James turned to the study door and opened it. "So I bid you goodnight. I go to meet with the Sons of Liberty, a group of right-minded leaders who believe, as do I, that we must speak and act in good conscience for our rights."

"That will bring you down, surely," John said, staring hard at James. "You will be in the gutter—with the mob. Let me not hear of such talk."

"All right, you will hear nothing. And yet you have taught many of my friends and leaders in the community: Samuel Adams, James Bowdoin, John Hancock, Henry Knox, Robert Treat Paine—all have learned their lessons from you, and have learned well."

"Enough. They err in this; they are deceived." John spoke gruffly, with effort. James had hit a nerve and he knew it.

"Good-night, Father. I will see you another time." James stepped out of the book-lined study, feeling a weight drop off his shoulders. Now he had spoken, his ideas were clear, and he would continue to act and think as he chose. *It is better to make oneself known,* he thought; *a rose by any other name would smell as sweet, as Shakespeare would say.* He passed through the kitchen, where his mother was sitting by the fire mending a shirt. She looked up at him and smiled.

"When are you going to bring your little one by for me to see?" she asked cheerfully. Mary and James's third son, whom they had named Joseph, was nearly a year old.

James placed his hand softly on her shoulder. "Soon enough, we'll bring the little fellow over for a visit. You just saw him a week ago."

"I can't get enough of him. Bring your wife and children soon, James. Maybe to dinner, next Sunday?"

"Yes, Mother, that should be fine. Good-night." James kissed her on the cheek and went out the front door into the sweet summer night.

It is sometimes hard that I must continue teaching in the same building as Father, but at least he knows me for who I am, James thought. *That much is clear.*

Chapter 6

Burned in Effigy: Andrew Oliver, Stamp Commissioner

AUGUST 14, 1765

James stood at the edge of the large crowd in Boston's South End. Dockworkers, stonemasons, beggars, and townspeople of all sorts were gathered in the grassy space before the Liberty Tree to stare with fascination at an object hanging from its branches. The large elm tree at the corner of Essex and Orange Streets had become a rallying point for expressing discontent with British policies. James peered up at the branches of the old tree, thick with summer leaves.

He saw dangling there, shifting slightly in the breeze, a straw-stuffed figure. The black hat and coal-marked mustache characterized the effigy as none other than Andrew Oliver, the designated Stamp distributor for Massachusetts. Beside the effigy hung a British cavalry boot, painted green on the bottom, a devilish doll leering from its top holding a sign with the crudely painted words "Stamp Act." Everyone in the crowd recognized the double pun: the boot for the Earl of Bute, the Prime Minister who stationed ten thousand British regulars in the colonies; the green paint on its bottom for George Grenville, the Prime Minister responsible for the Stamp Act.

James shifted his feet, looking about him in curiosity. All manner of people had come to the spectacle, many summoned by Ebenezer Macintosh, a sort of leader of the common people, a cobbler and veteran of the Seven Years War. Throughout the throng he recognized many of Boston's merchants and civic leaders, some disguised as tradespeople in pants and jackets or with hats pulled down on foreheads.

Andrew Oliver, an older, established merchant who had at one time controlled the Long Wharf, had agreed to be the stamp distributor under Governor Bernard. *That was his mistake,* James thought. *He doesn't recognize fully the dislike the people have for the taxes that will come with the stamps.* That he was hung in effigy showed the hate and scorn many had for Oliver's support of the stamps.

Most in the crowd knew that the display had been organized and likely put up by the Loyal Nine, a group of merchants, town leaders, and citizens concerned with the rights and prosperity of the citizens of Boston. The dangling effigy represented a public display of disapproval for the Stamp Act. Many in Boston fretted over the unreasonable requirement to purchase a stamp, an official paper representing a paid tax, for common transactions of life. No one could get married or buy or sell land, purchase a newspaper or pay for an advertisement, without a stamp. The Stamp Act was universally disliked and resented.

"How did that get there?" an older gentleman standing near James asked, nodding towards the hanging effigy.

"As far as I know, last night the Loyal Nine and others met, probably at the Green Dragon Tavern. They built the straw man in the night and hung him here. A good caricature of Andrew Oliver, don't you think?" James answered.

"Looks just like him, I'd say. Hold—there's the sheriff and his men. Wonder what he wants," the older man said.

The sheriff of Boston, along with his deputies, cut through the crowd. "Come, enough. You've had your fun. I'm taking him down," he said in a commanding tone.

Before he could reach up to the noose holding the straw man, a dozen hands restrained him.

"No you don't, Sheriff. Come on, we're going to keep him dangling there a while longer."

"You'd best be on your way," added a huge carpenter. The sheriff shrugged his shoulders, motioned to his men to leave. Without a backward glance, quietly they left through the crowd.

"The stamps aren't here yet, are they," the older gentleman said to James.

"No, they're supposed to arrive later this fall. If this turmoil continues, imagine what the protests will be like by then." James and his fellow bystander exchanged looks and nodded thoughtfully.

Through the afternoon the crowd surrounding the dangling straw figure grew. James was starting to think of leaving, when towards evening a shrill voice said, "Let's take him to Town Hall." Cheers and shouts echoed approval. James recognized Ebenezer Macintosh, the cobbler popular among the working class people of Boston. The little fellow seemed always to be at the center of a group, his crude and colorful statements drawing the attention of many. James had little regard for Ebenezer Macintosh, whose appeal for most was somewhere between comedy and pathos. Yet he recognized his power over many.

The crowd, laughing and jeering, cut the dangling scarecrow down from the tree and hoisted it high on a pike. The procession started up the street heading to the wharf area, Andrew Oliver's effigy swinging high above them. James followed in its wake, curious about what might happen and what direction the events of the night would take.

"Down with Oliver! Down with unfair taxes," the mob chanted. They passed through Marlborough Street at the east corner of School Street, jeering and shouting.

A burly artisan slapped James on his back. "A lucky thing we have justice for the stuffed man. The real Oliver had better learn his lesson."

"Yes, indeed," James agreed heartily. At the same time, he hoped the crowd's actions would not result in violence, yet he knew if he were to speak, his own words would have little effect on the possible damage they might inflict. He walked on the edge of the group, careful to stay in the background. If need be, he wanted to be able to melt out of sight, disappear. The potential for real danger was certain, he realized. Part of him wondered what he, a respectable Boston schoolteacher, was doing in such a group. But curiosity drove him on, and also a certain sense of sympathy for those in the mob. He, too, disagreed with the unfair taxes of the Stamp

Act. His ways of expressing disagreement might have been different from those who walked the streets, clamoring in protest, but in a general sense he agreed and stood in solidarity with the group.

"Here's Oliver's Dock," cried a sailor in an aged blue hat, pointing to a wharf at the harbor. "And here's the office where he will collect the duties," he added, motioning to a small one-story wooden building.

"Let's take it down; let's burn it," excited voices called. A scrawny dockhand waved a burning brand aloft, and stepping forward, touched the wooden structure. The empty building crackled and roared in bursts of flame, sending up shimmering heat waves in the twilight. James watched the figures of the crowd waving their hands in approval, black against the bright bursts of flame. The sight was both invigorating and appalling.

Before the blaze died down a harsh voice cried, "Let's go to his home! We need to stamp it out with our special stamp."

"No, we need not," someone in the crowd said. "We have made our point. Let us not cause further and unnecessary harm." James recognized the speaker, Benjamin Edes, printer of the *Boston Gazette*, one of the Loyal Nine.

"Aye, but we must," countered several voices. The crowd wheeled, departing down the street towards Andrew Oliver's fine home. A few hung back, turning away. Tired and hungry, James too thought it was time to go. Still, he decided to linger on the outskirts of the mob. No official control would stop this crowd from acting as it chose.

At Andrew Oliver's home the throng set fire to his fine coach and stable house. Stones clattered on the sides and shingles of the house and a window crashed, splintered. Light showed at an upper window for a few minutes and the curtains moved. Then the light was extinguished and the house darkened. Jeering and taunting, those in the crowd threw the stuffed figure they had been carrying down to the street, lopped off its head, and set it ablaze.

Torched, a short, intense flame shot up from the curling effigy that lay writhing in a heap. Bright, glowing sparks spiraled upward, whirling in the hot currents.

Not wishing to be questioned or directly connected to those acting in such lawless fashion, James found a secure position on a hill across from the scene. From there he watched the sweaty faces, the transfixed glares, the grins of enjoyment, now bathed in the lurid red glare of firelight. No one could dispute the unpopularity of the stamp collector, he thought. Despite the destruction of this night, the sooner everyone knew how dangerous it would be to collect the taxes and hand out the stamps, the better.

James stared at the hot ashes smoldering on the ground. A straw hand writhed in savage contortions as it submitted to the flames. *Like the swiftness of fire is the act of the mob,* James thought, *and in some ways as destructive yet also as free.* Like flames, such an act could chastise and purify, if not allowed to burn out of control. He had had enough and turned to make his way home.

The mob dashed through Andrew Oliver's house, ripping out pictures and furniture while the occupants left quietly from a back way. The ransacking continued for hours.

The next day, Andrew Oliver respectfully declined his appointment.

"This Is the Place to Affix the Stamp."
Library of Congress Prints and Photographs

A Mansion Meets the Mob

AUGUST 26, 1765

The stars shone in the clear summer sky as James stepped out of the Green Dragon Tavern. He had been discussing the Stamp Act with Josiah Quincy, James Bowdoin, and other friends, while they shared a few pints of ale. Shouts and cries interrupted their conversation. The commotion sounded like it was nearby, in the north part of town where some of Boston's best and stateliest homes stood. James said good night to his friends and stepped out into the warm summer evening, walking down cobble-stoned streets to find the source of the din.

He peered up a side street between two tall rows of flowering bushes. At the far end of the street he saw a crowd of at least two hundred Bostonians—working class citizens, laborers, and street vagrants. The crowd, illuminated by torches held high, were attacking the grand home of Lieutenant Governor Thomas Hutchinson.

James stepped into the bushes. There he watched, partially concealed, as pitchforks, axes, and clubs smashed windows, tore down shutters, and ripped off clapboards. He held his breath when the front door yawned open, like a mouth in pain. People streamed in, laughing and shouting. Glass crashed in the night as a tall bookcase, books cascading in a heap, plummeted out of an upper window. James could hardly believe the lawless, violent display of disregard for property he was witnessing. Yet he recognized the anger that was the source of the action.

"Quite a sight, eh?"

James jumped, startled. He turned around to see a man leaning on a wooden crutch on the walkway just beside him.

The man grinned with good humor, one eye hidden behind a black patch. "I've got a brother there—he should be getting me something nice. Silver candlesticks, maybe, or even a gun. Not the place for me," the ragged man added in a cheerful manner, motioning to his crutch. James noticed the man wore an odd assemblage of rags, jacket too short and pants too long.

"I'm Jabez Tuttle. O say, look at that chandelier. Now there's a nice find," the ragged man went on, peering in excitement at the spectacle. A dribble of drool ran down his bristly chin.

"It is quite a busy scene," James agreed. He was not sure what to say. He could not take his eyes off the destruction he watched, yet was glad he was safely out of sight, at a distance.

"They're dealing with Lieutenant Governor Hutchinson's home—it's him who's allowing the Stamp Act, you see. He should have known better." Jabez's voice rang with the authority of conviction.

A crash resounded as someone on the porch of the house swung an axe into a wooden case. Bottles of wine glinted in the moonlight. The wine was quickly picked up by those nearby, many of whom appeared to James to be already drunk. A stream of ransackers poured out the front door, some bearing brass candlesticks, others framed pictures, china dishes, and silken clothing. One beautifully framed portrait of a young girl, probably Hutchinson's daughter, landed on the lawn outside. The portrait was ripped from its gilt frame and stomped on by people shrieking with laughter.

"There's a nice one," Jabez said genially, as two burly men descended the steps carrying a green baize-covered settee. "Now I'd like that," he added with enthusiasm and a twinkle in his good eye, motioning with his crutch to a fine writing desk carried off by a tall thin man. The lucky individual swung one arm like a windmill as he trotted past, fending off competitors while he balanced the delicate piece of furniture with the other.

James shivered. The disorderly, drunken crowd had taken the reins of revenge and abandoned any law. In fact, they were nothing more than marauders and thieves. Dissension against the Stamp Act had no doubt been the spark for the mob's anger, but overtaking that had been greed, envy, and desire for revenge. Cultivated fruit trees in the garden met the axe; even the ornate cupola at the top of the house crashed to the ground.

"Quite a night, eh?" Jabez said cheerfully.

James agreed quietly. "Yes, I'd say they are having a fine time." Clearly, though, this destruction went beyond protest to vandalism. The passions that had flamed the burning effigy of Andrew Oliver over the Stamp Act just twelve days ago had smoldered hot in many minds and now burst into violent action.

"My brother should be back soon," Jabez continued, confidently. His tone was calm, chatty. *He might as well be commenting on an arm-wrestling contest,* James thought.

"That Lieutenant Governor Hutchinson and his fine ways should know not to force a tax on us—not one like that Stamp tax. This'll teach 'im."

Jabez Tuttle fairly danced a jig with his crutch in his excitement. "Here comes my brother now," he cried happily. "We'll see what good things he has found for me. Good night to ye." He stepped nimbly into the street as a torrent of people raced past, carrying in their arms all manner of valuables. On the lawn of the ruined home a huge bonfire flickered, bold in the night, while shingles ripped from the roof cascaded like falling leaves. James shivered in the warm night and turned back between the bushes to find another way home. The anger of the people was an enveloping flame, a punishing brand. He had seen enough for one night.

Lieutenant Governor Thomas Hutchinson had been writing a detailed history of Massachusetts, laboring with rare documents to craft a history for the benefit of the citizens. *If destroying that monumental work had been a goal of any of the participants of the night's chaos, they have certainly succeeded,* James thought. Furthermore, Lieutenant Governor Hutchinson had not supported the Stamp Act as the former governor, Governor Bernard, did. In fact, he stated his opposition to the Act before its passage, saying it would be bad for the economy of Massachusetts. Yet someone clearly wished to punish him for his position as governor. *The mob strikes again,* James thought, hurrying through the dark streets to home.

Chapter 8

Chewing on the Stamp Act

NOVEMBER 11, 1765

"So you think these protests and obstructions of law are going to amount to something, eh, James?" John cleared his throat and tugged at his stiff shirt collar. He reached for another of Abigail's flaky tarts. His face was beginning to assume the florid color it gained when he was about to launch into one of his discourses at school. "Here, sit down and have some tea. I was just going to pour some." John motioned James to the straight-backed chair near the fire and reached for the teapot.

There was an awkward silence. James hesitated, wondering if he could leave without offending his father. He hadn't meant to stop at his parents' home; he had needed to pick up the cape he'd left behind at school when his father saw him and motioned him in. He didn't want to listen to one of the old man's tirades on the subject of the current situation, which, brief though they were, were rather like holding one's hand on a hot stove for comfort.

"I'll just have a small cup. Thank you, Father," James assented, sliding uneasily into the tight caning of the ladder-back chair. The warm tea steamed in the cup and he picked it up, feeling its heat through the thin bone china his mother preferred. It had been a long day, and his vocal cords were still somewhat scratchy from the dressing-down he'd had to give the second and third form. Their conjugations were muddled, and their understanding of the intransitive form of the Latin verbs was simply appalling.

He frowned at the memory and sipped the tea. Warmth spread through his system and he sighed. The tea was as good as always; his mother demanded the best East India Company tea, even if his father's salary didn't permit the finest in imported furniture.

"Have a tart—excellent apple filling." John handed the plate to James, who took the sweet suspiciously. He doubted he had an appetite at this time, but his mother's baking was always superior. This confection was light and evenly baked. He found himself biting into it with gusto.

"Your sisters Abigail and Priscilla will be by this Sunday, and your mother's cooking a roast—be sure you come and bring Mary and the children. We will celebrate Abigail's new baby." John looked affably at James. Maybe this visit will not revolve on his father's particular political beliefs, James dared to hope.

"I will be sure to tell Mary. Tell Mother we will plan to come."

"Have you ever heard of such a name as Cadwallader?" John rolled his eyes, and both men laughed.

"You are referring to Governor Cadwallader Colden of New York, no doubt," James said, smiling with amusement at the unique name.

"It's not a name I'd suggest for Abigail's new baby." John laughed again at his joke, then grew serious. "The papers today told of the latest abuses in New York. It seems people feared that Lieutenant Governor Cadwallader Colden was going to enforce the Stamp Act by force of arms. Huge crowds paraded an effigy of the governor through the streets, like the parade here in Boston on August 14. They carried the printed Stamp Act on a pole topped with a grinning death's head, bearing a scroll inscribed with the words 'The Folly of England and the Ruin of America.'"

"Yes, I read about that," James said. "The crowd attacked his home. They seized his coach and sleigh and smashed the expensive conveyances before burning them on Bowling Green near Fort George on Manhattan. They also burned effigies of the governor and his lieutenant."

"They burned an effigy of the devil, too, not that that was appropriate," John continued gruffly. "This happened on November 1, just a few days ago, the same day the Stamp Act passed by Parliament under Lord Grenville was set to go into effect."

"But remember that the crowd in New York had been inflamed by harsh talk," James said. "Major Thomas James of the Royal Artillery in New York promised that the stamps would be crammed down the throats of New Yorkers. You know they have quite a contingent of regulars stationed there under General Gage, the commander of British forces in North America. Evidently the Major's threat inspired fear in many minds."

His father was quiet, thinking over the situation in New York, so James continued. He was not sure his father understood the measures those who protested the Stamps had taken in order to prevent violence. "Merchants in New York agreed to boycott all British imports until the repeal of the Stamp Act, while the New York Sons of Liberty warned merchants and citizens against using the stamps. They posted placards around town reading, 'First man that either distributes or makes use of Stamped Paper let him take care of his House, Person and Effects.' However, an angry crowd paraded through the streets, broke windows and lamps, and marched on Fort George, demanding the stamps be handed over to them."

James sipped his tea, savoring the pungent, slightly bitter brew. "The crowd rushed to Major James's home and tore it apart, ruining his garden." He finished the tart and glanced warily at his father. What would his opinion be on the subject?

"Similar unprincipled violence destroyed the home of our Lieutenant Governor last August," John said, his voice on edge.

"Yet peace and resolution are on the minds of many," James said. He'd better bring this discussion to a close. He didn't wish to make his father upset. "The Stamp Act Congress just met in New York earlier last month. Nine of our colonies sent representatives; the resolutions they agreed on were sent to the king and Parliament by the end of the month. More colonies would have sent delegates, except their royal governors forbade their legislatures from meeting to choose any. That alone is a crime against people's rights! It is always beneficial when opinions can be shared in public."

"People do have rights. Yet order must prevail. The stamps themselves are perceived as the problem. Yet does not Parliament have the right to impose taxes? Stamps or no stamps, taxes are a fact of life." John's voice rose as he became upset, and James set down his teacup. *This subject can't come up without our going at it head to head,* he thought.

In a voice he hoped was reasonable and quiet, James said, "It was the Massachusetts legislature that initially suggested working with the other colonies to agree on resolutions. A unified response is the only way we can get sufficient strength to stand up to the unreasonable demands of Parliament."

"Don't forget, Parliament needs the money that taxes raise," John said. "They must maintain armies here that work for our defense."

"Yet, Father, are we not capable of defending ourselves?" James responded. "Every colony has a militia. And we did not vote for those taxes. Basic rights, as Englishmen, dictate that we should refuse to pay taxes to which we have not consented. John Locke asserts that government cannot take from any man his property without his consent, and that means taxes. I am sure this was the main point of the Stamp Act Congress that just met: taxes imposed on people without their consent are unconstitutional."

John frowned at James. "It is a crime and a shame," said John, setting his teacup down with a force that rattled the saucer, "that officials must bear the anger, violence, and intolerance of an undisciplined rabble. What will happen next? What will happen to law and order and peaceful rule?"

"Not all protests are undisciplined," James countered. "Remember what happened the day before the New York protests began, on October 31. In Newport, Rhode Island, in a serious attempt to protest peacefully, townspeople celebrated a mock funeral for North American Liberty. The newspaper announcement for the funeral predicted the demise of North American Liberty and then arranged for a funeral procession for all his true Sons. The announcement added that disorder and riot would not be tolerated."

He continued, "In Boston most were aware that the date of November 1, the date the Stamp Act took effect, and November 5, Pope's Day, when we remember the evils of papacy, were close together, which was a poor choice of a date for an unpopular tax, if I do say so myself."

"Ah yes, Pope's Day. That opportunity for our north Boston mob and our south Boston mob to join in parades under the leadership of that self-proclaimed scoundrel from the gutter 'General' Ebenezer Mackintosh. Each day for a week 'General Mackintosh' dons his blue and gold uniform, probably scrounged from the sea trunk of some unlucky traveller, picks up his cane and speaking trumpet, and takes up leadership of a couple thousand paraders. Filled with good food and wine provided by the merchants of the town who wish to avoid smashed windows at any cost, the whole parade sallies through the streets in a joyful and peaceful mood. Then they celebrate the destruction of effigies early in the afternoon, and have the whole lot cleaned up and home before nightfall. Quite a display of public showmanship, if you ask me." John's face sagged with weariness. He tapped his fingers on the table in front of him in exasperation.

"Pope's Day," John added, "started over a hundred years ago in England as Guy Fawkes Day. People celebrated the failure of the plot hatched by Guy Fawkes to blow up the House of Lords and with it, King James. Fawkes wanted to restore a Catholic monarch to the throne. Now it's more likely people would want to blow up the house of the governor, though certainly not the king's house." John paused at this unorthodox thought, his face churning with disapproval, and picked up his teacup.

He finished his thought. "Today Guy Fawkes Day is known as Pope's Day, to beware the control of papacy. But royal tax stamp collectors are not the evil some imagine, and I can't think that the dates of November 1 and November 5 being close together would cause a negative attitude towards the stamp tax just because its passage was near to Pope's Day," John said.

"Oh heavens, Father, I'm sure that is not a major objection to the stamp tax." James stood up and picked up his cape. He tried to calm the irritation in his voice. "The Stamp Act is an evil unto itself. Remember what happened when first the stamps arrived. All the vessels in the Boston harbor lowered their colors and folded their flags to signify mourning. A unified response came a week ago in the *Boston Gazette*, the paper printed by Benjamin Edes and Peter Gill. These were the Resolutions of the House of Representatives of Massachusetts Bay." James pulled a worn paper from his pocket and unfolded it, conscious of his father's glaring eyes.

He read out loud:

> *Whereas the just Rights of His Majesty's Subjects of this*
> *Province, denied to them from the British Constitution,*
> *as well as the Royal Charter, have been lately drawn into*

> *Question; In order to ascertain the same, this House do UNANIMOUSLY come into the following resolves:*
>
> 1. *Resolved. That there are certain essential Rights of the British Constitution of Government which are founded in the Law of God and Nature, and are the common Rights of Mankind... Therefore,*
> 2. *Resolved. That the Inhabitants of this Province are unalienably entitled to those effectual Rights in common with all Men: And that no Law of Society can, consistent with the Law of God and Nature, divest them of those Rights.*

"I know," interrupted John, scowling, "some think we have the right to impose taxes on ourselves, confirmed by our great document the Magna Carta, and no other body of Englishmen have the right to impose those taxes. Well, I can tell you that His Majesty and His Parliament do have the right to impose taxes upon us, and we as his subjects have the responsibility to pay them. Any that object to that are unpatriotic and just downright foolish. What is all this nonsense? Just another way to avoid responsibilities of English people."

John wiped his mouth with his napkin in preparation for another verbal volley, but James stood up. Speaking in a controlled, calm tone, he said, "The taxes are a burden. That they are also against our rights is a debate that is not yet settled. Thank you for the tea, Father. I will let Mary know we are welcome here on Sunday. We are surely eager to see sister Abigail's new baby. My greetings to Mother."

Before his father could say anything, James picked up his cape and turned to the door. "Good night, then," James said.

"Good night," he heard John say as he shut the heavy door. On the porch James breathed in the fresh, cold November air, counted to three. *That was not easy,* he thought. *It is best we ended the talk when we did. And many events are happening,* he thought. *No matter how stuck in their ways some are, things will change.*

From the VOTES *of the House of Representation of the Province of the* Massachusetts-Bay, MARTIS, 29 *Die* OCTOBRIS, *A. D.* 1765. *In the House of* REPRESENTATIVES.

ACCORDING to the Order of the Day, there being a very full House, the following Draft, which had been laid on the Table was *particularly* considered, and thereupon *Voted.*

Whereas the just Rights of His Majesty's Subjects of this Province, derived to them from the *British Constitution*, as well as the *Royal Charter*, have been lately drawn into Question : In order to ascertain the same, this House do UNANIMOUSLY come into the following Resolves.

1. *Resolved*, That there are certain essential Rights of the *British* Constitution of Government which are founded in the Law of God and Nature, and are the common Rights of Mankind----Therefore

2. *Resolved*, That the Inhabitants of this Province are *unalienably* entitled to those essential Rights in common with all Men : And that no Law of Society can, consistent with the Law of God and Nature, divest them of those Rights.

3. *Resolved*, That no Man can justly take the Property of another without his Consent : And that upon this original Principle the Right of Representation in the same Body, which exercises the Power of making Laws for levying Taxes, which is one of the main Pillars of the British Constitution, is evidently found.

Resolved, That this *inherent* Right, together with all other essential Rights, Liberties, Privileges and Immunities, of the People of *Great Britain*, have been fully confirmed to them by *Magna Charta*; and by former and later Acts of Parliament.

"Resolutions from Massachusetts."
Boston Gazette November 4, 1765, *Early American Imprints*

Chapter 9

Under Liberty Tree: Andrew Oliver Forced to Resign

DECEMBER 17, 1765

The notice, short and direct, screamed on the door of the bookshop, *Stop! Stop!* James paused in his walk to school to read the post.

"The True-born Sons of Liberty, are desired to meet under LIBERTY-TREE, at XII o'Clock, THIS DAY, to hear the public Resignation under Oath, of ANDREW OLIVER, ESQ., Distributor of Stamps for the Province of the Massachusetts Bay."

James thought quickly. If he left school during lunch, he could walk to the Liberty Tree and see something of the humiliation of Andrew Oliver. The notice continued with finality: "A Resignation? YES."

Andrew Oliver, official Stamp Distributor for the British government, had resigned in August, pressured after his house was plundered and his grotesque, straw-stuffed effigy consumed in a crackling blaze. This ceremony under the Liberty Tree was to be a formal chance to make the town's position regarding the stamps clear. Oliver's official commission had arrived on November 30, and the Sons of Liberty wanted it made clear that he had indeed resigned: neither Oliver nor anyone else would be selling the hated stamps, tied to taxes not chosen by the colonists themselves.

James went into the bookstore and bought a *Boston Gazette*. He opened it with difficulty in the chill December wind, freezing rain driving against his face, and glanced through the paper as he stepped up the cobblestone street towards school, his breath coming in frosty puffs.

One article from New York, dated November 12, caught his eye. The Sons of Liberty in New York had carefully carried all the stamps a ship had just brought to City Hall, where confined behind official walls they would not alarm the people nor stir up trouble.

James remembered his discussion of the Stamp Act in New York with his father about a month ago. The two had done their best to avoid conversation specific to taxes since, and in fact had enjoyed meals together on a couple of occasions. It was amazing, James thought, how much he could enjoy agreeing with his father on some levels, while being completely opposed to him on others.

But what a wise group were those Sons of Liberty. Here in Boston the group included many town leaders, a larger association than the original Loyal Nine. Among them were Benjamin Edes, the printer; John Avery, merchant; Thomas Crafts, the painter; and other prominent Bostonians. Samuel Adams visited with the group often, as did John Adams, his cousin, the lawyer. James had heard many of these citizens speak at town meetings. He counted many as his associates and friends; he appreciated their point of view, protective of liberties, cautious, yet seeking action.

Reaching the school, James put the newspaper away. Students filed in and soon the room was quiet, the only sound the scratching of pens as students worked through their Latin or Greek lessons. John in his part of the room heard older students give recitations, their original compositions. James tried to concentrate on his younger students reading aloud. When the clock struck twelve noon, James stood up. "Lunch time; you may get your food out." His students picked up buckets from shelves and cupboards, uncovering buttered bread, cold cuts of meat, and apples. Postponing his usual dive into the sausage and biscuits in his lunch sack, James put on his coat and scarf. He looked across the large square room at his father, who had pulled his own lunch container out of a drawer and was inspecting the contents.

"I am going for a brief stroll. Master Lovell, please take charge in my absence." His father looked up and nodded yes, though he frowned in disapproval. *No matter,* James thought. He stepped out the door, meeting a cold, driving rain, and pulled his hat down more securely.

He walked the four or five blocks southeast towards Liberty Tree near the Boston Common, lengthening his strides with his long legs, tugging his hat tightly against the chilly downpour. A large crowd, maybe a couple thousand, gathered around the stately old elm, bare branches dark with rain. Under it, members of the Sons of Liberty gathered around a hastily-erected platform.

Andrew Oliver, his black hat dripping, stood head bent in the midst of the group. From the glimpse James caught of him through the crowd, he stood bowed with fatigue, his thick body drooped with discouragement. The former merchant and provincial assembly member, who with his brother had once controlled Boston's Long Wharf, had taken the unpopular position of Stamp Commissioner for Massachusetts and suffered as a result. James remembered seeing his fine house ruined by the mob last August.

The notice posted earlier by the Sons of Liberty brought out a large crowd that stood about the common near the Liberty Tree, including many women and children. James turned to a young lady standing near him in the crowd, her bonnet sodden, her arms crossed severely over her cape. A little boy stood shyly near her, clinging to her skirt. "Has the swearing of Andrew Oliver concluded?" James asked her.

"Just now, yes. He swore he would never serve as Stamp Commissioner. Then he signed the paper. It's a good thing, too; we want none of those stamps." The woman spoke firmly though shyly, her face set with a scowl.

James tipped his hat to her, rain pouring off of it. "Thank ye, ma'am." There wasn't much more he'd see here. Clearly, Andrew Oliver's days as Stamp Distributor were over. James took one last look at the forlorn figure of Andrew Oliver, shivering in the freezing rain, glanced at the speaker addressing the crowd, and turned to go back to school.

He dashed through the rain-soaked streets to the schoolhouse. Opening the door, he saw to his surprise that his father was not in the southwest corner of the school by his own desk, but rather stood in the northeast corner at James's desk. In fact, he had his hands in James's desk drawer, which was partly open. John started and shut the drawer at once.

"Just checking for something," he muttered, and quickly returned to his corner of the room. The boys were already quietly at work at their benches, books open.

"Certainly," James said. He looked at his father, a question on his face, but the Master did not return his look. James took off his dripping coat and sat next to the stove, his wet shoes cold. *What could the old man have been looking for?* He had a few notes in his desk from meetings with the Sons of Liberty. *A list of names, maybe. Why on earth would he want those?* He glanced again at his father. Master Lovell was checking a student's writing with great concentration.

It is not important, he thought. *Father would have no need to check up on me. He knows my opinions. All the same, I'd best be careful what I keep in that drawer.* James returned to his desk and his own students' papers, but the thought of suspicion lingered.

Chapter 10

Stamp Act Celebration

MAY 19, 1766

On Monday morning the schoolroom pulsed to a racer's tempo. Church bells pealed throughout Boston and guns cracked the spring air. Boys fidgeted and squirmed like worms on a hook, spoiling their Greek translations. James felt the same excitement himself.

By mid-morning the tedious school day nearly caused him to lose his patience. He barked at poor Isaac, who stuttered, and made William stand in the corner for nearly an hour for his immoderate laughter. Particularly annoying, William would neither explain his laughter nor stop. Instead, he grew red in the face and coughed until he nearly choked. James's upraised arm and threatening gesture, usually effective on even the most stubborn of students, influenced William not at all.

Meanwhile, James's father grew ominously more and more quiet, directing his students with sullen fierceness and pointed thrusts of his ferule. The din outside continued: carts rumbled past; crowds thronged the streets in a steady tramp; horses nickered; hooves rang on cobblestones.

On Friday, news had arrived on John Hancock's brig *Harrison* that the British Parliament had repealed the Stamp Act. The Sons of Liberty immediately sent riders to Newport, New York, and Portsmouth with the news. Throughout Boston the outpouring of joy was spontaneous. Church bells scarcely stopped clanging. Flags flapped in the wind and red hangings festooned doorways. The bookstore on Marlborough Street not only decorated its sign with white cloth but placed hand-lettered statements in its windows: "Long Live Liberty!" Bunting, ribbons, and all manner of festive adornments sprouted on houses and shops.

That morning at the bookstore James picked up a paper and glanced at the news. On that day, May 19th, a celebration would be held on the Boston Common. The Stamp Act had been repealed by an act of Parliament.

That was enough. He tucked the paper under his arm and ran to school.

"Father, should we not dismiss school? There is to be an official celebration," James said as he walked into the empty schoolroom early in the morning. "Many of the boys will be absent, attending that instead. Should we not send all home at once and support the glad occasion by our presence?" As master of the school, John made decisions that were beyond James's control. Being merely the usher, a teacher subordinate to his father, was an arrangement he often found irksome—if not downright detestable.

"I see no reason," answered John sourly. "The boys are here to learn and it's our job to teach them. They can attend the festivities soon enough if their families choose to take them."

Glorious News,

Juſt received from *Boſton*, brought by Meſſrs. *Jonathan Lowder,* and *Thomas Brackett.*

BOSTON, Friday 11 o'Clock, 16th May, 1766.
THIS Inſtant arrived here the Brig Harriſon, belonging to John Hancock, Eſq; Captain Shubael Coffin, in 6 Weeks and 2 Days from LONDON, with important News, as follows.

— From the London Gazette.

Weſtminſter, March 18th, 1766.

THIS day his Majeſty came to the Houſe of Peers, and being in his royal robes ſeated on the Throne with the uſual ſolemnity, Sir Francis Molineux, Gentleman Uſher of the Black Rod, was ſent with a Meſſage from his Majeſty to the Houſe of Commons, commanding their attendance in the Houſe of Peers. The Commons being come thither accordingly, his Majeſty was pleaſed to give his royal aſſent to An ACT to REPEAL an Act made in the laſt Seſſion of Parliament intituled, an Act for granting and applying certain Stamp-Duties and other Duties in the Britiſh Colonies and Plantations in America, towards further defraying the Expences of defending, protecting and ſecuring the ſame, and for amending ſuch parts of the ſeveral Acts of Parliament relating to the trade and revenues of the ſaid Colonies and Plantations, as direct the manner of determining and recovering the penalties and forfeitures therein mentioned.
Alſo ten public bills, and ſeventeen private ones.

Yeſterday there was a meeting of the principal Merchants concerned in the American trade, at the King's Arms tavern in Cornhill, to conſider of an Addreſs to his Majeſty on the beneficial Repeal of the late Stamp-Act.
Yeſterday morning about eleven o'clock a great number of North-American Merchants went in their coaches from the King's Arms tavern in Cornhill to the Houſe of Peers, to pay their duty to his Majeſty, and to expreſs their ſatisfaction at his ſigning the Bill for Repealing the American Stamp-Act, there was upwards of fifty coaches in the proceſſion.
Laſt night the ſaid gentlemen diſpatched an expreſs for Falmouth with fifteen copies of the act for repealing the Stamp-Act, to be forwarded immediately for New York.

"Glorious News."
The London Gazette. March 18, 1766. *Early American Imprints*

James replied, "The London merchants petitioned Parliament to repeal the Stamp Act. We didn't line their pockets by buying their goods, as long as we were taxed with the stamps. We hurt the British merchants enough that they lobbied Parliament for the Stamp Act's repeal. We stood together and we prevailed!"

"For certain, a celebration is in order," James continued. "We knew for the past month that Parliament had acted, but now we have confirmation. Surely we should gather in celebration for our freedom from the oppressive tax."

"We have our job to do," intoned his father in a dour manner. "After school's done, the boys may join their families."

"I understand Paul Revere has crafted something of a display, an obelisk. Cannon are set to fire on the Common, and there will be speeches aplenty."

"Go later, if you wish," John responded. "I am confident no parent wishes the boys excused from school early."

James retired from the conflict, fuming, to his desk in the northwest corner of the spacious room. A few students sauntered in, noisy and unusually distracted.

But throughout the big room many desks remained empty. After reprimanding Oliver twice for losing his place in reading and forcing Ben to recopy his passage three times for its errors, Master Lovell looked up and met James's eyes across the room. He shrugged his shoulders as a particularly loud gunshot resounded from the street, followed by the brisk beating of drums.

"All right, boys, you may go. Tomorrow's another day," the Master said reluctantly.

James followed right on the heels of the students, who lost no time in grabbing their jackets and running for the door. He turned to look at his father as he grasped the brass door handle.

"I'll see you tomorrow. Good-bye." His father looked calmly down at his desk and took out his worn copy of Bunyan's *Pilgrim's Progress*.

"To be sure," he said. "I may join the festivities later, if it suits your mother."

James saw a twinkle in his eyes. It puzzled him that his father could be on the one hand so dead set against the notion of defeating an unfair tax, and yet on the other hand might actually enjoy the town's commemoration of the tax's demise. *It just goes to show,* he thought, *we are all complex characters.*

Pushing past townspeople surging through the streets, all heading in the direction of the Common, James reached his home.

"Mary," he called. "Get your scarf, something to picnic on, and the children. We are going to the Common."

"I was wondering when you'd come," she answered from the kitchen. "I'll be ready in two minutes."

James found his son in the front room stacking blocks. "Come get your jacket, Jemmy. We're going to the celebration." Jemmy, at four, was tall for his age, with dark hair and straight, serious eyebrows like his father's. His gray eyes lit up with excitement.

Mary appeared in the doorway, handed James a basket of bread and sausage, and scooped up little John. "Here, you take Johnny and the basket. I'll get Joseph." She wrapped Joseph in her shawl, the youngest at nearly two, while James arranged Johnny in one arm and the basket of food in the other. Johnny, a sturdy three-year-old, stared at his father, curiosity winning over fear. Jemmy jumped up and down with excitement.

"I like nothing better than going on a walk with you," Mary whispered in James's ear as he held the front door open. Her red curls bounced under her bonnet. Little Johnny pulled James's ear and laughed. It was going to be a fine day.

The surge of people carried them down the streets and to the common. In days gone by the common was a grassy field where citizens of Boston could let their cows and sheep find pasture. Now, a group of heavy iron cannons pointed solemnly into the harbor. Throngs strolled about visiting and laughing. British soldiers, their uniforms brushed and shoes polished, leaned on their muskets. Many in the crowd sported their own firearms. Banners fluttered from houses. In the harbor, flags on the ships whipped and crackled in the breeze. Gulls wheeled and cried overhead in the bright sunshine.

At the center of the common stood a tall seven-sided pyramid bearing painted figures and designs. James and Mary followed the crowd that assembled around this impressive display, staring up to its peak high above their heads. Hundreds of candles glowed within its oil-soaked paper covering, emitting a rich light that shone through the detailed images on the paper. The crowd circled in wonder and admiration. Paul Revere himself, artisan and silversmith, had created this obelisk for the occasion.

"Look, there is America—in the figure of an Indian chief, protected by the angel of Liberty," James explained to his family. "And there is Satan delivering the Stamp Act while Lord Bute, the British Prime Minister, and other British officials watch. That scene depicts the beginning of the oppressive Stamp Act," he explained.

"Now look over here." Mary and the children followed him to the other side of the glowing obelisk. "Here an angel brings an aegis, a shield of divine protection, while the eagle feeds its eaglets in the Liberty Tree."

"There's America, Daddy," said Jemmy, pointing up at the Indian chief.

"Right it is," James said. "And this last is the funniest of all, for King George III dressed as a Dutch widow ('...you know that means a lady of ill repute,' he said under his breath to Mary, who startled and smiled) now introduces America to the Goddess of Liberty. We have our rights as free men here, fairly won by our heritage as Englishmen."

"It is beautiful," Mary said, admiring the carefully painted images. "And see the inscriptions: 'Our FAITH approved, our LIBERTY Restor'd, our hearts bend grateful to our Sov'reign Lord,'" she read.

"See, up there is King George, and other royal personages," James said, pointing high on the painted sides.

A cannon's boom shuddered the air and Joseph squealed in alarm.

"Come, let's sit down and eat," James said. The family found their way to the shade of trees and settled with other picnickers to watch the celebrations.

Bands, speeches, and cannon fire filled the afternoon. Some celebrants had passed by John Hancock's splendid house, where he had opened a pipe of wine for the enjoyment of any who came by. Others wandered the crowd with baskets, taking donations to bail out all those in jail so they might participate in the festivities. Joseph, Johnny, and Jemmy stared with wonder at the crowds, the soldiers fine in red uniforms, the speakers in formal black coats. As the afternoon deepened to evening, they fell asleep, nestled in a blanket on the soft grass.

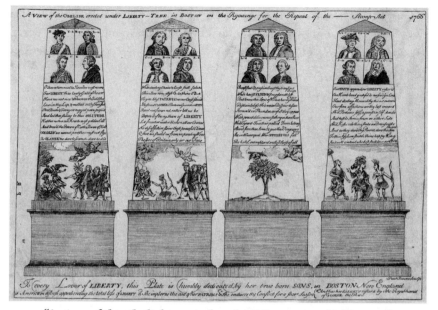

"A view of the obelisk erected under Liberty-tree in Boston."
Library of Congress Prints and Photograph

James left Mary with the children to find some of the Sons of Liberty that he knew and to visit with these acquaintances, toasting the great day with wine and accolades. When he returned to Mary, he brought her sweet rolls offered by a vendor, which she shared with Jemmy and Johnny, now awake and refreshed from their naps.

The sun sank behind high, rosy clouds. Purple and gray gave way to midnight blue. Stars danced over the dark sky, while the roaring peals of cannon from tall ships in the harbor drew exclamations of delight from the crowd. Smoke billowed across the water, silvery and luminous. Then the obelisk, shining in the dark, crowded field, illuminated by its hundreds of candles, hosted an awesome sight. From the middle of the tall figure, twelve rockets shot out. Fireworks of red, green, and blue spiraled upwards while the crowd roared. Whistling lights burst high into thousands of tiny gold stars, falling in light, filmy flakes like rain on the delighted onlookers. A whiff of gunpowder mingled with the lilacs on the spring air.

Just as that excitement died down, a second round of rockets burst forth from higher up in the obelisk, and again many in the crowd held their breaths and stared as the fireflies of the display burned, shrieked, and fizzled. James picked up Johnny and held him high to watch the sight, while Mary cradled baby Joseph, still sleeping, and Jemmy stood close beside her, his mouth open.

Then a final round shot of crackling rockets jetted forth from the top of the figure. This time there was no containing the joy of the crowd. Many stamped and clapped: "Long live Liberty! Long live King George!"

Music followed the fireworks, fife, horn, and drum playing popular songs. Jemmy and Johnny, excited and energetic, raced in circles with other boys. James watched the celebrations with contentment, glancing from the delighted townspeople to his happy wife with deepening appreciation of the peace the repeal of the Stamp Act should bring.

At eleven o'clock, twenty-one rockets exploded in the darkness. Gold and red sparks whirled into the sky and descended slowly on the delighted crowd. The booming echo resounded from the other side of the harbor. Horns blew, drums beat, and general applause filled the air.

James felt a tightness in his throat. He swallowed with difficulty and looked at the crowd, the ships at anchor, the flags fluttering. This was his country, his people. Long might they celebrate!

The obelisk had one more surprise in store for the entranced spectators. The horizontal wheel built into its top began to whirl. Sixteen dozen serpents, long strands of fireworks, shot out one after another, rising in shimmering trails, leaving phosphorescent crimson, pink, and blue paths illuminated in the sky. The excited crowd clapped and cheered. The last shouts died down, then the gathering turned to leave. James picked up the food basket and Joseph, who was now fast asleep.

"Come on, Mary. We'll go home," James said, cradling Joseph in his arms with the basket.

"I had a wonderful time," she said, her face glowing with excitement. "It's too bad we can't have a terrible tax repealed every day."

James laughed. "We surely have much to celebrate," he agreed.

They followed the crowds heading to homes. The streets gradually emptied, revealing bits of ribbon, crumpled handbills, and cast-off bread crusts littering the way, final remains of the procession that had passed through.

James knew the obelisk was to be placed under the Liberty Tree the following day. He looked forward to seeing again the delicate, detailed paintings on its sides. But at one in the morning, the masterpiece caught fire. James was startled to learn the beautiful pyramid with its carefully painted images had burned to the ground. Whether arson or accident caused the fire no one ever knew. The obelisk left behind a pile of ashes and memories of the joyful celebration of freedom for those who had seen it.

Chapter 11

Merchants' Agreement, Faneuil Hall

OCTOBER 28, 1767

The town meeting was unusually tense. Workers, merchants, artisans, lawyers, and, yes, schoolteachers, thought James, crowded Faneuil Hall. The tall, stately structure with its rows of regularly-spaced windows had been a gift to the town of Boston from Peter Faneuil, a wealthy merchant. Market was held here, gatherings social and at times serious, and formal meetings of Boston's town leaders.

James decided to attend the town meeting because he knew the topic of discussion was the Townshend Acts, a concern to Bostonians since word of the new taxes had arrived that summer. On June 29, 1767, Parliament had passed these Acts, reviving taxes all thought long banished. James had read the notice of the Acts printed and distributed by the king's agents with dismay.

He watched the Hall fill from his vantage point near the front. Samuel Adams, a leading figure in the Sons of Liberty, was talking loudly with his neighbors. Samuel Adams had just two years ago been elected to the Massachusetts legislative body. Next to him was James Otis, a respected lawyer who, a couple of years ago, had participated in the Stamp Act Congress in New York. James recalled that Samuel Adams and James Otis had graduated from Harvard at the same time.

John Hancock, merchant and participant in the Stamp Act Congress, sat in a conspicuous position near the front of the hall, looking relaxed yet serious. Nearby, James saw John Adams, lawyer and author of protest statements on the Stamp Act, concern twisting his placid features. Hundreds of merchants and workers filled the Hall, their talk raising a crescendo of sound.

The Townshend Acts, named after the Chancellor of the Exchequer Charles Townshend, filled the void of the Stamp Act. The colonies' relief had been short lived indeed. The repeal, called the Declaratory Act, had in fact contained the seed for future taxes, declaring that "the King's majesty...with...parliament assembled, had...full power and authority to make laws and statutes...to bind the colonies and people of America, subjects of the crown of Great Britain, in all cases whatsoever...." The colonies, celebrating the repeal of the hated Stamp Act, had overlooked the controlling wording of the Declaratory Act.

Enacted to raise funds for His Majesty King George's military, especially for the French and Indian War, the Acts placed a tax on all manner of items: lead, glass, paper, paint, and tea from Great Britain. The Acts also stated the British government sought to prevent "the clandestine running of goods in the colonies and plantations." *That does not sit well with our merchants,* thought James. *Smuggling, or trade avoiding the excessive duties charged by the British, is in fact a way of life for our merchants. Our courts do not take charges against smuggling seriously. Ships bring goods from France, Spain, or Italy, cheaper and not taxed, much preferred here in the markets over expensive British goods that are taxed, to boot.*

He glanced at comfortable John Hancock, prominent at the front of the room, smuggler extraordinaire with his fleet of ships.

The Townshend Act cleverly taxes goods not currently produced in the colonies or produced in very limited quantities, James reflected. *Therefore, we must import them. But as Ben Franklin, visiting in London, told Parliament in its debate on the Townshend Acts, Americans must become producers of just these articles and so obtain freedom from tyranny.* James hoped some action might result from this meeting. *People are rankled to be tools of a faraway Parliament raising money for its own purposes,* he thought.

Voices hushed and the crowd quieted as Samuel Adams and James Otis rose to speak. "We need to encourage the manufacture of those goods the Chancellor of the Exchequer attempts to tax with this act," said Samuel Adams. The crowd fell silent and listened with respect.

"If we keep buying the imports that are already expensive and made more so by the addition of taxes, we allow ourselves to become further impoverished," responded James Otis. Clapping and stamping greeted this statement.

James Otis continued. "Chancellor of the Exchequer Charles Townshend attempts to reign in imperial debt with this act. For our own good we must agree not only to cease buying imported tea, glass, paint, and lead, as well as other articles stipulated by the act, but we must actively promote the creation of these articles by our own artisans and merchants. So doing will strengthen our communities and avoid the support of a government that seeks only to increase its own well-being."

"Yes, yes," many said. "Aye, aye!" This discussion was going as he might have hoped, James thought, as he raised his own voice in agreement.

Paul Revere, silversmith and artisan, stood to declare, "The colony of Massachusetts can make glass and paint as fine as any imported."

Heads nodded; clapping swept through the hall. Others stood to speak.

"Our commerce has suffered; we are impoverished by the articles we are forced to buy from Britain. If we make our own, we become independent," a stout businessman said in a strong tone.

"We must agree together to ensure our independence and liberty," someone added.

"Huzzah! Yes. Yes."

"Should we not invite other towns in Massachusetts? Together we are strong," stated a voice from the back of the throng.

"Huzzah! Yes!" Loud applause followed. The stamping of feet echoed in the large room.

"We should invite other colonies, as well."

"If you can get your wife to give up her tea…" someone near James said, and then laughed loudly.

"My wife will give up what I want her to give up, don't you fear." James heard an angry response from close by.

An elderly man sitting near James began to cough. Annoyed, James strained to hear. Over the crescendo of hacks and coughs, he heard, "... especially the manufacture in the colonies of glass and paper—these must be encouraged. We conclude: Let a committee prepare the statement as resolved by this town meeting, that the merchants and people of Boston will avoid buying those items taxed by the British, and will instead buy locally made goods."

"Your votes, gentlemen. All in favor?" The town meeting erupted in assent. "Aye, yes." James loudly said "Aye" as well, but his voice was lost in the sound that carried from the great hall to the streets nearby. He got up from his seat, not unhappily leaving his coughing neighbor behind, and started towards the door. Solemnly the meeting broke up. Amid hopeful discussion, the members filed out.

James brushed against Josiah Quincy, lawyer and writer, as he left. He clapped Josiah on the arm. "A good business there. We will seek the support of the other towns in Massachusetts—and then the other colonies."

"Together we stand," Josiah agreed. His dark, intelligent eyes looked at James approvingly. "As the woodcut of Benjamin Franklin says, 'Join or Die.' Like that severed snake, each part a separate colony, we are strong only if together. Let us hope others will join us in non-importation."

"I agree; in due time we may find ourselves a union," James said, his heart suddenly full. Hope for the future seemed possible, with wise decisions such as those his fellow townsmen had just agreed upon. Hope for a peaceful and fair system, without taxes that seemed to benefit only those on the other side of the ocean. *In working together we may find that peace yet,* he thought.

"Join or Die."
Library of Congress Prints and Photographs

Chapter 12

Troops Come to Boston

OCTOBER 1, 1768

The act accompanying the repeal of the Stamp Act, titled the Declaratory Act, not only had made Parliament's authority over the colonies clear, but also had annulled the resolutions and acts of the Provincial Assemblies, which had asserted the colonies' right to recognize taxes set by their own representatives. *More than the obelisk has disintegrated since the night when we celebrated the repeal of the Stamp Act,* James thought. *In fact, our way of life and ability to set our own laws is threatened.*

James set his book down and stared out at the sea of boys, heads down, reading their Homer. Some appeared truly absorbed in their studies, but young Martin seemed far more interested in the state of his fingernails, and Thomas explored a deep scratch on the desk in front of him. James sighed and picked up his book again. Outside, a bell rang, then the rattle of far-off drumbeats resounded brightly, breaking the quiet afternoon. Passersby in the street shouted.

The ships must be coming, James thought, *bringing the British troops from Nova Scotia.* The largest British garrison in North America was there, some four hundred miles to the north on the coast at Halifax. Unwanted and unneeded, these troops would be a demonstration of British power, intended to quell any disturbance that might disrupt the proceedings of the Vice-Admiralty Court Act. The courts created by this Act would prosecute colonial smugglers without a jury, their guilt or innocence determined by a judge alone. *What has happened to the traditional right of Englishmen to trial by jury of their peers?* James wondered.

Troops would arrive under Colonel Dalrymple, though their departure would leave the British garrison at Halifax, Nova Scotia, barely manned. At least, that was what the paper said. No one knew how long the redcoats would be in town. The mere thought of an increased armed presence was repugnant to James, as it was to most Bostonians.

The boys looked up from their texts as an especially loud burst of drumbeats echoed from the harbor. A church bell pealed, then another.

"May we go to watch?" asked Samuel. All knew that the troops were due that afternoon.

James looked across the schoolroom at his father. "It's nearly four o'clock," the schoolmaster said with a sigh, his thick white eyebrows punctuation marks of dismay. He shrugged his shoulders, then turned to the boys. "Irregular, but yes, you may go. *Deponite libros.*"

Put down your books, James thought. He watched as John set his own book down on the desk with an irritated thump. The boys grabbed their coats and nearly tripped over one another in their haste to leave. "I hope they make welcome for Colonel Dalrymple," John said glumly.

"The Townshend Acts are an unpopular, unenforceable encroachment on the rights of Americans," James observed with displeasure, as the students scrambled for the door. He seldom talked about such matters with his father, since he knew well his father's disapproval of all actions or attitudes that questioned traditional authority.

Master Lovell did not answer, but began piling up the books on his desk in an effort to straighten it. James took a deep breath and continued. "You will remember that customs officials seized the *Liberty*, John Hancock's ship, in June of this year of our Lord, 1768. Their action angered many. The ship may have been doing what authorities term 'smuggling.' Yet local merchants recognize importing goods from countries other than Britain as the only way to do business. Merchants should be able to trade with whomever they like. Unfortunately, to operate profitably, as does Hancock, ships must avoid the infernal taxes that exist on so many luxuries—and necessities."

His father looked up from his task and sat down heavily in his chair. His response came bitter and direct as he glared at James. "Yet the purpose of the revenue raised by the Townshend Acts, as the document clearly states, is to defray the expenses of defending, protecting, and securing the British colonies. Why should anyone object to contributing to his or her own defense? Smugglers like John Hancock only reduce the funds available that support the common good."

"To make a profit, the taxes must be avoided," James explained. Reasonably, he thought, he continued. "And those taxes were not agreed upon by our local merchants and business people."

Another idea occurred to James. Though he knew the turn the conversation was taking, he decided to keep speaking. "As you may know, Hancock's ship was unloading when the customs officials arrested the captain and took charge of the ship. The seamen and shippers at the wharf cried an alarm and soon a crowd gathered. Before long, the customs officials found themselves mauled and slapped by the hands of the crowd. They were lucky to make their escape to Castle William, to the British fort at the island in Boston Harbor."

"I am well aware of the facts of that case and the unlawful behavior of that mob," responded John in disapproval. "In fact, such mob violence is not to be tolerated. There is no excuse for going outside the law."

"Don't forget, it was town leaders, including John Hancock himself, with Samuel Adams and Joseph Warren, who stepped in to persuade the rioters to disband. They, too, regretted the crowd's unlawful actions," said James. He felt this point, recognizing the town leaders' pursuit of peaceful actions, would surely meet with his father's approval. "It is a pity people are driven to act in such disregard for lawful process, but many are disturbed by high-handed authority."

"In fact," James continued, reaching for his jacket, "the convention held here in Boston not long ago discussed in calm and lawful manner many of these proceedings. Two hundred delegates from all over these colonies agreed that stationing soldiers here for the purpose of enforcing customs duties on paint, tea, glass, and lead would be despicable. Yet their peaceful resolutions are ignored, and the troops still come: Colonel Dalrymple and his two regiments, the 14th and 29th, together some 700 men, are now sailing into our harbor." *It is time we conclude this conversation,* he thought.

There is no point in annoying my father further, as there is bound to be little agreement between the two of us on this topic.

"I suppose," John said in a calm voice, "if you must pay attention to that sort of thing, you are right in the details. But you are not right in the attitude of disrespect and disregard for governmental authority, when that authority is central to the well-being of this colony. Really, James," he went on, his tone anxious and thoughtful, "you are asking for trouble, if you insist on looking at every action of government as if it were meant to harm your friends and fellow citizens."

James sighed and stood up. Of course, his father cared about him. Yet in these matters he could not possibly convince him to share his point of view. There was no use in talking.

Outside the church bells were pealing vigorously. "I'm going, Father," James announced. He picked up his coat, buttoning it against the early October wind. "I will see you tomorrow." He smiled at the older man as he left, knowing there was so much he could not explain and could not make clear. It was useless to pursue the argument further.

"Good night, then, if you must go," John said. He sat down dejectedly in his chair and picked up his book, his brow wrinkled with concern. More than likely, James knew, John would remain in the schoolroom for a while, tend to the stove, read his book, then go home. James knew his father could not understand the changes about him, whether spoken or published in the papers. Even as he cared about the old man, he recognized he must make up his own mind about the affairs of the day, and the events spoke to him so clearly he had little choice.

The sky glowed a deep, rich blue, as the sun's descent behind pale, translucent clouds illuminated the darkening sky and shone silver on the water. James joined the crowd—somber, thoughtful townspeople walking to the Long Wharf. The bells ceased tolling. Shops closed; business people left, locking their doors.

The big ships of the British navy, like great white birds, folded their sails at anchor, rocking not far off the wharf. Red-coated soldiers climbed into launches, group after group, filling them and rowing to the wharves. *Red-backs*, thought James, *a description that matches not only their coats, but also all too often their beaten bloody backs.* Many of these lads had been commandeered into service in the army, waking up after a night's drinking to find themselves enlisted for the "King's Shilling," a token bonus paid by His Majesty for enlisting. With extremely low pay and cruel discipline, it was a wonder that the Crown's soldiers were as brave and faithful as they were. Yet many would serve the British army throughout their lives, earning the name by which they were often called, "regulars."

The lines of soldiers marched down the Long Wharf to the rat-tat-tat of drums and the whistle of fifes. They lined up along Market Street, the brass buttons on their uniforms shiny, the facings on their coats, gaiters, and cross belts newly whitened with pipe clay. Their muskets, oiled and shined, stuck rigidly to their sides like inverted crutches. Their expressions held fixed and firm, though some must have been relieved to be off of the ships. The townspeople crowded the edges of the street, watching glumly, quietly. Little talk scattered in the crowd; for the most part people stood silently, waiting.

James's heart sank. This sudden influx of soldiers could not bode well. The convention with delegates from many colonies had just ended peaceably, yet now a challenge had come to the orderly operation of the town. The hated taxes would be enforced and Boston kept in line; never mind about the dissidents in New York or Pennsylvania. Boston had caused trouble for speaking out against oppression, so Boston would be punished. Where this would be taking them, James did not know.

As the setting sun peeked beneath the distant clouds, sending pink and gilded rays across the quiet sea, the troops formed ranks and stood at attention. Colonel Dalrymple, splendid in a white uniform, saluted Governor Bernard and the officials from the other towns. A growing whisper passed through the crowd. The troops will be quartered—quartered? James looked at Castle William, the island with its fort, two miles off in the bay. *That would be the logical place,* he thought, *barracks and beds there. But quartered? In private homes and in public buildings? Resentment and bitterness will be the result,* he thought, suddenly aware of the growing dark, the rumble in his stomach. The brief ceremony ended; the troops turned, formed lines, and filed off to a staccato drumbeat, a tinny fife, to their new quarters, some to temporary tents set up on the common.

James and others turned, started for home. He noticed a detachment of soldiers heading for Faneuil Hall. No doubt some would make that city meeting place their home. Others would end up in private homes, the Manufactory House, inns. *Boston has become a city occupied*, he thought. *This will change things.*

"A view of part of the town of Boston in New England and Brittish [sic] ships of war landing their troops 1768."
New York Public Library Digital Collections

Chapter 13

Non-Importation: The Shop of Abigail Whitney

OCTOBER 2, 1768

Walking down Union Street to market, the red and orange leaves of early autumn brightening the way, James passed shops selling all manner of goods. The baker had just set fresh loaves in his window; James caught a whiff of warm spices and his mouth began to water. Through the window of the candle maker's shop he spied some lovely cream-colored tapers and reminded himself to get some for Mary's table.

He looked out at Boston Harbor, the sun sparkling on calm water. An image came to his mind of dockworkers struggling against the press, forced against their wills up a plank to a ship. The struggle was still going on, James realized, but these days in different forms.

He heard men shouting, doors slamming. Through the rustling maple leaves he glimpsed Abigail Whitney, seller of imported damasks, calicoes, and linens, standing at the door of her shop. Mary was quite fond of Abigail's shop, where she could count on buying threads, buttons, needles, and all manner of necessary items—*as well,* James thought, *as a good many unnecessary items such as fans and necklaces.*

Abigail was standing on her front steps, her hands on her hips, her young daughter just behind her, shouting at a small crowd gathered in front of her steps. Their helper, a young man James recognized as a former pupil of his, stood looking helplessly at the crowd from the bottom of the steps. *What was his name?* James tried to remember. *Stuart?*

"You heard the talk today, Abigail. No more British imports." A stout man pointed directly at her, waving his hand energetically.

"My customers demand the items," Abigail responded defensively. "Where else can they get quality shoes, pins, lace, or buttons? They are not made here in Massachusetts or elsewhere in the colonies."

"They will be," was the retort. Around him the others in the crowd agreed, shaking their heads. "You'll have to find products to sell made here in the colonies."

James approached the crowd and walked to the front. Abigail recognized him. "Mr. Lovell, your wife shops here. Tell these men that we are only trying to make a living and our customers appreciate the quality goods we sell," she said.

James frowned. "Abigail, I can see that it will be difficult, but you'll have to change your stock. The town of Boston has agreed to non-importation until the duties on all imported items are repealed. We didn't vote for the tax so we shouldn't have to pay the tax. As difficult as it is, I'm afraid you'll have to put these items away for a while and find others to sell."

"We could always set fire to the stock," a voice from the back of the crowd threatened.

"Aye—or have your name published in the newspaper as a violator of non-importation," said the stout man. "A public reminder would result in a boycott of your store, and cripple your business."

The true Sons of Liberty

And Supporters of the Non-Importation
Agreement,

ARE determined to resent any the least
Insult or Menace offer'd to any one or
more of the several Committees appointed by the Body at Faneuil-Hall, and
chastise any one or more of them as they
deserve ; and will also support the Printers
in any Thing the Committees shall desire
them to print.

✍ AS a Warning to any one that shall
affront as aforesaid, upon sure Information given, one of these Advertise-
ments will be posted up at the Door
or Dwelling-House of the Offender.

"The True Sons of Liberty and Supporters of the Non-Importation Agreement." 1768, *Boston Gazette. Early American Imprints*

"Stuart," James ventured, relieved when the young man turned to him. *Good for me for remembering the name*, he thought. Sometimes it was tricky to remember every student's name, years later.

"I am sure you can help Abigail Whitney and her daughter find other goods to sell. You've a good head on your shoulders." James suddenly remembered the time Stuart had tried to play a trick on Master Lovell and had been caught red-handed hiding the lesson book. Presumably Stuart had a reliable side as well.

"Come, let's go. Good Mistress Whitney needs time to restructure her stock," James said, turning to the crowd and waving his hand in farewell.

To his relief the group dispersed, some complaining and speaking roughly. James had seen shops in Boston and elsewhere targeted for refusing to abide by non-importation with refuse, signs, or effigies. *Surely townspeople could boycott merchants in a peaceful manner*, James thought. *Non-importation will put pressure on the British to change the laws, but I would hope not through cruelty to individuals.*

IMPORTED from LONDON,
By Abigail Whitney,
AND TO BE SOLD at her Shop in Union-Street,
A large Affortment of Goods,
among which are the following Articles, quite low for the Cafh :

BLUE, green, and cloth-coloured EnglifhDamafks, neweft fafhion ftriped and flowered Luteftrings, Mantua Silks, cloth-coloured changeable, and green Mantua-Silks, rich Tobine Luteftrings, rich cloth colour Ducapes, plain and fprigg'd, rich Broglios, Meffihets and Crapes, fprigg'd and plainPoplins, plain and ftriped Camblets, beft double Camblets, figured Stuffs, Taffities, Perfi ns, Bengals, Alamode, figured MoJes, lace & fnail Trimming, handfomeAffortment Patches, Chints and Callico, Furniture Callicoes Lawns, Cambricks, Irifh Linnens and Sheeting, filk Gloves and Mitts, beft Bath Lamb Gloves and Mitts, fprigg'd and plainGauze, Fans, Necklaces, fine Bag hollards, 3-qr. and 7 8 hs Garlix, white Lace, a variety Broadcloths, German Serges, Ratteens, Kerfeys, Bays, Flannels, Swanfkin, Half-thick, Velvets, worked, thread and cotton Hofe, Morines, Callimancoes, Shalloons, Durants, Tammies, Worfled and Crewels, Canvas and yellow Holland, fewing filks, Threads, Tapes, Ribbons, twift & mettal Buttons, Mohair, filk and Hair, and fcarf twift, fhirt Buttons, Horn and Ivory Combs, filk linnen, lawn and gauze Handkerchiefs, Damafks and Diaper Table cloths, napkin Diaper, Buckrams, Cord and Braid, Englifh Shoes and Clogs, ftriped cotton-Hollands, cottonChecks, coloured Fuftain, Thickfe's, half-yard, and yard-wide, flowered and plain Dimothy, 6, 7, 8, 9, and 10 qr. Blankets, Duffils, good Wool-Cards, a goodAffortmentLooking-Glaffes, Curtains, ready made Bed quilts, with many other Articles not mentioned.

"Abigail Whitney Goods."
Massachusetts Gazette*, March 1768. *Early American Imprints

Chapter 14

Non-Importation: Tea, Glass

NOVEMBER 18, 1769

Mary pulled a pan of flaky brown rolls from the brick oven by the side of the fireplace. She set the pan by the loaves of bread cooling on the table, the family's bread for the week. A tantalizing odor filled the kitchen, toasty from the fire she'd fed all morning. The hot coals dwindled to piles of ash in the small brick oven, their job of baking the rolls finished.

"Can I have a roll?" Joseph jumped in excitement, nearly knocking over the butter churn standing near the table. He reached out a chubby hand to the warm rolls.

"Yes, you may." Mary pulled her skirts away from the fire as she reached to stir the stew bubbling in a pot, then knotted them up to keep them from the darting flames.

A crash sounded from the window at the end of the room, followed by a tinkle of flying glass. Shouts resounded from outside.

"What in heaven's name?" said Mary in alarm. She glanced through the window to see Johnny, Jemmy, and James Jr. dashing towards the house, slipping and sliding on the snowy walk. Joseph ducked behind his mother, his attention momentarily distracted from his half-eaten roll.

"It was a ball," Johnny stammered, opening the door. His face, already flushed from his play in the brisk air outside, reddened with embarrassment.

"It bounced off the tree—I didn't mean to," said Jemmy, running up beside his brother.

"We were just playing catch," added their older brother James Jr., stepping into the kitchen and stamping the snow from his boots. James Jr. had joined the family a couple of years ago, leaving his grandparents Hastings to become part of James's family so that he could attend the prestigious Boston Latin School. Calm and self-possessed, he often seemed lost in his own thoughts. He was not like his younger siblings, energetic and talkative, but he was self-reliant and unusually confident for his age.

"You shouldn't have been throwing a ball so near the house," said Mary. "What would your father say?" Mary liked James Jr. and rarely criticized him.

The door to James's study opened and he stepped into the kitchen. "What's going on?" he demanded. The three boys stared at him, flushed with misery.

"I see: the window's broken since you were playing ball near the house. Now we will have to board it up. There is no glass to be had, because we will not buy taxed British glass." James looked severely at the culprits. Already the crisp November morning had brought inches of snow outside on the ground while cool air flooded through the broken pane of glass, chilling the pleasantly warm kitchen.

"The sooner you board it up the better," said Mary, covering the rolls with a cloth. "I don't want baby Mary to catch a cold." She glanced at Mary sleeping peacefully in her cradle a safe distance from the fire. "William, too, has had the croup lately, and needs not be sick again." The two-year-old looked up from the blocks he was heaping at the mention of his name, then continued his efforts.

"Just hurry," she said with a smile. "Then we can have our dinner."

The boys glanced at each other, then began unbuttoning their coats. "Wipe your feet off," said their father sternly. "Put those wet boots by the fire."

"We'll have glass made here in the colonies before we know it," James said, turning to examine the broken window. "The non-importation agreement must be putting a terrible hardship on the British merchants. Shiploads of perishable goods rot in the warehouses, and cargoes of items meant for market languish in storage buildings, since no one will buy them. Before long Parliament will feel the pressure."

Mary did not answer, but nodded in understanding as she bent to stir the bubbling pot of stew again.

"Yes, we've had protests by a few Boston merchants," he added. "The publisher John Mein posted his opinion in the *Boston Chronicle*. Mein disagrees with non-importation and upholds the tax laws, but we can't all be wealthy bookbinders. Rejecting imported goods is the only way to let the authorities know that we refuse to accept the taxes," said James.

"So we will have to live with one less window," he added, his glance severe on James Jr., Jemmy, and Johnny. "You can help me board it up. James Jr. and Jemmy, go into the pantry. You may find some boards there. Bring them to me. And Johnny, fetch me the hammer and some of the longer nails."

"Don't worry," he added to Mary, a slight twinkle in his eye, "we'll have our window back when all this is resolved. Parliament will recognize our demands are just, we are within reason, and we deserve a voice in assigning our own taxes."

"John Mein was one of those attacked by the mob, wasn't he?" asked Jemmy, who sometimes read his father's newspapers.

"Yes," James said, "and he barely escaped tar and feathering. Those will do fine," he added, taking the boards that James Jr. and Jemmy handed to him. "The crowd was after a customs informer, as well as Mein. He received a blow from a shovel, so the royal guards took him to the guardhouse for protection. Johnny, thank you for getting the hammer and nails.

"I'm sure your grandfather would be concerned for Mein's safety," James added. "He reads the *Boston Chronicle* if he reads any newspaper. His views and mine don't agree, and…."

"Really, James, as if we didn't know that well enough." Mary looked at him with mock seriousness. "I thought you and your father were agreeing on matters in perfect peace."

"My views are not your grandfather's, but we love him all the same," James said to the boys. He set a board against the broken window. "Hold this board in place, Jemmy. All right—not a bad fit."

A few bangs later the window was dark with boards and the room began to warm again.

"Tea, James?" Mary poured a cup of steaming water from the kettle. "Here. And set this braided cloth against the gap in the door. It will keep the draft out," she added, giving Jemmy a length of stoutly braided goods. "Yes, we can drink tea from a plant growing in our swamps and bogs, though I do miss good East India tea." She picked up a newspaper clipping placed on the mantel and read it out loud.

> *Throw aside your Bohea and your Green Hyson Tea*
> *And all things with a new fashioned duty:*
> *Procure a good store of the choice Labradore*
> *For there'll soon be enough here to suit ye*
> *These do without fear, and to all you'll appear*
> *Fair, charming, true, lovely, and clever.*

"*The Boston Post-Boy* offered that rhyme, and I think it charming."

James took a sip and grimaced. "Labrador will have to do. We can enjoy imported tea when the time comes that we are not forced to pay taxes which benefit an empire."

"An empire that brings soldiers here, soldiers that cause problems," added Jemmy helpfully.

"The royal guards protected John Mein the publisher, which no doubt caused disappointment to many. Enough. Come to eat. We'll do our best with what we have; then some of you may split wood while I go to market," said Mary, setting cheese and sausage by the rolls on the table.

James Jr. came to the table right away, followed by the other boys. Taller and four years older than his brother Jemmy, James Jr. fit in well with the other boys. He was physically strong and quite capable, James thought. At school he managed well. His Grandfather Lovell seemed to be more than a little rough on him, however.

The other day Master Lovell had suddenly picked up his ferule and struck James Jr. hard, not the usual once or twice, but five times. Whatever he had done obviously did not deserve that punishment. James Jr. had borne the striking silently though he winced, but his expression shot daggers at his grandfather. James had spoken up from across the room. "Sir, you have flogged that boy long enough!" Grumbling, Master Lovell sat down and James Jr., to his credit, composed himself and returned to his place.

The next day, however, he had refused to go to school. "I will transfer to Master John Proctor's Writing School. He at least will not beat me for no reason," he said, his face glowering like a thunderstorm. James Jr. stood in the doorway of the home, looking out at his father who was about to leave.

James stopped on the steps of the house and turned around. He regarded James Jr. seriously. "If I thought it would really be best for you to transfer, I would help make the arrangements. However, consider that if you intend to go on to Harvard, you will need to stick with the Boston Latin School. It can prepare you best for the higher education you need so you can use the good mind God gave you. Just remember, Grandfather Lovell is an old man, set in his ways. Who knows what upset him? I often do not know myself. Just be polite, and he'll probably never do that again."

James Jr. looked down and shrugged. His troubled face calmed. "All right, Father, I will try. However, I will not be punished for mistakes I don't make."

He's strong and capable, James thought. *He will be all right.* James tousled his son's thick brown hair.

"You'll be fine, my boy. I am proud of you. Now it's time to go to school."

James Jr. tugged his coat on and shut the door to follow his father. Sighing with relief, James turned his head into the winter wind. *I tell my boys to remember their grandfather loves them,* he thought. *I sometimes don't know where I stand with him myself. However, we must do our best to get along. I will watch him, and if any more unnecessary discipline comes James Jr.'s way I will speak with him.*

Shaking his head at the memory, James took his seat at the table to enjoy Mary's good cooking. "Who knows where these issues will take us," he said to her. "Surely the royal authorities will see the unreasonableness of demanding we pay taxes to which we have not agreed. Meanwhile, we must do our best to get along with those with whom we disagree, like my father. Pass the stew here and I will serve it."

Chapter 15

Christopher Seider,
Victim of Violence

FEBRUARY 22, 1770

"Have you heard the news?" James picked up baby Mary from her basket by the table. She twisted her face into a little grin, looking at James intently, then knotted her forehead and began to cry. Mary looked up from the onions she was peeling. Tears streaking her own face, she set her knife down and shook her head.

"These are so strong. They've been in the bottom of the bin since September. I've hardly been out of the house all day. Little Mary has the croup and even Joseph and William are fretful. Here, hand her to me."

James passed the sniffling child to Mary. As many children as now filled the house, six altogether, someone was bound to be ill from time to time, he thought. The child's storm of tears died in a whimper as she reached eagerly for the bit of maple sugar in a cloth that Mary offered, her eyes red and puffy.

"Teething, I'll expect. A drop of peppermint would help," said James. He reached over and rubbed Mary's gums gently with his finger. Mary rewarded him by stopping her cries and sucking on his finger in interest.

"Before you tell me the news," Mary said, settling baby Mary back into her basket and taking up her knife again, "let me remind you that we are nearly out of potatoes, we have no carrots, and the flour bin is quite empty. These strong onions are the last of them. I've been to market three times this month, and the place is so disturbed, I left each time buying scarcely a thing.

"On marketing day, Thursday, shops that were importing British goods were ringed with crowds, customers smacked with dirt clods, windows besmeared and sometimes smashed. A few shops even had tar and feathers thrown on them. I will tell you, James, I do not feel safe even shopping there." Mary shook her head and looked intently at James, her face worried.

"I hurried by, hoping to find a safe place to buy my goods. Someone had put signs up on windows or doors stating 'Importer.' I saw some shop-keepers trying to take down these signs, but the crowd harassed them with clubs and sticks. There are merchants here who do not import, of course, but such was the lawless, rough nature of the crowd that I did not care to stay to find them." Mary's words tumbled out in a rush and her face flushed with emotion.

"I especially avoided the shop called the Brazen Head," she added. "The notice in the paper said that the owner, William Jackson, was an importer, and any Sons and Daughters of Liberty should not buy goods there. I have shopped there in the past, but this time I did not even try to go into the store."

James listened thoughtfully, but before he could speak Mary continued her tale.

"True, in the market soldiers arrived shortly after each incident of people throwing refuse or smashing a window, but by the time they came, the ones doing the damage were already gone," Mary said. "The soldiers walked about, hoping to find the leaders of the crowd.

"I am not a lover of violence. These are precarious times, unlawful acts endangering everyone who needs to be in the street. Either you shop your-self or you go with me," she concluded, her voice sharp with exasperation.

"The news I have to tell you relates to that trouble," James said. "Yes, I will go with you to market Thursday next, as school will be out early, as it usually is, to allow for market time. I had not thought your difficulties so great. Forgive me.

"The soldiers that have been quartered here for two years now, four regiments—the two from Nova Scotia and two from England—are here to guard the customs commissioners that no one wants, chosen by royal offi-cials as decreed by the Townshend Act." James got up and began to pace the length of the kitchen, up and down in front of the fire. Little Mary stared at him from her basket and sucked harder on her cloth-wrapped sugar.

James continued, "The soldiers are at loose ends. They know they aren't required or wanted, and they're defensive. And worse, people are upset because they're quartered all over. Officers are in homes, soldiers in warehouses or inns."

"They were moved out of Faneuil Hall not long ago," Mary agreed. She swept the chopped onions from the table into the pot of beans.

"The soldiers don't have enough to do," James said. "General Dalrymple, the commanding officer who brought them down from Nova Scotia, can't drill them properly or keep discipline as they're too scattered, so they get into mischief. They cause problems in the streets, acting rude when they have no reason.

"Take the terrible incident stirred up by Ebenezer Richardson, the customs informer," James went on. "People hate the man for assisting the customs commissioners who seize imported, often smuggled goods so they can't be sold. He reports to the attorney general and the customs board, who are all royal officials. Just the other day, Richardson tried to pull down an effigy that had been placed as a warning over the door of Theophilus Lillie, a merchant who was selling British imported goods in his shop. On Lillie's shop a sign stating 'Importer' had been posted. A crowd of young men and boys gathered, angry and ready to fight."

Mary listened intently. "So, that was how that trouble began," she said, nodding.

James took another turn with his pacing. "Yes, my dear, and an ugly event it turned out to be. The crowd saw Richardson attempting to take down the effigy, an ugly straw-stuffed caricature of the shop owner, really, and went after him, throwing rocks and taunting him. They chased him to his home where they continued to throw rocks, smashing and breaking his bushes and windows. Richardson shut his door and then poked a gun out of a broken window and began firing shots into the street. Two of his shots struck and killed a boy, Christopher Seider, eleven or twelve years old."

"I heard about that. It was a dreadful thing," Mary said. Her brow wrinkled in worry.

"The crowd went wild then, broke down his door, and pulled Richardson into the streets." James stopped pacing and bent to add wood to the fire. Outside cold winds blew, but inside near the fire the family was warm and snug.

He returned to his pacing. "Someone grabbed a rope and threw it over his chest. They dragged him quite a ways, as he screamed and shouted for help, the crowd threatening with loud cries to hang him. William Molineaux, a merchant who has always argued against importation, saved him. He convinced the crowd not to extend their anger to violence, but to take Richardson to jail. And they did, though I'm sure his neck still smarts from the thought of a rope. They took Christopher Seider's body to Faneuil Hall."

James laughed softly, but no humor was in his voice. "Our Boston crowds are always stirring up trouble, but half the time they have right on their side, and they are the people. They speak for the liberties of all of us. "

"So, what did the redcoats that loiter about the streets do in all of this?" Mary asked. "Did they stop the mob?"

"I'm glad you asked," said James. "One would think this kind of violence would be a perfect opportunity for them to earn their keep. In fact, soldiers did come and try to restrain the crowd as they were attacking Richardson's house. However, they may have made the matter worse, as they first threatened the gathering, then fired over their heads. That may have given Richardson the idea to pick up his gun. In any case, it appears his was the shot that killed the boy Christopher Seider. For a fact, the soldiers didn't help.

"There's going to be a public funeral in a few days, and you can bet everyone will turn out. The bells will toll all over town, shops will close, school will be out. It will be a day of mourning for all of Boston."

James sighed and made another turn on the creaking boards of the kitchen.

"No," he went on, "things have come to a pretty pass when we have soldiers, whole regiments, strolling the streets. Their presence aggravates the crowds. They walk around swaggering and bothering business establishments, or use the detested Writs of Assistance brought to life again by the Townshend Acts to search in private homes and warehouses without warrants for taxable goods. We'd keep law and order better on our own. Charles Townshend and his infernal Act have stirred up a pretty kettle of fish, and there's no denying it."

Chapter 16

Burial of Christopher Seider

FEBRUARY 26, 1770

Somber crowds filled the streets. Men, women, and children, dressed in their best clothing and wrapped against the chilly winds of February, walked solemnly under the icy gray sky up the hill to the burial ground. The funeral at Faneuil Hall that morning had been packed. Now mourners carried the body of Christopher Seider past the Liberty Tree at the edge of the common up to his resting place at the Granary Burial Ground. The whole town, it seemed, had turned out to honor Christopher Seider, a martyr at age eleven to the cause of liberty.

James walked with head up in the procession. Jemmy, Johnny, and James Jr. walked beside him, looking about them curiously. *There must be at least two thousand people here,* James thought. The line of those solemnly walking to the burial ground extended at least a mile. At the front of the procession marched some five hundred schoolboys, some James knew from classes at the Boston Latin School. Six of Christopher Seider's friends bore his coffin. Inside fine carriages rode well-to-do citizens, pulled by matched teams of horses.

The Liberty Tree bore a wooden sign hanging from a low branch: "Thou shalt take no satisfaction for the life of a murderer; He shall surely be put to Death." The Sons of Liberty had been busy, James thought. The inscription went on: "Though Hand join in Hand, the Wicked shall not pass unpunished. The Memory of the Just is Blessed."

British regulars lined the way, their boots polished, their uniforms brushed, looking grave and detached. The air crackled with tension and sorrow.

Reaching a stopping place near the burial site, the crowd stood back in respect as the casket passed, lifted high on the shoulders of the young pallbearers. James read on its head the Latin inscription *Innocentia Nusquam tuta*: Innocence is nowhere felt. James Jr. pointed to the Latin and read it quietly to his brothers.

Of course, James thought. *Where youthful innocence should flourish we have pain and sorrow.* He remembered hearing that young Seider lived after he was shot for a brief time. The boy had spoken clearly and politely to Dr. Joseph Warren, the doctor who attended him. In fact, he had shown bravery and calmness throughout his ordeal.

Peering through the crowd, James read at the foot of the casket *Latet Anguis in Herba*. The serpent lies hidden in the midst of the grass, he translated. He glanced approvingly at his young sons, standing near him, apprehensive and aware. *How grateful I am for each of them,* he thought. The ball that struck Christopher Seider could have struck any one of them. He shivered at the thought. *Or it could have struck me, had I been there, for that matter.* He looked back at the rows of British soldiers lining the path, their muskets at attention in defiance. *We may have more to mourn before these troubles end,* he thought.

Chapter 17

The Boston Massacre

MARCH 12, 1770

James walked in and shut the door firmly behind him, a flurry of snow swirling in. The March wind blew keenly from the east, moaning and whistling down the chimney.

"I went to the bookstore this evening. Such carrying on as everyone is doing over the massacre a week ago. True, it is a sad occurrence. The *Boston Gazette* gives an account of the horrific tragedy." James shook snow off the heavy coat he wore and placed it on the stand by the door. He settled himself in the comfortable chair by the fire.

"That is all anyone is talking about: the nightmare of King Street running with the blood of citizens," Mary said, setting down the flax she was carding and filling the kettle from the crock of water.

"British troops shooting townspeople is a tragedy, an affront to our liberties," said James. "People are furious. But redcoats have filled this town for two years, and we've seen confrontations in the street over and over."

"At market last week some boys threw stones at sentries and then ran off laughing," said Mary. She shook her head in disapproval, her curls bouncing. "I heard a soldier arguing with a merchant. The language he used! I had to walk away, though I would have looked at the merchant's goods." She picked up the steaming tea kettle from its hook over the fire and poured hot water into James's cup.

"It's common for the lobsterbacks to be teased," said James. "We didn't ask for these soldiers, and they do little good." He picked up his teacup, wrinkling his nose as he inhaled the musky scent of Labrador tea.

"The redcoats only serve to make people angry," Mary agreed, taking a sip from her teacup. She stood up to tend to the fire crackling in the hearth, careful to keep her skirts from the flickering flames. "Now supper will be ready soon. The soup is nearly finished." She lifted the lid and stirred the steaming ham and potato soup in the large iron kettle, a pleased smile on her face.

"About dusk a week ago, near the Customs House, the violence erupted," said James. "Maybe the boys and apprentices threw rocks or snow at the sentries there to tease them. But that gave the soldiers no excuse to fire at the crowd. When soldiers are stationed in a law-abiding place with no need, there is bound to be frustration and anger. They say a soldier got into a fight at John Gray's ropewalk the previous week. Why a soldier would pick a fight with anyone just working is beyond me, but perhaps the worker did start the fight, not the soldier. We may never know. By Monday evening, last week, the argument had developed into an outright brawl."

He took a folded newspaper from his pocket and spread it out. "Here's what the paper said."

"What are you reading?" asked Jemmy, coming in from the front room, curious. Johnny and Joseph followed. James Jr., across the hearth, set down the book he was reading and listened.

"All of you, sit down. You need to hear this," said James. His voice assumed the importance it often bore in the schoolroom.

The Town of Boston affords a recent and melancholy demonstration of the destructive consequences of quartering troops among citizens in a time of peace, under a pretense of supporting the laws and aiding civil authority; every considerate and unprejudiced person among us was deeply impressed with the apprehension of these consequences when it was known that a number of regiments were ordered to this town under such a pretext, but in reality to enforce oppressive measures; to awe and control

*the legislative as well as executive power of the province,
and to quell a spirit of liberty.…*

James stopped and looked at his family. He set his newspaper down on the table. "That pretty much states it. The soldiers are here as oppressors, but it was pretended they are quartered among us to aid the civil authority. We have Governor Bernard and his appointed Commissioners to thank for the soldiers' presence. In reality, such a demonstration of power cannot serve to help support peace."

"A redcoat spit on my friend two days ago when he walked too close," Jemmy agreed, looking at his father intently.

"I think their uniforms are quite fine," said Johnny thoughtfully.

"Fine their uniforms may be, but their presence is unnecessary and causes great trouble," James said sternly.

"The paper says that on Monday evening last, four youths, Edward Archbald, William Merchant, Francis Archbald, and John Leech passed a soldier in an alley who was carrying a large sword. Edward told William to take care of the sword. He may have been joking, but in response the soldier struck Edward on the arm and then stabbed through William's clothing. The sword pierced his cloak and grazed his skin near his armpit. William struck the soldier, but someone nearby ran to the barrack and returned with two armed soldiers."

The boys listened attentively. James Jr. closed his book, stood up, and came over to the table next to James, picking up the newspaper in curiosity. James glanced up at James Jr. *He is nearly as tall as Mary,* James realized with a start. *Before long he will be twelve years old.* Taking a big drink of his Labrador tea, James continued. "A brawl then followed between the boys and their friends and more soldiers. The soldiers poked and jabbed with cutlasses and bayonets, even though the boys were unarmed. A passerby, Samuel Atwood, saw the soldiers rushing after the boys and asked if they intended to murder people. One answered, 'Yes, by God, root and branch.'

"The tussling continued until thirty or forty boys rushed into King Street, where Captain Preston and a group of soldiers stood with fixed bayonets. Boys threw snowballs, the soldiers threatened with bayonets, and the paper reports that Captain Preston then gave the command to fire.

"Seven, eight, or as many as eleven guns, so says the paper, were fired." James looked around at his sons, who were listening with round eyes.

"Those soldiers should have gone inside and ignored the boys," James Jr. said wisely. "They made it worse by getting angry."

"A thoughtful comment, my boy." James nodded his head in agreement. "Indeed they did make it worse. Three of the townspeople died outright, another not long after. Others are grievously hurt and near to death. The result was tragic."

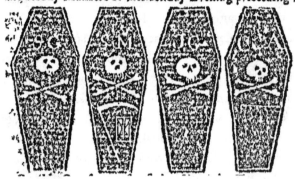

"Bloody Massacre of March 12, 1770."
Boston Gazette, **March 12, 1770.** *Early American Imprints*

"I remember being wakened by the church bells that night, wondering what the alarm was," Johnny said.

"Lieutenant Governor Hutchinson met late that night with town members and members of His Majesty's Council in the town house," said James. "The Lieutenant Governor assured them he would deal with matters the next day. Captain Preston was arrested and put in prison around three in the morning, and the soldiers who fired were imprisoned shortly afterwards.

"But one good thing happened," James went on. "Lieutenant Governor Hutchinson requested that Colonel Dalrymple remove both regiments from the town and confine them to barracks at Castle William until other orders come. He recognized that the soldiers were just causing trouble in the town."

"Removing the regiments from the town should help keep the peace," James Jr. said thoughtfully.

"I think you are right there," said James.

"Two days ago we went to the funeral for the four who were shot and killed by those soldiers." Eight-year-old Jemmy looked down with importance at Johnny, who was, at seven, just one year younger than he. "I got to go with Poppa and so did James Jr."

"I got to stay home with Joseph," said Johnny, giving Jemmy's arm a pinch. Three-year-old William looked at Johnny and laughed. Jemmy pulled his hand back in a threatening motion towards Johnny.

"Stop that," said James. He gave Jemmy a severe look. Jemmy squirmed and moved farther away from his brother, his face reddening.

"The hearses lined up in King Street. There were so many fine carriages. John Hancock's carriage was beautiful, with matching gray horses. I saw one carriage trimmed in red velvet. They marched up the hill to the Burying Ground," said James Jr.

"Such a crowd Boston has never seen," said James. "There were perhaps ten thousand people in attendance."

"People were so sad," added Jemmy. "Some were crying."

"They put the bodies into one grave," said James soberly. "The town will make a special marker to commemorate them, no doubt."

He unfolded the paper and found another section. "The important thing is this: the court has appointed John Adams to defend the soldiers. As a lawyer he is known for his shrewdness and honesty. That means they will get a real chance at a trial, not just a trumped-up verdict.

"Here," he said, rustling the pages. "In this paper Captain Preston, reported to have given the command to fire, states his thanks for the defense that has been appointed to him. From the Jail these are Captain Preston's words:

> *Permit me through the channel of your paper, to return*
> *my thanks in the most public manner to the inhabitants*
> *in general of this town—who throwing aside all party*

and prejudice, have with the utmost humanity and free-
dom kept forth advocates for truth, in defense of my
injured innocence, in the late unhappy affair that hap-
pened on Monday night last; and to assure them, that I
shall ever have the highest sense of the justice they have
done me, which will be ever gratefully remembered, by
their much obliged and most obedient humble servant,
Thomas Preston.

BOSTON-GOAL, Monday, 12th March 1770.
Messieurs EDES & GILL,
*PERMIT me thro' the Channel of your Paper, to return
my Thanks in the most publick Manner to the Inhabitants in general of this Town——who throwing aside all
Party and Prejudice, have with the utmost Humanity and
Freedom stept forth Advocates for Truth, in Defence of my
injured Innocence, in the late unhappy Affair that happened
on Monday Night last : And to assure them, that I shall
ever have the highest Sense of the Justice they have done
me, which will be ever gratefully remembered, by
Their much obliged and most obedient humble Servant,*
THOMAS PRESTON

"Boston-Goal [Jail], Monday, 12th March, 1770."
Early American Imprints

"It is a mark of freedom that we respect law and that we honor the dignity of everyone, even those accused of murdering innocent civilians. We should be proud that these soldiers will be tried in a court of law," James added.

"Come, your supper is ready. Jemmy, get the plates," said Mary. "I will look at the paper after dinner, James. I'd like more spermaceti candles for our lamps. There may be a notice of those for sale in the paper."

"They are costly, but we will see. I have some tutoring in French arranged in order to take in a bit more cash. Children, take your seats at table."

Of all things, James thought as he tasted Mary's savory ham soup, *we must guard against the loss of our liberties. The removal of the regiments is a good step, as is the trial of Captain Preston and the other soldiers. The preservation of law is the foundation of freedom, so we do well to bring those accused of firing to trial, though we condemn the tyranny that brought the soldiers to our streets in the first place. My family's peace is so important to me,* he thought, looking down at the heads bent to their meals. *Law and liberty still reign here; the trial should prove that.*

Chapter 18

Boston Discusses the Massacre: *A Short Narrative*

APRIL 15, 1770

"Listen to this," James said. It had been a full day at school. Classes had gone well with a few interruptions from Francis, who had a violent cough, and Charles, who had to run outside twice with an upset stomach. Otherwise, the boys worked diligently, and for once James had no need to threaten or chastise the scholars for want of effort.

Now it was nearly dismissal time. James had just finished reading *A Short Narrative of the Horrid Massacre*, the town's collection of depositions for witnesses and participants in the Boston Massacre. Shortly after the dreadful events, the town meeting had chosen Joseph Warren, James Bowdoin, and Samuel Pemberton to obtain the facts of the situation. They had turned over the task of getting depositions to justices of the peace, who had taken ninety-six statements.

Of course, the goal of *A Short Narrative* was to convince the townspeople of the guilt of the soldiers. Even though copies were not to be distributed within Boston, town officials reasoned that providing copies for neighboring towns would do just as well for release of information. While he usually did not talk about happenings in the town at school, James decided to discuss *A Short Narrative* with the students.

"Tell me what you think of this," James said. The boys stopped their reviews of the assigned readings, shut their books, and turned to him, their attention focused.

James read a statement aloud from the introduction to *A Short Narrative of the Horrid Massacre*: "'While the town was surrounded by a considerable number of his Majesty's ships of war, two regiments landed and took possession of it; to support these, two other regiments arrived some time after from Ireland: one of which landed at Castle Island, and the other in the town.'"

"The troops stayed here for nearly two years," said Lewis, a lively boy in the second form.

"They were everywhere. Until this week, we couldn't go to the shops or the common without seeing the troops," added James Jr.

"So, you all know the difficulty." James picked up the pamphlet again. He was proud of James Jr. for speaking up. A good student, he was usually shy.

"'Thus were we, in aggravation of our other embarrassments, embarrassed with troops, forced upon us contrary to our inclination—contrary to the spirit of Magna Carta—contrary to the very letter of the Bill of Rights, in which it is declared that the raising or keeping a standing army within the kingdom in time of peace'—by the way," he added, interrupting the reading, "what again was the Magna Carta and why was it important?"

"The Magna Carta was the great charter that the knights and lords of King John forced the king to sign after the Battle of Runnymede in England in 1066. Since it limited the king's power, in a way it was the beginning of Parliament," said one of the older students, Daniel. Heads nodded and a murmur of agreement went through the group.

Across the room Master Lovell, who had been checking on work in the garden, returned and looked inquiringly at the discussion going on. Usually the boys would be reading at this time. He sat at his desk and shuffled his books to one side, his head cocked to listen.

"So, the Magna Carta is the beginning of what we know to be English liberty and rights," James said. "Therefore, it was a very important document for all of us." He continued reading.

... keeping a standing army within the kingdom in time of peace, unless it be with the consent of parliament, is against the law—and without the desire of the civil magistrates, to aid whom was the pretense for sending the troops hither: who were quartered in the town in direct violation of an act of parliament for quartering troops in America: and all this in consequence of the representations of the said Commissioners and the said Governor....

James looked up. "Quartering troops then, as *A Short Narrative* reminds us, means forcing troops on civilians without their consent. You know the royal troops stayed in houses, in warehouses, and often in inns."

"My father had to take officers into our inn," said William. "He told me to be polite to them, but he didn't want them to stay there."

"That was unquestionably a problem for your father and for others," James said in agreement. "The soldiers have presented a problem for a very long time. Now we are all witness to the violence such armed men can bring. Here's one of the depositions from the night of the massacre." James read aloud from the paper, glancing at his father across the room. Master Lovell looked as though he'd like to speak, but instead he shook his head and said nothing.

Benjamin Frizell, on the evening of the 5th of March, having taken his station near the west corner of the Custom-House in Kingstreet, before and at the time of the soldiers firing their guns, declares (among other things) that the first discharge was only of one gun, the next of two guns, upon which he the deponent thinks he saw a man stumble: the third discharge was of three guns, upon which he thinks he saw two men fall, and immediately after were discharged five guns, two of which were by soldiers on his right hand; the other three, as appeared to the deponent, were discharged from the balcony, or the chamber window of the Custom-House, the flashes appearing on

the left hand, and higher than the right hand flashes
appeared to be, and of which the deponent was very sen-
sible, although his eyes were much turned to the soldiers,
who were all on his right hand.

James cleared his throat. "You can see that many details are unclear even to this person who was present. More than once he says he 'thinks.' That is because he is not certain. There were too many things happening for him to be sure of the events, and this is true for most of these deponents whose testimonies are included in *A Short Narrative*. People heard guns fire; some state the fire came from the soldiers, some believe they saw fire from the middle or upper story of the Custom-House, which stood behind the soldiers. We may never know what happened to be sure."

Taking advantage of the quiet that lay in the schoolroom, the students' obvious interest, he continued. "Another deposition from *A Short Narrative* hints that inciting violence was on the solders' minds even before the incident." James glanced at his father, who was squinting nervously in his direction.

Daniel Calfe declares, that on Saturday evening the 3d
of March, a camp-woman, wife to James McDeed, a
grenadier of the 29th, came into his father's shop, and
the people talking about the affrays at the ropewalks, and
blaming the soldiers for the part they had acted in it, the
woman said, the soldiers were in the right; adding, that
before Tuesday or Wednesday night they would wet their
swords or bayonets in New-England people's blood.

"That statement indicates pre-meditation," Henry, an older student, said thoughtfully.

Master Lovell stood up and coughed. Before he could say anything, James concluded, "We can be proud that we have restored order and peace, that the soldiers accused of murder will have a trial, that the soldiers are removed from the town. Making decisions to ensure law and equity in the spirit of Magna Carta is our priority." The boys silently listened, their faces grave and serious. James glanced at his father, whose face darkened as he pulled his watch from his pocket.

"You may be dismissed," said John, his voice gruff. "Good night, boys."

"Good night, sir," said one after another of the students to both teachers, picking up coats and bags before departing out the heavy door.

Soon John and James were alone in the square, spacious room. "Did you have to devote so much time to reviewing the unfortunate events that have happened in our town lately?" said John, his eyebrows knitting in concern.

"It is their town and they need to know what is happening just as much as you or I." James stood up and picked up his coat. He put it on over his waistcoat, smoothing the collar and adjusting his cuffs. "I believe we can promote their wisdom not only by their studies, but by their knowledge of the difficulties we face."

"You think we have difficulties?" John's voice rose, his cheeks flushed red. "We have difficulties only because people do not show respect for the king's troops. Unemployed boys have nothing better to do than to heckle the troops until they fire in self-defense. What is honorable or patriotic about that?"

"I have to agree with you, Father, that the scuffle arose out of idle mischief. Yet troops stationed here for two years have caused nothing but ill feelings, quartered as they are here without need, wandering about the streets leering at the inhabitants as if they were criminals instead of self-respecting citizens." James chose his words with care. He did not wish to inflame his father's anger.

John picked up an old exercise book and in his frustration began shredding it into fine bits, the pieces falling into a heap on his desk. "We have the finest system of government in the world. We have a governor that hears our requests and acts on them. We have a court system and the best schools in the colonies. We are permitted to worship as we choose. What else could we want?"

James paused before speaking. He considered his words carefully. "We petitioned the king to remove the unnecessary, harsh taxes. We humbly addressed the king with the utmost courtesy. He ignored—perhaps didn't even read—the petitions. Instead, we received troops quartered in our town. I don't think that is a just response to a reasonable request."

"But," he added, seeing that his father was about to add to his argument, "the matter is not for us to decide. Also, surely loss of life should be avoided at all costs. The courts will decree the response for those who fired on the five who died. The response will affect our students' futures, indeed the futures of us all.

"Therefore, I thought it best for the students to have some time to discuss the event. Good night," James said, standing up. "I hope you have a pleasant evening, Father." He bowed slightly to his father, walked to the door, and left. *It is not always easy to work with one's father*, he reflected, descending the stone steps. *Particularly in this matter, we do not see eye to eye, not at all. I did well to end that discussion peaceably.*

Chapter 19

Spinning and Tea

JUNE 30, 1770

"So, Mary, no tea in the house?" James settled into his favorite chair. It was early in the morning, and a welcome westerly wind blew in the open window, freshening the warm June air.

"No, not a bit of bohea. We have Labrador and peppermint. Which would you like?"

"Labrador doesn't always sit so easily with me. I will have peppermint, please," James answered.

"With some honey from our neighbor?" asked Mary.

"That will do very well."

Mary brought him a steaming cup and settled near him with her spinning wheel. She drew flax fibers through a comb—a wicked-looking toothed object—then placed the bundle of combed strands on the distaff by the wheel. Dampening her fingers in a bowl of water nearby, she fed strands into the aperture of the spinning wheel as it whirled, its treadle clicking. The smooth thread rolled onto the bobbin. Soon her fingers were flying as the wheel twisted the flax fibers into a thread. "I have just this bit to finish, then I am putting away my work."

"The spinning goes well?" James asked.

"I find that this wheel does better than the smaller one," she said, gesturing to the large wheel in front of her. "Today I'm going to the Reverend Tuttle's. Twenty-five of us are meeting there with our spinning wheels. It's to be a spinning bee to make yarn for the widows and poor of our parish.

The lack of imported British cloth has hurt them greatly. I can give my time to that cause."

James took a sip of tea. "Did you notice the apples forming on the trees? Cider will be good this fall. I so much enjoy a good cup of cider. When will you return from your spinning?"

"I shall be back by evening. I'll take William and Mary with me. James Jr., Jemmy, Johnny, and Joseph may stay here. They have the garden to tend and the chickens to feed. After all, James Jr. is twelve years old now, Jemmy eight, Johnny and Joseph both seven. The responsibility will do them good."

The clicking of the spinning wheel stopped. Mary turned to James. "I imagine you would like some breakfast." She reached into the cupboard and took out some cheese and bread. "Cut yourself some of these." She gave him a quick kiss on the cheek, leaving behind the scent of her favorite rose-scented lanolin, and went to the storeroom to get a sack of flax.

Peppermint tea is not so bad, James thought. *I'll get used to it.* He called to Mary, "The merchants of Boston agreed on a resolution earlier this month to continue with non-importation until all duties on every product are repealed. They sent their resolution to the merchants of New York, expecting agreement."

"I am so pleased you can spin and make some of our clothing," he added. "Non-importation of all goods hurts the British merchants. Imagine: loaded ships arrive at our docks and must return home with full cargoes because none will buy them, so no profits are yielded to the merchants. Those merchants will soon make their voices heard in Parliament." James stirred a spoon of honey into his tea and bit into the cheese and bread.

Mary returned from the storeroom with a bundle of flax fibers. "Jemmy can help me carry the wheel to Reverend Tuttle's. Then he'll return to help his brothers. I'll be leaving shortly."

James nodded with approval. "Measures taken here in Boston have made an impact," he said. "We have made enemies. Two days ago, on June 28th, the *Massachusetts Gazette and Boston Weekly* printed a British plan to cut off Boston's communication with the colonies. Furthermore, the plan would deprive the people of Boston of their firearms. They must think we are inclined to violent protest." James chuckled, remembering all too well the mob ransacking Lieutenant Governor Hutchinson's fine mansion. "Governor Hutchinson, too lenient for Lord North, King George's Prime Minister, is to be recalled and replaced by Governor Bernard," he added.

"Enemies we do not need, but we must be firm in our stance, of course," Mary agreed. "Come, Jemmy, she called. "I need you to help me."

James adjusted his waistcoat, a recent product of Mary's spinning and weaving. The cloth was dyed a rich brown with walnut shells. True, the fabric was not as fine as the linen imported from England, but it was soft and serviceable. He and his children would wear homespun.

BOSTON, June 8.

AT a Meeting of the Merchants and others in Trade, on Monday last, a Letter received by Express from the Merchants at New-York was read, proposing some Relaxation in the Non-importation Agreement: The Subject-Matter of this Letter was maturely considered and debated; and it was thereupon Resolved still to adhere to the Non-importation Agreement, without the least Deviation until the Revenue Act imposing a Duty on Tea, &c. was totally repealed: And the Trade further Voted, That the standing Committee should immediately inform the Merchants of New-York of this their RESOLUTION; and the Express returned on Tuesday last with this Resolution.

"Boston, June 8: At a Meeting of the Merchants."
The Massachusetts Gazette and *Boston Weekly*. Thursday,
June 28, 1770. *Early American Imprints*

Boston Massacre Trial Begins: Captain Preston

OCTOBER 24, 1770

The Queen Street Courthouse, a stately building adorned with a cupola, swarmed with townspeople and red-coated soldiers. The long-awaited trial of those accused of murder in the shootings on King Street on March 5, known as the Boston Massacre, was about to begin. A buzz of excitement filled the air—mutterings, conversations, even a spatter of laughter. Samuel Adams, his hair tied back in a queue, looked up at James from his seat near the front of the room and smiled. James Bowdoin, a classmate of James's from Harvard chosen by town leaders for the Governor's Council for his strongly patriotic views, also caught his eye and nodded a greeting.

"Look, there are the judges." Jemmy wiggled on the bench next to his father in his excitement.

"Be quiet," James said impatiently. He had taken Jemmy, James Jr., and Johnny with him, telling them "This will be an event you will always remember." However, there were few children in the courtroom. From their seats in the balcony, James and his three boys could see the whole proceedings. School was out for the day but would resume tomorrow. James himself would not be able to attend the trial daily, but could arrive in the afternoons to hear the result of the day's proceedings. The boys would attend perhaps only this once.

The judge Benjamin Lynde entered the front, splendid in his black robe and white powdered wig. Lieutenant Governor Thomas Hutchinson had declined to judge the trial. John Adams, attorney for the defense, took his place near the front, his wig slightly disheveled. He glanced in a thoughtful manner at the row of eight white-faced British soldiers seated behind him, shook hands with Captain Prescott who bowed appreciatively, then took his seat.

"That's John Adams," said James Jr., a note of respect in his voice.

"Yes," James nodded, "he's one of three counsels for the defense. He doesn't earn any approval from some in this town for taking on the case of those accused of killing citizens, but in his mind everyone deserves a fair trial, and I agree."

Behind Adams came his fellow attorneys, Josiah Quincy, Jr. and Robert Auchmuty, who also shook Preston's hand, nodded to the soldiers, and took seats next to Adams. The four townspeople accused of disrupting the peace sat to the side of the soldiers, looking more bored than worried. The soldiers, on the other hand, shrank in their seats and looked as if they'd melt out of sight if they could.

The attorneys for the prosecution, Robert Treat Paine and Samuel Quincy, the older brother of Josiah Quincy, entered, their wigs freshly powdered and papers in hand.

"It's going to begin!" Johnny poked Jemmy with an elbow.

"Be quiet now. You're here to listen," James growled.

Following a rap of the officer's gavel, all in the courtroom rose and conversation ceased. The craftsmen, merchants, sailors, and officers who crowded the benches and balcony stood with respect, waiting for the judge to speak.

During the long summer, tensions over the Massacre had risen and feelings ran high. True, having the 14th and 29th regiments out of the city and lodged at the island in Castle William had been a great improvement. No more was Boston, a town of some fifteen thousand, throbbing with four thousand soldiers.

But the conflict had continued in print: the *Boston Gazette* offered frequent opinions on the cruel actions of the soldiers. The town had collected depositions from witnesses and participants in the violent night, printed by Benjamin Edes and John Gill of the *Boston Gazette* at town expense. *A Short Narrative of the Horrid Massacre* made clear the injustice of armed soldiers inflicting violence on helpless civilians. Copies were sent throughout Massachusetts to influence public opinion, though not directly released in Boston. Most importantly, forty copies of *A Short Narrative* were sent to London, as town leaders hoped to influence official British policy and have royal troops removed altogether from Boston.

Finally, Paul Revere's colored engraving, created just three weeks following the March 5 event, depicted the soldiers firing on an undefended crowd. The sale of "The Bloody Massacre Perpetrated in King Street in Boston" had been a match set to straw, sparking anger for British brutality from everyone who had seen it.

"The bloody massacre perpetrated in King Street, Boston, on March 5th, 1770 by a party of the 29th Regt."
New York Public Library Digital Collection

Revere's engraving emphasized the horror of the confrontation. He had portrayed the soldiers as bullies, standing in their red uniforms in a line, firing in unison on a horrified and unarmed crowd. Behind the soldiers appeared their commander, raising his sword to give the order to fire. Three victims lay on the ground, blood gushing from their wounds. Two others were carried away from the scene of carnage. The engraving presented the scene differently than any account of the events, serving its purpose in inflaming many in Boston with fury for the slaughter of innocents.

The other side likewise had entered the public debate with its own publication. Lieutenant Governor Hutchinson required a justice of the peace who agreed with the British point of view to collect another set of depositions, generally from the same witnesses and participants. The published collection, *A Fair Account*, changed few people's minds about who was guilty. *A Short Narrative* had done its work. The town had been stewing over the events and the war in the press since March, and now it was late October.

Looking about him at the balcony and the seats below, James saw a crowd eager to listen, yet strangely enough, here and there he saw empty seats. *Or maybe not so strange,* James thought. *People know what they think of the situation. They've read the depositions, they've read the statements of the opposition. They know what they think and they've long since made up their minds. The people expect that justice will be served. Foreknowledge has calmed and eased the situation; having the whole story exposed in the press has been a deterrent to thoughtless antagonism.*

"When will they start?" Johnny asked impatiently.

"Hush. It is beginning now."

The Clerk of the Court called for attention. "His Majesty's Superior Court of Judicature, begun and held at Boston within and for the County of Suffolk, on the twenty-first day of October in the Tenth year of the Reign of George the third by the Grace of God of Great Britain, France, and Ireland; King, defender of the Faith and so on." The Clerk of Court spoke in a haughty, nasal tone, reciting the formal opening.

James found himself yawning. He had not slept well the previous night, and the quiet chamber was proving a restful spot. He sat up straight, resolved to pay attention to the proceedings.

A juryman, taking evident delight in his role, read in a pompous voice the charge against Thomas Preston, captain of the 29th Regiment. Preston was accused of ordering his soldiers to fire maliciously on the unarmed Crispus Attucks, the first to fall. In a few days, James remembered, a second trial would likely follow for the remaining soldiers. Yes, the other soldiers had petitioned to have their trial at the same time as that of their captain, but the judge had overturned their request.

"Tell us what happened on the night of March 5," said Robert Treat Paine, a lawyer who had travelled the seas. He spoke directly to Captain Preston. "Five citizens of Boston lie buried in the Granary Burial Ground: Crispus Attucks, Samuel Gray, James Caldwell, Samuel Maverick, and Patrick Carr. Our purpose is to assign guilt if such can be assigned."

Captain Thomas Preston stood. In a voice that shook slightly, he recalled the lone sentry standing at the customs house, the taunts and insults exchanged between the sentry and passing apprentices, the sentry's frantic call for help when a group of boys and vagrants threatened him with snowballs. Preston had been just up the street about fifty paces at the main guard station. Preston stated he ordered those soldiers with him to form a relief party, to advance with bayonets fixed but guns unloaded, and to form a semi-circle around the lone sentry, placing their backs against the customs house. But once there, the soldiers could not get out of their positions. Cornered, the soldiers loaded their guns.

Sitting with the townspeople, James listened carefully in the still courtroom. Apparently, the soldiers were struck with clubs and snowballs, then so taunted with dares to fire that three or four did discharge their rifles into the jeering ruffians who surrounded them. Captain Preston said he asked the soldiers why they fired, and they responded they had thought they heard the order to fire. His face twisted in passion, the captain assured the courtroom he had never given such an order.

Captain Preston bowed and took his seat, his brow sweating. The courtroom buzzed with excitement. Someone shouted out, "He's guilty!"

"Quiet, quiet," said Judge Lyndes, banging his gavel. "Counsel for the prosecution, call your witnesses."

A number of witnesses took the stand to speak in turn. "How much longer, Father?" asked Johnny. He wriggled impatiently on the bench next to James.

"We'll go soon. Hush," James said sternly. He pulled a piece of bread and cheese from his pocket. "Share that with Jemmy, now," he said.

Ebenezer Hinkley, a townsman, spoke first. "I heard Captain Preston shout 'Fire.'" The listeners drew in their breath in amazement at his words.

"The Captain did order 'em to prime and load. I heard him distinctly as I was just four feet off," said Peter Cunningham, coughing profusely, overcome with his own importance.

"Thank you. Next," said the clerk of court.

William Wyatt, a young apprentice, took the stand next. Loudly, he said, "I heard the officer swear until the soldiers did commence firing." William Wyatt stepped down, glancing contemptuously at Captain Preston. *Apprentices will sneer when they may*, thought James, *particularly when they think they have the upper hand.*

The afternoon sun's long, rosy rays beamed through the tall windows of the courthouse. It was nearly evening. As the judge banged his gavel for the conclusion of the day, James motioned the boys to follow him. The crowd shuffled out of the room, buttoning coats against the cold.

Over the next few days, more witnesses were called. James attended the trial as he could at the end of each school day, but he did not try to bring his boys back. One afternoon, he listened as witnesses for the defense spoke in turn.

One was Richard Palmes of Boston. The courtroom was quiet; outside, the October wind picked up and began banging a loose shutter on the clapboards, over and over.

"Did you hear Mr. Bliss speak to Captain Preston?" asked John Adams.

"I did," replied Richard Palmes.

"What were his words?"

"He asked Captain Preston if he would not fire. Shortly he swore and ordered him to fire."

"And at the time of the firing were there also objects thrown at the soldiers?" asked John Adams, with exaggerated calm.

"I did see a piece of snow or ice strike Montgomery." Richard Palmes spoke softly, thoughtfully.

"Can you say that Captain Preston ordered his men to fire?" Here John Adams looked shrewdly over his spectacles at Richard Palmes.

"Sir, I heard the order 'fire,' but as to who said it, I cannot say." Richard Palmes looked down at the floor, then stared straight at John Adams.

"And you are not sure that Captain Preston ordered his men to fire?" Adams turned to the judge with these words.

"I think it so," Palmes acceded.

"No more questions at this time, Your Honour."

The witnesses for the defense continued. James Woodall said, "I saw sticks and ice thrown at the soldiers."

"Very good," said the clerk of court. "Next."

"Once firing had commenced, Captain Preston stopped a soldier who was going to fire and said, 'No more firing,'" said Edward Hill.

"Thank you," said the clerk of court. "Next."

Jane Whitehouse smiled as if enjoying her moment in court. "I heard the command to fire, but I am positive it was a man standing behind the soldiers, not the captain." She curtsied before returning to her seat.

Newton Prince, a black member of the South Church, said, "The people in the crowd jeered at the soldiers, calling 'em lobsters. They dared 'em to fire. Yet they were not ordered to fire." He shrugged his shoulders and returned to his seat.

The testimony continued for six days. At length on October 30, John Adams was called to summarize the case for the defense. It had been clear to all those who attended the trials that even those present on March 5 differed in their opinions about any order to fire. As John Adams's eloquent summary stated, proof did not exist that Preston had ordered the troops to fire. Therefore, it was the jury's duty to find him innocent. In just a few hours of deliberation, the twelve-man jury—sequestered for the six days of the trial with a meager diet of biscuits, cheese, cider, and hard liquor—acquitted Captain Preston on all charges.

Walking home, James thought the trial had gone remarkably smoothly. Little opposition had disrupted the proceedings. The next trial, however, would present a more delicate dilemma. Someone would have to pay for the lives lost. Captain Preston was not to blame. Yet James realized that self-defense alone could not be the motive, lest Boston be thought the home of murderers and criminals. How the lawyers would resolve this he could not be sure, only that the next trial, that of the soldiers, might prove more lively and contentious.

Chapter 21

Boston Massacre Trial: The Soldiers

NOVEMBER 27, 1770

The trial of the soldiers started on a Tuesday. James came daily after his teaching duties. Master John refused to discuss the trial with him, mumbling something about "Street ruffians should show more respect." James could see his point of view, but the trial was an important event that would prove the triumph of law over passion. James knew which he'd rather have in charge: he'd support the law any time.

In the crowded courtroom, the eight soldiers—Corporal Williams Wemms, James Hartigan, William McCauley, Hugh White, Mathew Kilroy, William Warren, John Carroll, and Hugh Montgomery—squirmed in their seats. The stone jail in which they'd been detained for nearly nine months was just behind the courthouse. They wore their uniforms, brushed and whitened with clay powder, but grime from months of confinement bled through the powder like a sooty fireplace under a quick sweeping.

As the day wore on, witnesses gave statements. John Adams, Robert Auchmuty, and Josiah Quincy, the defense attorneys, emphasized that the soldiers had been acting in self-defense, imperiled by a mob that meant them mortal harm. Shooting in self-defense warranted a lesser charge than murder, possibly only manslaughter. For the prosecution, lawyer Robert Treat Paine held a well-thumbed copy of *A Short Narrative* in his hand, which he consulted from time to time. Both sides referred to a detailed map of the King Street setting drawn by Paul Revere showing the bodies.

James could see the difficulty was pinning down exactly what had happened. Just as in the trial of Captain Thomas Preston, the prosecution could not specify which soldiers shot whom. All that could be proven was that the soldiers were the ones with the weapons, and they had perpetrated the shooting of the five slain citizens. Samuel Quincy, prosecutor, focused on Private Matthew Kilroy. "He's a willful, malicious murderer," were his words. In addition, he accused Private Hugh Montgomery of shooting Crispus Attucks, the black man who had fallen first, though the evidence was unclear.

"Samuel Quincy cannot pin guilt on any one of them, though of course he can imply guilt," mused James as he helped James Jr. fill the wood box that night. "Of Private Mathew Kilroy, he said, 'Here, gentlemen, is evidence of a heart desperately wicked and bent upon mischief.' The evidence is thin, but he must do his job as a prosecutor."

"He's doing what he must," said James Jr., hefting a pile of kindling into his father's arms. "When civilians are shot, someone must take the blame."

"Hearing all the evidence is the court's job," said James. "This is what abiding by law is all about. The message to the British, though, is that no one is above the law. We uphold the law here. We would expect no less if citizens shot soldiers. They should respect that."

"Here, that's enough wood for the night. Thank you, James," he added, following his son into the warm house.

One day, an unusual witness was admitted for the defense. Dr. John Jeffries had treated Patrick Carr's wounds as Carr was dying from injuries suffered in the massacre. He presented Carr's dying statement. James listened closely, knowing that Dr. Jeffries's testimony would be sure to have significant weight.

"Did you attend Patrick Carr to treat his wounds?" asked Samuel Quincy.

"I did." Dr. Jeffries appeared calm and unruffled.

"Was he able to speak with you?"

Dr. Jeffries responded, "He told me that when he lived in Ireland, he had often seen soldiers suppress the action of mobs by firing on the people. Never had he seen soldiers bear so many taunts and insults before firing."

"When was he last able to speak?" asked Samuel Quincy.

"On the day he died he spoke in the late afternoon. He gave his forgiveness to the man who shot him and knew the man had fired in self defense." Dr. Jeffries bowed and took his seat. The courtroom buzzed with comments. The dramatic statement of someone who had died as a result of the shots in question, provided by his attending physician, moved many listeners.

A redcoat testified he had heard soldiers of the 14th regiment complaining about the treatment they had received in Boston. He said some thought blood would soon run in the streets. Someone in the courtroom shouted out in protest, and the judge banged his gavel.

So many soldiers, James thought. *They come to make a living, desperate for work. They find themselves serving where they have no ties, no loyalties. Then, of course, when they are treated harshly, they are fearful.*

John Gray, the owner of the ropewalk, spoke for some of his apprentices who were involved in the March 5 altercation. He stated clearly that he'd made efforts to avert violence.

"I, John Gray, realizing that my men had spoken rudely to soldiers, told Colonel Dalrymple that I would do everything in my power to keep my workers from further insulting them. For his part, the colonel assured me he would do his best to prevent a disturbance."

At John Gray's testimony, James warmed with pride. Here was a business owner who had chosen peace over rancor. He would not let insults keep him from maintaining order.

For the defense, Josiah Quincy explained the soldiers' efforts to maintain peace. Waving his hand for emphasis, he said, "These soldiers shouted for the crowd to stand off, but warned that if the crowd molested them they would fire."

The courtroom was silent for some time after Josiah Quincy's words. Some nodded. Yet others scowled and stared stony-faced at the judge. *Anger still is what many feel,* James thought. He twisted in his seat, hoping for a peaceful end to the disturbance. Glancing at the British redcoats, glum and weary from the days of the trial, grimy from confinement in the Boston Stone Jail, he was sure they, too, hoped for peace.

On December 5, John Adams summed up the trial with its forty witnesses for the defense. He encouraged the jury to make their decision on the basis of facts, not emotions. He reminded them that if the soldiers were struck with snowballs, oyster-shells, or sticks, they had a right to protect their lives; therefore, the offense should be manslaughter, a lesser charge than outright killing.

Well-stated, thought James. *John Adams is a clever lawyer. He has assigned some blame, and blame there clearly needs to be, but in the case of self-defense, manslaughter is a more appropriate charge than murder.*

On Wednesday, December 5, the jury reached its decision. Six of the soldiers were found not guilty. But in loud tones, the foreman of the jury announced, "Your Honor, we find Private Mathew Kilroy and Private Hugh Montgomery of the 29th Regiment Foot guilty of the charge of manslaughter." Cheers and raucous shouts greeted the announcement. The judge pounded his gavel. "Sentencing will be December 14. Take them away."

John Adams, Robert Auchmuty, and Josiah Quincy shook hands, looking relieved, but tired, then greeted the lawyers for the prosecution. To James, it seemed as though they were glad the proceedings had gone as well as they had.

He turned to Oliver Wendell, an acquaintance sitting near him. "The verdict is perhaps entirely appropriate for the crime."

"Most appropriate," Wendell agreed. He shook his head. "The sentencing will be interesting. It is not over yet."

"No, it unquestionably is not over," James agreed.

Chapter 22

Sentencing of Kilroy and Montgomery

DECEMBER 16, 1770

Walking home from church about two weeks after the trials, Jemmy asked James, "What was the final verdict?"

"Two soldiers, Mathew Kilroy and Hugh Montgomery, were found guilty of manslaughter. The others were acquitted," said James.

"And they will be punished?" asked Johnny.

"They already have been," James said. "On Friday at the courthouse they 'prayed the benefit of clergy.' That is an old custom that may be used to give relief in a severe punishment. The person facing the punishment has to prove he can read Psalm 51, verse 1: 'Have mercy upon me, O God, according to thy loving kindness: according unto the multitude of thy tender mercies blot out my transgressions.'"

James added, "The person may read or recite from memory the verse. Either way, the accused will face a lighter sentence."

"Then what was the lighter sentence?" asked James Jr.

"Sheriff Stephen Greenleaf of Suffolk County branded them each on their right thumb with an 'M' for murderer."

"How'd you like to have a brand on your thumb?" asked Jemmy. "Sizzle, sizzle—ouch!" He and Johnny poked each other and rubbed their thumbs together.

"Well, I suppose that was better than the alternative," James Jr. said wisely.

"Much better," said James. "The alternative would have been hanging. The 'M' is used so that in the future, the person can never again claim the benefit of clergy."

"So, they are set free," said James Jr. "I didn't think they were completely guilty. I mean, after all, there were people taunting them and throwing things at them." He glanced at his younger brothers as if to say he was aware of much more than they.

James Jr. looked away quickly, but James had seen the look he'd given the others. So had Jemmy. Without a second's thought, Jemmy picked up some snow and packed a snowball, aimed it at James Jr.'s back and fired. James Jr. whirled. In a moment he had scooped up an armful of snow and pulled open Jemmy's coat, then stuffed the snow down his back. Jemmy's face turned beet red with laughter and then froze in shock as the cold snow melted on his skin.

"No one likes to get hit without hitting back," James Jr. said seriously. Jemmy shook the snow out from his clothing and reached for more snow in retaliation.

James interrupted him. "Enough, enough," he said sternly. "Better you throw snow at those blackbirds there"—he pointed to a fence—"but we're not going to start a riot here. Let's get home."

The boys straightened up and continued the walk. Jemmy let his snowball fly at a tall tree, causing a branch laden with snow to dislodge its burden in a heap on the ground. He shrugged and joined the others.

"Overall, the court could not prove who fired the shots," said James Jr., returning to their topic. "So punishment is rather out of the question."

"All in all, I am glad things turned out as they did," James said. "The soldiers have rejoined their regiment, the 29th. General Gage wrote to Lieutenant Colonel Dalrymple to have the men march to Rhode Island. From there, transports took them to New Jersey. Colonel Preston has left Boston for Castle William to join his regiment, the 14th, which is to remain stationed there."

"Why did we have soldiers here to begin with?" asked Johnny.

"Remember, the 14th and 20th Regiments were called here in October of 1768 from Halifax to keep the peace. The Townshend Acts were so unpopular that Lieutenant Governor Hutchinson thought he could not enforce them without armed assistance. Indeed, he has not been able to enforce them." James chuckled. He turned to James Jr. and Jemmy. "Do you remember seeing the regiments all come in on the ships and line up near the wharf?"

Jemmy nodded. "I do remember. We were able to leave school early." He grinned.

"Yes," said James. "Yet the 64th and 65th Regiments, which came from Ireland in November two years ago just after the 14th and 29th arrived, found the situation calm and peaceful. General Gage wisely decided to relocate the additional troops to New York the following summer. I wish he had been wise enough to remove the 14th and 29th Regiments as well."

"Then the violence might not have happened as it did," said James Jr., a hopeful tone in his voice.

"Right you are. The troops didn't really have a specific role to play. They were supposed to keep the peace, but that is difficult when people are upset about unreasonable rules and taxes. Apparently they didn't succeed. All right, boys, we are nearly home," James said, stamping his feet on the snowy walk. "I'm sure there will be a good supper waiting."

"They clearly didn't keep the peace," James Jr. said. "They were taunted and maybe even dared to shoot. When they did shoot, that caused bad feeling."

"People will remember the Massacre for years to come," James added. "It shows the difficulty of keeping armed troops in a civilian population without specific guidelines. In fact, those who were slain are seen as martyrs, in many people's eyes.

"It is difficult to ignore that blood has been spilt—civilian blood—in this conflict," he said, opening the gate to their walkway. "That is an important event, regardless of what else occurs."

Chapter 23

Oration for the Boston Massacre

APRIL 2, 1771

"Have another tart, James. The quince preserves are from our bush," Abigail said. She held out the silver tray of the jam-filled pastries he so loved. His mother had invited James to bring little Mary for breakfast. James had not minded bringing Mary. He knew seeing the child would make his mother happy.

Savoring the last of the tart, James pushed himself back from the table and wiped his chin with his napkin. In his lap, two-year-old Mary reached for another bite of pastry and bit into it, her eyes sparkling. He passed his hand over her golden curls. Sometimes, with six boys, his one daughter was a great thrill to him.

"I can't at this time, Mother, but thank you for inviting Mary and me. The breakfast was excellent," James said. "I was invited by the town committee to speak at the first anniversary of the Massacre. True, we are a few weeks from the actual anniversary, but the event scarred us all, so its commemoration is vital.

"Therefore," he said, picking up little Mary, "I must be off to Faneuil Hall."

"James, you can't be serious," his father said. His white, bushy eyebrows arched in disapproval. "What possible good could it do you to speak on such an occasion? And what credentials do you have for public oratory?"

"I gave an oration at Harvard to commemorate the passing of Henry Flynt, the long-time tutor. The speech was well received, I think," James said, bristling.

"But in this case the soldiers who fired on King Street did so in self-defense, a fact proven by the trials," his father said. "This speech puts you at risk for taking a public stand against authority. In fact," John went on, his voice grave and serious, "Your very life could be in danger. I do not like the idea of your speaking out on this occasion, no, not at all."

"All the more reason I should speak," James said, adjusting his ruffled shirt and picking up his black hat. "Words temperate yet honest are just what the people of Boston need at this time. Hundreds will be there, and I pray my words reflect the spirit of insight and justice. Blood running in the streets of Boston—innocent blood—is nothing to be ignored. Yes, I welcome this opportunity to speak. Good day to you each, and thank you for the excellent breakfast, Mother."

"Good-bye, James," she said, "and bring little Mary back to see me soon." His father, shaking his head doubtfully, turned back to the table to finish his breakfast.

James left Mary at his house and picked up his notes. The day was fair, light clouds scudding across a blue sky. Apple blossoms and lilacs freshened the air. On the walk to Faneuil Hall, he was joined by dozens also making their way to the meetinghouse. Carriages clattered by, drawn by shining horses. He recognized prominent citizens along the way, Sons of Liberty, merchants, tradespeople. Some tipped their hats to him in greeting.

What an occasion this is, James thought. *I am fortunate to be making this statement on behalf of the town. I must be sure my words inspire but do not inflame. Those guilty of the shooting of innocents are punished, but we are left with the charge to uphold liberty, personal rights, and safety.* His throat tightened but he pushed back his fears. *I have been over my notes to a great extent,* he thought. *I hope my words ring true with my listeners.*

"How are you?" James Bowdoin said as James entered the stately Faneuil Hall, already crowded with over a hundred people. Older than James, he served on the Massachusetts General Court and had penned much of *A Short Narrative*, introducing the depositions of witnesses and participants to the event.

"I am well, thank you," James responded. He smiled to see his friend and tipped his hat.

"I am pleased you will be our speaker today," James Bowdoin said thoughtfully. "But it seems our meeting place is crowded to the point of discomfort." The two made their way to the front of Faneuil Hall, where Samuel Adams, John Adams, John Hancock, and other leaders were assembled. Dozens of people continued to file through the door, pushing and jostling. Their voices echoed in the large meeting room. Soon every seat was taken. Samuel Adams turned to James Bowdoin, a question on his lips.

"What do you think of meeting in a larger place—the Old South Meeting House?" James Bowdoin asked. James looked about at the throng, pushing up to the walls and filing out the door.

"I am in favor of the move, to be sure. So many listeners must be accommodated." James smiled encouragingly.

"All adjourn to Old South Meeting House," Samuel Adams announced loudly to the group.

The gathering filed out of Faneuil Hall and made its way to the stately Old South Meeting House, where white seat boxes and balconies were soon crowded. Finally, there remained only standing room in the aisles and against the back. James made his way to the elegant pulpit overlooking the audience. The church bell pealed a summons. James took out his papers and spread them on the reading desk of the pulpit. He removed his hat and looked out over the crowd. Beads of sweat stood out on his forehead, and he took out a handkerchief and wiped his face. This was no time to be fearful or worried, he thought. He must be calm and express a sense of dignity even as he felt the pain and apprehension of everyone present at the occasion.

The Reverend Dr. Charles Chauncy came up and stood by his side. His expression fierce and determined, his white hair flowing to his shoulders, the long-time minister of First Church and avid supporter of personal rights looked over the crowd. All became quiet. He offered a prayer both compelling and eloquent. Then Dr. Chauncy bowed to James, shook his hand, and descended the pulpit to his seat. A buzz of comments settled, and the assembly grew quiet again.

James spoke from his notes and from his heart. His brown hair, brushed carefully, was tied back with a black ribbon, and his gray-green eyes scanned his audience with sincerity. "The horrid, bloody scene we here commemorate, whatever were the causes which concurred to induce it on that dreadful night, must lead the pious and humane of every order to some suitable reflections."

The multitude listened intently. Outside a dog barked, but inside the big church not a word could be heard except those of the speaker, as every head bent in his direction. Some drew in their breath at the memory of those shot. "The pious will adore the conduct of that Being who is unsearchable in all his ways and without whose knowledge not a single sparrow falls, in permitting an immortal soul to be hurried by the flying ball, the messenger of death, in the twinkling of an eye, to meet the awful Judge of all its secret actions," James continued.

James spoke of the importance of keeping and upholding the English liberties to which they were entitled. "Our fathers left their native land, risked all the dangers of the sea, and came to this then-savage desert, with that true undaunted courage which is excited by a confidence in God. They came that they might here enjoy themselves, and leave to their posterity the best of earthly portions, full English Liberty."

"We have seen and felt the ill effects of placing standing forces in the midst of populous communities." The thought of the redcoats, standing on every corner, parading on Boston Common, struck many listeners with familiar apprehension. "One article of the Bill of Rights is that the raising or keeping a standing army within the kingdom in a time of peace, unless it be of consent of Parliament, is against law."

Taxes not agreed to by the people were a major problem, he reminded his listeners. "England has a right to exercise every power over us but that of taking money out of our pockets without our consent." Yet, he added, cautious not to inflame the crowd and raise their anger further, "We are rebels against Parliament—we adore the king."

He continued with his fervent hope that the king listen to the colonies' appeals for justice. The king should cause justice to prevail. Forcing back a lump in his throat, James clearly stated that a tax forced by Parliament was "not only illegal in itself, but a down-right usurpation of his prerogative as King of America."

Resounding applause greeted these words. James smiled, reassured and relieved. His audience was with him. John Locke would approve of his point, he felt sure.

"The design of this ceremony was decent, wise, and honorable. Make the bloody fifth of March the era of the resurrection of your birthrights, which have been murdered by the very strength that nursed them in their infancy."

Calling himself a Son of Liberty, he closed with an appeal to heaven: "May the all wise and beneficent Ruler of the Universe preserve our lives and health, and prosper all our lawful endeavours in the glorious cause of freedom."

The chamber resounded with clapping, shouts of "Huzzah, Bravo," and the stamping of feet as all stood in respect. James bowed. For a moment the hope of freedom, the vision of a society ruled by law, appeared to him as a shining beacon, a place of light. He stepped down from the pulpit, men clapping him on the back, the ringing of applause filling his ears. Great relief flooded him that his talk had been greeted with such strong approval. How proud he felt to have so clearly expressed support and encouragement for the town.

"I can assure you that you have the thanks of our town and of each of us," Samuel Adams said, shaking his hand. "You have expressed well the feelings and elements of the hour."

"I am most grateful for the opportunity," James said, bowing. "We can only hope that our resolve to create a society free from oppression and persecution will bear fruit."

"I agree with that," Samuel Adams said sincerely.

James walked through the crowd, shaking hands and smiling. As he made his way home, his steps were light, his heart happy. What an honor it had been, to speak for his town, his people.

Chapter 24

Boston Tea Party

December 17, 1773

BOSTON, DECEMBER 1, 1773.

GENTLEMEN,

THE Committee of Correspondence for this Town had just prepared their Letter covering the Proceedings of the Town at their two late Meetings of the 5th and 18th ultimo, when a Ship arrived from London with Part of the East-India Company's Teas : This induced us to forbear sending the Letters until we could procure some further Intelligence. On Monday last this and the neighbouring Towns as one Body convened at Faneuil-Hall, 'till the Assembly were so numerous as occasion'd an Adjournment to the Old South Meeting-House, where it was computed there was upwards of 5000 Persons, and then came into a Number of Votes and Resolves unanimously ; a Copy of which being handed to us by a Committee of that Body, we now forward to you, and are with great Esteem your Friends and humble Servants.

By Order of the Committee of Boston.

William Cooper Clerk

"Boston Tea Shipment. December 1, 1773."
Early American Imprints

"Did you hear?" James stepped into the front door of his home, his eyes shining.

"Yes, my dear. Neighbor Wendell informed me early this morning as I was sweeping the walk. News travels fast in our town," Abigail responded.

She picked up the kettle whistling on the fire and poured hot water into her teapot.

"They did it, they did it!" James chortled. He laughed, picking up little Thomas, and swung the startled toddler around in a circle. Mary realized how seldom she heard James laugh, and smiled in pleasure. He was usually so serious!

James set two-year-old Thomas down, who reached up his hands. "More, Da," Thomas said, pleading.

"No, not now, Thomas. Go play with your toys." Thomas dutifully walked off to his box of toys, in the corner by the warm fireplace, and proceeded to roll his little wooden cart across the floor.

"Have some tea, James." Mary poured him a cup from her flowered teapot, which had once belonged to her grandmother in Scotland. "Tell me the news."

James inhaled the spicy odor of peppermint and reached for his cup. "You know we had a meeting yesterday on the tea question, at the Old South Meeting House. There were probably over five thousand there. In the afternoon John Rowe, who sometimes votes Tory and sometimes patriot, stood up and apologized for his part ownership of a tea vessel. He then asked the crowd if 'salt water would make as good tea as fresh.' Of course everyone there understood he meant the tea should end up in the sea. They cheered, clapped, and huzzahed their approval. Later, someone remarked that a good Tory had been won over to our side."

James raised his cup and sipped the steaming peppermint tea.

"This is much better than Labrador, Mary," he said. "I really am not fond of Labrador. In fact, if truth be known, I prefer black bohea tea. I'll drink peppermint, however. Of course no one now in Boston would drink bohea."

"Nearly no one," Mary corrected him. "I am sure there are a few who cling to remains of the trade, though it may not be to their advantage to sip the beverage in front of their neighbors. Yes, I'm glad we have peppermint. So, what happened?"

"Last night was the fourth meeting at the Old South Meeting House about the tea question," James said. "The thousands who crowded the Meeting House yesterday were in agreement that we should not yield to the new tax, even though as a bribe the British offer us cheap, high quality East India Company tea. Incidentally, of course, the British would like to help out the ailing East India Tea Company, its warehouses filled with tons of unsold tea after years of boycotts."

"The British plan is to set an artificially low price on the tea, hoping to coax us into purchasing it," Mary said. She reached for a paring knife and a basket of apples and began slicing the fruit into a pie crust. "But what was said at the meeting?"

"The meeting started at Faneuil Hall," James said. "There were so many in attendance, it was decided to move it to Old South. There are three ships moored at Griffin's Wharf with cargoes of tea. The ships' customs duty must be paid within twenty days of arriving in port. Yesterday time had run out. It was the twentieth day for *The Dartmouth*. Captain Rotch of *The Dartmouth* complained he would be ruined if he had to return to London without unloading his tea. Finally, he appealed to Governor Hutchinson, who said he must pay the customs duty."

"He must have been really worried about the loss of profit for his voyage. What happened next?" Mary asked. She sprinkled cinnamon on the apples, then dowsed them with honey from the canister on the table.

James took a long swallow of his tea, then set down the delicate cup. "After the meeting, a group of leaders retired to the Green Dragon Tavern to make preparations. In the night, individuals painted up like Mohawk Indians came to the wharf. They stepped on board the *Dartmouth*, told the crew they would do them no harm, and proceeded to hoist the one hundred and fourteen chests of tea onto the deck, hack them open, and toss the contents into the harbor. They did the same with the other ship and its chests of tea. The third vessel was a brig; its captain begged them not to take his tea as he also had crates of other goods on board. But they insisted they would be very careful not to hurt other cargo, and only take the tea, which they did. Then they threw the contents of those chests into the sea as well."

"So, Boston Harbor is awash in tea." Mary smiled at the thought. "And all went well?" she asked. She placed a mound of dough on the table and began rolling out a top crust.

"Yes, indeed!" James said. "Very well, as the people were so careful. One man did fill his pockets, but he was treated very roughly. The crowd tore his coat off of his back and drove him up the wharf through the hundreds of people waiting there, cuffing and kicking him as he went through."

"It sounds as if the people had the final word on the tea question," Mary said thoughtfully. She crimped the pie crust together, working with quick fingers.

"We had four meetings on the tea. We met on November 29, 30, December 14, and now this last, yesterday, the 16th," James said. "Of course I could not attend them all, but I was present enough that I understood the proceedings. You know, these meetings, on issues that affect those in the town, are remarkable. Each time those who attend meet all day, breaking only for a noon meal. People have come from all around, even twenty miles away. The issues stir people because they realize their rights are threatened.

"Many at the meetings are working people, who come and go as their jobs permit," he added. "That, of course, is somewhat my situation.

"Samuel Adams leads these meetings. As principal member of the Committee of Correspondence, which sets up the meetings, he encourages and listens to all opinions. We have the extraordinary circumstance of common men from all employments speaking up, having their voices heard, and taking a stand right next to men of substance, means, and education. Such equality among various elements of society is amazing and would be unheard of in Britain. Governor Hutchinson sometimes stares in disbelief as the opinions of journeymen, poorer artisans, shopkeepers, and even apprentices are heard and weighed.

"John Locke would be proud of the society we are encouraging in Boston," James said. "We are joining in 'a body of the people.' Locke would say that if the ruler—meaning the king, of course—was not respecting that trust, then the people had the right to look to Heaven and change their form of government. I wonder if that change might at length be necessary.

"Repealing the Townshend Acts is all right, but the British err in keeping a tax on a single item just to prove a point. It smacks of control and despotism, and our people will not stand for it." James laughed and finished his tea in one long swig. "My, that pie will be tasty." He watched as Mary slid the pie into the brick oven. "I look forward to it. Thank you, my dear, for listening and refreshing my day. I must say I feel much better about tea!"

"I am proud of you, of course," Mary said, looking at her husband thoughtfully. "You must realize, though, that the British are still in control. We may win a point here or there, but their government is still our government, and their jails our jails. I hope you may be careful, my dear."

Chapter 25

The Tar and Feathering
of Malcolm

JANUARY 25, 1774

A large crowd thronged the usually peaceful street in the market district. Sailors, artisans, and working people raised their fists and shouted, their voices ringing against brick buildings. Fresh snow filled the stone-paved roadway, trampled by the passing of feet and carriages.

"The customs official Malcolm should be hanged!" cried a burly seaman.

"Tar and feather 'im," bellowed another. "He's worn the black jacket before in New Hampshire but that warn't enough. Here he is, a-beatin' someone who's 'is better. He'll learn this time!"

On his way home from market, James stopped near the edge of the crowd, wondering what the commotion was about. He recognized the shoemaker George Hewes standing at the center, his apron patched and his tan jacket worn and frayed. Hewes had been in every sort of scrape. James remembered testimony from the Boston Massacre trials that Hewes knew personally four of the victims of the Massacre. He declared he had been standing next to the sailor James Caldwell when Caldwell was shot, and had helped transport him to a doctor. James remembered Hewes's statement at the trials—that he and the others "were in the king's highway, and had as good a right to be there" as the soldiers. Also, he remembered

Hewes saying, rather proudly, he had received a blow on the shoulder from a soldier's club but had refused to leave.

The shoemaker's words, shrill and strident, peppered the crowd like grapeshot. "My name's George Robert Twelves Hewes and I'll thank ye to listen to my story." Those in the street stood curious and quiet, looking with concern at the blood-spotted rag wrapped around the shoemaker's head.

"Speak up, my man," said a carpenter loudly. "We're with ye."

"I was just walkin' down Cross Street, going back to my shop from my dinner. You know I am a shoemaker." Murmurs of assent rippled through the crowd and a few chuckles.

"Well, here comes this John Malcolm that is a customs official. He was swearing at a little boy who was pushing a sled, threatening him with his large heavy cane. I stopped, and thinking to prevent the murder of the youngster by the rascal Mr. Malcolm, said to him, 'Mr. Malcolm, I hope you are not going to strike that boy with this stick.'

"Malcolm responded rudely to me that it was none of my business. I asked him, 'What did that child do to you?' Malcolm said to me, 'Damn you, you vagabond, don't you know you should not speak to gentlemen in the street?'"

"I said to him, 'I am not a rascal nor a vagabond. I may not be rich, but my credit is as good as yours.'"

Some in the crowd cheered at this statement. Hewes's voice barked on.

"Malcolm turned beet red at this and swore, and said that I would never be as good as he was."

"Then I knew how to answer him, I did. So, I says to him, at least I'd never been tarred and feathered, nor would I be. This Malcolm is a customs official; he takes bribes and deals in British goods contrary to our agreements. He got what was coming to him when they painted him black in New Hampshire, I'll warrant that."

Hewes paused and looked fiercely about the crowd. Shouts of "Hear, hear," and "Good for you" rang out. James thought Hewes looked like a little red-faced turkey cock, strutting with self-importance.

"You see, I remembered he'd had the devil's treatment last November in New Hampshire. This buffoon Malcolm had seized the brig *Brothers*, part of the business of being a low-down customs official, but the good people there would have none of it and he got the treatment for scoundrels, the black jacket."

"That's when Malcolm picked up his big cane and hit me hard in the forehead." He pointed to his rag-wrapped wound and winced.

The crowd hissed and booed, hanging on Hewes' every word. *The odd thing is that someone like Hewes, a simple working man, could get so many people to listen to him,* thought James. *Surely this involvement of common folk with public affairs is unique to us here in the colonies, certainly here in Boston. I can't imagine a shoemaker stirring up a crowd in England or France. Governments there control folks much more tightly.*

Hewes pushed aside the white rag wrapped about his head to reveal a swollen, angry bruise with a deep purple cut.

"He hit me so hard that I'm knocked out, and I lay there in the street some time. When I come to, Malcolm and the boy had disappeared.

"Now I must go get a doctor for this," Hewes continued, covering his wound. "The stroke he gave me, I am like to bleed to death. Excuse me." He turned and disappeared into the crowd.

"What do you say? Do we allow wretches like this customs official Malcolm to misuse honest citizens here in Boston?" a seaman shouted.

The crowd bellowed back, "No, no." Sticks and clubs waved in the air.

"We'll deal with 'im—and we'll get 'im tarred and feathered so it will stick," shouted another voice. "What do you say, Captain Godfrey?"

"We'll do worse, if he doesn't change his tune," the first seaman said fiercely.

James could readily see the direction in which this mob was heading. The opportunity to punish the customs official who had struck the shoemaker was too good to miss. Hewes had only been trying to protect a boy from being struck by Malcolm. Besides, simply the fact that Malcolm was a customs official earned the crowd's hatred. He took taxes in the name of the Crown, taxes that hurt honest citizens. The mob in Boston had taken control in so many situations, the power to maintain law and order had become theirs.

A well-dressed gentleman joined the group. James recognized one of the town lawyers. "Would it not be better to turn Mr. Malcolm over to the law?" he asked those in the crowd. "Let the courts deal with him."

"Not so, no, no," many shouted back. "What course did the law take with Preston or his soldiers, with Captain Wilson or Richardson?"

"Was justice done?" asked an angry voice.

"The judges showed preference to the soldiers and customs house officers. No, we must take matters into our own hands. Deal with 'im ourselves," answered someone.

"Come on—let's get the knave," bellowed Captain Godfrey.

The crowd swarmed up the street. James followed at a distance, cautious not to be swept up into the doings of the rabble. At the same time, he was curious. The actions of the mob were unpredictable and often regrettable, but there was no doubt they had a voice and a will to see justice served.

At Mr. Malcolm's home workmen beat and kicked at the door until a thick-waisted, gray-haired individual opened it. His face turned white when he saw the crowd.

"You perhaps know Mr. Hewes?" stated a working man in an old tri-corner hat. "We'll teach you to treat him like dirt."

Malcolm's expression twisted with fright. He slammed the door shut and locked it. The crowd surged around the house to the back. Rocks and sticks pelted the windows and doors, sounding like gunfire.

James stood across the street, watching at a distance. Malcolm stuck his head out of an upper window, waved a pistol at the crowd, and shouted, "Go away, if you know what's good for you." A flying rock clipped his head and he slammed the window shut.

George Robert Twelves Hewes and a burly policeman appeared at the edge of the crowd, the little carpenter's head dressed in a thick, wide bandage. "Here's Constable Hale, ready to do the right thing. Let him arrest that scoundrel John Malcolm. My cousin, Dr. Joseph Warren, has dressed my wound," he added, pointing to his new dressing. "He recommends the constable serve a warrant on him. He told me I was the luckiest man he knew, to have survived the blow the rascal gave me," Hewes said with a spiteful sneer.

"No, no, let us teach him a lesson," said several voices. Hewes and the constable stood watching at the edge of the crowd, then disappeared. James didn't see where they went. He had forgotten that Hewes was in fact Dr. Joseph Warren's cousin. *What an amazing society we have,* he thought, *that a common workman is related to one of our finest leaders and physicians, and he can count on that physician for help.*

Suddenly, an upper window opened. "I've got Malcolm and he's coming down," someone shouted from the window. The crowd roared approval.

Malcolm, ropes wrapped about his body from shoulders to knees, descended from the upper window, lowered by another length of rope. A horse cart clattered into place, into which the crowd dumped his thick body.

"Here, get his shirt off. And jacket," said Captain Godfrey, removing enough of the bonds to be able to grasp Malcolm's clothing. Hands reached in, roughly yanked off his jacket and shirt.

"What are you doing?" Malcolm shouted. He struggled but a dozen hands held him tight.

"Get his shoes too," someone suggested.

"Right enough." The shoes were passed back in the crowd and disappeared from sight.

"We're giving you a jacket that will fit—and well." Laughter and jeers followed this taunt.

"Feathers needed," someone shouted. A fellow ran into the house and came out bearing two pillows, which he tossed into the cart. Malcom's wife could be heard wailing.

The whole procession set off for Henchman's Wharf. James and other curious onlookers followed at a distance. The mob grew as it went, people waving fists, shouting and jeering at the helpless figure in the cart. At the wharf, two strong workmen hoisted an iron kettle of hot tar up to the cart. A pungent, oily stench rose into the chilly January afternoon in clouds of steam. James imagined the inky substance just off the boil, bubbles still rising to the surface. Not long ago it had been hanging over someone's fire. He shivered at the mere thought of the hot liquid being applied to a person's bare skin.

"Here, hold him," said Captain Godfrey. Hands confined Malcolm in the cart, while others daubed his chest with the sticky, steaming liquid, ignoring his protests and cries for help. Then they poured more on his back, shoulders, and finally, his head.

James saw the horrific liquid envelop the pink body of the merchant and scald as it went, scorching his skin. He smelled the harsh tar, the burning flesh, the reek of blood. Malcolm screamed and writhed, twisting in pain. The smell was almost enough to make James gag, even from his vantage point across the street. What a revolting spectacle this was. His stomach turned queasy, but he decided to stand his ground. Then the crowd tore open the pillowcases of feathers and threw them on the hot tar.

The mob pulled the cart with its burden, Malcolm's head rolling from side to side, to Butcher's Hall, then to the butcher's market on Main Street near the Old South Meeting House. On King Street they pulled the unfortunate Malcolm from the cart and proceeded to beat him with a heavy rope. James was almost relieved to hear Malcolm swearing and cursing, reviling his tormenters, showing he was surviving the torture. *What would these people stop at?* he wondered.

"Now it's off to the Liberty Tree. He's going to renounce his commission in customs and swear he'll never have another." The crowd shouted and jeered at its captive.

Jostled and tumbled like a strange, downed bird, Malcolm sank into the cart. A few blocks later, however, he seemed to recover his strength, for he sat up and said, "I couldn't swear I'd never have another commission. You couldn't make me!"

"What? You don't see reason yet? Then it's off to the gallows with you," responded someone in the crowd.

Malcolm put his head down on his knees and moaned. James could see through the tumult of people the inky-black figure bespeckled with dirty feathers. *It is a wonder he argues at all,* James thought. *Such an ordeal as he's been through is enough to make most men faint outright.* The crowd carted the blackened figure to the Liberty Tree, then to the town gallows hanging on Boston Neck, then back to the Liberty Tree, then to Butcher's Hall, then to the ferry at Charlestown, then to Copp's Hill. At each site they pulled the trussed and tied Malcolm from the cart and beat him.

By now it was growing dark. The evening star glowed in the sky and the wind picked up, chill and frosty. The crowd reached the gallows set up near the jail. A workman threw a rope over the dark, heavy frame of the scaffold.

Sitting up in his sled, a grotesque, shapeless figure, Malcolm screamed, "You'll never hang me!" James was amazed at his determination. He had

had nearly enough of watching the spectacle, but resolve to see if Malcolm would survive his ordeal kept him at the scene.

Perhaps struck by his bravery and spirit, those in the crowd merely taunted and jeered, taking turns lashing him with the heavy knotted rope. No one reached for the noose swinging ominously from the gallows.

"You're finished, in any case. You'll not treat good citizens as though they were dirt," said Captain Godfrey, his voice solemn.

"Here, he won't change his tune? He won't forswear customs knavery?" said one of the biggest sailors. He took out a huge dagger. Glinting in the streetlight, it was a formidable instrument. James wondered if it were all over for the unrepentant Malcolm. He held his breath.

"We'll cut his ears off! Here, lay him down," commanded the sailor, holding his huge knife up high.

"No, no," screamed Malcolm. "I relent. I foreswear—I do swear—that I'll resign my post. I'll never take another. I'll leave. Just take me home."

"Well, well, you can sing another tune. Come, lads, let's take this miserable lump to his door."

"Yes, all right. We've taught him his lesson," agreed some.

James watched the remnants of the crowd hauling the cart with its wretched cargo up the street in the moonlight. *In a day or two I'll read about this in the* Boston Gazette, he thought. *But to see it makes all the difference. We cannot underestimate the power of the mob. They will not be abused or trampled, so they give one of the first lessons of liberty: have respect for free men. Even if this kind of lesson is so cruel as to make one shudder,* he thought. *Surely, though, under fair laws such behavior would end.*

James shivered in disgust and turned to walk home. He was not sorry he had watched, but he was glad the gruesome spectacle had at length come to an end. He knew some actually survived the cruel punishment of tar and feathering, though not without scarring. *Apparently, Malcolm is one who will survive. And,* thought James, *if someone had not threatened that bully Malcolm with his ears we might be here all night. The crowd has its strengths, but so do those loyal to the Crown and the ways of authority. Liberty will not be won that easily, after all.*

"The Bostons Paying the Excise-man or Tarring & Feathering."
Library of Congress Prints and Photographs

Chapter 26

Rising Tensions in the Schoolroom

APRIL 17, 1775

James entered the schoolhouse early in the morning. The first cocks had crowed; the sun was rising over the sea, brilliant and gold. The day promised to be fair and pleasant. He was angry. He had stopped by the bookstore on his way to school to see if any news had been posted or published. A British sentry standing pompously near the corner, his red service hat at a ridiculous tilt, had halted him. Pointing his long musket like a poker directly at James, he snarled, "Where do you think you are going?"

"I am on my way to teach the young minds of this community proper behavior and the respectful attitudes towards authority of the Greeks and Romans." James held his tongue, but words of anger, acid and sharp, tumbled at the edge of his lips.

"See to it that you do," the sentry had laughed, spitting on the cold ground.

"God save the king," James responded, turning and going on his way. Did he really mean that? He realized briefly that the polite form of respect no longer held the meaning it once did.

His students had more discipline and respect for themselves than any of these soldiers seemed to possess. In January, the slick ice on their sledding run—which started at Beacon Street, crossed Tremont, and ran down School Street—was ruined by ashes thrown out by General

Haldimand's servant. The general, one of General Gage's officers, lived on School Street. The boys formed a committee and made a formal complaint to General Haldimand, requesting that the ashes not be thrown into their sledding path.

General Haldimand had listened and then quietly asked his servant to cease throwing the ashes in the street. The general told the governor about the request, who replied that it was "impossible to beat the notion of liberty out of the people, as it was rooted in them from their childhood." *That is true,* thought James. *Even our students demonstrate beliefs in personal rights and freedom of thought.*

James entered the schoolroom. Across its expanse, his father rummaged through books on his desk, apparently trying to locate the text for the day. His white wispy white hair appeared unusually unruly today, escaping from the confines of his smoking cap. John looked up at James, bushy eyebrows lifted in caution.

"Are not the students coming soon? Let us get the fire going, then, to ward off the morning chill," Master Lovell said.

"At least we have the firewood brought from the country by James Greenleaf's parents, and not the firewood that the regulars use, hacked from the trees that grow on the Common," James growled.

"You seem to find the actions of the British army deplorable," said his father with considerable calm, "yet consider the necessity. To control the unruly actions of those who oppose good order, quartering troops has become necessary."

"Necessary?" James slammed down his fist on his desk and lost his temper. "No more necessary than the sentries' massacre of unarmed civilians. No more necessary than maintaining a hated tax on tea just to prove that law is above reason. No more necessary than Parliament rejecting petition after petition. There is nothing needful about turning over rule already orderly, followed in due process, and according to British law, in favor of rule that is arbitrary, ignorant of rights, and dictated by an unfeeling legislature and king a thousand miles away." He stared in disbelief at his father. *Surely the old man could see the point?*

"Our common has been stripped of trees, and tents line its greens," James continued, his words an outraged flood. "Troops lodge in our very statehouse. Our Sabbaths lose their quiet to military music, the sound of fife and drum interrupting every prayer. Indeed, many of our churches are rendered unusable, ill-fitted for worship through desecration, steeples torn down or pews ripped out. Some, as the Brattle Street church and the Hollis Street church, have been turned into barracks for the regulars.

"Faneuil Hall, given to the town of Boston by Peter Faneuil, is turned into a theater for the amusement of General Howe," James went on. "Why, you yourself gave its dedication speech some years ago, Father," he retorted, his gray-green eyes shooting sparks at the silent schoolmaster. "If I recall rightly, your words were something like 'May this Hall be ever sacred to the interests of Truth, of Justice, of Loyalty, of Honor, of Liberty.'" He paused and shook his head.

"I recall the performance of *Zara* at Faneuil Hall, the tragedy by Voltaire," Master Lovell said in a voice devoid of emotion. James wondered what he was really thinking. "I was invited to see it. General Burgoyne himself wrote the prologue and epilogue to the play. The proceeds from its performance went to benefit the widows and children of British soldiers. What harm could it be to present a worthy endeavor to benefit those in need?"

"And what of the widows and children of those killed by the British?" James continued, his voice rising. "Yet moderation has been the constant for the leaders and citizens of Boston. The Provincial Congress has continued to conduct its affairs with the order and due process to which it was always dedicated. General Gage set a date for the prohibition of further town meetings, yet those in charge merely suspended the ending of the meeting, keeping the same meeting alive indefinitely so as to avoid his ridiculous order.

"Now the Provincial Congress has assumed the role of the Massachusetts legislature, banned since May of 1774. Its Committee of Safety has the power…." James paused. Some words were better left unsaid. Would it help to share with his father that the Committee of Safety could call forth the militia, if needed? He choked back his thought.

"Something good will come of this yet," John responded quietly. James paused, angry thoughts rolling through his mind. He looked at his father. Stubborn and regressive though he knew the old man to be, he still loved him. He knew he shouldn't shout at him; it did little good. Much of what

James himself was, as a teacher and a seeker of knowledge, he knew he owed to his father. Yet now Master John Lovell was blind to the truth, blind to change. His father looked to the past, to what had been a stable way of life. That way of life was crumbling. James knew he could not choose that path. A different one awaited him.

"Even now, Boston is ringed with minutemen from the country," said James. "All are watching to see what the next move of the regulars will be. Tories, many of whom are your friends, Father, have come here seeking the protection of the British troops, and find themselves held here. They are like sailors on a wind-tossed sea awaiting the coming storm.

"Meanwhile, I help my friends who have left Boston," he continued. "I care for the property of Nathaniel Appleton, keeping the keys and records for his candle factory and his warehouse. My cellar is filled with the furniture of Oliver Wendell, who has left for a time. I do what I can to ease the difficulties of friends of mine afflicted in this duress, and I do not leave. In fact, Father, I have shown myself steadfast in the face of calamity, though Heaven knows I question sometimes the wisdom of that course."

He paused, wondering at his father's grieved yet stony look. Master Lovell was silent, but James's words poured out. "I have written my friend Joseph Trumbull in the country just lately to thank him for an offer of lodging, yet tell him I intend to remain planted in my present dwelling. However, I plan to send some of my boys to help hoe his corn. Staying in the country, my boys can breathe fresh air and work in a serene environment, not languish in a battle between hostile braggarts and those of us left in Boston trying to uphold personal rights.

"And," he continued, another thought coming to him, "what was General Gage's coach doing here the other day, at your house?"

"I did some business for him," Master Lovell said, his voice quiet.

"Of what sort? What could you possibly do for General Gage?"

"My services, James, are quite helpful. Consider my experience in writing, for example." Master Lovell turned to his stack of books on his desk and began searching for something buried in the pile.

James wondered if his father were telling him everything he knew. Before he could say anything else, a knock came on the front door. "School's beginning. The boys are here," James said.

James swung the heavy door open, waved the students in, and picked up his *Cheever's Accidence* for the first form and *Aesop's Fables* for the second form. Across the room Master Lovell greeted the older boys, set them to exercises with *Ward's Lily's Grammar* or translations from *Caesar's Commentaries.* Whatever his father might be keeping from him, he clearly had no intention of revealing it. John had also kept his temper remarkably well, smoldering rather than raging. *These difficulties anger me,* James thought, *and so I become inflamed. I had best be more controlled, lest I be a firebrand without discipline.*

Chapter 27

"War's Begun and School's Done: *Deponite Libros*"

April 19, 1775

The shrill of fife and beat of drum awakened James at early dawn. Outside, the thud of tramping feet, the rumble of carts, and the clip-clop of horses' hooves on cobblestones signaled the advance of British troops on nearby streets. James left his house at Chapman Place early, telling his children as they readied for school he'd see them soon. He glanced quickly up and down his street, then turned the corner on School Street to the Boston South Latin School. He could see the regulars forming in long lines on Tremont Street. The muskets of the redcoats shone, their brass glittered, and they stared rigidly ahead with the attention of men headed off to a serious encounter. Mounted officers barked commands, riding up and down the even rows of soldiers.

James reached the corner of Tremont Street and stared. As far as he could see, the column of regulars stretched, heading down to the mall by the common. An officer with a white plumed hat trotted past him, his gray horse jerking his head, prancing. The officer sneered at James, his lip curled in disdain, then shouted, "Lord Percy's Brigade, form. Advance." The columns began to move, lined in unison, to the beat of drums.

James turned and walked the half block to school. General Gage's troops were on the move, more than likely marching to Concord. Hadn't he heard in the Green Dragon Tavern the night before that troops would be sent to Concord to capture the stock of gunpowder and arms there? At the time, the words—spoken in hushed voices over tankards of ale—had thrilled him with alarm, but then again the speaker did not seem one of authority, and perhaps it had been just a rumor. James had not taken the story seriously. He opened the school door.

"Father," James called. At the opposite side of the room, dim with shutters still drawn, John stood up.

"We have action outside," John said, in a calm voice.

"So it seems." James stood with the door open. Outside the first boys to arrive at the school gathered, their faces white and serious. "We will have to close the school," he said to his father.

"I agree, but for how long will the school be closed? That we are at war seems increasingly obvious." John walked over to the door and stood at James's side. He spoke in measured tones to the students clustered on the step.

"*Deponite libros,*" John said firmly. Put down your books. Those were the words that signaled the end of every school day. What could they mean now, early in the morning? The boys stared open-mouthed at Master Lovell for a minute. Then they turned and ran for their homes.

Harrison Gray Otis, a quick lad of about ten, turned and smiled briefly at James. "Good-bye," he said. Then he turned and darted down the street.

"Good-bye," James called after the fleeing students. "When will we see them again?" he asked his father. He didn't really expect an answer. Neither knew what the situation would be.

John said firmly, "The school is closed, for now, at least. We have a war on our hands, and who knows what might develop. For the students' safety, they must remain at home."

"Certainly," James responded. He looked at his father, the rumpled hair under the smoking cap. "I will be going home. I hope you and Mother will be safe."

"We'll be safe enough, for the time being. I hope you, Mary, and the children fare well also. Good-bye, then."

"Good-bye." James left the building, walked across the street and down to his house. The file of troops was still advancing down Tremont Street, their steps an even tramp, officers' commands insistent and firm.

He stopped to watch the regiments march past. There might have been a thousand of them. From farther down the hill, James heard the strains of "Yankee Doodle." The redcoats sang this popular new song to make fun of the patriots. The words came up to him from the distance.

> *Father and I went down to camp,*
> *Along with Captain Gooding,*
> *There we see the men and boys,*
> *as thick as hasty pudding.*
> *Yankee doodle keep it up,*
> *Yankee doodle, dandy,*
> *Mind the music and the step,*
> *And with the girls be handy.*

There would be trouble; one could hardly expect that so many armed men, on a mission to gather ammunition in hostile territory, could come home without challenging others in a fight. Armed conflict could signal a major change in the tensions that were developing around Boston.

Chapter 28

What Happened at
Lexington and Concord

APRIL 20, 1775

The next day, neighbors and shopkeepers speculated continually about the march of the British on Lexington and Concord. In the evening, James went to the Green Dragon Tavern to learn the news. Gathered at a table in the dimly lit room, he recognized several who were involved with the Sons of Liberty. James drew up a seat near them, tipping his tri-corner hat in greeting.

"Two days ago, on Tuesday, April 18th, General Gage ordered the capture of John Adams and John Hancock, our leaders who have fled to Lexington to be safe from arrest."

The speaker was James Bowdoin, who had collected depositions from witnesses to the Boston Massacre. Possessed of Bachelor's and Master's degrees from Harvard, he served on the Massachusetts Provincial Congress's executive council. Elegant and precise, he spoke gravely in a low voice, his words distinct and clear.

"Aye, we heard that rumor. Adams and Hancock were safer in Lexington," someone said.

"So when British agents rode through Lexington asking the where-abouts of Adams and Hancock, of course our militia began to muster, even before they heard any British troops were coming," said James Bowdoin quietly.

Heads nodded in approval.

All listened intently. James looked about. No regulars sat at tables in the tavern, enjoying a tankard of ale or playing a game of dice. *Perhaps the 4,000 redcoats posted in Boston are all busy,* he thought.

"In the afternoon General Gage ordered Lieutenant Colonel Francis Smith to proceed with haste and secrecy to Concord. Their spies had informed them that colonial militia had collected ammunition and arms at Concord, west of Lexington, to keep them safe and out of Boston. Gage wanted Smith's troops to seize and destroy all military stores. However, the militia had already moved most of these supplies to safer places in towns nearby." James Bowdoin looked about at the circle of listeners, his face half hidden under his black tri-corner hat.

"They spread them out in several towns," agreed another speaker.

"Yes," he said. In the dim light of the flickering fire, James could scarcely see Bowdoin's features. "Two nights ago, April 18, Dr. Joseph Warren, president of the Committee of Safety for our Provincial Congress, received intelligence that the British troops would take boats from Boston to Cambridge across the bay and from there travel west to Lexington and Concord. He told William Dawes, a young tanner, and Paul Revere to ride to Lexington and Concord to warn the provincial leaders to flee and to call out our militia.

"Revere and Dawes split up, thinking their movements would go more unnoticed. Dawes rode south on land. He left Boston at the Neck, the strip of land joining Boston to the mainland, and traveled over the Great Bridge spanning the Charles River to Lexington. Revere gave instructions for signal lanterns to be placed in the Old North Church that he could easily see across the Charles River. If one lantern were hung, the signal would mean the British would advance by land over the Boston Neck and then march to Concord. If two lanterns were hung, that would mean the redcoats would cross the Charles River by boat to Cambridge, the shorter of the two ways, and then proceed to Concord. Revere himself crossed the Charles River on the north by rowboat, and slipped past the warship Somerset undetected. He landed safely in Charlestown and then rode to Lexington, warning almost every house as he went." James Bowdoin paused in his tale to take a long drink from his tankard. No one moved. James sensed the tension of those listening, all quiet with interest.

"A brave and fortunate ride, Paul Revere had," someone commented. Others muttered agreement.

"In Lexington, the riders ran into a British patrol," Bowdoin continued. Outside, James heard shouts and the beating of drums, but the noise was far away.

"Revere was captured, Dawes thrown from his horse, and Samuel Prescott rode on to warn Concord. Over five hundred British troops were coming. Towns throughout the region warned others of the danger, sending messages with bells, alarm guns, bonfires, and trumpets, rallying the militia in villages throughout the region."

"Can you imagine the terror those villagers were feeling?" someone said. Others agreed.

"To have British troops advancing on homes with intentions to take weapons by violence, that would be a terrible situation," came an answer.

"The militia have been drilling for months," said someone else.

"Yes, and a good thing they have. There's fighting yet," was the answer.

James Bowdoin regarded the listeners seriously. He continued, "British troops quietly loaded into boats at wharves on the western end of Boston Common Tuesday night. They crossed the channel and early in the morning marched the seventeen miles to Concord. The warning sounds of colonial drums, trumpets, and fired alarms from nearby towns must have alerted them that they had lost the advantage of surprise and the militia would be waiting.

"When British regulars arrived, they faced the minutemen on Lexington Green. A British officer shouted to the minutemen to disperse, but no one moved. Then a shot rang out, no one knows from where, and before the minutemen could run, eight of their number lay dead. The rest ran to cover."

"How awful," said someone. "It would seem that war is not far off."

"Indeed it is not," agreed Bowdoin. "The day got worse after that.

"In Lexington the British set fire to houses and shops, plundering as they passed. They shot and killed even the elderly, the unarmed, and the young. My report came from one who followed the British back to

Cambridge and slipped through to Boston early this morning. He says the British mangled the bodies of those they killed in a most shocking way."

Groans and hushed whispers greeted this statement.

"The Concord militia, who knew their ammunition and cannon were safe elsewhere, joined with militia from Acton, Bedford, and Lincoln. About four hundred of them faced the hundred or so regulars holding the North Bridge outside of Concord.

"A shot rang out, more than likely from the outnumbered British. Before anyone could stop the action, dead fell on both sides. The British retreated to their main force, leaving our militia in control of the North Bridge," said James Bowdoin, his voice low.

"About noon, the British assembled to return to Boston. By this time companies from all around the region had gathered. Joseph Warren was with them, having slipped through early that morning. But they didn't form a line of attack. Instead, securing themselves behind walls, trees, and gullies, our militia fired on the retreating British. The British, exhausted and running low on ammunition, were in full retreat, hit hard by rifle fire all the way." James Bowdoin permitted himself a broad grin, his teeth flashing in the flickering firelight. Then he became solemn again.

"Good for our side," someone said.

"Apparently, yes," Bowdoin continued. "Gage sent reinforcements, though. Yesterday morning, the 19th of April, about nine in the morning, Lord Percy's brigade of a thousand troops left Boston. You all heard them, marching out as they sang 'Yankee Doodle.' Percy did reach Lexington in time to join Colonel Smith's men, exhausted and fleeing, but unfortunately for him Percy had not thought to bring extra cannonballs or ammunition.

"General Gage sent a wagon full of ammunition and cannonballs after Percy, but we heard some older militia, too old to join the minutemen, had ambushed the wagons. The older soldiers killed some of the British, while the others ran off. Then the militia threw the ammunition into the river." James Bowdoin smiled broadly.

"Good for those old boys," someone chuckled.

"So, Lord Percy's men joined Colonel Smith's in the rout back to Boston, all with low supplies of ammunition. The militia pursued them, firing from behind stone walls, trees, and buildings. Townspeople joined in when they could.

"By nightfall yesterday the regulars had made it to the hills of Charlestown, where they collapsed. The big guns of the *Somerset* protect them there. They must have been exhausted from two days' march without sleep and the strain of combat. No doubt they earned any pain they may have felt, however, those dogs." James Bowdoin broke off and gulped from his tankard. His voice sounded strained from weariness.

Heads nodded around him, listeners agreeing, "Yes, yes." James nodded in agreement. It served the British forces right, for attacking where they had no business.

"Some say the regulars will build barricades on Breed's Hill. The first shots of war have no doubt been fired," James Bowdoin resumed.

"The militia carried flintlocks used against Indians and were led by those who served under General Wolfe at Quebec, so they were not entirely unseasoned. Knowing the British were the aggressors, killing their friends and neighbors and ruining their property, must have inflamed them. For every one of our militia that fell, more than two British were shot, so we can be proud of our minutemen.

"We can be proud of our leaders, as well," he added. "Joseph Warren fought alongside the militia at Lexington and joined in the rout of the British back to Boston, though he has no combat experience."

"He did show remarkable bravery," James said.

James Bowdoin nodded. "I hear a musket ball pierced his wig. He is busy now organizing the militia watching Gage's forces at Breed's Hill."

James Bowdoin seemed to have finished, for he sat back and folded his arms, staring at the group in thought. James finished his drink and stood up. "Thank you for your report. The more we know, the more we can prepare for whatever comes next. I hope our brave boys out in the field watching the regulars have a peaceful night of it." He tipped his hat before leaving the group. "Good night, then."

"Battle of Lexington."
New York Public Library Digital Collections

Chapter 29

The Siege: Burning of Hog Island, Taking of Noddle

MAY 28, 1775

Ever since the shots at Lexington and Concord on April 19th, tension between the soldiers and the residents of Boston ran high. James avoided casual outings into town, as did everyone else. British regulars walked the streets and performed daily drills. When he did walk to market, he avoided the soldiers strutting by. Filled with self-importance, they pushed townspeople out of their way, snarling as they did so. On the grassy common where people usually strolled and children played, the British cannon bristled in iron formation, ready to respond to any possible attack by the militia.

Militia from towns near and far now ringed the city on the surrounding hills. Farmers, carrying their Brown Bess muskets, had marched to the outskirts of Boston from Connecticut, Pennsylvania, and even Virginia. The presence of so many militia, some 15,000, James had heard, made the British fearful and uneasy. The British forces, though better armed and trained, were outnumbered by the multitudes of citizen soldiers encamped around the town.

But the townspeople within Boston remained patient, calm, orderly. Town meetings continued. James had heard Samuel Adams was in Philadelphia with the Second Continental Congress. He hoped that assembly would make good decisions to better the situation.

James Jr. had decided to leave the city to join the militia. James was proud of him for his decision, though he worried for his son's safety. The younger James had explained to his father before leaving that he planned to tell the British soldiers watching the Neck that he was going to help his uncle, Rufus Bent, and his cousins in the country. Then he hoped to find friends near Dorchester to the west. The British were watching those leaving Boston carefully, so James Jr. had not been able to smuggle out the family's old musket with him. However, at seventeen, he was tall, strong, and well-able to take care of himself. Mary smiled in approval at the news that James Jr. would join the militia, though she looked grave when she hugged him good-bye. "Be careful, son," she said. "We are looking forward to hearing report of your safety."

"Come, Father," called little Mary from the street one early May day. James set down the book he had been reading with Thomas, just four, and followed six-year-old Mary outside.

"There, across the bay. See the smoke?" A thick black cloud of smoke billowed up. The dark clouds looked as though they came from near Castle William, the British fort to the south at the entrance to Boston harbor.

It might be a ship on fire, he thought, *but then again, a cloud of smoke that large at this distance must be something burning bigger than a ship.*

"I think it may be a fire on an island. Come, Mary, let's go back in. Thank you for showing me the smoke." James took Mary's hand and led her and Thomas back into the house.

"Mary," he called up the stairs, "I'm going to the wharf to find out about that fire across the harbor."

"Be careful," she called back. "If you see any potatoes or cabbage for sale, be sure to get some. We have almost no vegetables remaining, and there is nothing but lettuce yet in the garden."

"I will be sure to look," James responded, putting on his hat.

Since the Boston Latin School had been dismissed on April 19, when the conflict had erupted at Lexington and Concord, school had not been in session. James saw little of his father. True, he greeted the older Lovell each Sunday at church. James's mother always stopped to visit with the children and Mary. Occasionally he passed his father working in his garden or walking to market. James had no wish to cut ties with him, but the schoolmaster already seemed cut off, wrapped in his own thoughts, unaware of the passions that filled the city. H*e clearly lives a separate life from me,* James thought.

Somehow, he did not miss school much—there was always plenty to be done. Today, for example, he had time to help Mary by going to market, when usually his day would be spent in the busy schoolroom.

The morning sun sparkled on the water, fresh and bright. The May weather had turned pleasantly warm. A steady breeze threw scents of blooming flowers and ocean spray, tinged with smoke from last night's cannonading. Light clouds scudded high in the deep blue sky.

A number of people filled Market Street, talking about the fire. For once, few regulars were in sight. "What is burning?" James asked a peddler, who carried pots and pans hanging from his back.

"Hog Island," the man laughed, showing a remarkable set of pale gums in his jowly mouth. His collection of wares tinkled and jangled.

"The militia from Massachusetts and New Hampshire slipped over to Noddle's Island to take cattle from the British," the peddler continued. "They chased 'em back to Hog Island. The militia set fire to the houses on Hog Island, right this way of Castle William. You can be sure the British are hopping mad. The admiral sent a schooner to catch 'em, the six-gun *Diana.* But before he could fire the guns, the schooner ran aground on the island and then the rascals set fire to that, too! The militia got away with all the cattle from both Noddle and Hog Islands, and just three wounded. A pretty day's work!" the peddler said, poking James in the ribs. His pots clanked and clattered.

"An excellent effort," James agreed, stepping back from the peddler a few inches and watching the thick dark plume soar. Noddle's Island lay just to the east of Boston in the harbor, Hog Island just beyond. Both had proved convenient places for the British to keep supplies of cattle to feed the regiments.

"I got my news from a British soldier I heard grousing at the tavern," the peddler said, swelling with importance. "An actual participant in the event, you might say." He puffed with pride, looking to James for all the world like a strutting rooster.

"Now, could you use a pot? A dish?" the peddler asked, turning around to display the startling array of pewter pots dangling on his back.

"No, thank you, my friend. I need to find some potatoes," James said, remembering Mary's request. "But thank you for the news. It is good news, indeed."

He turned from the peddler, who spat into the dusty street and, clinking and clattering, turned and shuffled away.

James walked towards Market Street, passing groups of grim-looking British soldiers. He wondered what anyone could do to confuse the plans of the British. They were at a disadvantage, bottled up in Boston like flies in a wine decanter, and they knew it. Outnumbered, they nevertheless had superior firepower in cannon and ships, and posed a danger for the wary militia gathered around the town.

What would his friend Josiah Quincy say about the situation? Co-counsel with John Adams at the Boston Massacre trial proceedings, Josiah was so concerned for the cause of freedom that he had gone to London, where he contacted those politicians he knew to be sympathetic, urging them to speak out for better treatment for the colonies. But to James's sorrow, on his return trip Josiah had been overcome by tuberculosis and died, at just thirty-one years old. This had happened a month ago, in April, just before he would have reached Massachusetts. *We have lost a great friend and strong voice for liberty,* James thought.

He looked up from his musings. Ahead in the street he saw his sister Elizabeth, dainty and pretty as always, neatly dressed in her burgundy velvet cape, arm in arm with a British officer. *A captain, likely,* thought James, noticing his splendid plumed hat and gilt handled sword. The fellow appeared totally lost in fascination with his sister. She smiled sweetly back, her chestnut curls swinging. James had no wish to talk with the officer, so he turned without saying anything and walked the other way. Elizabeth had not seen him, and for that he was glad. He had no idea what she was doing. *Why would she want to spend time with a British officer?*

Whatever game she was playing, he didn't want her to see him while in the officer's company. It was bad enough that she was walking with a British officer, apparently wrapped up in their conversation, but at twenty-five Elizabeth was unmarried and very much an independent young woman. His glimpse of her set him to worrying. He hoped sincerely she would be careful of her choices.

He walked quickly down a side street towards the market. Either his sister was really fascinated with this British officer, or she had some other object in mind. She had always spoken in favor of the rights and liberties of Massachusetts' citizens, and she supported non-importation. *Possibly Elizabeth was amusing herself,* he thought, remembering the young officer's carefully trimmed mustache and look of adoration. Her arm had been very tightly held in his. If she was playing a game, he hoped she would be careful.

At market James bought potatoes and onions, scowling at their high price and poor condition, then headed home. So little food had been available at market. He'd have to speak with Mary. What food they had must be carefully used, as supplies were growing short. He could take the boys and go fishing. Fish for the table would be a welcome change.

He wondered what he could do to help the militia and those coordinating their movements. He was a schoolteacher, not really fit to go join the militia. In fact, he had little experience in weaponry. Besides, if he did go, what would happen to his family? Reading and writing were his stock-in-trade. James frowned in concern.

Then an idea occurred to him. He was not familiar with weapons, but maybe he could make his occupation as schoolteacher an asset. No one would think of him doing anything unusual. They would never, for instance, imagine he might be able to view the movements of the enemy, or assess troop strength. Maybe he could turn the situation to his advantage, to be of help to the Sons of Liberty and those uniting in support of opposition to British oppression. James quickened his steps and smiled to himself. Yet even as his thoughts raced and he hurried home, he was careful to avoid the street where he'd seen Elizabeth strolling with her plumed, besotted officer.

Chapter 30

An Accomplice

JUNE 6, 1775

In an unpredictable course of events, the casual encounter James made at the tavern turned out to be a great help to his predicament sooner than expected. On a warm June evening, he walked along Boston's wharves, surveying the ships anchored there, listening for any news he could gather. For over a year, since the Boston Port Act had closed the harbor on June 1, 1774, trade and commerce had come to a standstill. As punishment for the Tea Party, ships could no longer transport manufactured products from Britain or other countries into Boston. Any goods caught were confiscated. As further limitation on trade, the Continental Association the previous fall had agreed the colonies would continue to pressure Great Britain through non-importation. No British goods could be sold in shops without severe punishment from local authorities.

Meanwhile, General Gage with his troops tightened the noose, erecting bulwarks on the Neck for whatever conflict might arise. Four cannon stood guard at the only entrance to Boston by land, to keep patriots out but not to prevent the occasional raid on farms and food by the British.

Making his way through the streets near the wharves, James watched a coaster from South Carolina and one from Pennsylvania unloading sacks of rice and flour. Trade in food from other colonies was still permitted. In fact, many colonies, in sympathy with Boston, had been sending extra food into the port on ships navigating the coastline.

He stepped into a quiet, dark tavern on Prospect Street for a minute to get a drink, then nearly bumped into a shadowy, silent figure sitting on a bench under a dirty window.

"Watch where you're goin', mate," the man said gruffly.

"My apologies," James said, and stepped back. He heard a lilt in the fellow's voice. Was that an accent, perhaps? He paused and looked closely at the dark figure. His gold earring, scarred face, and worn coat, greasy with age, suggested a seaman. Maybe he served the British.

"May I buy you a drink?" James said, impetuously. He might be able to find out some news, if this was indeed a British sailor.

"I can always use a drink," the man said. His voice was low and husky. *Canadian?* James wondered. *Not British, likely.* His hawk-like nose gave his indistinct face a twisted, brooding look.

"Are you a sailor?" James asked. He handed the fellow a mug from the tray of a passing servant and sat down on the bench beside him. Around them, a few British regulars lounged at tables or gathered by the cold hearth, laughing and jesting. None paid James any attention. He glanced at the thick, rough brand on the dirty hand as the man reached for his drink. So, the man had been in trouble with the law—a thief, maybe.

"I am that, sometimes. I come down in His Majesty's fleet from Halifax as a cook's assistant. The British sent reinforcements from Halifax some time back, soldiers and ships. They about cleaned out the garrison up there."

James remembered the surge of redcoats from Nova Scotia a few years ago, troops arriving under Colonel Dalrymple. Their arrival had without doubt put the town on edge.

"I was traded off to other British ships around Boston, though I've also crossed the big water once. Still, I am not navy, though I'm stationed on the *Somerset,* man-of-war. I'm in the kitchen most days. Pressed, I was, in Halifax. I once fished with my father."

"Ah, a tough business," James said sympathetically. He wondered how he might convince this sailor to help him.

"I have no love for the British," the man said gruffly. "They did this to me." He held up his thumb. James stared at the twisted, rough mark of the brand that spanned the length of it. "I was just taking bread I was entitled to—my portion. And they took me from my home, four years ago, and there's no goin' back.

"Besides," he added in a gruff, low voice, "my father came to Halifax from Massachusetts. So that makes me really part of New England, you know?"

James nodded agreement. He took a long sip from his tankard and decided to take a chance.

"You ever see things? Hear things?"

"I hear all kinds of things," the man admitted. He said in a hoarse whisper, "I bring General Gage his dinner, sometimes, and help clean up as well. On Castle William I serve in the scullery, and on 'is ship too."

"Could you maybe report to me any changes, any plans you hear of?" said James cautiously.

"Aye, I could do that." The fellow's black eyes twinkled fiercely under his grimy yellow cap. "Where would I find ye?"

"Here. In the back of the tavern. I'll check in every day or so, to find you," James answered.

"I can only come a couple times a week. The rest of the time I'm slavin' in the scullery. Zach's my name."

"That's good, Zach. My name's Jemmy, to you. And I'll be most obliged if you can help me get that information—anything we can do to obstruct these British overlords."

"Here's my hand on it." Zach extended the dirty appendage, a pleased grin on his face, and James clasped it, feeling the surprisingly strong grip, the rough scar.

"Be safe," James said, rising to go and tossing down the last of his drink. "My thanks to you."

"My thanks to you as well," Zach responded, sinking back into the shadows. In a grave, low whisper, he said, "Who knows what good we might do? The situation must change."

Chapter 31

A Window into British Plans

JUNE 10, 1775

James set out for the tavern on Purchase Street near the wharves around seven o'clock in the evening. The old tavern was a favorite meeting place for British regulars and sailors, while few from Boston felt comfortable there these days. The streets swarmed with soldiers, as ships with reinforcements for General Gage's occupying troops had arrived the day before. James slipped through the busy streets, head down and eyes averted, as he passed groups of them, fresh from Britain. Inexperienced and brash, the young regulars strutted by, congratulating each other on their new station in life, all the while longing for their chance to prove themselves heroic. These recruits, most from impoverished families back in Britain, had never experienced the hardships of fighting; in their minds, the opportunity for adventure as well as good pay lay just before them.

Shouts of bravado and cheers echoed in the dusty tavern, which was filled with carousing British soldiers. Regulars in their red coats and sailors in dark blue mingled, offering raucous toasts.

James stepped in through a back door, nearly tripping over a knot of three British soldiers playing a game of dice on the floor, foaming mugs of beer in their hands.

"Here, watch where you're goin'," snarled one.

"Excuse me," James said quietly, sliding past the group. The last thing he wanted was to provoke a confrontation. Reaching the back of the tavern without further incident, he looked about cautiously. The place was mill-ing with soldiers: young, inexperienced, and brash. Through the throng, he saw a lone figure near the opposite wall sitting on a low bench, face half hidden in a hood. *He might be Zach, holding a drink,* James thought. He pulled his hat down low and made his way across the tavern, keeping near to the wall. A few soldiers looked up at him in surprise, and laughed to see a Boston gentleman in their midst.

Approaching the solitary figure, James looked closely under his hood. Yes, it was Zach. Deep olive eyes looked back at him in recognition. Then without a word, the sailor stood up and walked to the back of the tavern. He pushed open a low door entering onto an alleyway and stepped out into the night. James followed, not too close behind. Out of the corner of his eye, he thought he saw faces turn in his direction, eyes following him, but he put down his head and kept moving forward. One regular swore and spat when he saw James, sneering at him unpleasantly. But before anyone could pursue him, James opened the back door and slipped out, latching it quietly behind him.

Stars sprinkled overhead; the moon shone brilliantly over the water. The black figure stood in the shadow of an overhanging roof across the alley. James quietly walked up to him and moved into the darkness near his acquaintance.

"I have a word," Zach said in a whisper. "Yesterday General Gage met with the new generals who just came."

"Generals Burgoyne, Clinton, and Howe," James said under his breath. "They call them the 'three Bow-wows.' They bark as loudly as the top dog."

"Yes, they're the ones. The plan they agreed to was General Gage's. On Sunday, June 18, they plan to march out Boston Neck and occupy Dorchester Heights." Zach motioned in the direction of the hills to the south overlooking Boston. "From there...." Zach didn't need to finish his statement. James easily added the words.

"From there the British guns could command the town. It would be only a step from that, to occupying the region." James drew his breath at the thought of the audacious plan. "Thank you, my good man," he said, taking several coins from his pocket and handing them to Zach.

Zach took the coins without comment and tucked them away, pulling out a folded sheet of paper for James as he did so. "I do this for the pleasure of seeing British plans unravel. They've been no friends to me. But thank ye."

"I may see you again." James put out his hand and grasped Zach's tough, leathery palm in a handshake. He glanced at the written note and pocketed it. "Good luck to you, then. Be safe." He returned Zach's steady gaze as the sailor acknowledged the gift with a nod and a hint of a smile.

Then he turned and made his way down the alley. His breath came light and fast as he realized he'd just received news from a reliable contact. *And,* he thought, *the news was worth every minute of the risk. Still,* he reminded himself, *I had best be very careful.*

Several British regulars stood arguing behind the tavern; from their shrill words and volleys of curses it was clear they had had too much to drink. They paid James no attention as he walked quickly away from the waterfront towards home.

The breeze blew off the harbor where His Majesty's ships rested like dark cormorants, flags fluttering. Fresh salt air revitalized James's spirits, and he breathed deeply, feeling a connection to his home, his hopes, as he paced through the dusky night. Half an hour later he reached a handsome house up the hill, its door framed by a decorative arch, a luxuriant rose bush perfuming the night. James made his way around the dwelling to the back, ignoring the barking of a spotted dog that raced towards him and sniffed him suspiciously. Through a small window he could see a kitchen fire crackling. He knocked on the back door five times. A black servant wearing a white turban opened it a crack and peered out.

"I must speak to Dr. Warren," James said quietly.

"Come in, sir," she answered politely, motioning James across the braided rug to a chair by the fire. In a few minutes Dr. Joseph Warren, president of the Safety Committee for the patriot cause, entered.

Joseph Warren's smooth face and even features looked troubled. Gray circles under his eyes revealed restless nights. He had assumed a central position of leadership for the town and the Massachusetts province; now his tireless work for the cause of liberty was beginning to wear on him. James had known Joseph Warren for many years and admired his exuberance, his ability to speak, his work on the part of those laboring for freedom. Dr. Joseph Warren had graduated from Harvard the same year James had concluded his own post-graduate work there. James suddenly remembered him speaking in a Roman toga just this past March, the 5th anniversary of the Boston Massacre; his oration had been dramatic, focused, and heartily cheered by the crowd who gathered to listen.

"Hello, my friend," James said, standing. He was relieved to see Joseph Warren. He smiled for the first time all night and felt a sense of peace.

"It is good to see you, James," said Joseph Warren, extending his hand. His calm face, usually serene and secure, was pale with worry and lack of sleep. "Have you news?"

"Yes. It may be of great importance. I have word from a reliable source that General Gage and his compatriots will be marching troops out of Boston Neck on the night of June 18 to occupy Dorchester Heights." James spoke with a thrill of importance.

"This is news, indeed." Joseph Warren's eyes opened wide with alarm. "Think of thousands of British regulars in Boston. If they could get to the heights, what power their army would have." He turned to pace in front of the fireplace. "With those just arrived under Gage, their numbers are some-where near 10,000. But we have the chance to make use of this news, since we have an even greater number of militia encircling Boston, in Roxbury, Cambridge, Charlestown, and the surrounding area. There are more than 16,000 militia, reports say."

James thought of the men encamped about Boston, drilling during the day, watching the British movements, sleeping in tents or rough shelters. He remembered that his son James Jr. would more than likely be with them.

"A goodly number, Dr. Warren," he said, nodding agreement. "My own son, my oldest, has joined them, I believe, though we have had no word from him."

"Good for him. And they now have a leader," continued Joseph Warren. "George Washington, from Virginia, has just been appointed commanding general of all the patriot forces, and we have other generals as well. There are old Israel Putnam and Artemas Ward, both of whom saw combat in the French and Indian War; and William Prescott, another veteran of that conflict. I'll bet they can stir the place up. They expect me to play the part of military commander. I'll do my best, though I'm not the one most suited for it, I greatly fear." He turned and looked at James steadily, his brown eyes calm and clear.

"Time is on our side, if we can use it to our advantage," Joseph Warren continued. "I'll tell the committee of this news. Thank you, James. I knew we could count on you. If you find out anything more, please get word to me again."

"You may be sure I will. I am concerned for your safety, as well," James said. "Your role is important to our forces." He regarded Joseph Warren with concern and extended his hand for a final handshake, handing him a folded sheet of paper. "This is the note from my contact with the news. The source is dependable."

Joseph Warren tucked the paper in his pocket. "Would you take a bite of food before you leave?" He motioned to a side table holding a silver tray of bread covered in linen.

"I've had little to eat for hours, so yes, thank you." James picked up a tender, buttery roll, nodded his thanks, and stepped out the door that Warren opened for him into the night. "I had best be going. Thank you for your attention."

"Good night," Dr. Warren said in a low voice. "Take utmost care of yourself."

"A most good night to you as well, and safe travels," James said, tipping his hat. He slipped into the alley. If he were careful and stayed out of the light, he might avoid both the watch and the British. Stepping carefully through alleys and side streets, avoiding the lamplight, he made his way home through the soft June night.

How right Patrick Henry and John Adams had been, James thought, as he walked. *A year ago they concluded we must fight, if we couldn't otherwise rid ourselves of the oppressive measures placed upon us by the British government. Closing the port of Boston and bringing this horde of soldiers here is more than likely the straw that will break the camel's back and usher in armed conflict. We will see.*

The moon shone brilliantly through high, light clouds. James glanced at the harbor, where, like a huge mirror, the calm sea threw back the light of the moon. He imagined the thousands of militia encamped around Boston in the shadowy hills. *We may have a surprise for the British yet,* James thought.

Chapter 32

A Message

JUNE 14, 1775

It was a long, weary night, full of unexpected developments and difficulties. After eating a supper of fish and potatoes, James left Mary and the children at home and set out on his mission. He had congratulated Johnny on his excellent catch of cod.

"Any food that helps our family is truly a blessing, Johnny," James said, polishing off his portion of crisp cod. *Mary could make any food tasty*, he thought. Even the well-cooked fish, however, had not stopped the pain of the stomach distress that gripped him. Lately he had endured several bouts of the sharp discomfort that seemed to come and go, torturing him with painful cramps. Right now, though, he could bear the discomfort. He determined to ignore it and undertake his quest.

"Must you go, again?" Mary asked, concern wrinkling her brow, as he adjusted his hat.

"Joseph Warren is counting on it. General Warren now, though he isn't much of a military man. Yes, my dear, I must," James said. "Go back to the table, Jemmy," he added, speaking to his son who appeared, worried and quiet, in the doorway. Jemmy nodded and returned to his seat.

"General Warren survived the attack at Lexington and Concord back in April, and he can best figure out the strategy for defense of the land across the bay on the Charlestown peninsula, or wherever the British might attack," James added. "And he will be better than the old Generals

Israel Putnam or Artemas Ward at explaining the layout of the defense to the men.

"You know," James continued, bending to adjust his shoe buckles, "less than a week ago more British regulars arrived on transports, so there are upwards of 10,000 here in Boston. They mill about the city, hoping for a conflict. But there are over 16,000 militia ringing Boston—minutemen from Pennsylvania, Rhode Island, Connecticut, New Hampshire, and more—so the British are, in reality, trapped. Whoever makes the first move, that's the issue. This siege becomes a game of chess."

Mary picked up two-year-old Charles, who reached out to grab his father's hat and nearly knocked it off. Charles smiled and tugged a ringlet of his mother's hair.

"Your bravery had better not border on foolhardiness. We need you here as well," Mary said. "What would we do if the British noticed you paying more than passing attention to them? Besides, you know how your father would react if he knew your doings." Her blue eyes looked at him anxiously. Lines of weariness left tracks on her cheeks. *These days have not been easy on her either*, James thought.

"You do not need to worry, my dear," James answered, straightening up. "I am careful, as always. The British have more on their minds than noting my movements. And as you surely know, my father and I parted ways on that score long ago. He has his views, and I have mine."

He smiled and handed his hat to little Charles for a moment, who examined it thoughtfully. "At least you can be sure no one is taking seriously General Gage's ridiculous proclamation of two days ago—that if we lay down arms and submit to British rule peaceably, all will be pardoned. Most definitely not our leaders, Samuel Adams and John Hancock. Does the general really think we will agree to such foolishness? We intend to have our rights and liberty, though it means conflict. Enough of tyranny and despotism.

"I have contacts in Boston, safe contacts," James continued, "and Joseph Warren has need of knowledge. It is better with little said." He gently took his hat back from Charles. He needed to leave soon.

"Mary, if you see British frigates under sail or hear guns firing, bring the children in to the house and keep them there. You'll be able to see what's going on from the widow's walk up on the roof. The rails will protect you from slipping, and the roof is quite flat and sturdy there. If the British should start an advance on militia camped outside of Boston, you will know it. The latest reinforcements are quartered at Castle William and in the town; there are redcoats everywhere. They may risk an attack soon.

"I must be going. You'll be safe here. I will return as soon as I can." He gave Mary a quick hug and kissed her cheek. "It's not much I can do as a schoolteacher with a rebellious stomach, but I do what I can. Good-bye."

"Please take care of yourself," Mary said, her voice nearly trembling as she shut the door.

James walked down the streets, keeping in the shadows as much as he could, heading to the wharf district. He entered an alley leading to the back of the tavern on Prospect Street. Slipping in the back door unobserved, he sat down on a shaded bench in the rear of the tavern. The din of soldiers carousing and drinking sounded in the front of the tavern. Clearly, they were too involved in revelry to notice him. After a few minutes, a silent figure stepped in from the back door and sat down next to James. A gold earring dangled beneath his long black hair, tied back in a queue.

"You have it?" James asked quietly.

"Of course," was the response. The Canadian accent.

It's good to see you, Zach, James thought.

"Thank you for your help." He held out a hand and placed in Zach's outstretched palm a few coins. The sailor took one and fingered it, admiring its shiny yellow glint in the dim light. Then he slipped the coins in his pocket and handed James a folded slip of paper.

"It's for the good of all that I do this," he said in a whisper. "The sooner the British realize they cannot have their own way and treat the colonies like belligerent children, the better." He bent his head low and turned to face James. Choosing his words carefully, Zach spoke so quietly James had to cock his head toward him to listen. "What we know is that 2,500 British troops on barges with cannon will land on the Charlestown peninsula on the northeast point. General Howe will send ships to fire hot shot on Charlestown. To those wooden buildings, we can guess what that would do."

"When? Do we know?"

"In two days' time—June 16, if all goes well."

James slid the note Zach had given him into his pocket. He drew in his breath. "Thank you, my friend. I must be on my way. Be safe."

He shook Zach's hand firmly and stepped out of the tavern. In the inky darkness no one saw or questioned him. Down the street, a group of red-coated British soldiers stood under a street lamp, their voices high with excitement and rum. Remembering the curfew, James ducked into an alley.

Crossing streets quickly and sticking to back ways, he travelled north-ward to Hanover Street. When James reached the silent, dark home of Dr. Joseph Warren, his hands were shaking. He had been to the patriot leader's house several times, and each time he had been unobserved. He prayed his luck would hold.

No dogs barked at his approach, for which he was thankful. On the first knock no one came, and James was about to leave, having remembered the lateness of the hour, when the turbaned servant opened the door, a candle in her hand. She bent curiously towards James. "Dr. Warren is not in. May I give him a message?"

"Yes, with my thanks. Tell him this note is of utmost importance." He bowed slightly to the servant, handing her the folded paper. As a member of Dr. Joseph Warren's household, he assumed the servant could be trusted to deliver the note as soon as she was able. She smiled and closed the door.

One more trip—home, this time, James thought. *It is late, very late. Or very early, depending on how one thinks of it. I shall be glad to arrive home safely. I sorely need a good night's rest.*

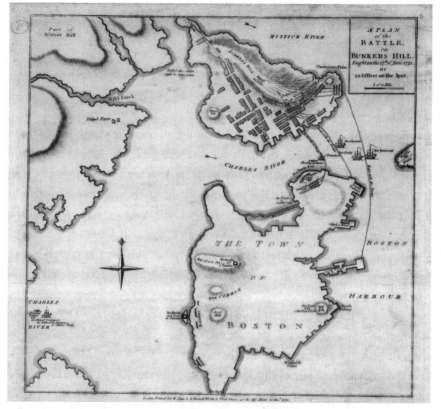

"A Plan of the Battle, on Bunkers Hill fought on the 17th of June 1775."
Library of Congress Prints and Photographs

Chapter 33

Bunker Hill

JUNE 17, 1775

Restless thoughts kept James awake. More than once he climbed the steep stairs to the widow's walk on their roof, where he had a good view of the town and harbor. He did not know what he was looking or listening for, but as nothing had occurred the previous evening, this was surely the night when the conflict might begin. The air was still, calm; stars sprinkled the nearly cloudless sky, and moonlight revealed the hills across the bay and the rippling sea. On Charlestown Peninsula men under the command of Colonel William Prescott, assisted by Israel Putnam's Connecticut soldiers, dug through the night, constructing earthworks, redoubts, fortifying fence lines at the top of the hills. *Who knows what role Dr. Joseph Warren will assume?* James wondered. The militia depended upon this citizen general, though he had little experience in battle.

Once in a while James thought he heard the ringing of shovels on rock under the starlight, but it was difficult to say for sure. The attack might come on Breed's Hill, the first and lower of the two hills on the peninsula facing Boston from the northwest, or on Bunker Hill, the taller. Farmers Breed and Bunker had taken their cattle and left, giving ground to the army. To the west of the high ground on the peninsula lay the town of Charlestown, also a possible target for the British advance. The three generals with their subordinates were tired of playing the waiting game; they would attack with the strength and might of the British troops and navy. Secure in superior firing pieces, soldiers, plenty of ammunition, and swift ships outfitted with cannon, the British knew they could ferry troops with barges wherever they pleased. Meanwhile, their heavy ships could pick out militia or structures by firing cannon from farther out on the water.

General Gage, General Howe, General Clinton, and General Burgoyne might not agree as to plans, but they would unite in action. William Howe, brother of Admiral Earl Howe, was the most senior of the three, so James thought it was his plan they would likely pursue. Henry Clinton, experienced in combat in the Seven Years War, had been summoned by King George to assist with the siege in Boston. Thomas Gage was Commander-in-Chief of British forces in North America, so he had the most to lose if this attack did not go well. *General John Burgoyne is not in charge, so he probably will not see action in this battle. This is how their plans will likely unfold*, thought James.

James could hear the watchmen's cry of "All's well" from the British ships. He pulled a blanket around himself and sank into an old chair on the roof. Sometime during the night, he began to doze fitfully. Towards morning the sky lightened; streaks of rose and gold brightened the horizon as the stars faded. The clatter of gunfire woke him with a start. Barges filled with red-coated soldiers were gliding into the tip of the peninsula, dotting the sea with floating red islands.

James threw his blanket off and stood at the rail, his heart in his mouth. He could make out the big heavy-gunned frigates, the *Lively* and the *Falcon*, making their way towards the southern tip of the Charlestown Peninsula. To the east, more ships sailed northward to provide men and firepower, the goal being to flank the Americans at the neck of the peninsula and cut off their retreat. By the time the sun was well up in the sky, the first booms of cannon echoed across the bay, sending up clouds of white smoke.

Jemmy and Johnny, so alike they could almost be twins, tall and gangly for their ages at twelve and thirteen, appeared on the roof next to him. Joseph came behind them. "What is happening, Father?" asked Jemmy.

"Be still and watch. The British are attacking the militia positioned on the Charlestown peninsula. If you look closely, you can see all those red-coats arriving on barges, forming lines, hauling cannon into position."

The boys watched, fascinated, huddled close to their father. Mary came up and put her hand on James's shoulder, little Charles in her arms and the three younger children crowding against her. "We have the advantage of preparation there, do we not?" she asked. Charles hid his head against her as the sounds of firing resounded. William, Mary, and Thomas clung to her skirts, their eyes round with curiosity and fear.

"That we do," James answered. He squinted into the morning light, looking across the bay. "The redoubt the militia has dug is a square cut into the earth, more than likely at the top of Breed's Hill, the first hill closest to the water. In addition, the fence lines will be reinforced as barricades for protection. Our forces were wise to choose the closer hill to fortify. If they had not, the British would come charging up, take that high ground with no difficulty, and then have the advantage to pursue the second hill."

The family watched, transfixed. From their housetop they could see red British lines form and move up the hill, and they could hear the roll of drums and shouts echoing across the water. It looked to James as if cannon swung into position to the right of the advancing troops. Suddenly, shots echoed out and the dark figures at the top of the hill fired back. Clouds of smoke engulfed the scene as firing echoed from hills and across the harbor. The boom of cannon resounded, while to the west, smoke and flames erupted from the wooden buildings of Charlestown.

Mary gasped in horror. "They are burning Charlestown!"

James looked at the leaping flames with worry. "Yes, the hot shot from the *Lively* and the *Falcon* is setting those fires. The ships will also prevent militia in nearby towns from coming to the aid of those in the conflict. I imagine the British are fearful of snipers who could use the buildings as convenient hiding places. Yet how cruel and reckless, to put to the torch an entire village." James shook his head in sympathy. The children watched in shocked fascination as the smoke rose, black and thick, from the burning structures.

"How awful for the people who live there!" Mary said. "I hope they are all right. Perhaps they could leave."

"I imagine they would have gotten word in time to leave," James said, hoping he was right. "Don't worry. I am sure they would have left if at all possible."

Mary hugged little Charles tightly, who began to cry. "Come, children," she said, motioning to William, Mary, and Thomas to follow her down the stairs to the house. "We have watched long enough."

Jemmy, Johnny, and Joseph remained on the roof with their father. "Do you suppose James Jr. is somewhere fighting?" Joseph asked.

"I should not be too surprised, except he was not to be in Charlestown but rather in the countryside. We will find out later, I expect," James said. In fact, he had a sinking feeling every time he thought about James Jr. He hoped his son's good sense and strength would keep him out of danger.

Throughout the long day the firing continued. James watched as the red row of advance, hundreds of well-trained regulars, formed a line of attack three times and surged up the hill. Twice the line was pushed back towards the water from the heights, repulsed by a straggling force of darker figures, but the third time the relentless red surge continued, rushing up onto the hill in a wave. Though James stared, the thick smoke and confusion of movement made it difficult to tell just what was happening. Hand-to-hand and bayonet fighting probably engulfed the scene, but he could make out no individual movements. Nonetheless, James could not bring himself to leave the roof, nor could the boys. Mary came up, bringing them water, bread, and cheese, but they remained a captive audience to the smoke, noise, cannon blasts, and flames on the far side of the harbor.

As the sun sank into the west, columns of dark smoke poured out of Charlestown and the hills across the bay. The roar of cannon ceased, and barges bearing red-coated figures began the trip back to their quarters on the town side of the water. The conflict was over. The British would not pursue the Americans. They could retreat to the countryside beyond the Charlestown peninsula. *But what terrible wounds they must have borne,* James thought. No doubt many were suffering from the ordeal of the day's fighting. He felt ill just knowing what carnage must have been suffered in the battle.

On the other hand, he felt a sense of pride in the strength of the militia. It had taken the British three successive assaults to gain the heights. *The patriots have shown they could fight, and that might be the greatest victory of all,* James thought. He stood in the advancing starlight, weary but exhilarated. His tired family had long gone downstairs and taken rest.

He watched the fires burning on Breed's Hill, the red glow smoldering and flickering in the dark sky. *So many lives had been lost today.* Above, the stars twinkled in the solemn night sky. James saw a falling star, then another. For a moment he imagined a thousand stars falling, a vision of light and glory descending on the ruins of the battlefield. He hoped his vision was for the good. *By all that's holy, we've beaten them, even though good men have suffered and died in the fight. We will prevail.*

"Battle of Bunker's Hill."
New York Public Library Digital Collections

Chapter 34

After Bunker Hill

JUNE 18, 1775

The next day clouds of ash lay over the town, dropping in acrid flakes on houses and streets. Black smoke hung like a plague over Breed's Hill and the ruins of Charlestown. Townspeople stayed in their homes, under curfew from the British, but the news of the battle passed from one dwelling to another. The British had taken Breed's Hill and Bunker Hill but had paid a huge price to do so. Nearly a thousand British soldiers lost their lives charging up the fortified terrain, repulsed and beaten back time and again by a determined and sturdy militia. Outnumbered and out of ammunition, the patriots had retreated, joining the militia that ringed Boston in the countryside. They had lived to fight another day. James and his family drifted from one activity at home to another, amazed and stunned by the events, tired from little sleep.

From a neighbor, James heard that reinforcements to the patriot militia had attempted to come up through the Charlestown peninsula neck; however, they had been repulsed by live fire from Admiral Graves's ships waiting just at the northern edge of the peninsula. So it was fortunate Generals Artemis Ward and Israel Putnam had escaped with their men.

The rumble of British carts echoed in the streets, carrying dead and injured, towing cannon to new sites. Shouts and groans echoed in the warm air. The stench of smoke from charred buildings in Charlestown drifted in the air, bitter and sharp.

In the afternoon James opened his door cautiously, wondering what he could do. Could he get word to the militia about the British losses? If he could overhear the soldiers talking, he might find out valuable information. However, his stomach was acting up most painfully. He could not eat the food Mary prepared. All he could tolerate was a little plain bread and water.

His neighbor Oliver Wendell walked down from the corner of School Street and knocked on the door in the late afternoon. James opened it and welcomed in the stout businessman.

"Have a seat," James said to his friend, motioning to a large armchair.

Oliver Wendell sat down heavily. He looked at James with concern, his black eyebrows knitting together, and fidgeted a minute before he spoke. James took a seat near his visitor to listen. "I am sorry to bring bad news," he said at last. His face became very solemn. "I have heard that Dr. Joseph Warren died in fighting with the militia in defense of Breed's Hill. He was struck by a shot to the head."

James wiped his forehead. The thought of losing the clever, honorable Dr. Warren made him feel deeply sorrowful. He again felt the painful stomach distress that was eating at his insides and tried to shrug it off.

"I am so sorry," James finally said, after some moments of silence. "I cannot imagine how we can replace him. He was leading those men, was he not?"

"I hear he in fact had relinquished command of those militia troops to Thomas Knowlton, saying he had not enough experience to act as leader. Rather than seeking safety, however, he took up arms alongside the militia."

"He never should have been in that fight," James said. "He was no soldier."

"Yes, but the defense of that position was important, as he knew," Oliver Wendell explained sadly. "The militia were sheltered by entrenchments dug into Breed's Hill, but even that position fortified by wooden walls was not enough to hold off the waves of British troops."

"I am sure he did his best and fought bravely," James said, his voice thick with sorrow. "He will be greatly missed, not only as president of the Massachusetts Provincial Congress, but as an effective leader."

"The militia showed the British regulars they could fight, for certain. General Gage and General Howe may claim victory, since they did take Breed's Hill and Bunker Hill, and burned Charlestown, but our militia lost fewer men and gave those redcoats a good fight." Oliver Wendell took a handkerchief out of his pocket and blew his nose loudly.

"I heard that General Howe himself led the British charge up Breed's Hill," James said. He gave a hollow cough.

"And if that is true, is that not foolhardy and reckless in a leader?" Oliver Wendell said, his voice critical. "After all, he commanded an advance right up the hill straight into cannon and musket fire. Those British have little respect for any save their own egotistical ways of doing things. Somehow General Howe survived, but numbers of his men did not. He had to call for reinforcements. Apparently, he did not think our militia capable of real fighting, and I am glad he found out otherwise. General Clinton and four hundred marines arrived and saved the day for him."

James nodded, appreciating the bravery of the militia. "Perhaps he will have more respect for our armed forces from now on, even if they are not all clad in uniform."

The portly Oliver stood to go. "He certainly should. What this will lead to no one knows, but it is certain the fight is on. I must be going. I will bring you more news if I receive it."

"Good-bye. Thank you for coming. Stay well," James said. He bid good-bye to his friend with a handshake and shut the door, thinking of Josiah Quincy—who had died coming back from a visit to Britain—trying to sway those in authority to sympathy for the colonies. *Now here is another lost leader,* he thought.

James paced across the floor and stared out the window at the smoke still rising from the ruins of Charlestown. Beyond a doubt, the information he himself had supplied must have helped the militia prepare for the attack on Breed's Hill and the firing on Charlestown. Zach's report that on June 16 the British would advance on the Charlestown peninsula had turned out to be fairly accurate, as it had come, in fact, on June 17.

Mary and the children had gone to the garden to weed the new plants in the morning sunshine. With the scarcity of food, the garden's yield was important. James could not settle down to join them, however. All he could think about was the situation in Boston. He wondered when he could leave to find out more news. When would it be safe? Also, he was especially worried about James Jr., concerned for his welfare.

A knock sounded on the door. James opened it to find his sister Elizabeth wrapped in her burgundy cloak, standing on the step.

"Hello, James," she said, her blue eyes shining.

"Come in, come in, my dear. You are brave to be out and about at this time. If the soldiers had cared to stop you they could have." James held the door open as she entered, giving Elizabeth a hug. He was most surprised to have her come to his house. Elizabeth slipped off her velvet cloak.

"Our forces have survived despite the best of the British," Elizabeth said. Elizabeth's actions were very independent, self-assured, and brave to the point of foolhardiness, James thought. Under that lace bonnet and those fetching curls was a strong and indomitable spirit. If she had been a man, he would have thought her reckless.

"Are Mary and the children well?" she asked in concern, pulling off her gloves.

"Quite well, as a matter of fact. They are in the garden presently, and I am sure will be delighted to see you. But what brings you here today?" James motioned to a chair. "Won't you have a seat?"

Elizabeth settled herself in the chair, sliding her cloak over her lap. She removed her black bonnet and smiled at him.

"I just thought I'd see how you and your family were faring," she said.

"We are all fine," James said. "It is James Jr. that I am concerned for. He is in Cambridge, or was, I believe, until this recent conflict began. He went there a couple of months ago to meet up with the militia. Possibly he attempted to join the fight on Breed's Hill, but unless he was there at the beginning, any reinforcements trying to aid the militia were stopped by British fire from ships."

"I hope he was not in that engagement," Elizabeth said. Her blue eyes lost their look of merriment and her face appeared serious and concerned.

"Without doubt, we hope he is safe," James continued. "However, he is seventeen and well able to take care of himself. We could see the waves of soldiers streaming up Breed's Hill from the roof of our house, and the firing of the cannon. It was especially horrible to see the British warships, the

Lively and the *Falcon,* blasting their guns into Charlestown, their hotshot putting the town to the torch while preventing escape and aid."

"I admire James Jr. for his service," Elizabeth said, nodding. "I surely hope he will be safe."

"He left Boston when the British allowed those loyal to the patriot cause to depart, saying he was needed by his uncle Rufus Bent in Milton. However, he really intended to go join the militia in the hills near Boston. The British let him go, but he could take no weapon with him since they would have confiscated it."

"That was when orders from General Gage allowed some sympathetic to the patriot cause to leave," Elizabeth said. She settled more comfortably in the chair, took a deep breath.

"And some loyal to the British to come in," James added, remembering his father's friends who had come to stay with his parents. "You can be sure," he added, "that James Jr. found a weapon, if he made it to the militia lines."

"But how does it happen that you were strolling arm in arm with a British colonel not long ago?" James ventured, looking guardedly at his sister.

"Oh, Colonel Cleveland?" She laughed. "I was introduced to him by one of Father's friends, and indeed he can be charming. There is something about a man in uniform." Her voice trailed off. She gave James an impish smile.

"And there are so few young, unattached men in Boston these days," James said pointedly. Elizabeth laughed and said nothing.

"Still, how could you find pleasure in the company of one who is part of the British army?" James glared at her. Elizabeth was hard to chastise, but he had to point out how the situation looked to him.

Elizabeth was not to back down. "You might realize, my dear brother, that our younger brother Benjamin received employment from the British. In fact, he was made officer in charge of ordering shot and cannon for the British guns," she answered.

"Benjamin? What on earth does he know about ordnance? He'd be better off preparing for the ministry. All he likes to do is read scripture or talk about biblical stories."

"Nonetheless, I persuaded Colonel Cleveland to employ Benjamin. Or, rather, I suggested it, and he took me up on it. I would hate to think my company had any influence on his hiring considerations." Elizabeth looked pertly at James, who scratched his head. *Why would she want Benjamin to be Officer in Charge of Ordinance?*

"You might also hear, my dear James, a story going the rounds before long. Apparently insufficient cannon balls of the correct size were ordered for the conflict. Twenty-four-pound shot arrived rather than the twelve-pound required. In fact, the story suggests that cannon balls were scarce during the battle, so the British were somewhat hampered because all they had was grape." She laughed.

"Grape? You mean small shot was all they had to use with the cannon? That would be indeed a waste of large artillery. You're not suggesting Benjamin has anything to do with that supply?" James stared at her, then smiled.

"Oh, I am not suggesting or explaining anything. Yet Benjamin was the one responsible for the ordering, and Benjamin has been told not to return to his position by an irate Colonel Cleveland. So, I will remain at Father's, finding pursuits to occupy me there, rather than go forth elsewhere and perhaps further upset the colonel." Elizabeth's smile was smug, coquettish.

"Indeed, you should stay far away from public areas or anywhere Colonel Cleveland might see you," James said in concern. "Do not go again anywhere near the British quarters. Who knows what might happen if any thought you were involved with the specific ammunition orders for the battle?"

Elizabeth laughed and blushed slightly. "Oh, clearly not. I would never venture to be so bold. And now," she added, "may I visit Mary and the children?"

"Of course. Allow me to take you to the garden."

A surprise, she is, James thought. Yet even though she had influenced Colonel Cleveland to hire Benjamin as Officer of Ordnance, and even though Benjamin seemed to have done a poor job of fulfilling his duty, she did not mind Colonel Cleveland's company, he sensed. *Women are strange,* he thought, opening the door to the garden.

Chapter 35

Brother Benjamin

JUNE 26, 1775

Mary put away the stockings she was knitting, took a lamp, and, exhausted, quietly went to bed early in the evening. James gazed through half-shut eyes at a candle flickering on the mantel, the shadows dancing on the ruddy fireplace bricks.

What was his brother Benjamin really thinking? His freckled face and bland blue eyes held a world of secrets. He had been dismissed from his post with Colonel Cleveland as Officer of Ordnance, but then enlisted with the Royal Artillery. In his few conversations with James, he scoffed at the patriots, saying the militia ringing the city would be forced to yield to the British sooner or later. Twitching his new red moustache with pleasure, Benjamin strutted about the town in his fresh uniform. James had seen him playing dominos in the square with the regulars, laughing and joking.

James remembered when Benjamin was eight years old. He had been sent by their mother to gather eggs for old Mrs. Winslow, whose rheumatism kept her home. James wondered whether Benjamin would stick with the task, since racing his new dog had become his sole interest in life. The whippet he had convinced their father to let him keep—a slender, spotted canine—won most of the races that Benjamin set up for him. Gathering Mrs. Winslow's eggs was no easy task, since her hens laid them all over her wreck of a barn, lacking proper setting boxes. James thought Benjamin would take his whippet along on the errand and the dog would further slow the work by finding his share of the eggs.

But Benjamin had produced an overflowing basket of eggs, delighting Mrs. Winslow with his efforts. Then he read aloud to her from the Bible for an hour, for which she thanked him heartily. She had sent him home with a basket full of muffins and gooseberry preserves. A good student, Benjamin rarely was in trouble at school, excelling in his studies. Still, from his experience, James had always thought of him as undependable.

Whatever Benjamin was really thinking, his loyalties clearly lay with the plans of the British. James watched the candlelight flicker, casting long shadows in the dark room. *Benjamin probably just thinks his bread is buttered more if his loyalties reside on that side. More fool he*, he thought.

In the morning, Mary scraped the flour barrel and sliced the last of the salt pork for dinner. "Go to market and see what you can get, James," she said, her voice pleading. "The carrots and beets in the garden are still new. Lettuce is in, but potatoes and onions will be a while yet. I can go borrow from Mrs. Winslow. She told me at church she still has potatoes left. But we are nearly out of everything."

James walked cautiously through the occupied town. Broken windows winked from buildings, casualties of sniping attacks, some covered with hastily tacked-on boards. Many residents had left Boston earlier, when General Gage permitted departure, and their homes stood empty, locked and still. British troops, frustrated and angry, vandalized and broke into houses, pillaging freely. Many of the residents feared departing from the town and losing their valuables. Staying was equally hard, however, with food shortages making survival a daily struggle. Recognizing the community's dire state, General Gage had just reissued permission for townspeople to depart from Boston. So hundreds sewed their silver into quilts or jackets for protection and prepared to abandon their homes.

His older boys, Jemmy and Johnny, just a year apart and so much alike he often thought of them together, also left, invited to Cambridge by his friend and classmate Joseph Trumbull. Joseph had written him in April, offering rooms for James's family, and he had responded saying he might send a couple of his boys to help hoe corn. Again, Trumbull had contacted him, writing that he could use help with the haying and extra hands to bring in the garden. So Jemmy and Johnny, twelve and thirteen years old, packed their leather satchels and walked the miles to Cambridge, passing the British checkpoint as they did so. James worried for the two, but he was grateful for his friend's assistance as their absence meant two fewer mouths to feed at home.

Nearly fourteen thousand British troops were quartered throughout the city, in barracks, churches, warehouses—while just six thousand citizens remained. The troops fought amongst themselves, settling grudges with violence. Dirty, disorderly, and often ravaged by smallpox, they were so ill-disciplined that their officers publicly flogged the worst of them in vain efforts to impose order. Caring little for Boston or its traditions, the troops chopped down the Liberty Tree and carried that venerable old elm off for firewood, despising the freedom it stood for. They hacked off limbs from the beautiful shade trees lining Boston's streets to make fascines, bundles of wood to improve fortifications.

Dried blood stained the middle of the street where carts had rumbled following the battle on Breed's and Bunker's Hills, bearing British wounded just ten days ago. The regulars who walked the streets were grim, angry, spiteful. Across the harbor the smoke had cleared from the ruins of Charlestown, revealing bare, desolate ruins of buildings, black and charred.

Walking past a tavern hosting a few British regulars, James heard a snatch of song. He stopped to listen.

> *Our conductor, he got broke*
> *For his conduct, sure, sir;*
> *The shot he sent for twelve-pound guns,*
> *Were made for twenty-four, sir.*
> *There's some in Boston pleased to say,*
> *As we the field were taking,*
> *We went to kill their countrymen*
> *While they their hay were making.*
> *For such stout whigs I never saw, -*
> *To hang them all, I'd rather,*
> *For making hay with musket-balls*
> *And buck-shot mixed together.*

A burst of laughter rang out. *Benjamin's gaffe with the wrong size of cannonballs had garnered poetic acclaim,* James thought.

A rough voice said loudly, "And General Howe had it right. Colonel Cleveland was spending all his time with Schoolmaster Lovell's daughter. Making hay, he was." The fellow laughed rudely. More seriously, he added, "I don't begrudge a man his time with a lady, but not when it complicates our ordnance."

Elizabeth's friendship is remembered, but Colonel Cleveland seems to bear the brunt of the blame for the mistakes, though Benjamin has not made any friends for himself, James thought. Yet though his brother had been dismissed from his ordnance position, somehow he gained another duty, with the Royal Artillery.

The soldiers' voices died down, and James walked quickly past the tavern towards the market, glad that Elizabeth was safe at his father's.

He had little hope he would find much at market for sale, yet perhaps there might be a sack of last year's potatoes, at a high price, no doubt. Everywhere James saw signs of the recent conflict. Regulars strutted past him, their weapons held close. He passed a British soldier leaning on the arm of his companion, a rag wrapped about his eyes. Townspeople glanced furtively here and there as they walked quickly by. No one dared linger as loiterers would be stopped. Under martial law, all must be in by ten at night or be taken under arrest.

James remembered Johnny's comment that the battle had been a kind of Pyrrhic victory. "Don't you remember, Father?" Johnny had said. "King Pyrrhus had prevailed against the Romans but he lost men he could ill afford to lose. One more such victory would undo him, he said."

James answered Johnny, "You are so right. The British too won a kind of Pyrrhic victory, as they lost many men in taking Breed's and Bunker's Hill. Our militia proved how well they could fight." With pride, he reflected that likely James Jr. would have been at the battle, if he could have been there.

At market, the few stalls offered little food. James saw trays of fish for sale, terribly expensive, sacks of stale flour, mounds of old and suspiciously moldy potatoes. Salt fish was very expensive, as was salt pork. The British troops kept all the beef raised locally, captured any cows they could find, and still lacked food themselves. It had been months since James had been able to get milk for his children.

James decided to take his boys fishing at a quiet spot as soon as he could find an opportunity, far from the turmoil at the British posts, if he could find such a place. He bought a sack of dried beans, some salt pork, and a sack of flour, then grew anxious as he realized his purse was almost empty. *The situation must improve,* he thought, returning to his home. *It can't get much worse.*

Chapter 36

Arrested

June 29, 1775

"Another fish cake, please?" Little Thomas wiped his chin with the back of his hand.

"Mind your manners. You may share one with William." Mary cut the golden sphere in two, lifting the fluffy white fish onto Thomas's plate. What Mary couldn't do with salt cod couldn't be done, James thought. She had a complicated ritual of soaking, then pounding the dry, hard fish; mixing in flour and sometimes potato; and finally, frying the cakes in fat from salt pork. Fishcakes were one of the family's favorite foods. Mary had been delighted when James found a box of salt cod for sale at market.

She picked up a wooden cutting board bearing a loaf of bread, golden though irregular in shape. "Would anyone like a slice of bread? Mary helped knead it."

"Yes please," said Joseph, William, and Thomas at once. Six-year-old Mary beamed with pride as her mother sliced the loaf.

Everyone was nearly content, when a jarring knock on the door jolted James to attention. He opened the heavy oak door to the still June evening.

A stout, red-coated officer stood in the doorway, a thick sheaf of papers in his hand.

"James Lovell, schoolmaster?"

"Yes," James answered, his chest suddenly pounding.

"You're to come with us, sir." The heavy officer breathed an oniony blast in James's face.

"On what charge?" James answered in alarm.

"That's a matter for the courts to say. I am just here to get you. I am Sheriff Joshua Loring. Here, Major Cane, search his things and gather up all his papers before we take him and leave." The stout sheriff turned to his companion, a colorless individual thin as a stalk.

"Search? Where's your warrant?" James asked.

"You seem to forget," Sheriff Loring said with a humorless laugh, "that we need no warrant. Go on, Cane."

James's heart turned over in a beat. What had he done to be arrested? Major Cane pushed around the table and vanished in James's study, where he began rifling through his papers. "You'll find nothing there," James called. Joseph jumped up, waiting to see what he should do, while the other children sat at the table, open-mouthed. Little Charles started to cry, his tears loud and frantic. Mary reached to pick him up and held him close.

"Where are you taking him?" she asked, her voice raspy with fright.

"To jail, where the traitor belongs. You'll not see him free for a long time, if ever."

"You have no right to be here. I've done nothing wrong," James protested fiercely.

"Hold your tongue," Sheriff Loring said, putting his hand on the sword that hung, long and sharp, from his belt. "You wouldn't be wanted in Provost Prison for nothing."

"You have no reason to arrest me. What is your charge?" James backed up across the room. For a moment he thought of reaching for his musket, which he kept under the bed. No, it wouldn't do to provoke violence with his family there. He'd have to go along with the soldier and trust that any weak charges they might try to impose would not stand in court. Biting his tongue, he glared at the heavy officer. Sheriff Loring took a length of rope from his shoulder, pulled handcuffs from his pocket, and stepped to James's side.

"That's it. You come along nice and peaceable now. The charges will all be made clear in due time." He smiled a wicked, forced grin at James, who suddenly was reminded of a rat, obese from eating carrion. The sheriff grabbed James's hands and forced them into the handcuffs, then tied the rope to them in a tight knot.

"How can you do this? You can't take him. He hasn't done anything wrong. He's innocent!" Mary said, her voice trembling. She crossed the room and reached for his arm, grasping it tightly, as if nothing could part her from him. Her face twitched with anxiety as she fought to hold off tears.

Thomas began sobbing. William reached for Joseph's hand, while Mary ran to her mother's side and clutched her skirt. Joseph, at eleven— nearly big enough to imagine starting a fight—glared stonily at the sheriff, while he drew himself up to his full height beside William and Thomas. The children huddled together near the table, their faces pale with fright. James's heart sank, yet he could do nothing to save them from the fear that each felt.

"In case you don't remember, there is a state of warfare going on. British troops are challenged by ruffians who haven't the uniforms to cover their backs. Your husband here is just another traitor whose intentions undermine the authority of the British government and the king," said the pudgy sheriff with a merciless snort.

"You can't prove I have done anything wrong, because I haven't." James felt his forehead beading in drops of sweat. He looked anxiously at Mary.

"How are you coming with that search, Major Cane?" Sheriff Loring called. The sounds of drawers opening and papers fluttering came from the study.

Joseph looked at his father and silently mouthed "Should I...." James shook his head. The last thing he wanted was for any violence to occur around his children. If Joseph were thinking of grabbing the musket, he didn't want him to.

"Here we are," Major Cane said, appearing at the door of the study with a bulging canvas sack.

"I need to see what you've taken," James answered. "I am helping a friend, Oliver Wendell, store his furniture and personal effects while he has left for the country. Some of the paperwork you may have taken would be his accounts, for which I am responsible."

"Oh, that," said Major Cane icily. "I left that in the desk. Where else would you have papers stored?" he asked shrewdly.

"Be sure you search the whole room, Major. I'll just check around here." Sheriff Loring gave James a severe look as he rummaged about the kitchen, tossing the contents of Mary's recipe box on the floor, thrusting a few schoolbooks off of their shelf, and even pushing the family Bible off of its place of honor on the mantel to the brickwork of the fireplace, where it landed with a thump. Joseph sat down, clutching Thomas, who clung to him, sniffling. Mary peered from behind her mother, eyeing the sheriff's movements, while William, tears running down his cheeks, left his chair to stand by Joseph, his eyes never leaving Major Cane.

The gaunt major began rifling through the bookshelves in James's study, flinging books to the floor. He found a wooden box on a middle shelf and emptied the letters and documents from it into his sack, shaking the contents into the bulging canvas. Then he climbed the stairs. James heard him banging about, probably in his bedroom. A few minutes later he stomped down the stairs and came out into the kitchen.

"All right, that's enough," said Sheriff Loring. "We're taking you and these papers to Provost Prison, where you'll await hearing." He tugged at James's knotted hands. In spite of himself James nearly swung at him. It would be so easy to bash the tubby Sheriff on the head and then kick him to his knees. But Major Cane was armed, and James knew he'd end up getting his family harmed.

"The law is on my side," James said to Mary. "I have no recourse but to submit for now and wait until my innocence is proven. My dear, I should be home in just a few days." He managed to hold back the tremor he felt in his voice. Mary, pale and distressed, choked back her sobs and unwillingly released her grip on his arm. "Tell my father what has happened. Children, mind your mother." They nodded silently, their eyes big with fear.

"Come on, come on. We haven't all day. Let's get going, you slow son of a jackass." Sheriff Loring mumbled something and laughed unpleasantly. He ushered James out, jerking him with his rope. Major Cane followed with his sack, giving the family a nasty leer as he left. The door slammed shut behind them.

In Boston Jail

JUNE 29, 1775

Sheriff Loring and Major Cane forced James the block and a half to the Stone Jail, just behind the Court House on Queen Street. Cruel tugs on the rope fastened to his handcuffs kept him lurching from one step to the next. Passersby looked at him curiously and then turned quickly away. A few redcoats glared at him with gleeful malice. The high, barred windows on the Stone Jail stared out like narrow eyes, clotted with spiderwebs. James remembered reprimanding boys from school for using slingshots to fling dead mice and birds at the small windows. For a moment, he remembered doing the same thing himself when he was young.

The squat, heavy building was formed of thick cuts of granite, its door double slabs of oak studded with nails, a narrow set of bars positioned in a top opening. A rough yard covered with sparse grass ran the length of the front, guarded by a high stone wall topped with iron bars that curled inwards in sharp spikes to prevent any escape.

James followed Sheriff Loring through the iron gate into the yard. The stench of filth and decay rose from refuse in its corners. The heavy door to the jail swung open.

"Another rat for the cage?" asked a British sentry cheerfully, prodding James with the butt of his rifle. Major Cane and Sheriff Loring ignored the joke and shoved James into the dark, dank hall.

"Over here. Get in here, at once." Major Cane pushed him into a small, windowless room, lit only by the light from the open door. Two pale, startled faces looked up at him from the fusty walls. James thought he recognized one: the son of Benjamin Edes, the printer. Young Peter, it might have been.

"On what charge are you putting me in here? What have I done?" James protested as the gaunt officer unlocked his handcuffs.

"They'll have a charge for you. Never fear. Traitor to your country, that's what you are, and you deserve to hang. And you *will* hang. Now get in there and keep your mouth shut." The officer slammed the thick door with a bang.

A small window set with iron bars in the top of the door gave little light. James sank to his knees. The stomach trouble that had bothered him for months now erupted in painful spasms, and he doubled over in the corner of the cell, overcome by retching and miserable pain. Emptying his stomach helped, briefly, though he was embarrassed for others to see his illness, and he straightened up.

"Are you all right?" a voice asked sympathetically. James turned to see a well-built, tall youth, strong features dark with grime and dust.

"Yes. It will pass. I am sorry about my sickness. And you are…."

"I am Peter Edes. Do not worry about the illness. It is nothing we haven't seen here before." Peter grinned cheerfully. "We have a slop bucket you can use. Here, this will be your pallet." He motioned James towards a piece of canvas thrown over a layer of hay.

Peter continued his explanation. "My father is Benjamin Edes, the printer. I have been in jail for ten days now, not charged with any offense since there is none they can charge me with. A public display of excitement would be the only issue, since I was observed shooting a rifle in my joy that the British onslaught on Bunker Hill had cost them so dearly. The hangdog looks on their faces and the carts of dead and wounded that passed our door warranted at least some merry display, though they claimed to be the victors. But I have done nothing wrong."

James shook his hand. "I am James Lovell, schoolmaster. I have not been informed of the charge I have for my imprisonment, though my firm support of the principles of liberty that have been part of our cause from the beginning no doubt has something to do with it. And you, sir?" He turned to the other face.

"I am John Leach, master of a school for navigation in Boston. I've sailed around the world three times, but I have no knowledge of why I am imprisoned. Some British soldiers observed me drinking to the health of the American army before the breaching of Bunker Hill, but how that warrants my imprisonment I do not know. I was taken to jail just minutes before your arrival." John Leach appeared a calm, thoughtful individual, his brown hair neatly held in a black ribbon and his clean ruffled shirt revealing order and care.

"How long will it be before we are charged?" James asked, controlled fury in his voice.

"I hope soon, though I have been here ten days with no formal hearing." Peter Edes spoke quietly, yet his voice held little hope.

James put his head down in his hands. *How could he provide for his family? Mary would be having their eighth child that winter. Surely he could prove his innocence. He had in fact done nothing wrong, nothing according to written law. Having opinions was not illegal. And supporting those opinions could not be wrong, Though as to that,* he thought, *anyone who did not agree with British law and rule and the power of King George could be thought to be in the wrong. He was most definitely guilty on that account.* He shut his eyes in the dark cell and waited, miserable and sick, for the pain in his stomach and his head to subside.

Chapter 38

Provost Prison, Boston

July 2, 1775

Heat waves churned the steaming air in Boston prison. Dancing light from the hallway thrown by a brilliant sun fell through the bars of the cell door, confusing James and making him dizzy. The first days he had spent in the prison he had been unable to keep down the coarse food tossed in his cell by the jailer, who jeered and made unmentionable gestures, chucking the old bread upon the ground. His weak stomach returned in full force, and for a time all he could do was gasp on the cold stone and wait for the nausea to pass.

At length he was able to sit up. Across from him sat Peter Edes, his elfish grin inspiring. The eighteen- year-old apprentice to his father leaned calmly against the stone wall, examining a colony of ants moving dirt into a heap. John Leach snored on his pallet. Even at rest, the fifty-year old Leach seemed in command, long years at sea before opening his navigation school having given him the ability to relax in any situation.

"The food here is disagreeable, is it not?" Peter smiled, showing bright white teeth.

"Most certainly is," James agreed. He reached over for the bucket of brackish water and found its wooden dipper. The lukewarm water was stale with bugs and scum floating on its surface, but he managed to gulp down a dipperful. He settled back against the granite wall, feeling the comfort of its chilly surface on his burning skin.

"I should like to tell the warden of this jail a thing or two about civil treatment and hospitality," Peter said with energy. "I've enjoyed the comfort of these walls for ten days longer than you, already, and I think I'd like to check in to a different inn." He laughed at his little joke.

"I'm sure the warden should oblige. Meanwhile, he could tell those biddies next door to pipe down." James smiled faintly.

The screams and sharp words from a pair of women in a neighboring cell had been echoing in the prisoners' ears since daybreak. Their offensive language rivaled the epithets used by the guards. Curses flew from their mouths like ammunition as they screamed blasphemies against each other, their surroundings, the guards, their families, and their friends. *Women in a jail*, thought James. *What sort of women would end up in jail? Not the nicest sort*, he reflected.

On top of that, the stomach distress that had plagued James for months continued, wrenching him in torture. The din that echoed from the room next door did not help matters. *The shrews probably deserve each other's company*, he reflected, moving some of the straw to create a more comfortable seat.

John Leach yawned and sat up. "I should like to go outside to the yard. It is hot, to be sure, but it would be nice to see a bit of daylight before it is dark."

"Is your wife coming?" James asked.

"No, I think, but I have hope she will before long. Poor thing, she has a mile or more to come each time and the weather is so hot. If she is not let in, it will be very distressing to her."

Mary had come to the jail that morning, bringing James a basket of food, cold ham and rolls. The guards laughed, took most of the food, then threw a couple of rolls and a portion of the ham butt into his cell. James had seen her frightened, pale face as she stood in the door of the yard. Her worried eyes had searched the jail's windows in vain for a glimpse of him. "No visitors for your husband," the guard said, waving her away as he took her basket. "He's a sorry one, a traitor to the Crown, and sure to hang." He laughed, snide and spiteful.

Mary turned, her head downcast in dejection. James called through the small barred window at their door, "Thank you, my dear." He did not know if she heard him, but he was very grateful for her visit. Her gesture touched him, for he knew well that food at home was scant. He divided the food amongst himself and his cellmates, managing to eat part of a roll and a bit of ham before his stomach overwhelmed him again with distress. Peter and John shared the remaining food, glancing at him with worried looks.

From the cell next door came the continual commotion of loud, coarse women quarreling. In the hot late-afternoon their argument reached a crescendo, curses mixed with thumps and shrieks. "Damn you, Lila," one screeched. "You got me here, you wretch. Now you'll pay."

"Not I, you baggage," came the answer. A loud whack ensued, followed by a string of curses.

For certain, James thought, one could not choose one's jail mates. His stomach rumbled again. *Who would have thought that he, a respected teacher and town leader, would be thrown into the Provost's Prison? Of what was he accused? When would he know?* Persistent thoughts swirled through his mind.

"At least if your wife isn't allowed inside, she'll be spared the noise we endure," John said with a crooked smile, sitting down not far from James on the hard stone.

"I'm with ye. Those crones are worse than sailors," Peter said cheerfully. He stretched out his long legs on the stone floor and raised his thin arms high.

"So, damn it, as the neighbors say!" Peter grinned briefly at James, who smiled in return. Nausea gripped his stomach again. *Would it ever settle down?*

He relaxed against the hard stones, felt their coolness even as warm, stagnant air blew in from the narrow opening in the door. Flies buzzed and hummed in the room, jumping from the buckets of refuse to his arm. One continually landed on his cheek; James brushed it off repeatedly.

"It's hot enough to cook an egg, out there," James remarked. "That's what my mother might say on a blistering day." The thought of food made him ill, and putting aside his attempt at humor for another day, he leaned back against the cool stone and shut his eyes in weariness.

toll. *Master Lovel taken up and put in jail, which is in consequence of some letters found in doctor Warren's pocket; master Leech also. Released out of prison 4. Mr. Hunt saying, that he wished the Americans might kill them all, was confined in jail. Eleven dead of the wounded prisoners at Charlestown. Col. Parker dead, having declared, at his last hour, if he got well he would do the same. The officers say,* Damn the rebels, that they would not flinch.

Extract of a letter from Cambridge, July 12. *Virginia Gazette, August 11, 1775. The Omohundro Institute of Early American History & Culture.* Massachusetts Historical Society

Chapter 39

Provost Prison:
A Long First Month

JULY 19, 1776

The days dragged on, settling into a kind of routine. One day the unshaven, filthy jail keeper opened the door and announced, "William Starr. Make room for him." A tall, gaunt individual collapsed, groaning on the hard floor. William Starr found a place against the cell walls and leaned back against the stone until his eyes became accustomed to the dim light. He proved quiet and complained little, though it was evident the bandaged wounds on his arms caused him suffering.

Another day a rotund figure tumbled into their cell, a hefty shove from the pockmarked jailer nearly knocking him off balance as he entered the narrow chamber. "Get in there, Mr. Hunt, and never leave," the jailer shouted, banging the door shut behind him.

"Why are you here?" Peter asked the newcomer, making room for him on the pallet on which he sat.

"I am John Hunt. I just said I wished the Americans would kill all the British," the chubby fellow said, sinking to his knees. He looked about him at the crowded, small room with despair.

Really, thought James, *what an absurd pretext for putting someone in jail. Half the population of Boston could have said the same thing, only they didn't have the poor luck to say it in the hearing of someone who would report the words.*

Mary came several times each week, bringing food. Sometimes it was just a loaf of bread, other times she managed a portion of sausage or a baked fish. The jailers kept most of it, passing on crusts of bread and some of the meat to James. Usually they allowed her to speak with James through the barred cell door. Her face pale and frightened, she told him about the children, the constant struggle to find food, the ceaseless patrols of the British soldiers. James feared for her safety as she arrived, but he was always glad to see her. For a few minutes he could forget his own distress as he imagined the children with Mary, safe at home.

One day, the jailer tossed in a small basket of food, slamming the door shut as he left. Mary's face, white and fearful, appeared on the other side of the iron bars of the heavy door. "A British officer came to our door last week and told me I had a week to leave the house as it was required for lodging for officers." Mary choked back tears but managed a weak smile. James shuddered at the thought.

"My dear, what will you do?" he asked, greatly concerned.

"I have accepted the offer of Dr. Joseph Gardner on Marlborough Street for rooms for the children and me," she said, smoothing back her red curls under her bonnet. "We move tomorrow."

"Dr. Gardner is most kind to offer you room," James said, somewhat relieved at the sympathetic gesture. "I remember when I saw him last. He counseled me not to leave the house as my stomach distress was causing me great affliction."

"I will be able to serve as housekeeper and cook for him, so he thinks the arrangement will suit him well. He is unmarried and has room for us. I can bake and wash, and so earn our keep there. But think ... we must leave most of our furniture and belongings behind." Mary caught her breath and then composed herself, fighting back the worry that threatened to consume her.

"Bring to me the packet of papers that Oliver Wendell left in his desk," James said. He thought quickly. "It should be in the cellar with his belongings. It lists his personal property that I promised to care for. The jailers should allow you to give me those papers." The heavy thump of a guard's steps sounded in the hall outside his cell. Mary turned to go, her face twisted in worry.

"Good-bye, my dear," he said, his voice breaking. "Come again when you can." His fingers brushed hers through the bars. He sank to his knees as the guard gripped her arm to hurry her down the hall, her muffled protests sounding as she left. What else could he do? He could only hope Mary understood how much he appreciated her visits and her help. He could say or do little else.

James put his head down and cradled his forehead in his hands, pain rolling through his system. He looked up to see John Leach staring at him with concern.

"James, Mary left these rolls and roast beef for you," John Leach said, pointing to the basket.

"Not now, thank you," James said, his face white. "You eat them."

John glanced at Peter Edes, John Hunt, and William Starr. They looked sympathetically at James, who lay down on his pallet and shut his eyes.

Early on the 18th of July, a Tuesday, Sarah Leach sent a messenger to John with the sad news that his son Tileston, just seven years old, had died of a fever. The news was a great blow to the navigator. When he was thrown in jail, Tileston had been healthy. John wrote General Howe a letter asking permission to go to the funeral, but the Provost William Cunningham told him he was denied. "What, and next you'll be wanting to go to tea with the king?" the sneering provost said.

When he learned of Tileston's passing, John slumped down on his pallet and shut his eyes. His cellmates spoke in whispers, respectful of his sorrow. Before long the guards swung wide open the door to the cell, letting blazing sunlight into the dark recess. The prisoners blinked. They had been confined to their narrow, dim room for days with no yard privileges. The previous night the provost told them to prepare for trial, apparently no bluff because now a group of jail keepers strutted into the hall, chains clanking in their hands, to lead them to the courthouse.

In the sudden sunlight, Provost Cunningham shouted, "Get up on your feet, all of ye. You blackguards, get in line here. Come on, hand over your wrists. We're chaining you up. You're sure to go to the gallows now. Get in line."

James, John Leach, John Hunt, Peter Edes, and William Starr stood, trying to conceal their alarm. Stumbling and rubbing their eyes, they followed Provost Cunningham into the yard, lining up behind a tall fellow who introduced himself as Mr. William Dorrington. With him were his daughter, young son, and a nurse.

"How long have you been in here?" Peter asked William Dorrington quietly.

"Four days. I'm the manager of the smallpox hospital in Boston. They've got me on some trumped-up charge. I really don't know what." William Dorrington's voice was sour. Peter shook his head sympathetically.

"Be quiet, there! No talking." Provost Cunningham and the group of guards walked up and down the line, handcuffing all and linking them together with a long heavy chain. They set off in a snaking, clanking line towards the courthouse on Queen Street, just on the other side of the jail.

Throughout the long afternoon, James and his jail mates waited in the back of the courtroom, handcuffed, while prisoners were taken to the bench. Officers shouted questions at one inmate after another. One or two from James's own group were led to the front to answer questions, then returned. No one questioned him, however.

William Dorrington, his daughter, and the nurse, all called to the stand, stood meekly, looking at the shriveled old prosecutor. William Dorrington's daughter twisted her shawl nervously, coughing. "You are accused of blowing up flies with gunpowder. We know these explosions were in reality signals to the American army during the battle at Bunker Hill."

William Dorrington sighed. "Why would I want to use gunpowder to blow up flies? That would be a tragic waste of good ammunition. And what purpose would I have to send signals to the army? You have no proof that I was doing anything illegal, or that I was sending signals at all."

"Nonetheless," the wizened prosecutor said, "that is the charge. You will give up your personal belongings, including bed and bedding, until such time as we can settle this matter. Next."

William Dorrington, red in the face and perspiring, huffed back to his seat and sat down.

The flies buzzed and the judges dozed and the jailers laughed and ate crackers. James remembered the times he had been in the courthouse. A place of law and order it had been, a place where the British Constitution had been upheld. But now the army had made it into a mockery, a place where ruffians were in charge. He could imagine no honest treatment for the prisoners there, though he had to persist in hope.

The following day, Wednesday, July 19th, again James and his cell-mates were handcuffed and linked to their chain, right behind William Dorrington and his family. Three sailors, tattooed and filthy, joined their manacled group, along with several thieves and housebreakers, surly fellows who had been helping themselves to valuables from Loyalist homes in absence of the usual order in Boston.

After a long morning, during which James and his jail mates waited anxiously for their questioning, Major Moncreif, a British officer, came forward to the stand.

"Your Honor," he said to the bewigged judge, who set aside the dish of nuts he had been cracking, wiped his mouth, and looked in the Major's direction, "I must call Captain Symmes of the Regulars to the stand. He has information about the prisoners, James Lovell and John Leach."

James and John sat up in alarm and looked at the tall, disheveled figure. The regular's red uniform was caked with mud and his hair hung long and ragged on his shoulders. James had never seen Captain Symmes before. He looked at John Leach, who shrugged his shoulders.

"Captain Symmes, come to the stand."

The captain slouched his way forward and stood leaning on the stand, looking in a bored manner at the judge.

"What do you know about the prisoners, James Lovell and John Leach?"

"I know that Lovell is a spy; we have it from good authority that he was passing intelligence to the rebels."

"And Leach?"

"He, too, is a spy, taking plans and turning them over to the rebels." Here Captain Symmes turned to John Leach and pointed.

"Is that the man James Lovell?"

"It is."

James stood up. His voice cracking with anguish, he said, "Your honor, obviously Captain Symmes does not know what he is talking about. I am James Lovell. And without proof of his words, which does not exist, an honest court would not even consider this case."

"Be quiet!" thundered the judge, now fully awake.

"Can you get proof, Captain Symmes?" the judge asked.

"Yes, of course, I will get proof. I'll bring it before long." Captain Symmes meekly turned in some embarrassment and went back to his seat.

"Very well, then. Next case."

The afternoon grew hotter and hotter. No one else questioned James, John, or any of their group. William Dorrington was called to the stand again.

"You, sir, are charged with blowing up flies as cover for signals for the army. How do you plead?"

"I wouldn't do such a foolish thing, begging your Honor's pardon." William Dorrington puffed up with indignation.

"Even so, you are charged a fee of three dollars for the inconvenience you have caused us. You may have your personal belongings back when such fee is rendered. Case dismissed."

William Dorrington came back to his son and daughter, shaking his head. "Do they think I am made out of money? I have almost no cash. It will take me days to find or borrow some." The jailer grabbed his handcuffs unsympathetically and chained him again to the group.

About two o'clock in the afternoon, Provost Cunningham stood up and yanked on the long chain. The prisoners rose to their feet. "Come along now, it's back to the jail for you," he announced. Four other jail keepers, armed with cudgels and daggers, surrounded the prisoners as they paced the few steps back to the Stone Jail.

"In you go. A nice piece of work, today," remarked Provost Cunningham sarcastically. He slammed the cell door shut, leaving the prisoners in darkness again.

James sat down on his thin pallet, aching with discouragement. He glanced over at John, who leaned his head back against the thick stone wall, his eyes shut. So far they hadn't charged John or Peter Edes or James himself with anything specific. *How could it be right to hold people without a definite charge? The letter he had written Joseph Warren stating what Zach told him about the British troop strength and movements was surely information anyone in Boston could have seen and noted. If that is the evidence they have of my efforts on the patriot side, it is not enough to keep me in prison,* he thought.

"Could we appeal to someone? Sheriff Loring?" he asked.

John opened his eyes and smiled wryly. "Don't you know? Sheriff Joshua Loring has his position due to the beauty of his wife. At least, General Howe finds her beautiful. The arrangement works well for the sheriff. Loring gets a job, she gets special treatment. He wouldn't change it on scruples of guilt or innocence for some prisoner, no matter what the truth might be. General Howe wants you in jail: you are in jail." John Leach laughed hollowly.

"I see," James said. "Then I'd best write letters. Someone, perhaps General Howe, will listen."

He leaned back against the hard stones, felt their coolness even as the flies buzzed in the warm, stagnant air that flowed from the hall, thick with the foul smells of refuse and waste.

As the days crept by in jail, James felt more useless than ever. If he were free, even then he was not sure he could be of much help to the forces standing up against the British army. His health would not permit him to serve in combat, and he was no good with a weapon. Yet he did have strengths. What he could do was write and speak in support of the effort to obtain freedom. If he could get out of prison, he could find some way to use those talents. James turned over on his thin pallet, seeking relief from the questions that plagued him and the constant pain in his stomach. *I must not despair,* he thought, *and I must find a way to help our brave patriots prevail.*

Chapter 40

Provost Prison:
The Second Month

AUGUST 23, 1775

Day after day followed, unbearably hot, yet still the prisoners were kept confined in the foul jail. July passed and the days melted into August, even more miserably hot. In the stone rooms, scarcely a breath of air stirred. Buckets for waste overflowed before the jailers carried them out, sloshing and spilling half the contents onto the floor. There was no washing water. James was often sick, and so worn with weakness that his cellmates had to coax him to drink the warm drinking water, rancid though it was.

He asked for and got writing paper, pen, and ink. After much consideration, however, he decided not to write to Sheriff Loring. Corrupt and treacherous, the sheriff not only owed his position to his wife's illicit relationship with General Howe, but also abused the power of his position horribly, dictating unnecessary ill treatment of the prisoners.

Instead, he wrote to Major Cane, the officer who had arrested him, protesting his innocence and pointing out the lack of evidence and testimony against him. One day, a Major Small was admitted to James's cell; the pompous red-coated officer handed him a letter from Major Cane. The major had responded that he had no part in the government's decision to imprison James, and had no control over the matter. James thanked Major Small, obtained more paper from the provost, who sneered as he handed it over, saying "Little good this will do you," and wrote another letter to

Major Cane, denying any possible charges against him. This time, Major Cane did not answer.

James wrote to General Gage as well, reasoning that the general might bring about a change in his situation. General Gage did not reply. For a time, James's lack of success, coupled with his illness, made his days miserable and deepened his discouragement.

On his good days, James thought about his agreement to help friends with their property. His neighbor Oliver Wendell had left Boston to visit his family in Newburyport in January. Oliver Wendell, lame and often ill, had asked James to care for his furniture and other possessions. James had, in addition, agreed to watch the property of Nathaniel Appleton and Henry Prentiss, business friends of Oliver Wendell. But for a time the jailers denied him paper, so all he could do was wait and worry.

For a short while before his arrest, James had thought that he might move his family out of Boston for safety. He made a thorough inventory of Oliver Wendell's belongings, listing furnishings and even china, and wrote Oliver to explain that should he end up leasing his home, he would ensure their safety.

Then he had added a short note, addressed to his friend. The words came back to him often, during the long, tedious days in jail, sometimes in a fever:

> *And now, Dear Sir, as to the most important Point. Be confident in the Deity, throw off an anxiety which is evidently undermining your Health. This country, nay, this very town, will soon rise to glory and peace from its present condition; therefore, take the best care of your health, that you may yet again as heretofore be a great public ornament and private blessing.*
>
> *God Almighty defend and cherish all you and yours; to whom pray me and my wishes.*

Those words might just as well have been written to me, instead of by me, he thought. *I must have hope. The country, the town, will recover. I will be released, and yes, I will be able to help the cause.*

That day James fell asleep hoping for a change. He woke feeling refreshed. For once, the incessant swearing and screaming that went on in the nearby cells had ceased. Maybe the inmates had been let into the yard for a breath of air. A crack of sunlight from the evening's rays fell into his corner, lighting up the dark space. He remembered his garden at home, little Mary bringing him a new carrot, his wife pulling fresh bread from the oven. He would be back with them, he knew.

In late July the jailers escorted the cellmates to the courthouse on three separate days and held them there for hours each time. During the long afternoons they sat in silence in the rear of the courtroom, no questions being asked of them. The jail keepers cursed and kicked them going and coming, yanked on their chains, forced the handcuffs to bite into their wrists, and compelled them to sit for hours without rest or drink. Still, no charge had been made against any of them.

In August the prisoners had been allowed to use the yard once. Even that dirty, ill-kempt enclosure had seemed pleasant, for the cellmates could walk about, stretch their limbs, and inhale clean air. Peter Edes had turned somersaults on the grass until he rolled on a dog's droppings.

But that was only once. Since then they had been confined to their cell, the doors locked. The jailers would not even open the doors to give them food, but passed bread and tankards of water through the bars. They didn't much care when the drink or food spilled clumsily on the floor.

John Leach was much saddened when his wife Sarah came. She was allowed to enter the room for a few minutes—an arbitrary decision on the part of the jailers, it seemed to the prisoners, for there was no explanation as to why she had been permitted inside the cell. It was clear she was terrified to be there, for she said little and would not sit down beside John on his thin pallet. The provost interrupted their visit, swore at John, said he was a damned rebel, and told her not to come back. She left with tears in her eyes.

Two days later Sarah returned, bearing a note she had obtained from General Gage.

*Mrs. Leach has the General's permission to visit her hus-
band, provided she carries in no letters nor brings any*

out, and the Provost is always to hear the conversation.
R. Donkin, Aid de camp. August 12, 1775.

Bravely, Sarah returned the next day. This time she seemed less afraid, embraced her husband, and sat with him for a few minutes while the other cellmates did their best to ignore the couple. She brought John Leach a note about his neighbor rolled up in an extra pair of stockings. The note was discovered, however, so after that, clothing brought to the prisoners and even food was searched constantly. Sarah continued to come for brief visits when she could, but the five in their cell were mistreated all the more in consequence of her bravery.

A week later in mid-August, the swearing and abuse about them reached a fever pitch. John Leach, who had served on many ships, commented that the language they all overheard was worse than on any man-of-war he had experienced. The filthy water in the pail was hot and brackish, yet the jailers left it until every drop was gone. James felt ill, his head dizzy from heat and hunger. John Leach reminded them that though they had been in a dreadful place, God had sustained them. They were not terribly sick; they would survive; they should put their trust in God. Peter, John Hunt, and William Starr nodded in agreement. James could do no more than shut his eyes. John Leach took a strip of cloth, wrung it out in water, and placed it on James's burning forehead. It felt cool and pleasant. Finally, somehow, he was able to fall asleep.

One day the guards ushered in a marksman with the militia, Cornelius Turner. Through the bars the cellmates could hear Colonel Robinson harassing the new prisoner. "Now, Cornelius Turner, you think we are not serious here? We're serious enough to hang you, and that this day. Your only chance is to tell us what you know about the Provincial Army."

"I know nothing worth reporting," the sullen response came. Cornelius Turner, whom they could not see, sounded as if he were suffering from a bad headache.

"Then you might as well have your last rites, as you won't live through the day." Here a muffled groan sounded and chains rattled. Apparently Cornelius was shackled to a wall in the outside corridor.

"We've got the reverend of the army here to listen to you recite your crimes, just before hangin'. Here he is."

Cornelius spoke up. His voice was harsh, strident. "I have nothing to say. You are wrong to have arrested me. I am not part of the militia." His desperate words carried clearly to James and his cellmates, who listened anxiously.

"Come, come, my man," an oily voice said.

That must be the reverend, James thought.

"Just tell the jailer what you know and you'll go free. Otherwise, you'll be wearing a tight collar and regretting your silence."

"I cannot," Cornelius protested, with a shriek. "I truly am ignorant of any information about the Provincials. Please tell them to let me go."

"That I cannot do, unless you confess. What were you doing with that gun? How many of you are there?"

The questioning went on for some time. At length the reverend said, his tone wheedling, "I'll be back this afternoon. Just think this through. You'll be doing yourself a favor to speak up."

The door clanged shut, and apparently Cornelius was left to himself, because the cellmates could hear him muttering. Finally he grew quiet.

"Probably fell asleep, poor fellow. What an awful way to treat someone. I don't suppose they will really hang him," John Hunt said.

"We can surely hope not," said James. He sighed and leaned back. The close-quartered cell was so hot, the air so foul and stagnant, he had trouble breathing. His stomach was in full rebellion, and all he could do was wait for the spasms to subside. He must have slept, because before long he heard the smooth voice of the reverend haranguing poor Cornelius again.

"You'll do best to just admit your crime. Then you may go free. Otherwise, I'll not be responsible for what might happen to you."

"Reverend, you know as well as I that I have nothing to confess. Just tell them that and we'll be square."

Good for him, James thought. *He's a brave man, and deserves to go free.*

They must have taken Cornelius to another part of the jail and locked him up, James thought the next day, because no word of a hanging occurred. *That makes sense,* he thought. *They threaten but they are just trying to milk him for any information they can get. I hope they let the brave fellow go soon.*

The next day another prisoner, a Mr. French, entered the jail. "Here you go—best inn in town. Get in there," the jailer with the torn jacket said loudly, kicking French in the back, who groaned and swore.

"You British are all alike. No feeling, no respect. Go back home to your king," French said bitterly.

"Your king, you say? King George is your king too, and don't you forget it. For that, you will be brought out to the yard tonight. You must kneel in the sand and say 'God Bless the King' until the stars go home. Better rest up in this black hole, because you'll be busy tonight."

"I have rights. Where is the provost?" demanded the new prisoner, but the cell door slammed shut, and Mr. French's cries were extinguished.

An old Dutchman who had been released from jail nearly a month previous was brought back. The cellmates recognized his wheezing accent. "Get in here. You didn't have enough of us before?" a jailer said rudely.

"I only said that the regulars are thieves and robbers, which they are. They helped themselves to my corn and onions until there was nothing left. How am I supposed to feed me and my family? That garden was all I had. How can there be law and order when you defend criminals and thieves?" To James, the Dutchman's quiet tones sounded more sad than angry.

"You are charged a dollar for disrupting the peace and causing more trouble than you're worth. Pay up, then," the provost said loudly.

"But I have nothing. Not a cent," the old fellow said.

"Then you'll be kicked out of here. Get through those fellows and you're free." The Dutchman must have been kicked by each of the guards, because he cried and begged all the way down the corridor. Laughing and joking accompanied each blow.

Another day, a visitor came to the jail. "Here is the three dollars for William Dorrington," the cellmates heard him stammer in the hall.

"Oh yes, the one guilty of blowing up flies." The provost belched and then rattled his key chain. "Here. Release Dorrington and his family. But I'm keeping his bed and bedding a few more days. They're in use, one might say, and it's not convenient to let them go just yet. He may come back for them next week."

"You must give him his bed, as it is all he has," answered someone from a nearby cell.

"I must do nothing. Be out of here or be hanged," the provost snarled. Mr. Dorrington and his family followed their visitor out without a word.

The next day Mary came, a small basket of food with her. The jailer let her through and admitted her to the cell, holding the door open while she stepped in, then slamming it shut. When she saw James's weakness, she gasped. "Oh, my dear, you are so ill."

"Don't worry for me," James responded. Grateful for what seemed to be a change in the prison's policy of admitting visitors, no matter how arbitrary it was, he sat up against the wall, pale and wan, and smiled weakly.

"Here, sit next to me on my pallet." He motioned to the thin, straw-stuffed pad that served as his mattress. "It is good to see you, though I wish I could offer you a better chair."

Mary sat down dispiritedly beside him. A tear spilled down her cheek and she wiped it away quickly. The other cellmates nodded, then looked the other way politely.

James held her hand, noticing its rough redness. He looked with concern at her thin, care-worn face. "The baby does well, my dear?"

She smiled faintly. "Yes, all is well and I will be fine." James lifted her hand to his lips and kissed it. He looked at her closely.

A wave of emotion washed over her. Lips trembling, she said, "Jemmy and Johnny are still in Cambridge, where Joseph Trumbull has found them a family with whom to reside. Many there have fields and gardens, and such families will need help to bring in hay and garden produce. I miss them, but it is well they are in a good place." Her blue eyes misted with emotion.

"In addition, I must tell you that your brother Benjamin has set sail for England. He plans on becoming a minister." She glanced quickly at James.

James chuckled. "That would be just like Benjamin," James said. "He gets out of a hot place and slides into something else."

Mary laughed weakly and nodded agreement. "Here," she said, handing over the wicker basket to James, who glanced at the loaf of bread, cooked potatoes, and round of cheese, shrugged his shoulders, then pointed to the floor. Mary set the basket down and said to John Leach, "You are welcome to help yourself."

"Thank you," said the navigator, who began pulling out the contents and handing the food to the cellmates. James shook his head and looked away from the brown loaf.

"James, I have a question," Mary continued. She glanced anxiously at her husband. "I don't know if I should buy meat at the market. The British have a rule that only those who have signed their roll sheet 'Friends of the Government' may buy meat. Meat is very scarce, as are vegetables, flour, and nearly everything else. Should I sign?"

James stiffened in alarm. "In no way, Mary, should you sign. Do not argue when you go to market. Buy what you can, but sign nothing for the British. Trust to Providence. We may live with less meat than we like, but at least we'll live free. Ask no favors from those wretches who have taken control. They are not worth the food on their tables."

"Then that is what I will do," Mary said. "Thank you. I must go soon," she added, looking nervously at the door. Her voice breaking, she said, "I will come back before long to see you, I hope. Dr. Joseph Gardner, in whose house we are living, has been so kind to us. I am able to do household chores for him. I bake bread, tend to washing. His protection has been invaluable."

"We are both indebted to him," James said. He thought of the kind doctor, helpful to many in the community. "Please give to him my deepest thanks for sheltering you and the children. And, my dear, I think of you daily and pray for your health." He looked at her anxiously.

"I am fine, James," Mary replied. She smiled reassuringly. "I have no discomfort and am strong enough to do the work required of me at Dr. Gardner's, thank heavens. It is a blessing to be there, where the children feel safe, as do I."

"That is good news. Thank you for telling me." James leaned back in weariness against the wall.

Mary accepted her basket back from John Leach, who nodded his thanks. She looked at James with concern. "I wish you were feeling better. It worries me to see you so ill."

"You may be sure I will do my best to get through this sickness. By the way, have you seen my father lately?"

"He keeps to himself, as does Abigail," Mary answered. "He comes out of the house little. They must be all right, however, as he appears calm and comfortable when I do see him, usually in his garden."

"It is best to leave him to his own affairs." James frowned. "It is far better than having him give his opinions to you about my present situation. You could, I believe, go to him and Mother if you needed help." He thought a moment. "Yes, they would help you. But you are doing well enough. His disapproval of me would make a visit with him most difficult, I am sure." Mary nodded understanding.

"Besides," James added, "I seem to remember my father saying he sometimes does favors for General Gage. He may get favors, or rewards, in return. In any case, with such connections he seems to lack for little. Give my love to the children," he added.

Mary nodded and smiled. "Yes, I will be sure to." She stood, smoothed her skirts, and gave James a long, heartfelt look as she lingered, reluctant to leave. With a swift motion, she turned and knocked on the door. A jailer opened it and motioned her out. Without looking back, she left. The heavy door slammed shut.

Dear Mary, James thought. *She is so brave and able. I am so fortunate she is able to manage.*

"Here, have some bread. Mary brought it for you," John Leach said gently, holding out a piece of the brown loaf.

"I will try a small bit. She is a good woman to come here, though it must be hard for her," James said, accepting the portion.

"Aye, and for my wife as well, though she comes less often than yours. Without them we would be much less well-fed. That's Providence for you, supplying what we need." John Leach bit into a cold potato and smiled. The others also took some food, and for a while all James heard was the munching of his cellmates.

"Hey, I'm hungry," shouted someone from another cell.

"Who's that?" replied a jailer.

"I'm Dr. Brown. I've had no bread for two days. Get me the provost."

"If you please, Your Lordship," drawled the jailer. That afternoon he returned with the provost.

"And what is your complaint?" asked Provost Joseph Otis.

"I'm hungry. You have no right to starve people here."

"You can eat nail heads and be damned. We are not running an inn. Say, you are a doctor, aren't you?"

"Yes, I am," was the bitter response.

"We have a prisoner here whose leg is green. It should be taken off. If you'll do that for us we might find a bit of bread about here."

"This is not a hospital. You have no proper tools or assistance," said Dr. Brown, pointedly.

"If you don't take it off, he'll die anyway. What do you choose?"

"All right. I'll do it. You must get me a pan of hot water and clean cloths, as well as some warm rum for the patient to drink."

The provost opened the cell door for Dr. Brown and the two shuffled down the hall, followed by three jailers. "You'll get cold water and cold rum, and be damned if you don't like it," said the provost roughly.

The cellmates exchanged glances. Prison amputations rarely were successful. More often than not, the unfortunate patient died of disease or bled to death.

Horrific shrieks filled the next half hour, until a sudden silence indicated the prisoner had either died or fainted. James shuddered. *What a place to suffer such a wound.*

Dr. Brown returned to his cell a short time later. "One less prisoner is all to the good," a jailer said with sarcasm as he opened the heavy door.

"You beast," Dr. Brown answered. "If I had had proper equipment…"

"Shut up," the jailer said, shoving the doctor through the door. Dr. Brown fell to the floor with an audible thump. James sighed.

Some days James's illness bothered him more than others. On his good days, he asked for writing paper and pen. One day the jailer brought him those at his request, throwing them in through the window of the cell. "Suit yourself," was the curt comment accompanying the projectiles.

He wrote to General Howe, explaining his situation: he had been imprisoned, with no crime and no charge. This treatment was inhumane in the extreme. For days, he wondered if the general had received his letter.

A couple weeks later, in mid-August, he received a short, terse response. General Howe said nothing clear, but that he had noted James's letter and would take it under consideration. The letter, in fact, was a disappointment, as vague and meaningless as no response at all. His stomach rumbling, James wondered to whom else he could write.

He tried to ignore the racket that echoed from the room next door, nearly a lost cause. The swearing, abuse, and vile language from the women prisoners was shocking to hear. If anyone deserved callous treatment, perhaps they did. James doubled over in pain and shut his eyes.

One day John Leach's little son came, bringing him food. The provost showed him into the cell, then shoved him in so he nearly fell. "Join your miserable father, and be damned to you. You'll be locked up here soon, like as not."

"Here, William, you're a good boy to come see me." John held out his arms to the boy, who set his basket down and went over to his father to receive his embrace, his eyes wide with fright. "Are you all right?"

"Yes, Father," the child said, sniffling. He looked about at the anxious faces of the cellmates. "Mother could not come, but wanted you to have this." He pointed to the basket. James could see he was trembling and frightened.

"That's a good boy. You'll be all right. The provost talks a mean talk, but he won't hurt you. Here, we'll share this." John passed the basket of bread and sausage around among the men, who each took a piece and began to eat hungrily. James took a small piece and bit, and found he could manage the food.

"You'd better go. Jailer, let my son out," John Leach called.

"What's the hurry? He can just stay there with you."

An hour later, the pockmarked jailer opened the door. The swearing and cursing outside were terrible, but William picked up his basket and joined the jailer at the door. "Good-bye, Father. I will tell Mother you are well."

"Yes, my son. And God bless you," John said. The door clanged shut. "They don't know how I worry about them. How long must we be here?" He subsided in misery, and for a time all the cellmates were quiet, each lost in his own thoughts.

In two days William returned. John stood up in alarm. Outside he could hear the provost swearing. "You came back to see that villain John Leach? You dog, you deserve to be shot."

"No, no, my William, be brave," John said quietly. In a minute the door opened and the jailer pushed the boy in.

James's stomach rebelled. He lay down and shut his eyes. He refused the food that John Leach offered him, and rolled towards the wall.

"Guard, we have a sick man here," Peter Edes called.

"He can hang. We have no time to deal with sickness," said a jailer roughly, who came to the cell.

"Dr. Eliot came to the gate and offered to help. We heard him yesterday," said Peter.

"You're hearing things," the jailer answered rudely. "No one would want to treat such as you. You are not worth the bread we give you."

"And Sergeant Neal and Corporal Royal got locked up for giving you fresh air and water. Serves them right, showing pity on scoundrels such as you," the provost shouted, coming up beside the jailer and joining the abuse. "I say, even if you're dead and rotten, you're staying in those cells."

I seem to remember, thought James, *that British law says a man is innocent until proven guilty. I seem to remember that a man deserves a trial by a jury of his peers. But what does all that matter, when might makes right and the law is thrown out?*

I understand why my father does not come, James's thoughts went on. *He has his life, his beliefs. But surely he cares about me. Did we not work together, teach together, for years? Despite his differences in view, I wonder why he does not try to see me. Then again, maybe he is fearful that if he came, someone might think he sympathizes with the American cause. He wants to be seen as a good Loyalist. He thinks when this is over he may be rewarded for his faith in British power. He does not realize what a big change is coming. I must not hold it against him,* he thought. *He is weak in his own way.*

James rolled over in pain. Sometimes the illness overcame him, to the point he could hardly tell what to think. At such times his worries about his family and about his own condition became oppressive. In truth, he knew, much more of this treatment would be extremely difficult to bear. He shut his eyes.

Chapter 41

Provost Prison: Third Month

OCTOBER 4, 1775

In late August the heat grew intense, the moist, rank air nearly suffocating. The prisoners were shut up all day, as they had been for weeks. Finally, one blistering day, they were again allowed out into the yard. James and his fellow cellmates stood on the grass, blinking in the bright sunlight. Birds fluttered and squirrels chattered, scampering up and down an oak.

"Here, we have the latest statement of your Provincial Committee, just for your pleasure," said Provost William Cunningham, grinning an evil smile. He opened a folded note in front of James.

In Council, August 23, 1775.

The Committee are of opinion that in case Mr. Hicks and Mr. Jones, two persons now in custody in Concord, can by any means procure the release of Messrs. James Lovell, John Leach, John Gill, William Starr, and Peter Edes, from prison in Boston, and their removal from Boston, the said Hicks and Jones, with three others, such as the major part of the Council shall consent to, who are now in custody by order of this Government, be discharged.

SAMUEL ADAMS, per order.

"And I suppose they are of the opinion that all prisoners should receive a pension, and a carriage, and a gardener," the provost went on, waving the paper in front of the group. "None of you are worth the trouble it would take to bury you, and you had better remember that." He went into the jail, his helpers following him.

"So, they are taking notice of us," said John Leach.

"You may be sure we are missed. I would hope that such petitions may be effective, in time, to secure our release," said James. He felt dizzy being outdoors, the relief of breathing fresh air was so great. The small grassed yard was dirty with slop from the prisoners' garbage being thrust carelessly out the window, foul with peelings and waste the jailers dropped, just as was every other part of the prison; yet it was closer to freedom than he had been in a long while.

A guard in a dirty red uniform, his leather face scarred, came out and brandished a pistol at them. "Get back inside. Enough." He walked over to an older prisoner who had trouble getting up and kicked him soundly in the back. "Get moving."

"Who are you to kick me that way?" asked the prisoner, hobbling to his feet.

"I'm Sergeant Dyer. You'll get more of my boot, be sure of that. In with ye."

Dyer moved them all inside, cuffing several with his pistol and throwing young John Rowe to the ground. Within days he had kicked or beaten or punched nearly every prisoner in the jail. "Enough," growled William Starr. "The man is beyond belief. We must tell someone."

"No one has the right to torture us," Peter Edes agreed. "But to whom could we appeal?"

None of the cellmates had a ready answer for that question.

At the end of August, the prisoners had been given nothing for thirty-seven days but bread and water. Then, out of nowhere, for five days, the jailers started bringing out pails of pork, butter, rice, and peas, with wooden spoons and trenchers, setting them in the common room, and releasing all there to eat. They brought James a pail of fresh beef. "Here, you," said Provost Otis. "Maybe this will help you get over the trots." James nodded weakly and took the pail. No one knew what to think about the sudden change. Were the jailers under new orders?

In the middle of September, the prisoners' doors were opened and they were allowed out into the common room or the yard. Each cell received a couple of candles. In the flickering light, with fresh air moving in the stale rooms, James felt a little better. His stomach finally seemed to be on the mend. The summer's heat was at last waning.

Then the swearing began again—the jailers', some of the prisoners', and the women's shrill voices merging in the cacophony. The excessive profanity seemed a deliberate scheme encouraged by the jailers to cause misery to the prisoners. Yet James and his cellmates, refreshed by the light and the air, were able to rest more soundly than usual.

Jemmy and Johnny had been much on his mind. His heart ached for them, thirteen and twelve years old, dependent on the kindness of strangers in Cambridge. In the third week of September he asked for paper, pen, and ink, which a gaunt jailer thrust unkindly into the jail cell. "Write what you want, it will not help you," he said with a sneer.

"My dear boys," he began his letter.

> I charge you to reflect continually upon that one easy rule for your behavior, which I have repeatedly laid down for you—act in all cases as if I was present. You know I allow you all the diversions suitable for children, but your diversions too often grow into a rudeness which may be corrected by the imagination that I am looking upon you. And if I do, how much more ought you to be kept in order by the thought of the real presence of the great God, to whom you owe an obedience and respect infinitely superior to what is due from you to me, as his love, his care, and his tenderness towards you is infinitely greater than mine.

He told them of his stomach illness, making light of the condition, and assured them that if he were freed he would visit them. He asked the boys to thank the family who had opened a place for them, and suggested they write themselves to him, as it was more likely a letter from them would reach him in jail than would one from any older acquaintances. At the end of the letter, he wiped his streaming eyes.

> *To conclude, my dear Jemmy, be cautious of what language you make use. My dear Johnny, command your temper—and both my dear boys, be assured of the tokens of the continued love of your affectionate father.*

Signing his name with a deep flourish, he folded the paper and addressed it in care of Joseph Trumbull, Esq., of Cambridge. *I must be sure they receive my words of affection,* he thought. He handed the letter to a guard, his face revealing his concern so clearly that even the usually belligerent guard looked at him with sympathy.

"I'll do what I can to have it delivered," he said.

One day their door creaked open, and several guards entered. "We're here to check your valuables."

"What valuables?" asked John Leach.

"Any you have. Here, empty your pockets." In the cell all the men turned out their pockets. They produced William Starr's pocket watch, a wallet belonging to James, and John Leach's wedding ring.

"Off with that ring," said the pockmarked jailer, laughing.

"What—you would take my ring?" asked John in disbelief.

"Yes, of course. It's for a good cause. Hand it over or you'll give me your finger into the bargain." John shook his head and turned over the gold ring.

The jailers then held a mock sale with the collection of articles stolen from the men. Sheriff Loring served as the auctioneer, while Provost Cunningham, his son, and Sergeant Dyer bid for the articles. The prisoners looked on from their cell door in disbelief as their personal objects were distributed. None dared to speak up, though privately they groaned.

On Sunday, September 17, the guards forced the prisoners into a line, attached their handcuffs to a long chain, and marched the group off to Dr. Cooper's meeting house. A minister from Peterboro, he had been forced to leave his pulpit because of scandalous behavior, James recalled hearing from friends. Cooper had served in the patriot army at Bunker Hill but then left the army and joined the Tories. He preached against the ministers of Boston as speakers of sedition. True to Tory thought, he suggested that the colonists should be grateful to the British for protecting them from the French and the Indians. James listened to Dr. Cooper's bombastic speech with disgust. *His words do me no good,* James thought. His talk was worse than the poorest sermon he'd ever heard.

A dead prisoner was carried out a few days later. In the yard James and his group learned that another of the group held since Bunker Hill had died. "That makes only eleven left of the original twenty-nine arrested. Not such good odds for those who stay in the Provost Jail," Peter Edes remarked grimly.

At the beginning of October, Major Kemble came with an offer for the prisoners. "This offer for you to go free stands for Mr. Gill, Mr. Starr, Master Leach, and Peter Edes, but not to you, James Lovell," he said.

"Why not?" James asked.

"You're not the sort of prisoner we can set free," Major Kemble said vaguely. "Pipe down or you'll go back in your cell. Here's how you could be freed," he said to the others. "If you can find two men who would sign and give their word that you will not leave town, you may leave."

By October 3, most of those who had received the offer had found two witnesses willing to affirm in writing that they would not leave town. Mr. Gill had to find someone else since his second witness had been John Leach, so he located another signator.

In their cell that night, John Leach said, "James, you can be sure I will do what I can to secure your release. You deserve freedom as much as any of us."

"You can count on me to help," said Peter. William Starr nodded his head vehemently.

"This has been a sorry situation," John said. "Our treatment has been worse than I could have ever imagined. We have been in here ninety-seven days, the first thirty-seven given only bread and water. Yet our captors deserve perhaps more of our pity than our contempt. They have not learned to treat others well because they have been abused themselves. They are, after all, fellow creatures made by God. As Alexander Pope said,

> *'Teach me to feel another's Woe,*
> *To hide the fault I see;*

> *That Mercy I, to others show,*
> *That Mercy show to me.'"*

James said, "You're a better man than I am, John, but perhaps you are right. However, I must believe that before long I will be out of this miserable place as well." He looked at the stalwart navigator with affection.

One warm fall day, the jailer with the torn jacket allowed James out to the yard for a visit with his wife. Mary approached James, her head and shoulders draped with a shawl. She was thin and pale, her face lined with concern and worry. She brightened when she saw James come over to her. He held her in a brief embrace, letting her go sooner than he would like, knowing the jailer would be watching and not wanting to give him cause to prevent their talk.

"It has been a few weeks since I've come," Mary said. "I have been tending to Thomas and Charles, both sick. We continue at Dr. Gardner's and all is well, though food is scarce."

James placed his hand on her shoulder. "I am so thankful. It is good to see you, my dear. Come, sit with me under the tree." He motioned to an elm in the yard, away from the watchful eyes and ears of the British guard who stood by the door of the jail.

James helped Mary sit under the tree, aware of her swelling form, the baby growing.

"You are thin and pale, but the sickness seems better. Am I right?" Mary asked, searching his face anxiously.

"Indeed, I am better. We have had some decent food from time to time, as well as the chance to come to the yard and be in the fresh air, so I am feeling healthier," James answered.

"I have news," Mary said quietly. She lowered her voice to a whisper. "The petition to King George, approved by the Second Continental Congress, asking for reconciliation, has been dismissed by the king. He would not even read 'The Olive Branch Petition,' as some called it. It would be a last chance for us to make peace before this conflict becomes a war." Mary shook her head regretfully.

"It already is a war," James responded. He frowned. "Those soft of heart in our Congress, including the illustrious Farmer who penned the petition, would have the problem dismissed with a wave of the royal hand. John Dickinson of Pennsylvania, who uses the pen name 'The Farmer,' does not speak for many. Denied our rights, what choice have we? Be glad General Washington is drilling the militia, as we shall have need of them," he said bitterly.

"They say he is a very good commander," Mary said. "He keeps strict order and puts discipline even into the country volunteers from the south. James Jr. is still with the militia. Jemmy would like to join as well, but I have convinced him to remain with Joseph Trumbull at Cambridge for the time. He is too young for such notions. It grieves me to know either may see warfare."

"James Jr. will be fine," James responded. "Do not fear for him. He is as likely as any to survive the conflict. We should be proud of him. I wish I could join him. Nonetheless, I think you are right to keep Jemmy from enlisting."

"Your older brother, John, has joined a regiment of the British Loyalist Volunteers," Mary said.

"That would suit John well," James said gloomily. "He is always quick to defend British rule."

"As perhaps would your father, but I have not spoken with him in some time. He, your mother, and your three sisters yet at home keep to themselves most of the time, though I have seen Elizabeth at market occasionally. We are not going to church these days. Leaving the house often is not safe."

"It is just as well you do not see my father," James answered, with some resentment. "He would help you if need be, but at the same time he would no doubt remain critical of my actions."

Mary continued with her news. "The troops desecrate the city. The Old South Meeting House, where you gave your oration on the first anniversary of the Boston massacre, has been gutted; its fine pews and pulpit pulled down and taken out; dirt and gravel spread on the floor. General Burgoyne has ordered it to be used as a horse riding school for the Seventeenth Dragoons." Her voice held a note of disbelief. "They have set a long bar down the middle as a vault for jumping. And in cold weather, for heat they burn the library of the pastor."

"That is disgusting," James said. "What terrible treatment of a venerable, elegant building."

"Even worse, the Old North Church has been pulled down for firewood. They seem especially vindictive towards churches other than Anglican," said Mary. "And also for firewood, the regulars have chopped down many of the lovely oak and maple trees on the common."

They were both silent for a moment, considering the devastation of their town.

"Good-bye, my dear," he said at length. "The provost is coming to get you. It saddens me to think of the cruelty these troops practice. But I am grateful to you for coming and bringing me food. It makes all the difference to me—that and your company."

"You are doing better, I think," she said. He stood and helped her to her feet. "You are in great need of the food. I will return when I can." She picked up her basket, wrapped her shawl about her, and smiled at James. *Dear Mary,* James thought. *How much I owe to her constancy and assistance.* He put his arm around her to escort her to the gate, ignoring the rude glance of the provost. His heart followed her out as the iron gate clanged shut.

On October 4 the provost came to the cell. "Well, fleas will fly and so will you. Leach, Edes, and Starr, you may go. Hunt, we're moving you to another cell."

The prisoners looked at James. "Not you, I guess," said Peter Edes, sympathetically. "However, you may be sure that many on the outside are aware of your situation and are working for your freedom."

John Leach shook James Lovell's hand. "Take care of yourself, my friend." William gave him a handshake as well, and Peter a tight squeeze, before they joined Mr. Gill in the corridor. Together they filed out into the pleasant light of day. James was left alone in his cell.

Why was he not set free? James wondered in discouragement. His heart sank. After all this time, the letters he'd written, the release for his cellmates—and no one had yet liberated him? He sat down on his pallet. It seemed so unfair. The emptiness in his cell was strange after his cellmates had left. He resolved to endure on his own, though his heart ached, as he had no choice.

Chapter 42

Provost Prison: Winter

MARCH 9, 1776

James remained alone for a week. Worse than being alone was the thought that he had not been given the same chance to leave as his cellmates had.

During the crisp October days, the provost opened the door and James was free to go outside into the prison yard, crunching red and orange leaves and smelling the tang of fall in the air. He paced the yard vigorously, trying to make up for weeks of inactivity. That night the filthy jailer tossed him a blanket and candles.

Sometimes, as the days went by, James woke with frost riming the floor next to his thin straw pallet. To his dismay, he still had not been summoned for an actual hearing, nor had he been charged with a crime. But before long he was no longer alone, as several captured militia were ushered in to join him in his cell.

Mary brought him a new shirt of homespun linen that she had made herself. She carried him scanty meals, remains of feeding the five children at home. Each time she came James felt enormous relief and pleasure. Her visits were the only bright spot in his tedious, painful days. It also cheered him to hear about the safety of his children and see that Mary remained strong.

Mary reported hearing from James Jr. that the militia drilled regularly. General George Washington visited the camps often on his fine horse. James Jr. and hundreds of others were digging entrenchments on the hills near Boston. It was dirty, hard work, hauling rocks and moving earth. Camp life bred disease, typhoid and smallpox being the worst of the scourges, and weeks went by without the chance to wash or change clothing. However, James Jr. was surviving in the militia and had remained healthy.

From Mary's reports, James could tell that Boston was starving, both the thousands of troops and the several thousand citizens left. At one time the master butcher, General Hewes, had only six head of cattle for the troops and the people of Boston. Even the most undesirable parts of a carcass were sold for good money. Salted meat, fish, or pork went quickly.

The lack of food in Boston served to explain why there was even less for the prisoners. James was heartily tired of eating dry, moldy bread. Occasionally the jailers brought bits of pork and beans or salt fish in the prisoners' bucket, just enough to keep him and the others from starvation.

The sounds of gunfire often echoed over the hills and harbor of Boston. It rang through the jail's stone walls at all hours of the day or night. Sometimes it was British shooting at the militia sentries; sometimes the militia firing at the British sentries. The British, who seemed to have no shortage of ammunition, often drilled and fired volleys in practice, so there was little quiet.

James again asked for writing paper, pen, and ink. What else could he do but continue to make his case known to the authorities? The pock-marked jailer handed several sheets of paper to him. "Here, don't thank me. But writing a letter isn't going to do you much good, not where you're going," he said with a smirk.

In mid-October the news reached the prison that General Gage had been dismissed and sent back to England. Tired of Gage's indecisive actions, King George appointed General William Howe the new commanding officer in North America. James wondered if a letter to General Howe might produce more results than his previous letters to General Gage. On October 16th he carefully penned a petition to General Howe. A very little, he allowed his hopes to rise.

Mary came to the jail before long, carrying General Howe's response. Dripping wet from a heavy rain, she wore an old cloak over her dress. She tossed the hood of the cloak back, her hair damp and tangled.

"James, I have received a letter for you from General Howe," Mary said, her voice holding a note of excitement. The jailer slammed his door shut.

James did not offer Mary a seat, realizing that in her present condition, it would be easier to stand than sit on the floor. He set her basket of food on the floor and took the folded letter from her with interest.

"It was delivered to me by Captain Balfour, Howe's aide-de-camp. You must write to General Washington to request you be exchanged for Colonel Skene and his son. Captain Balfour was clear on that point. General Howe very much wants to have Colonel Skene returned to him."

James's face lit up. He scanned the script on the fine paper in the dim light. Mary smiled and smoothed back her wet red curls, waiting for his reaction.

"Colonel Skene, I believe, is a retired British officer," James said. "He held an estate near Fort Ticonderoga on Lake Champlain, until he was taken prisoner. I will write to General Washington to request the exchange. Thank you, my dear, for conveying this excellent news." He gave her a kiss on her cheek.

"I understand that General Howe did think of exchanging me for Dr. Church, but something happened to the deal," James added. "This sounds like a more promising exchange. Dr. Church was a patriot trusted by Joseph Warren and others, but unfortunately he worked undercover as a scoundrel of a spy and turned his back on the patriot cause. I am glad he was discovered and arrested by our militia. I know General Washington has a great deal on his mind, organizing the Continental Army, but perhaps he will consent to facilitating the exchange. This is without doubt good news. Mary, do not give up. I will be home before long, I am sure."

"And how are you doing?" he asked, glancing at her in anxiety.

Mary gave him a long look. He felt sure she was guarding her words. "The baby is doing well, I have every reason to think. I am more than grateful for the employment at Dr. Joseph Gardner's, since not only am I able to feed the children better, but I find more peace in his secure establishment."

"Your employment there is a blessing." James said. At least she had some good things to report. Perhaps it was just his long absence that was troubling her. He sighed and looked down at a crusty loaf of bread in the basket. "I would so much like to be there, but I am doing everything I can to be freed. My heart yearns to be with you and the children. We must not be discouraged."

The jailer called from the hall, his rough voice a missile of scorn. "The visitor must leave now."

Mary wrapped her cloak tightly about herself, pulling her hood back on, and James reached for her. Without saying a word he clung to her, feeling desperate as he embraced her tightly. So many emotions rose within him. He missed her, longed for her and his children. She returned his hold fervently. Tears coursed down her cheeks. Then the jailer opened the door. Mary ignored him, but the jailer grabbed her arm roughly and pulled her toward the hall. "Come, you. Or you'll not be coming back in a month of Sundays," he said rudely.

James stepped back, tears in his eyes, letting her go. "Good-bye, my love," he called as, once again, the slam and clank of the jail cell door shut her out. In misery, he heard her footsteps echo down the hall.

In November, when the snow swirled under the door into the Stone Jail, wearing all his clothes in the unheated rooms and wrapping himself in his blanket, James sharpened the nib of his quill and wrote a formal letter to General Washington.

> *Provost's Prison, Boston, November 19, 1775.*
>
> *MAY IT PLEASE YOUR EXCELLENCY: I wish at this time to waive the expression of my veneration of your character, in a still lively hope that Providence will bless me with the opportunity of attempting it by the united sincere language of my eyes and lips, though even that must prove inadequate. Personally a stranger to you, my sufferings have yet affected your benevolent mind, and your exertions in my favour have made so deep an impression upon my grateful heart as will remain till the period of my latest breath.*
>
> *Your Excellency is already informed that the powers of the military government established in this town have been wantonly and cruelly exercised against me, from the 29th of June last. I have in vain repeatedly solicited to be brought to some kind of trial for my pretended crime. In answer to a petition of that sort, presented on the 16th of*

October, I am directed, by Captain Balfour, Aid-de-camp to General Howe, to seek the release of Colonel Skene and his son, as the sole means of my own enlargement. This proposition appears to me extremely disgraceful to the party from which it comes, and a compliance with it would be pregnant with dangerous consequences to my fellow-citizens. But while my own spirit prompts me to reject it directly with the keenest disdain, the importunity of my distressed wife, and the advice of some whom I esteem, have checked me down to a consent to give your Excellency this information. I have the fullest confidence in your wisdom, and I shall be perfectly resigned to your determination, whatever it may be. I must not, however, omit to say, that, should you condescend to stigmatize this proceeding of my enemies by letter, the correction might work some change in favour of myself, or at least of my family, which must, I think, perish through want of fuel and provision, in the approaching winter, if it continues to be deprived of my assistance.

I have the honour to be, your Excellency's devoted friend and servant,

James Lovell.

I know General Washington has a great deal on his mind, he thought, *but even so I shall be hopeful he may take the time to arrange an exchange for me.*

The days dragged on. Bitter winter weather settled in, harsh and cruel, piling snow in great drifts outside. Mary came seldom to the jail, and James missed her visits as well as the food she brought. Still, he knew that coming to see him in the snowy weather was extremely difficult and dangerous for her. He chewed the tasteless bread he was served and tried to imagine it was Mary's light, flavorful loaves.

Sleeping on the pallet on the stone floor was even more unpleasant in cold than it had been in heat. James knew himself to be luckier than some prisoners, who suffered from gout or rheumatism. These were not his complaints. Still, he had lost a great deal of weight and it was hard to remain in good spirits. On December 6 he wrote General Washington again. *I must risk offending him,* he thought. *I cannot mince words. Even though he may think me rude, I must express the desperation of my situation.*

> *Boston Prison, December 6, 1775.*
>
> *SIR: I address your Excellency upon a matter greatly important in its consequences to more than myself. And though I am personally unknown to you, I shall proceed without any other ceremony, than just to beg you would not attribute my abruptness to the consideration of the channel by which my letter will be conveyed, but to my embarrassment in an aim to express, by words, my real veneration of your publick character.*
>
> *Charged with being a "spy, and giving intelligence to the Rebels," I have been suffering the pains and indignities of imprisonment, from the 29th of June last, without any sort of trial.*
>
> *Captain Balfour, Aid-de-camp to General Howe, some time ago, directed Mrs. Lovell to tell me, from the Commander-in-chief, that I must obtain the exchange of Colonel Skene and his son, as the only condition of my enlargement; and I have waited weeks from that, in a vain hope of being enabled to write with more precision to your Excellency.*
>
> *I have no argument, but of a private nature, to make use of upon this occasion, and it is addressed to your Excellency's humanity, which I am well satisfied will attend the decisions of your wisdom. I myself am reduced to such a risk of life, and my family to such miseries, by my imprisonment, as to make both the objects of compassion to all who are not learnedly barbarous and cruel.*
>
> *I am, your Excellency's devoted servant,*
>
> *James Lovell*

Of course General Washington is very busy, he thought. *Yet I can hope he will receive this letter and effect the exchange suggested by General Howe.*

On December 9 he wrote a letter to his friend Oliver Wendell. Still worried about the papers Wendell had entrusted to him, he told his friend that the tenant who had been staying in Oliver Wendell's home had been forced out when the house on the corner of School Street was seized by the British and made into a barracks. Now that the soldiers had left, James would try to arrange for another tenant. Meanwhile, he had been sorting and packing some of Oliver Wendell's business papers, brought by Mary to the jail.

At the conclusion of the letter he wrote, "The wantonness of the exertions of military power against me and my most innocent family should excite all who are out of the reach of it to prefer death rather than to come under it." *I can hardly express the barbaric treatment of the British,* he thought.

One day in late December, after the heavy cell door had clanged shut and Mary had left, the latest letter James had written to the Massachusetts Provincial Committee tucked in her pocket, he heard her scream from the corridor. "What are you doing? Stop! Stop!" she shrieked.

He rushed to the jail door. It was locked. Through the small barred opening he shouted, "Guard! My wife! She needs help!"

"Now, now, Mr. Lovell, don't you be alarmed," the provost said, smiling in an unpleasant way, as he tromped down the corridor. "Your wife just meant to help you, but she's tried to take out a letter that was not authorized. She's been caught, see, and the letter you thought to smuggle out is going to go to the authorities, my fine gentleman."

James stiffened in anger. "She must not be hurt. She is innocent, as am I. She is not smuggling. She probably just forgot to show you the letter. In no way should she suffer for my presence in this pesthole. When I am out of here, I can promise you will pay for any harm you do to her." His voice rose in anger.

"Not so fast, you won't be going. Your wife is all right. She's on her way home. No more letters for you, though, or you'll not see your wife again. Do you hear?" The provost jangled his ring of keys at him, his forehead furrowed angrily. He turned and left James standing miserably in his cell, listening to the clink of the keys die away.

In early January the jailer with the torn jacket handed James a note. "Addressed to you, I see—but don't be too sure it means anything. The provost said you could have it, so more than likely it cannot help you." He laughed unkindly and left.

The note was from the Provincial Committee. General Washington had written to Congress, and Congress had recommended an exchange for him. After receiving the authorization from Congress, Washington had written General Howe, offering the suggested exchange. James's hopes soared for days. Finally, at last the exchange might happen.

One day in February his cell door opened and there stood Joseph. "A brat come to see you," sneered the gaunt jailer.

"Come in, come in," James said, giving Joseph a hug. Joseph had grown, James could see; at nearly twelve, he was no longer chubby, but almost as tall as Johnny had been at that age. "But all is well at home?" he asked anxiously.

"Mother just had a baby, a night ago. She is fine. Dr. Gardner was able to attend her, and she has a baby boy. She wonders if the name George would suit you."

"Tell her George is a splendid name and suits me fine. I am so pleased." For a minute the image of the contemptuous King George flashed before his eyes and he stiffened. Then, quickly, he relaxed. The name George was still an excellent one. It depended on the owner of the name to prove of sound character. Surely his son could be as fine a person as anyone.

"It was good of you to come." Joseph looked about the cell in some suspicion, eyeing the other cellmates who lay on their pallets or sat leaning against the walls. He shook the snow from his coat and stamped his boots a couple of times.

"It is no trouble, Father. I am glad to see you. We have no extra food at home at this time, Mother bids me tell you, but she hopes you remain in good health."

"Tell her I am indeed well, and thank her for her concern," James said. "And Joseph, I hope you read often and write on your own. One day you will be back at school and you must be prepared."

"I will, Father," Joseph said with a smile.

"Come, enough. Visiting is over," said the provost, opening the door to the cell. "Don't bother to come back. Visiting is for adults only." He frowned at Joseph.

Joseph hastily turned to go, wrapping his coat about himself tightly. "Good-bye," he said to his father. "I am happy I could see you."

"Many thanks for coming. I am glad to hear news of the baby. Give my love to the children and your mother." The door slammed shut behind Joseph. James brushed away a tear. *Joseph is brave*, he thought. *It is not easy to come to this place. If only I could see the others.*

One day before long the provost threw a scrap of paper into his cell. "Here, read this. It is a draft of a letter from General Howe to your George Washington. You have no hope after all." He leered at James, his smile cruel and sarcastic, and slammed the door.

Bitterly, James read the note.

> *Boston, February 2, 1776.*
>
> *SIR: In answer to your letter of the 30th ultimo, which was delivered with the seal broken, I am to acquaint you, that having lately discovered a prohibited correspondence to be carried on by Mr. James Lovell, the liberty, which I fully intended to have given him, cannot take place.*
>
> *I am, sir, your most humble servant,*
>
> *General Howe*

So Howe had already denied the exchange, since he had learned about the letter James tried to smuggle out. James felt his hopes come crashing down. What else could he do?

Worse than the poor food, freezing nights on a hard floor, and lack of communication about his imprisonment was his inability to do anything to help those working for freedom. The cause burned in his heart like a brand, bright and strong. If he ever got out, when he got out, he would do what he could to assist his fellow countrymen, he was more sure than ever.

Midnight on Saturday, March 2, the pounding of cannon woke the prisoners. Stiff, cold, and tired, they sat up, their ears ringing from the bombardment of cannon fire, far away but close enough that it seemed to shake the walls of their prison. A fierce barrage was in progress, coming from across the harbor. *Probably an attack resounding from the recent fortifications of the Americans at Dorchester Heights,* James thought. British cannon responded, thundering loudly, preventing sleep for all. Beating of drums, rumbling of carts, and cries of people threatened by crashing cannonballs filled the night.

The next night the firing continued, the cacophony even louder, and the third night the boom of cannon resounded again. James and his fellow prisoners could not leave their cells during the day. The jailers rudely shoved in buckets of water and hunks of old bread, then clanged the doors shut.

On the night of March 5, cannon fire again shattered the night in bursts and volleys. Terrified shouts of those whose homes were destroyed by cannonballs rang in the streets and church bells clanged in alarm. Then the wind picked up, moaning and howling like a hurricane. Sleet and snow whipped through the openings in the jail cell doors and hail pelted the stone walls. James sat up shivering, wrapped in his blanket. The shrieks of those under fire and the wail of the storm were too loud and worrisome to permit sleep. He half expected any minute to have a cannon ball burst through a jail cell wall. His only consolation was that the cannon fire must be coming from the patriots, since he suspected it was hitting homes and buildings where the British lodged. *Where had they gotten cannon and ammunition from?* he wondered.

Early the next day the pockmarked jailer opened the cell door, setting down a bucket of water so hard much of it splashed out. "Well, those filthy militia have done it," he said in disgust. "They've dug in the frozen ground and built redoubts and fortifications on Dorchester Heights so they can fire cannon anywhere. General Howe's cannon cannot reach that height. He was all set to advance the attack, send troops across to storm the heights that the colonials have fortified, but not with this. Maybe you've heard some of the attack…" His voice trailed off. James and his cellmates sat in silence. Their ears echoed with the pounding of guns.

"Somehow some colonial, Henry Knox, I think I heard, made it from Lake Champlain dragging cannon. All the way from Fort Ticonderoga on Lake Champlain, dragging cannon stolen from the British. Do you believe that? In this weather? Those militia are completely crazy. Transports of soldiers left Castle William to attack the fortifications in force, but then this has changed General Howe's plan." The jailer motioned to the swirl of snow that had followed him in the door as the wind howled. "The weather just isn't cooperating. Now he has announced we leave. Luckily for you, that means you go too," he said, an evil glint in his eye.

A couple of days later, the jailer set the bucket of water down in James's cell with a whack, tossed the chunk of bread next to it, and announced, "It won't be long 'til you're gone, out of here, all of you." James and his cellmates looked up anxiously. "We're leaving. Where we're going we're not sure, but prisoners go as well. You may find yourself swinging from a rope in New York yet."

"General Howe's taking all the Loyalists, too," he went on, in a matter of fact manner. "Someone's been crying to him they'll be picked apart by the rebels, as well they might be, so he's assembling a fleet to carry them all off. You—just pack your bags, because in a day you're gone." He chuckled rudely and swaggered out.

Where were they going? James wondered. *And the Loyalists?* That meant, more than likely, that his father and mother, perhaps the girls still at home as well, would be going. A glint of hope began to dawn for him. Perhaps this change would be an improvement.

The next day the jailer opened his door. There stood Mary, her face pale and worried. "I told her she could see you for just a few minutes. It may be the last time before you join General Howe in New York." He motioned her in with a rude gesture and slammed the door.

Her voice cracking, Mary said, "He told me you'd be moved with the other prisoners. I would rather you were kept here. At least you are close enough here for me to see you," she said. Tears streaked her pale face.

"Do not worry, my dear," said James, putting his arm about her. "Providence has cared for us so far and will still. Here," he said, handing her a bundle of papers, "take these and store them safely at home. They are the records of Oliver Wendell's and Nathaniel Appleton's belongings which we care for, as well as a few letters I have received."

"The colonials' barrage of cannon fire has worked all too well," he added. "General Howe has decided to evacuate all the British troops from Boston. Prisoners too are being taken. That means me, as you know. It also means that all the Loyalists will be evacuated, at their request. Many Loyalists are fearful of possible ill treatment at the hands of the patriots for having sided with the British. Of course, that means my father and mother and the girls still at home will probably also be taken."

"But how is the baby doing? And the other children?" James asked anxiously. He searched her face for good news.

"Baby George is no trouble. He is good and sleeps well. Little Mary has had a bad cold. I give her honey and vinegar to quiet her cough. Dr. Gardner administers inoculations against smallpox—when she recovers, I may ask him to inoculate her and the other children. There are risks in being inoculated, but catching the disease is worse."

"That is very good news. I would recommend the children receive the inoculations. Has the shelling hit anywhere near you?"

"Oh, it has been dreadful," Mary said. "Luckily, it has not hit any building that is near us. A block away, a house caught fire, but fortunately the snow put out the flames. But it has been terrifying, so that we could not sleep." James nodded. He knew all too well the fear that came with the whistle of cannon balls, the crash of walls, the cries for help of those hit.

The jailer with the torn jacket returned before they could say more. "Visiting is over," he said briefly. "Say good-bye. You probably won't see him again." He laughed when Mary gave him a frightened look. She glanced at James quickly.

"I will hope you are home before long so we can have George christened," she said, nearly in tears.

"Don't worry, I will do everything I can," James said. "And don't listen to the jailer. I'll do my best to be home as soon as possible." He gave her a quick kiss good-bye before the jailer could stop him. Mary turned and left with a tear on her cheek.

There is no use in alarming Mary, James thought, as he settled down to wait for the promised evacuation. *Probably, yes, I'll be gone for a while. But more than likely the absence will be short, I can hope. Maybe outside of Boston, without the weight of the siege and free from the worry of defending his troops from the thousands of militia nearby, General Howe will consider my situation more positively. An exchange for me might be worked out yet.*

Chapter 43

Boarding Ship

MARCH 10, 1776

The jailer with the ragged, torn jacket threw open their cell door early in the morning. "Get up, you lucky dogs. You're off with the royal fleet. We're boarding this morning. You and the Loyalists. General Howe is taking over a thousand Loyalists from this miserable town. They'll get the better berths in the fleet, but they have special places reserved just for you." He chuckled unpleasantly.

Handcuffed, the twenty-five or so prisoners in the Stone Jail filed out, shivering in the chilly March wind. Linked with a long chain, clad in light jackets despite the frigid temperature, they filed down the street, armed jailers in front and behind prodding the procession.

As they tramped down School Street, chains clanking, James glanced towards the schoolmaster's house. There was no sign of movement at his father's home, so his family must already have departed. James saw a gilded coach bearing royal insignia standing at the door. *General Gage's coach,* he guessed. *What is that doing there?* His father said he did favors for the general. General Gage was long gone, replaced as commander by General Howe. *Maybe,* James thought, *I don't want to know why that coach is there, or what Father has been doing. The gilded coach must have been given as a reward to him. In any case, it doesn't truly matter. If my father is taking his family with General Howe, he won't be able to use the coach anyway.*

Crowds filled the streets as the Loyalists threw what belongings they could onto carts, in a frantic haste to join the British ships waiting from them in the harbor. Families thronged down to the wharves, tugging their household possessions with them. *Think of what they must have left behind,* thought James, as he and the prisoners filed through the mass. Almost everything they owned would have to be abandoned: fine bedsteads, stately clocks, china sets, paintings, crystal chandeliers. *They are leaving their whole lives behind so they can follow the royal troops,* he thought. *They live in such fear of the actions of the rebels, as they call them, they would go anywhere.*

The prisoners stumbled along in a column through turbulent streets down to the harbor. The sun shone thin and light through scattered March clouds, a lemon slice on cloudy tea. A chilly wind whipped gray waves into froth. Gulls and albatross floated high overhead, scanning and waiting.

Loyalist families crowded anxiously at the wharves, carts in tow, lining up for assignment. Men, women and children clutched their belongings, calling out to one another, as officers barked orders and sea captains jotted names in their logs.

Frigates rocked in the harbor, sails furled, the Union Jack crackling in the breeze. Launches, crowded with passengers, ferried Loyalists to the assigned bigger ships where they scrambled aboard, their trunks swung up after them. Others boarded small privateers docked at the wharves. The big transports lay further out in the harbor with the men of war, ships of the line, hatches closed over fifty or more guns. Eight thousand or so troops would board soon, as well as the camp women of the army and their children, as Boston was evacuated.

James read the names of some of the bigger ships. He could see the *Resolution,* the *Eagle,* the *Sea Venture.* The *Empress of Russia,* huge and weighty, loomed farther out, her stern higher than the mast of some smaller boats, and the *Neptune,* boasting carved figurines on her prow. Dozens of other British ships of the line filled the harbor, as well as smaller privateers hired by the British. *There must be over a hundred ships,* James thought.

Filing through the crowds with the prisoners, James saw Dr. John Jeffries and Reverend Badger with their families walking towards the wharves. They tugged behind them carts piled with belongings. They were friends of his father's, well-known figures in town and Loyalists too, he knew. Their faces seemed frightened and distracted. He recognized William Coffin, the apothecary, and his wife; the prominent merchant

Benjamin Faneuil with his family, whose brother Peter had built the meeting hall for the town; and Benjamin Gridley, the judge. There was Sheriff Joshua Loring too, his wife conspicuous by her absence, probably situated somewhere comfortably on General Howe's flagship the *Chatham*. Many of the Loyalists were Harvard graduates, respectable people of wealth and position throughout the community. For all these Loyalists, life was about to change.

No one knew where the fleet was going, but rumor held it might be New York City, where Loyalist support was strong, or perhaps Halifax, the nearest garrison of the British. Halifax, to the north on the coast of Nova Scotia, boasted a harbor and fort, the Citadel. "Whether it's New York or Halifax you're headed to, either way," sneered the ragged jailer who walked alongside James and his fellow prisoners, "you're not likely to see the light of day in a good long time, perhaps never. Halifax has just suffered a bout of smallpox, they say. Hundreds have died. If that doesn't get you, the gallows will."

Jostling through the crowds, bewildered townspeople strained to see where they could line up to find passage on a ship, children crying, women clutching their children. A blue-coated naval officer spotted the file of prisoners. "Here, this is your ship," he motioned to them. "Get over here to this plank."

"They've got a private room for you, likely—and it's far away from the other passengers," chuckled the jailer. James and the line of prisoners clanked into place on the wharf. A mid-sized frigate waited, sailors running about, hoisting cargo and shifting the ropes. A second line, this of Loyalists, formed at a plank farther down the length of the ship. Prisoners and Loyalists looked anxiously at the captain, a thick-set, middle-aged man with a swarthy complexion. He barked orders to the sailors loading the ship, impressive in his blue coat with gold buttons.

Looking down the wharf, suddenly James recognized his father. His heart pounding, James stared at his father and family, who seemed at once nearby and at the same time very, very far away. John Lovell was in the Loyalist line for this same ship, looking up at the captain, squinting to see in the bright sunlight, his hand framing his eyes. Wind whipped his black coat and tousled his fluffy white hair, straggling from under his cap. Next to him were James's mother and the girls, Rebecca, Mary, and Elizabeth—bonnets tight, capes buttoned, clutching bundles and looking with concern at the plank to the ship. His mother clung to Rebecca as if unsteady on her feet.

They had not seen him yet. James tried to wave, his shackled hands holding him back.

"Come on, move this way." A sailor yanked on the chain linking the prisoners, while the jailers pointed up towards the deck. "Prisoners in the hold—step lively now. We've got more ships to load."

James glanced again at his family, just down the wharf. Suddenly, his father turned and looked at him. Recognition lit his face, and he raised his hand in greeting. James could almost see the old man's trembling hand. "You, there, James, we are leaving…." he called. A rough tug on the chain almost caught James off-balance. James found himself jerked back into the line of prisoners marching up the plank into the ship. He could not answer his father, nor could he look back.

James figured it would be the last time he would ever see his father. Stubborn, set in his ways, the old teacher followed the promise of a king to another land, and never would return. *While they will travel on this same ship,* James thought, *certainly they will not travel in the hold, as will I. I wonder how my father feels about that.*

A sailor pointed to a hatch that opened to stairs leading down. "Down those stairs with you," he said to the prisoners.

Walking carefully down the steep steps, James followed the line of prisoners into the dark hold. A swinging lantern revealed chests and furniture stored along the sides of the ship. More storage pieces descended by swaying ropes through another hatch. A few cannon stood between the stacks of trunks, left from days when the frigate had seen combat. Grimy portholes let in daylight, their surfaces splashed regularly by salty gray waves.

"Sit down, all of you," bellowed the jailers. The prisoners collapsed on lumpy, straw-filled pallets. More furniture and trunks descended into the hold with thumps and bangs. Footsteps and shouts echoed from deck as Loyalists clambered aboard.

The prisoners sat and waited throughout the long day. At nightfall sailors removed their handcuffs and chains, then locked leg irons on each.

James and the other prisoners grimaced at the tight, uncomfortable leg irons and James tried to ease his to the narrowest part of his ankle. The hatch door closed and with it vanished the starlight. A greasy lantern hanging from the ship's beam swung back and forth, casting dim shadows on the men, the cannon, the bulky trunks and boxes stashed along the sides of the hold.

A cook's helper, his head wrapped in a ragged blue scarf, brought down a big pot of stew, trenchers, and spoons. He ladled the stew into rough wooden bowls for each. The prisoners began to eat hungrily. Then to James's surprise, the cook's helper approached James. Wiping his hand on his grimy apron, he handed James a bowl containing some tough, cooked beef, smoking hot. "This is for you. Don't ask who ordered it," he said, with a wink.

James took the bowl quickly, meeting the curious glances of the prisoners around him. He thought of his father, his family, confused and frightened, sharing the space with others crowded in the mid-deck. Perhaps his father had spoken a word with the cook, slipped him some coins, asked for meat for James. Surely no one else on this ship would have thought to request a special ration for him. James ate a few bites, hungrier than he thought he would be, then shared the rest with prisoners near him, seeing their jealous looks.

Wherever his father and family were going would be their new home, perhaps permanently. Father had chosen the king and the familiarity of royal rule. His lot and that of the other Loyalist families, many among them merchants, doctors, lawyers, craftsmen, would be far from the home they had always known. They were exiles from their country.

The creak of the capstan signaled the ship's move farther out into the harbor. There it pitched at anchor for days, which stretched into a week. It would be twenty days before the fleet set sail for the open sea. In the dark of the hold—close, smelly, airless—the prisoners endured the time disconsolately. Where were they going? James thought of the many letters he had sent, the appeals. Surely, an exchange could still be negotiated. Maybe he could be traded for Colonel Skene, the British officer that General Howe had wanted returned. Perhaps another exchange might be possible. Surely, General Howe must see reason. Frustrated, miserable, the stale air in the ship's hold already causing prisoners to cough spasmodically, the leg irons biting into his ankles at each movement, and his thin straw pallet jumping with fleas, James lay waiting like the others, as if they were animals tossed in the dark, counting the days.

Arrival Halifax

APRIL 9, 1776

The black, airless time in the hold seemed to James to go on forever. The stench of the refuse buckets overpowered even the salt smell of the sea, provoking many prisoners to sickness. During the day the only light in the dark confinement came from the small portholes. In the evening, one lantern, lit for a couple of hours during the evening meal, shed a light as dim and fitful as the dark of a hideous dream.

At length the anchor cranked up, sailors shouted, and the ship began to move. Any movement was better than the ceaseless waiting, James thought. "We're sailing northwards along the coast. That means we're going to Halifax," a jailer told them. He spat and winked at the prisoners. "The lot of you will swing from a rope in Halifax, at the Citadel, most likely." James's stomach turned over. The thought of going to Halifax was worse than going to New York. For one thing, it was farther away from his home. At Halifax, the site of a British garrison, it was unlikely that there would be any rescue from prison unless it came from an exchange. Very well, he resolved, if his only hope was to plea for exchange, he'd write more letters, just as soon as he could.

Once a horrific storm blew in, the wind churning up immense seas. Thunder ripped the night. Blue-black flashes of lightening glared through the portholes, brightening the dark hold for an instant. The ship tossed and bucked like a wild thing. James endured, he knew not how. He tried to stay clear of the cannon rolling wildly on their chain tethers as the ship pitched.

He prayed and recited the psalms he knew. About him prisoners cowered, seasick and miserable. A trunk fell off a stack and cracked a prisoner in the head, causing him to lose consciousness for a while. The night passed, and in the morning the storm calmed, an eerie violet shining through the window. The ship sailed on.

It seemed like nine days later, though James was not sure he had kept track well, that the prisoners heard shouts above. "Halifax! Land ho!" Some time after that, the frigate dropped anchor and took its rest in Halifax's deep, open harbor.

The next morning shouts and thumps signaled the departure of the Loyalists. The prisoners waited anxiously as the passengers above disembarked, descending rope ladders or riding on slings down to smaller boats. Finally, the hatch door opened, letting in pale sunshine and fresh, cold air, and sailors hoisted up the stored furniture and trunks. *Somewhere above are my father, mother, and the girls,* James thought. *I hope they have made a safe passage; I do hope everything goes well for them, despite our differences.* He remembered the special ration of beef from the cook's helper, more than likely a gift from his father, never repeated on the voyage.

At last the hatch above their stairway opened, and a couple of strange jailers appeared in the entrance. One was enormous, paunchy, his jowls shaking as he walked; the other tall, thin, gaunt. "You're the new lot for the Hollis Street Jail. We've just the place for you," the heavy jailer said, a malicious expression on his blubbery face. "Come now, hold out your hands."

The jailers clapped handcuffs on each in the group, linked them with a long chain, and removed the detested leg irons. As a group, the prisoners climbed the steep stairs out of their hold, blinking on deck in the light of day. They'd been sequestered in the dark bowels of the ship for over three weeks. Dirty, foul with lack of washing, they stared about the harbor and land like creatures from another world. They saw a harbor crowded with the British fleet from Boston. Over a hundred ships rocked on the waves.

"That's where you're going," the heavy jailer informed them, pointing to a varied collection of wooden buildings, the rows punctuated by a couple of white church spires. The buildings of Halifax stood scattered along the edge of the harbor beneath a rounded hill. From the summit of the hill fluttered the Union Jack over the fort called the Citadel, a rough stockade of logs fortified by earthworks. "Hold on. Here's your launch," the jailer said, motioning to a smaller boat rocking in the gray water below. The jailers removed the long connecting chain from their manacled hands, none too patiently, and the prisoners carefully climbed ladders swinging from the ship down to the launch.

The harbor throbbed with sailors, troops unloading from massive frigates, Loyalists stepping down ramps from launches to the docks. Furniture and trunks landed onshore, dumped unceremoniously. *Where would the thousand or more Loyalists go?* James wondered.

James could see off to one side a couple of enormous transports. From their decks the 17th Dragoons led horses, squealing and whinnying, down planks to the land. Their coats shiny and sleek, the animals looked better fed than many of the troops. Along with them soldiers unloaded tons of hay. From other big transports, troops led cattle and sheep down wide ramps, walking provisions for the royal army. Hundreds of redcoats surged down the narrow streets, boisterous and shouting, searching for a drink of rum after days on board.

Children and women belonging to the army disembarked the transports last, for though General Howe recognized their existence and arranged for their transportation, they did not count as full individuals, but instead were issued half a ration of military provisions each day. Yet who else but camp women would wash the clothes of the soldiers or tend to their wounds? And children came along where there were women. Those James could see looked pitiful, poorly clad against the cold March air, some with no shoes or coats. Children in their mothers' arms wore blankets only. The women shuffled off to side streets to beg lodging, in tents, barns, wherever they could find a roof.

On the rickety wharf, the jailers linked the prisoners in chains. Salt spray wet and chilled them as whitecaps smacked the piers. "Come. Lucky you, you don't have far to go," the flabby jailer said, smiling crudely, jerking on the chain. Like fish on a hook, the prisoners followed the jailer through the crowds. Loyalists frantically called, trying to locate their families and possessions. Troops burst out of the ships, swearing and shouting, eager to find grog shops. Animals bawled and cried as they were led off to pasture.

James did not see his family, though he knew they must be somewhere in the throng.

But he had more immediate worries. Bound and cuffed, the prisoners followed the jailers' lead a short distance uphill from the harbor. With a jerk on the chain, the jailers turned down dirty, frozen Hollis Street, parallel to the water. The group stopped in front of a long, low wooden building, set off by a stone walled yard running the length of the front. A rough, thrown-together affair, the Hollis Street Jail faced the harbor.

"Home, sweet jail," the heavy jailer proclaimed, throwing open the door. A few vagrants and thieves blinked at them from the recesses of the long, dark room. James and the other prisoners filed in and sat in a row while the jailers jerked off their handcuffs, at last. James rubbed his chaffed and bruised wrists.

"Watch it," warned a prisoner, swatting an invisible speck on his side. "Lice, everywhere."

"We're no strangers to lice," James said. "Thank you all the same." The vermin had been everywhere in Boston Jail. The men stretched and found a spot to sit down. The jailers stomped back in, bearing buckets of water, dried fish, and bread, dropping them rudely on the floor before the prisoners. Outside, the wind picked up, howling and roaring, snow filtering in through cracks in walls and windows.

The prisoners ate like starving beasts. The food gone, they found here and there on the wooden floor lumpy pallets. James collapsed on the rough sacking. At least the floor wasn't rocking, the walls not pitching. It would be days before he regained his land legs. He shut his eyes and fell into a deep, exhausted sleep.

Chapter 45

The Hollis Street Jail

APRIL 10, 1776

The tossing of the ship, a constant in the weeks since he'd been thrust into the hold of a privateer, had stopped. James opened his eyes. Of course, he was in the jail at Halifax, led here in chains last night from the ship. Wearily he rolled over. The uneven wooden floor was cold and clammy, but at least it was stable. Only once during the nightmare of the voyage had prisoners been allowed to walk on the upper deck of the ship. Loyalists, passengers on the ship, had eyed the prisoners curiously and then stayed away. James had not seen his father or family on deck, though he had looked.

He sat up. Around him men slept near the walls of a long room, maybe sixty feet in length. Pale sunshine poured in between cracks in the boards covering the windows. The roof pitched up sharply above him. At one time the structure must have been a house, James guessed, but the British had knocked the walls out, boarded up the windows, added a stout lock and bar to the heavy door, and created a jail.

For furnishings the room had a number of tubs for the men's relief, kept in various stages of overflowing. The smell was appalling, acrid and foul. The newly-arrived prisoners lay sleeping, exhausted from the voyage. Someone coughed harshly.

James walked to the window near the door and looked out between the cracks. Not far away lay the harbor, the tall masts of frigates and sloops dense as a forest, ships floating at anchor. The sun was rising, faint and nearly transparent, through heavy gray clouds. Wind churned the sea into whitecaps, and gulls swooped and cried above the surf.

A lovely lady walked into his view, dressed in a black cape, feather-trimmed bonnet, and black muff. A small spotted dog trotted beside her. He watched her mincing steps along the road in front of the wharves. She bent her head against the wind, the feathers blowing and bowing. For a minute she glanced in James's direction. He wondered why she was walking near the jail. Then she turned and walked out of sight.

Down the street, from the other direction, he heard cries and shouts. A large group was gathering out of James's view. He heard someone say loudly, "Line up, folks. Just a bit and we'll have food for you. Form a line, now."

A prisoner came and stood next to him at the window. "What are you listening to?" he asked.

"Someone's talking about food," James said. "He says the people out there should get into a line. There must be quite a crowd there."

"That's the Hollis Street food handout. This here's the Hollis Street Jail, and that's the food handout," the prisoner, an older man with a long, gray beard and rough features, explained. "The British have so many Loyalists and evacuees from Boston and the colonies they have to give them food. There's not enough in the town. Of course, you have to be pretty hungry to eat that food. Nasty, it is, I've heard. Not much better than what we get. Peelings and parings from the officers' quarters, rotten potatoes they won't eat, salt pork or salt cod. Still, it keeps body and soul together. Also, I've heard the prices for housing in Halifax are outrageous. People charge for a room what most folks elsewhere would pay for a mansion. At that rate it won't be long 'til the lot of the Loyalists are beggars, glad to get any food."

"The people of Halifax are, for the most part, on the side of neither the British nor the Americans," the older prisoner continued. "Some, to be sure, would like to see Halifax and Nova Scotia join the Americans, maybe even become a fourteenth colony. Like Malachy Salter, a merchant who, for a time, tried to get businessmen to boycott imports of British tea. But others are for the British, being they hold the stronger card here in Canada. Either way, they are for themselves, so charging huge prices to the Loyalists doesn't hurt them a thing."

James nodded his thanks to the older fellow for his explanation, left the window, and hunched down on his pallet. Maybe his parents and sisters would be in those lines. His father had never been rich, and with the sudden evacuation probably had not had time to sell many of his household belongings. Besides, with so many leaving, who would have wanted to buy them? He thought of his family fondly for a moment, then realized they had made their choice; they would have to live with their surroundings. Had his father not been so determined that British ways were always the best, they would not be here. As a Loyalist, John Lovell had left Boston along with the other twelve hundred who had made the same decision: they thought that life in Boston would no longer be safe for those who had sided with the British. With an effort, James shut his mind to his family's plight and resolved to consider his own difficulties.

The ruckus from the lines outside died away. Calm descended on the street while a ray of sunlight, sparkling and warm, fell from the window crack above him on the men, some still sleeping, others stretching or sitting up, wondering what the day would bring. James thought of Mary and his children, far away in Boston. He remembered with gratitude Dr. Gardner, who had helped Mary with lodging, and Joseph Trumbull, who had taken care of two of his boys. He hoped fervently all were doing well. At least his own health appeared satisfactory. He did not suffer the persistent cough that some endured, nor did he have the sores that came with scurvy, a common problem for sailors and prisoners. The stomach distress he had suffered in the Boston Stone Jail had at length subsided. His wool coat, though filthy from constant wear, was serviceable, if home to a family of fleas, and his shoes whole if worn. He would persist, he thought defiantly. Whatever it took, he would appeal to even the most important general or official. He would be freed.

Chapter 46

New Arrivals in Halifax

AUGUST 5, 1776

Morning light shone through the boarded-up windows of the large jail room. The summer's heat had been oppressive for weeks. Smells ripened in the close, stagnant air inside the jail room, causing the prisoners to long for fresh air or a change of scene. James stood to stretch. Some poor wretch had taken sick in the night, groaning and crying; of the thirty-four prisoners in close confinement in the Halifax prison, most had scurvy and many suffered violent stomach distress.

Shouts sounded outside, then thumps near the door, causing all to turn and wonder.

A rough voice outside bellowed, "Stand back all, while we open the door."

James recognized the voice of the paunchy warden. The flabby bully took pleasure in kicking and abusing the weakest of the prisoners. "Out of my way," he would bark, stomping through the crowded floor with buckets of water.

The heavy door swung open; there in the bright sunlight of the summer morning stood one of the tallest, sturdiest men James had ever seen. He was dressed in what had once been a fine suit of dark silk, cut in a military double-breasted style. Over it was a dirty jacket of deerskin, fringed and worn. His bearded face was haggard and unwashed, his hair gray and long.

The large man stepped into the jail, ducking his head. The warden held the door open, looking with some amazement at the new inmate.

Behind him filed about a dozen other prisoners, all handcuffed, their dress filthy, unkempt, disheveled. They were followed by a group of guards carrying rifles.

"Stand at ease, ye devils, whilst I unlock your irons," commanded the paunchy warden, recovering his voice. He unfastened the giant's rusty handcuffs. The big prisoner rubbed his hands, then waved his arms in wide circles, looking about him with a pleasant expression.

Men sitting against the rough pine walls or lying on the stone floor gazed in curiosity at the new arrival. Even the guards stopped and stared in astonishment. He walked the line of excrement tubs in the middle of the sixty-foot structure, surveying the group in the thin light that shone through the cracks in the boarded-up windows. The warden unlocked the other prisoners, then turned with the guards and left.

The new prisoners each found a place, crowding in with others in the already-packed room. The big man walked over by James to a vacant space on the floor. He eyed James intently, seemed to approve, and then sat down, moving with ease for one so big, James thought.

"I am Ethan Allen of the Green Mountain boys, and a reviled prisoner of His Majesty's troops these several months," he introduced himself. "I've been to England and back, but they haven't hung me yet." Ethan Allen fixed bright brown eyes on James and held out his hand in greeting.

James met Ethan's handshake, marveling at the size of the man's hand. "I am James Lovell, of Boston. I am a teacher, or up to the time of the first shots between the British and the patriot cause I was one. I have been imprisoned now for over a year, here in Halifax going on six months. I wait every day for a return to my home through an exchange of prisoners. General Washington has written to me more than once and I hope soon the exchange will be effected."

Ethan Allen motioned to the prisoners who had come into the jail with him. "This is Captain Francis Proctor of Philadelphia," he said, introducing a pale seaman with a thin mustache who bore on his face the sores of scurvy. Francis Proctor acknowledged the introduction with a nod.

James nodded back in greeting, then looked about him at the fellow prisoners he knew. "I'll introduce you to some who are here in this prison. This is Consider Howland," he said, "and Jacob Taylor. Master Howland was commander of the privateer brig *Washington* and Jacob Taylor was his mate. They are waiting for an exchange to be freed, as am I."

"I am pleased to meet you all. I am in good company," asserted Ethan Allen. He nodded to each, and the prisoners smiled back.

James motioned to other men watching and listening from the sides of the room. "Here are some others you should meet. Richard Carpenter of Boston, Misters Bigelow, Kemp, Peak, and Sessions, all of whom fought at Bunker Hill."

The men nodded. "Pleased to meet you," said one.

"Here is Corporal Cruise and this is Cornelius Turner, both riflemen at Bunker Hill." The two men both greeted Ethan Allen. "There's Corporal Jeremiah Low, of Fredericksburg, John Gray of Arlington, Barnabas Castle of Saratoga, and Preston Denton, from Stillwater." James indicated several reclining forms in the back of the long room. "The sickness has them at present, but they'll be all right."

"I would like to share my story with you," Ethan Allen said. "It is a tale for strong constitutions, but I take it you have that!" He laughed heartily and the listeners smiled, nodding agreement.

"Not long after the militia at Lexington and Concord routed the British, my boys and I were at our favorite tavern, the Catamount, in the New Hampshire Grants, enjoying a drink or two of stone walls," Ethan Allen began. He evidently loved telling a story, for he warmed to his subject enthusiastically. "The Catamount is so named because outside the tall building is a pole bearing a mounted wildcat, warning anyone from New York or New Hampshire that we are independent and this is our country."

Ethan smiled and rubbed his hands together emphatically. James had heard about Ethan Allen, this bigger-than-life frontier woodsman and warrior. He and his Green Mountain Boys ranged the land west of New Hampshire, called the New Hampshire Grants, which were claimed by both New Hampshire and New York. The Green Mountain Boys wanted no part of either New Hampshire or New York. They wanted independence.

"We were talking at the Catamount about the war that was coming. I said, 'Boys, we should take Fort Ticonderoga.' This old fort was held by the British on the western shore of Lake Champlain. The ammunition, cannon, and guns left from the French and Indian War kept there would make a great addition to the Continental Army, I thought." He chuckled at the memory.

"Before I went to bed I told the men, by God, I'd like to take that fort. Next day, my brother Herman reported that the authorities in Connecticut had asked the Green Mountain Boys to attack Fort Ticonderoga. Which was exactly what I was thinking," Ethan added, winking and smiling.

"So we called up the Boys. Some came from Hartford, old soldiers from the French and Indian wars who knew the country well. Some settlers I called as we went. They grabbed their flintlocks and their bullets; I told them 'We're going on a big wolf hunt.'"

"On May 8 we had our council, just twenty miles from Fort Ticonderoga. I was elected head of the army. But we needed boats to get over to the west shore of the lake. That's when naturally we thought of the land and holdings of Colonel Philip Skene. He was a retired British officer who had rowboats, scows, and even a schooner. I sent some thirty men under a friend of mine, Sam Herrick, and told them to take the boats over to the eastern shore."

Colonel Skene, James thought. He sat up and listened with interest. What a coincidence. That was the retired British officer for whom General Howe had wanted him to be exchanged.

Men listened spellbound all around, caught up in Ethan Allen's tale. The August heat settled, bringing the stench in the dark room to rich fumes. Flies buzzed and bit continually, while fleas scampered about, causing one and then another of the men to jump or scratch.

"I sent a runner through the north," Ethan Allen continued. "He ran over sixty miles in a day and a night, calling the Green Mountain Boys to come to the fight. I had sent Noah Phelps as a scout to Fort Ticonderoga; he had gained admittance by pretending to want a shave. You know military men—they always have a razor about. Noah found out easily that there were fewer than fifty soldiers at the Fort. It was not in the best shape, outer walls broken down, no protection at all.

"Hiding in the timber, we were watching closely for the boats that Sam Herrick was supposed to bring from Colonel Skene's place, when here comes the gaudiest, most elegant officer you've ever seen, riding on a fine horse with plumed helmet and all, directly from Secretary of War Mott.

His name is Colonel Benedict Arnold, and he tells us that he'd been put in charge of our expedition. That was a lie, as we found out later, but naturally we paid him no mind. I said I'd been elected leader, but if he wanted to march with me that would be fine. So we had two leaders for our group, but naturally, I was the real leader." Ethan Allen laughed and the others nodded knowingly.

"We commandeered two boats and pushed off with eighty-three men in the early morning. I gave my boys a stout talk before they reached the fort. I told them they must move quickly for the attack to succeed. The men surely knew that attacking a British post could mean a hanging, yet none hesitated.

"We moved silently through the trees. When we reached the dark fort, I climbed first over the broken wall. A sentry fired at me and ran; I hit another redcoat advancing on me with my sword. He begged 'Quarter, quarter!' and I told him to take me to his commander.

"He led me up the steep wooden stairs; there at the top was Lieutenant Jocelyn Feltham, the second in command. Colonel Feltham had been surprised in his sleep and stood in his doorway embarrassed as could be without his breeches on." The prisoners listening broke into shouts of laughter at this.

Ethan Allen continued. "Behind me were Colonel Benedict Arnold, who did look right fierce, even if I knew better, and a dozen of my men with their muskets, yelling for blood.

"We must have been a frightening sight. But the British second in command held his ground and showed his metal. 'By what authority have you entered His Majesty's fort?' he demanded.

"I answered, 'In the name of the Great Jehovah and the Continental Congress.' I've been told these words were remembered, as I've heard them said back to me from soldiers who were there and even soldiers who weren't there."

James shook his head in amazement. No doubt this giant's words would be remembered, as bold as brass, taking the British fort in the first offensive move of the war.

"When I got nowhere with Lieutenant Feltham, I began battering down the door behind him. Pretty quick here comes Captain Delaplace. And he is fully dressed."

James and the others listening laughed again. Ethan Allen was certainly a diversion. James couldn't remember when he'd heard such a tale.

"Meanwhile, the rest of my boys down below had broken into the rooms, taken the arms, and rounded up the redcoats. We put under guard thirty-eight soldiers and twenty-four women and children. Not only that, but we found quite a bit of good strong liquor and rum. Not a bad day's work," Ethan added.

"I had some more complaints about my command from that Colonel Benedict Arnold with his fancy plumed hat, but Secretary of War Mott fixed that up for me and wrote out my commission. I was to keep command of the garrison of Ticonderoga until I had further orders from the colony of Connecticut or the Continental Congress." The men nodded approval. Some stared with open expressions of awe at Ethan Allen.

"My friend Sam Herrick, meanwhile, had taken control of Colonel Philip Skene's property down the lake, including the settlement of Skenesborough and a schooner. Now we had abundant vessels to deliver all arms and cannon to the east side of the lake. Later, Henry Knox, who had been sent by General Washington all the way from Boston to take them, retrieved the cannon and arms. He, brave soul, hauled them by oxen over the snowy Berkshire Mountains to General Washington. The Continentals used them to blast the British out of Boston and end the siege. Wasn't that a hell of a way to serve your country?" Ethan Allen laughed with delight at the bravery of Henry Knox and his own part in getting cannon to the American militia.

James well remembered the rounds from cannon that shook the Boston Stone Jail night and day in the final days before the prisoners left with the fleet to sail to Halifax. He shivered as if the thunderous blasts were smashing buildings nearby again. Now he knew Ethan Allen of the Green Mountain Boys, and had heard his story of how he had freed the cannon used by the Americans and made them available to Henry Knox.

Ethan Allen continued, "Within a few days, I sent the officers from the fort as prisoners to Connecticut's governor. Major Philip Skene, meanwhile, had returned from London with a commission as governor of Ticonderoga and Montreal, intending to raise a regiment of Canadians against the Americans. He was captured by Connecticut patriot militia, escaped, and was recaptured. He is now in American hands in Connecticut."

James listened to this explanation with interest. "Is Philip Skene a colonel or a major?" he asked.

"I meant colonel, since he was generally called that, though I believe at one time he was a major. And sometimes he is known as governor, since he controlled quite a bit of land around Skenesborough," Ethan Allen said with a smile. "Why would you ask?"

"General Howe had suggested I be exchanged for Colonel Philip Skene," James said. "That exchange fell through, but I assume it was the same British officer."

"Undoubtedly one and the same," Ethan Allen agreed, "and with any luck it may still happen." He looked at James thoughtfully for a moment.

"To resume my tale," Ethan Allen continued, "through one thing and another, sticking up for the rights of the Green Mountain Boys and fending off the claims of New Hampshire and New York to our lands, I ended up being captured by the British when I tried to take Montreal."

"You tried to take Montreal?" James's eyes grew big at the thought. Ethan Allen was either amazingly brave or a fool.

Ethan Allen laughed genially. Everything about him was big, James thought, even his laugh, which was so infectious Francis Proctor, John Howland, and others joined in despite their miserable surroundings. Some of the sicker men lying in the back of the room looked up in wonder.

"Yes, but I would have had help if those that promised to come hadn't failed to show up. Then, I might have succeeded. Overall it was a scheme that had less than perfect merits, and it got me captured. I was taken to New York and then to England. Though they threatened to hang me, they didn't, and I was given this fine suit of clothes and sent back here."

Ethan Allen paused in his story to take a drink of water from the nearby bucket, using the dipper set in it. He wiped his mouth with the back of his hand and continued. "I must say, though, this Captain Montague who has the charge of the ship I've been on is the most cruel and uncivil person in all of the British navy. Me and several of the prisoners had the scurvy desperately; I wrote Captain Montague repeatedly, begging for a redress of our grievances, but got no answer. Finally he ordered the guards not to bring him any more letters."

"I well know what it is like to be at a loss for help or decent treatment of any kind," James said, nodding agreement. "I was put in prison in Boston back on June 29 of 1775, and all the time since then I've had no formal hearing or charge. That's unfairness for you."

He added, "I have written to General Washington more than once, to the Congress, to the Massachusetts Council, to the *London News*, to the diplomat Arthur Lee, to General Gage and General Howe—in short, to anyone with authority who might be able to help. I am still waiting for a solution."

Francis Proctor, Howland, and Taylor all nodded. Their stories, though different, all told of mistreatment, neglect, and abuse since becoming prisoners of the British.

Francis Proctor said, "I once was with the English service. Since then I have changed my allegiance. For no good reason I was thrown into irons when first I came on board the *Mercury*, the vessel which bore us here until we were transferred to the foul prison sloop. There I was kept under close confinement for three months before we arrived."

Ethan Allen nodded sympathetically. "Aye, they're a sorry lot, and they treat prisoners as badly as ever could be," he said.

Suddenly, the door opened and a gust of fresh, hot August air blew in to the crowded room, easing the stench of illness and waste.

Ethan Allen stood. More than a head higher than any there, he looked with curiosity towards the open door. James stood up near his new friend.

"Come, yard's open," shouted the paunchy guard. The prisoners filed out the door, down the steps to the narrow yard confined within stone walls. Under the hot summer sun, on a wooden bench, waited the pail of water, basin of bread, and cold potatoes that were both breakfast and lunch. "Have at it, and a pox on you all," said the guard maliciously, slamming and locking the iron gate shut as he left.

Chapter 47

Unexpected Help in Jail

AUGUST 6, 1776

"The first thing we'd best do," Ethan Allen said in his energetic way early the next morning, "is to write to the Commander of Halifax, General Massey, and let him know of the foul treatment we are enduring."

"Aye, and petition him for some vegetables here before the scurvy takes us out," said Francis Proctor, whose flushed face ran with sores.

"I have paper," said James. He produced some from his bag and laid it on a board, smoothing out the creases. "You'd think they would have more respect for Americans. After all, we just declared our independence," he added slyly, a twinkle in his eyes.

All the prisoners had heard that the Declaration had been written and read aloud in cities throughout the colonies. General Washington had commanded it be read aloud to the American forces in New York on July 9. The stirring words had strengthened the hearts of the army. Filled with enthusiasm, crowds had pulled down royal statues, even one of King George that was later melted into musket balls. A recently arrived prisoner had brought the news to the Hollis Street Jail.

The prisoner had pulled a fragment of paper from his pocket. "Come, listen to the news," he had said. "The colonies have declared their independence." With difficulty he read from the scrap:

When in the Course of human events, it becomes necessary for one people to dissolve the political bands which have connected them with another, and to assume among the powers of the earth, the separate and equal station to which the Laws of Nature and of Nature's God entitle them, a decent respect to the opinions of mankind requires that they should declare the causes which impel them to the separation. We hold these truths to be self-evident, that all men are created equal, that they are endowed by their Creator with certain unalienable Rights, that among these are Life, Liberty and the pursuit of Happiness. —That to secure these rights…. .

He stumbled over "political" and "separation," but others in the group came to his assistance. "That is all I could get," he apologized. "I tore it from a posting." When he finished, there were shouts and cheers from the other prisoners.

"We have declared ourselves independent," said James, "and by the grace of God we may yet be so. But whether or not our British captors yet have respect for us, we do need fresh vegetables. We are in great danger of serious illness. The confinement of so many prisoners in such close space together with those who are ill causes us all danger of infection. Smallpox is once again raging in the town. One case in here and we would all be stricken. Those ill should be taken to the hospital."

Ethan Allen continued, "A further problem is in our jail we have not only gentlemen, officers, and political prisoners on parole or awaiting exchange, but also privates and those of lower ranks. Mixing classes in a military jail is uncommon and against the laws and customs of nations. We should be separated, and those of a gentlemanly status should receive better treatment."

James nodded in agreement. "We can add a request for that better treatment to our formal complaint."

"Yard's open, breakfast served," the tall, gaunt jailer called out. He opened the heavy door and the men filed out to the dry little yard. James looked over the wall at the ocean, sparkling in the August sun. The spars and masts of ships moored at dock loomed high, though the British fleet under General Howe had left in June for New York, leaving only a handful of troops to hold the Citadel. Flocks of gulls wheeled and cried overhead.

The men gathered around the bench, where the jailer had placed breakfast and lunch. Today, as usual, the food was bread, old, dry, and moldy, and a bucket of warm water. There was also a bucket with odds and ends of cooked potatoes and potato peelings. Ethan and James helped themselves to chunks of stale bread and a handful of potato scraps.

"I must tell you of one happy circumstance on that cursed prison sloop commanded by Captain Montague," said Ethan genially as he and James sat down in the sparse shade of a linden that overhung the prison side of the yard wall. The sand and thin grass of the yard were home to armies of red ants who crept up the pant legs of the unhappy prisoners. James slapped as they talked. Still, the open yard was a great relief compared to being inside the dark prison. James enjoyed the company of Ethan Allen. He seemed able to show good spirits no matter the situation. After months in jail, being around a cheerful individual felt like an inspiring tonic to James.

"Our voyage from England saw us suffering from boils, weak from stomach distress," Ethan Allen continued. "Captain Montague would do nothing for us. As we neared these shores, a prisoner saw at the side of the ship a canoe of Indians. He bought from them two quarts of strawberries, in exchange giving them nearly all his money. He ate all the strawberries and was so much improved in a short while he seemed to be nearly recovering.

"The others of us prisoners tried to get more fruit in the same way, but we could not. Then at length the doctor's mate of the *Mercury* came on board and gave me a vial of smart drops that I shared with the others. Though fresh vegetables were still needed to cure us, the drops helped, and for some men may have saved their lives."

Ethan continued in a lively manner, being in a talkative mood as he often was. *What a blessing those smart drops must have been,* James thought. He wondered what they were made of. Even so, fresh fruit or vegetables alone would cure the dreaded scurvy, which caused fever, painful sores, and even loss of teeth to afflicted individuals. The men sitting near James listened closely to Ethan Allen's story, nodding their understanding.

"I noticed our guard, Lieutenant Russell, seemed to have feelings of compassion towards us, for he often inquired of our welfare and brought us fresh water. Lieutenant Russell, in a friendly and polite manner, inquired after my well-being and showed anger at the rude and cruel treatment we were given. At length Lieutenant Russell conferred with the ship's surgeon. Together they reported the deplorable condition of the prisoners to Governor Arbuthnot of Nova Scotia. He had us moved to this jail on the following day.

"I am not sure this is the better place, yet," Ethan Allen added loudly, looking about the prison yard and its high stone wall, "but perhaps our situation will change. We were on the prison ship for six weeks. The sickest of us were taken to the hospital, while any Canadians in our group were put to work in His Majesty's service. Twelve others from that prison ship were judged well enough to be taken to this prison along with me."

Ethan sighed with disgust, considering the bare yard running the length of the long house with its boarded-up windows, pitched roof, rough wooden walls. James followed his glance and shivered in the hot August sun. He pulled a maggot out of the remains of his bread, inspected the rest, and took another bite.

"You may not believe it," Ethan Allen continued, "but this shabby prison is preferable to that foul prison sloop. Also, consider the heat of August can be born better here than the freezing cold of winter, which will soon be upon us and cause many prisoners' deaths. In fact, we'd best be away from here before winter."

Just then a barking sounded outside the prison yard. James stood on the bench in the yard and looked over the stone wall. A little spotted dog on the street below yapped fiercely at a black cat that crouched on the ground, hissing but otherwise unafraid. At the dog's side was the most beautiful lady James had seen in months. Her light blue, ruffled dress was stylishly adorned with lace. Her hair was piled up in an ornate coiffure, and two darkened beauty spots set off her face, telltale signs that beneath the stylish dots lay the scars of smallpox. He suddenly remembered an earlier glimpse of a lady dressed in black when he had first arrived at Halifax. Could this be the same woman? While he watched, she pulled out an ivory pick from a pocket and delicately poked into her piled hair. *Lice,* thought James, *I'll bet anything she's scratching.*

"Come, Sparky," the woman said. "We must be on our way." Sparky ignored her and continued his barking.

Ethan stood beside James on the bench. "Hello, Madam," he said politely.

"Oh, hello," the lady responded uncertainly. She peered up at the wall to see who was speaking.

"I am Ethan Allen of the Green Mountain Boys. This is James Lovell of Boston, a scholar and a schoolteacher."

"It is good to meet you both, though I cannot see you well," the lady answered cheerfully.

"Step up on that wagon to your right and I believe you'll be able to look over this fence and into the yard. Then you will be able to see us," Ethan replied.

The lady did so, dragging the little dog with her, ignoring its plaintive barks.

"Oh, my yes, I can see you," she said a minute later, perched on the seat of the wagon. She peered under her parasol at James, Ethan, and the other prisoners. "Are you all quite well?"

"No, madam, we are not," said James firmly. "We are in need of much better food than we are getting and that right away, for some of us are growing weaker by the day and are in desperate need of nutrition."

"Will they let me bring you food? I am Mrs. Blaeden. My husband runs a store here in Halifax and keeps us well supplied. I am a member of the St. Paul's Christian Charity Association. I am sure the Association would help me bring you some food."

James looked at the corpulent prison guard sitting on the steps of the jail. His broad sword rested on his knees and he dozed in the warm sunlight.

"They will allow it, Madam. They figure that any food we get is that much less they must give us. We would most surely be in your debt. It would be a true act of Christian charity. We would divide it amongst our friends, many of whom are awaiting a just and deserved parole," said James.

"Any food, particularly vegetables, fruit, and meat, would be very welcome," added Ethan Allen.

"Then I will endeavor to bring you some food, you may be sure," Mrs. Blaeden responded. "You poor wretches, so far from your country. I am

Canadian but understand that we have, in some ways, a common enemy, though I shall not speak of that at this time." She climbed daintily down from the wagon and turned to walk down the street. "Come, Sparky," she said, leading her yapping charge behind.

The prison guard woke up. "Come down from there," he said indignantly to James, standing up and shaking his musket threateningly.

"I am," James responded. He glanced at Ethan Allen as he stepped down from his bench, grateful he had joined in encouraging Mrs. Blaeden to bring provisions. The big Green Mountain Boy was a friendly spirit in a barren place, James thought. *Energetic, confident, and a fighter for his cause, he is a companion when one is needed. And yes, I think fresh lettuce or carrots would be a welcome change,* he thought.

Chapter 48

Surviving the Hollis Street Jail

August 7, 1776

The next day, James, Ethan Allen, and the other prisoners had the freedom of the yard in the early morning. Breakfast consisted not only of moldy bread and cold potatoes, but a couple of raw onions, which Ethan said were quite advisable for curing scurvy.

A sudden barking of a dog again brought them quickly to the fence. There was Mrs. Blaeden, Sparky at her side, and behind her two older women, shielded from the hot sun with parasols, and followed by a black servant with a wheelbarrow. "We have brought you something to eat," she said. "Will you arrange it that we may come in?"

Ethan and James exchanged glances. "We will see what we can do. Please be patient, Mrs. Blaeden. This may take just a minute."

Ethan walked over to the guard, who looked up from his bench at the tall figure towering over him. "See here, we have three kind women outside who want to give us some provisions. What do you think? You'd let them in, wouldn't you?"

The guard scratched his head. "I don't know. The next thing you'll want is for me to open the gate and let you help her bring the foodstuffs in. They may have written a Declaration of Independence down in Philadelphia, but that nonsense doesn't apply to you. But maybe her servant could come in if first you all go into the jail. As to the food—the less we have to haul to you the better, and you'll share it with me, mark my words."

Ethan whistled and all the prisoners in the yard looked up. "Come, boys," Ethan Allen said. "If we're in the jail, the good women outside of the St. Paul Christian Charity Society can bring us our dinner." The prisoners cheered and followed him into the Hollis Street Jail. The guard locked the door, his keys jangling.

Then he sauntered over to the iron gate and unlocked it. The servant pushed the wheelbarrow in through the gate. "You'd better not come in," the jailer said to Mrs. Blaeden and her friends. "It's not fittin' in here for women."

They nodded. "We'll wait outside," Mrs. Blaeden said. The guard slammed the gate shut and immediately locked it.

The servant unloaded the wheelbarrow. On the bench he laid out boxes of cold baked fish, carrots, apples, loaves of bread, and two bottles of wine. "Help yourselves," he said. "Compliments of Mrs. Blaeden, her husband, and the St. Paul's Christian Charity Society."

The prisoners inside the jail, peering through the chinks in the boarded up windows, gasped when they saw the spread.

"Tell your mistress and her friends thanks," the guard said. "You'd better leave now." The servant bowed and left through the gate.

The guard picked up a couple of apples and a bottle of wine for himself, then looked over the food slowly, munching on one of his apples. In no apparent haste, he turned, opened the jail door, and let the prisoners out. Ethan eyed the guard calmly, then stood on the bench to look over the wall. The guard glanced at the huge man towering over him and looked away, pretending to ignore him. However, he kept a firm hold on his musket.

Over the fence Ethan Allen said, "We send our thanks, Madam." Mrs. Blaeden curtsied and dipped her parasol in acknowledgment. "If you could bring more tomorrow, it would be ever so much appreciated."

"I'll certainly try to be here. It is a pleasure to help you. We believe in helping others at St. Paul's, whether Americans or British. Good day," Mrs. Blaeden responded. The other women smiled and nodded.

"Come, Sparky," she said. The three women turned and followed the servant with the wheelbarrow down the street, Sparky trotting behind on his leash.

"There goes an angel of mercy," Ethan Allen said, helping himself to fish and bread. "She may save us yet."

The prisoners ate until nothing was left, then stretched out in the shade of the jail, the door open to fresh breeze from the ocean. Times like this were hard to come by. James's stomach for once was content, and he shut his eyes.

He thought of his wife and children and hoped they were all right. True, he had written Mary, but it was unlikely any letter from her would be delivered to him. In fact, little word had come from Boston, but with General Howe and the troops gone, life had probably returned to something like a normal state. The Continental Congress was meeting in Philadelphia, and General Washington with the Continental Army was gathering at New York, preparing to defend the city from General William Howe's army and his brother Admiral Richard Howe's fleet.

The guard's comment about the Declaration of Independence had been said in sarcasm, but in truth the Declaration was the most binding statement to come out of the conflict. James felt proud of it and all it stood for. He was glad Congress had made a statement to the world about the intentions of the Americans.

In June he had written to Arthur Lee, foreign diplomat for the Americans, but had not yet heard back from him. He still had hopes that General Washington would arrange some kind of exchange for him. Every day of waiting was a hardship. Surely he would not have much longer to wait now.

Chapter 49

Scurvy, Fleas, and Letters in Jail

September 30, 1776

James's stomach growled. He rolled over on his pallet in the dim evening light and clenched his teeth in distress. He had managed to eat portions of the bread and potatoes brought by the guard in the morning, but months of scanty food had worn him down. Mrs. Blaeden, who with the ladies of the St. Paul's Christian Charity Society had brought baskets of nourishment daily for six weeks, had ceased her visits. A terrific storm beat on their wooden jail for days, driving freezing rain in rivulets down the cracks in the walls and spattering through the boarded-up broken windows. It was nearly impossible for James to find a dry place on which to place his pallet. It was also chilly, as apparently the water within the communal buckets would have to freeze over before the warden thought it cold enough to warrant some sticks of wood to burn in the fireplace for warmth.

A month ago the doctor had visited their jail, examining those who were ill with scurvy and dysentery, ordering that more vegetables be added to their daily allowance. Since then, cooked potatoes were provided frequently, with carrots on rare occasions. Ethan Allen's letter to Governor Arbuthnot had proven somewhat effective.

Yet now illness once more plagued the prisoners. The tubs lined up in the middle of the room saw such frequent use that their contents overflowed. Prisoners afflicted with diarrhea stayed up nightly, their moans and complaints waking James and others from sleep. In the storm, the jailers refused to try to empty the tubs, so their contents sloshed in puddles on the floor.

An older inmate, taken sick, coughed night after night; wracking, deep coughs that kept the crowded jail mates awake. Tuberculosis, James thought. The paunchy guard ignored their requests for treatment for the sufferer.

"What? Take such as him to hospital? When the hospital is filled with the smallpox and funerals are a daily event, dozens dying of disease and doctors laboring to keep up with the flow? He's better off here." The guard slammed the door.

"We're political prisoners, mind," Ethan Allen said, looking at James. "We're not criminals. And we're valuable for exchange, don't forget that. They'll listen, in time. We need to write more letters, so no one forgets we are here."

"You'd just think that they'd want to keep us alive, in the meantime," James fumed. "General Massey, our head jailer, is taking his time with the arrangement. But yes, we'll write letters."

James took out paper. He scratched his head and flicked off a few fleas. The incessantly-biting insects scurried everywhere, from the fashionable hairdressing of Mrs. Blaeden to the worn shoes of the prisoners. In the dim morning light he wrote to the Boston selectmen:

> *The treatment of prisoners here is not only scandalous by neglecting all distinction of rank but is also murderous by joining the nuisances and infection of a Hospital to the confinement and common miseries of a jail. That we have been even thirty-six and are now thirty in a single leaky room, the floor our bedstead, a thin flock bed and pair of blankets being the best provision for two, one has lingered and died in our sight through want of proper nourishment and one has been long near the point of death, not allowed the comfort of removal to a convenient place of attendance while several with fluxes go in a continual rotation to a tub through the night when we*

*are close locked in....To judge by appearances my life has
been aimed at in what I have been obliged to undergo.*

He folded the paper and added the address. The heavy jailer snatched
his letters from his hand carelessly, and James could only hope they were
sent. In any case, it was all he could do. He shut his eyes.

Lying back on his pallet, somewhere between sleep and daydreams,
he thought of his family. His father might be huddled in a rude apartment
in Halifax by a wood-burning stove, his mother nearby knitting stockings,
their purse of money growing lighter every day with the expense of basic
needs. Who knows, they may have been among those crowds receiving handouts of food from the British in the streets last summer. Their
crowded rooms would not be well-furnished, since they could only have
brought the basic items from home; his father's small writing desk, most
likely; and a couple of bedsteads. His father would probably not be able
to teach. He had done that for forty-eight years, and starting over in a new
place would be most difficult.

Mary and Elizabeth, bright, outgoing souls, would do well. Likely they
had made friends among the Anglican congregation of St. Paul's in Halifax
and would enjoy dinners out, cards, maybe even skating. Rebecca, more of
a homebody, would be helping her parents with chores, cooking, spinning,
cleaning. But both parents would be grieving the loss of their pleasant home
in Boston, the furnishings acquired over the years, the comfort of social
standing achieved through hard work and nurtured ideals. His mother, in
particular, probably longed for her fine china and silver candlesticks.

Halifax, as far as James could tell, was a rough frontier settlement, a
few merchants prospering with sales of rum to soldiers and sailors, while
blacks and Chebucto Indians made do with manual labor, fishing, or begging. In fact, it was far from the scholarly atmosphere of Boston. Yet his
parents had chosen their lives, he thought, remaining loyal to the rule of
Britain rather than accepting change. Now they were essentially refugees
in a new country. He could do nothing to help them.

The prisoners slept on, though some stirred and rolled in weariness.
James sat up and once more took out paper from his small bag, found his
ink and quill. He must write, must get help. To whom could he appeal that

he had not yet written? He had sent letters to General Gage and General Howe, two letters to Major Cane while in the Boston Jail, and then a second petition to General Howe. He had written to the Massachusetts Council and to General George Washington. The ink was scarcely dry on his letter to the Boston selectmen.

In desperation he began before the twilight faded. He wasn't sure to whom he would send this letter, but writing down the dilemma facing him seemed most important.

> *A parent and head of a large family in Boston, I was induced to tarry there while others fled from apprehended danger, in the early months of last year. An absolute decision of providence fixed my wavering intentions in April, and ties of honour succeeded to prevent my after removal. By the first, I mean the birth of my eighth child....*

"A Parent and Head of a Large Family."
Excerpt from letter. *Houghton Harvard Library*

> *Surely someone must see the unfairness of my imprisonment. In fact, General Howe is destroying my dependents, leaving them with no one to provide for them, despite the safeguards for someone not in the military written into the Mutiny Bill,* he thought to himself, furious at the realization. His pen moved on.

In August I even expressed my desire to be sent even in irons to Britain to be tried at Concert Hall by officers I had never seen.

'Tis not as a rebel that I am here. Other well-known rebels, the Select men and various Committee men, are with their wives and children while I was dragged away to Halifax.

I had broken no law, civil or military, at the time of my commitment. If my conduct was injurious, why was I ordered to depart the town?

His handwriting trailed off. James could write no more. He was tired and weary of the painful unfairness and helplessness of being in prison. Writing his thoughts down eased his torment for a while, but in the end would do little good if the right authorities did not see his words. He put the letter away to be finished another day.

Sometimes the thought of freedom, his family, his hopes to help the patriots in the war going on, seemed a distant flame burning on a dark night. He set his goal on that distant flame and tried to ignore the darkness all about him, resting his head as best he could on his thin pallet as he sought the blessed relief of sleep.

Chapter 50

Freedom: Going Home

NOVEMBER 5, 1776

James leaned on the railing of the upper deck of the *Lark*, watching the sun descend in clouds of orange and violet. Fresh wind blew on his face, and he inhaled deeply the scent of the sea, of lands beyond, of currents flowing across the ocean. Gusts whipped the sea to whitecaps, but still he lingered at the rail, wrapping his coat tightly about himself.

"Sailing from Halifax to N. York."
New York Public Library Digital Collections.

Now the stars came out; first the evening star, then the whole span-gled firmament. He could hardly believe his freedom, still, after nearly two weeks on board the *Lark*. He was going home, first to New York, then back to Boston.

The paunchy jailer had thrown open the jail door in early October and announced, "Well, boys, you're sprung. Read this." He handed James a note.

James read the note quickly. All eyes were on him. When he finished he turned to the group, his face relaxing into a wide smile. "General Massey says, in July, Congress approved General Washington's request that I be exchanged for Governor Skene. General Howe has agreed to this exchange. General Washington also proposed to General Howe a trade for Colonel Ethan Allen for any officer of the same or inferior rank, to which he has not yet agreed."

The jailer broke in, "And political prisoners join James Lovell in a trip to New York, and that means almost all of ye. All but you," he added, point-ing to two newcomers in the back. Cheers and loud applause greeted this announcement, while the two who would have to stay hung their heads and looked more dejected than ever. Ethan Allen clapped James on the back. "You have my congratulations. No one ever deserved freedom more."

"And you as well. Your prospects are much improved." James smiled back at Ethan, holding fast to the thought that freedom, a longed-for light in a dark tunnel, was now a little brighter.

The proposal for exchange, first suggested a year ago, had finally been approved. Colonel Skene would be released to the British, while James would be freed. In the next days, James felt his spirits lifting with the thought of being reunited with his family and his home. Yet he hardly dared believe the long-awaited release would at last occur. On October 12, all but the two prisoners who had to remain filed out of the jail at Halifax. The flabby jailer watched them go. "Good riddance to ye," he said, shaking his keys at them. "It's time you were gone." He held up a gold watch, ignor-ing the eyes on him, inspecting the time.

"There's my missing watch!" called out one of the released prisoners.

"Too late," the jailer laughed unpleasantly. "You set it down for the last time. I hope the lot of you drown at sea." He chuckled, thrusting the watch in his pocket.

"Let's go," called Ethan. "You can get another watch." Without a backward glance, the prisoners followed the officer in charge to the man-of-war the *Lark,* moored in Halifax harbor, and boarded the ship just at dusk. What a difference from the last time James had been onboard a ship, he thought. Confined in chains to a dark hold, the voyage to Halifax had been a nightmare. Now at the end of this journey, freedom awaited.

Captain Smith, a genial, thoughtful British officer, introduced himself to them, shaking hands. No one had to wear chains onboard the *Lark,* and all had freedom of the deck when wanted. Meals were ample: apples, potatoes, salt pork, brined beef, and good bread.

A Captain Burk was added to the prisoners, an American from an armed vessel captured in conflict. One night he came to the berth where Ethan Allen and James rested with their group. In a low voice he proposed a mutiny. "Come, let us take this ship. The ship's crew is in agreement; we will kill Captain Smith and the officers and take it. There are also thirty-five thousand pounds sterling in the hold. You can persuade the other prisoners to take our side, and then none will stand in the way." Captain Burk fixed his dark brown eyes intently on Ethan Allen and James.

Ethan Allen sat bolt upright. "That plan doesn't suit me, not at all. Captain Smith has treated us like gentlemen. My conscience could not bear harming him or the other officers. You had best forget that plan and disremember you ever thought of it."

James looked Captain Burk in the eye and shook his head. "I very much agree with Ethan Allen. Captain Smith has been as kind and gracious to us as an officer charged with holding prisoners could be. In no way should we repay his kindness with treachery. Such an act would amount to murder, since he has trusted us with our liberty and our movements. What say you?" James looked about at the others listening in the berth.

"We agree. We want no part of such a plot," said one. "We owe Captain Smith a debt of gratitude for his gracious treatment."

Another said, "As grateful as I am for the food and liberty given to us by Captain Smith, I would never want to repay him with mutiny."

"But it is too late. Since many know about this, the conspiracy will be found out," Captain Burk said in anxiety. "We must go through with it, or else hang for even considering the idea."

"If you so much as touch any of the officers or Captain Smith," Ethan Allen said, fixing Captain Burk with a malevolent stare, "you'll answer to me. I will guard his life at all costs."

"Then we shall not share the story further," Captain Burk said reluctantly, backing away from the big man. "No one must speak of this again. The conspiracy is over."

"You may be sure that is best," Ethan Allen said. James nodded in agreement. "Go back to your own quarters, and tell all the others nothing will happen. No one mentions this to anyone again," Ethan Allen said, a serious scowl on his face.

A day or so later, the lights of the big transports and British ships anchored off of Long Island came into view. The *Lark* sailed past a huge old hulk, rough and dirty. "That's a prison ship," said a crew member. "You don't want to end up there. They starve them there, then throw them overboard." James shivered.

The prison ship the *Scorpion* had once been a fireship, capable of aiming explosives with deadly force from her fourteen guns on either side. Now her iron mid-deck was rusted, corroding. Blood red it looked to James, as they slid by in the mist. The hinged iron gun portals were rusted too, looking like so many baleful eyes. The sides of the ship ran with smears, offal and foul matter. Dark, stained lines fell from the masts. A gallows stood on the upper deck. She rocked at anchor like a scavenger, a bird of prey, but she was a hell to hundreds of men, doomed to stay there until the end of the war—or death—freed them. James heard a single horrified shriek as they passed, as some poor soul felt his life's blood slipping away.

The *Lark* cast anchor further south off the shores of Staten Island at the entrance to New York harbor. Over a hundred ships rested in the harbor on their moorings, the fleet of Admiral Howe: men-of-war, frigates, great transports, hulks, privateers.

James waited anxiously for his release. Captain Smith came to Ethan Allen one day and told him that he had recommended him to Admiral Richard Howe and General William Howe as a gentleman and requested they treat him as such. Ethan thanked Captain Smith sincerely for his kindness. "You, sir, have been a pleasure to have for a captain," he said.

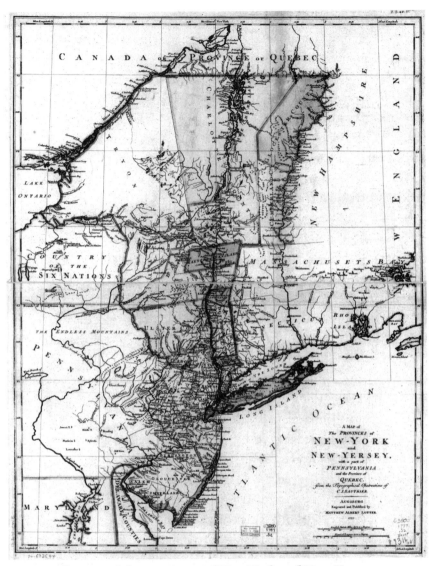

**"A map of the provinces of New-York and New-Yersey,
with a part of Pennsylvania and the Province of Quebec."**
Library of Congress Prints and Photographs

A group of British guards came in a rowboat to take Captain Burk. "He's wanted on a prison ship." Captain Burk protested, shouting and struggling, but they put him in irons, and he left, groaning. *Maybe the British caught wind of his plot to mutiny,* James thought. No one should be put on that hellish prison ship, but Captain Burk had a sly set to his character that might have caused suspicion to land on him, whether or not Captain Smith knew of his mutinous plot.

All the remaining prisoners were transferred to the *Glasgow*, a large transport, commanded by Captain Craige. The good recommendation of Captain Smith influenced the treatment of the prisoners, so they continued to enjoy decent food and free rein of the ship. All waited further orders or exchange.

On November 3, a party of British soldiers pulled alongside the transport in a small packet. "Our orders are to escort James Lovell, Esq., across Staten Island. From there he is free to travel home," said one. James took a deep breath. His head spun with happiness. In an instant he had buttoned his coat, thrust his papers securely into an inner pocket, and followed the redcoats.

He paused to say good-bye to his friend. "You may be sure I will help obtain your freedom, if such help is needed," he told Ethan Allen, shaking his hand firmly.

The big Green Mountain Boy returned the handshake and clapped James on the back. "Never a better mate could be found than you," he said. "A gentleman and comrade, you have made my miserable confinement palatable, if not enjoyable. I have been glad to make your acquaintance and will rejoice to hear you are safe at home, before long."

"That I intend to be," James responded. "Good luck with you."

"Good luck and God bless thee," said the giant, releasing James's hand.

James followed the direction of the captain and descended the side of the ship on a ladder. He stepped into a launch manned by sailors, where two British regulars greeted him. The soldiers escorted James to the ferry, where he and the soldiers climbed aboard. Then the oarsmen steered the ferry for the harbor on the east shore of Staten Island. The sight of the low, distant land: sand dunes thick with course grass; bushes flaming orange and crimson; falcons and kestrels soaring overhead, made James swallow, his heart beat fast. It had been so long since he'd seen his own country, or any countryside save the port of Halifax.

The sail filled with a steady wind; the ferry reached the shore about dusk, entering a small harbor. The British controlled Staten Island as they did New York, but most of the army was stationed at the north end of the Island. A few fishing boats were drawn up on the sandy beach; otherwise, the harbor lay quiet, peaceful. No one would think the British army was encamped just ten miles off, in New York.

The soldiers and James left the ferry at the harbor and headed into the countryside, following a narrow road. "We'll stay here before we cross the Island, tomorrow," said one of the regulars, a considerate fellow with a pale, downy mustache. He led the others into a clearing in the trees. He and the other soldier pulled packets of provisions from their pockets and set biscuit and dried beef on a large rock. James helped the soldiers gather a few sticks; the mustached regular brought out flint and knife, collected some dry grass and, striking the flint, soon had a little fire on which he set a tin to boil water for tea. James spread out the musty blanket handed to him under a scrubby tree and collapsed, bone weary, in the thick, sweet-smelling grass.

The next day he and the two regulars set off to cross the island. Farms lay quiet in the fall sunshine, sheltered by trees to which a few dried leaves clung. A farmer leading his oxen to pasture caught sight of the soldiers. He turned and quickly retraced his steps to his barnyard.

"You are lucky not to be going to prison in New York," said the friendly serviceman. The other eyed James suspiciously and said nothing. "Churches and warehouses have become prisons there, boarded up and holding hundreds of rebels tight, until the diphtheria, typhoid fever, small pox, or tuberculosis gets them. There's no food to spare for prisoners, so they often starve and are carted out by the dozens. I can't say I think they deserve such treatment, but then they are rebels, working to overthrow the government."

"You're the fortunate one," the other soldier said, eyeing James with disdain. "You're valuable enough to be exchanged. We're just following orders; otherwise, there would be no safe passage for you."

James nodded, but said nothing, keeping his thoughts to himself. He was indeed fortunate, he knew, but he was still in enemy territory. He must keep a careful eye on movements about him and stay out of conflict.

"They hang them, here, in New York," the sullen regular said, warming to his subject. "They hung a spy, Nathan Hale, just a couple of months ago. General Howe's army here is about 30,000 strong, and he takes no half measures in dealing with rebels. Last August he attacked the rebels' fortifications on Long Island. He would have been able to surround Washington's army, but the rebels slipped away in the fog." The soldier turned away from James in disgust and said nothing more.

James remembered hearing that the Declaration of Independence had been read aloud in New York to the American troops. As many obstacles as the troops had to overcome, they needed all the encouragement they could get. He had yet to read the whole Declaration, but he had heard some of the words. The stirring phrases remained vivid in his thoughts: "We hold these truths to be self-evident, that all men are created equal, that they are endowed by their Creator with certain unalienable Rights, that among these are Life, Liberty and the pursuit of Happiness." *What exhilarating words*, he thought.

They reached the far shore of Staten Island by late afternoon. "Here's where we leave you," said the friendly soldier. "We'll turn to cross the Island and take the ferry to New York. You'll take the ferry across to the mainland. Head north, and though you'll be traveling through Loyalist country, you may find someone willing to help a patriot. But you're on your own.

"If you run into the British army, show them this letter," the serviceman said, handing James a folded paper. "It explains your exchange."

"Here," the soldier called, hailing the ferryman, a wiry fellow with an enormous red beard and an old sailor's cap. "Here's a passenger for you." He motioned James to step onto the ferry and handed the ferryman a few coins. "Good luck to you," the soldier said with a cheerful grin, tipping his hat to James. The other regular turned and, grim-faced, without looking back, headed off to cross the island.

The ferryman set to work, and before long the craft was on the other side of the quiet channel. "Here you be, master," he said in a friendly manner, tipping his hat to James. "Head north to Elizabethtown—that's the stuff."

James thanked him and took to the road, keeping his eyes open for sight of British patrols. All he met, however, were farmers or local folk, and few of those. It felt good to walk, his legs limbering up and his lungs filling with good, fresh air. For a while he felt almost like whistling in joy at finally being on his way home. He swung his arms and admired every stone wall and thicket. But he felt himself tiring; after so many months of confinement, his legs began to ache with fatigue and his muscles cried for a rest. It was a relief when in the gathering dark under the stars he reached the crossroads of Elizabethtown and saw a white clapboard inn bearing a discreet sign, "The Yankee Harbor."

He knocked on the door, guessing from the name the innkeeper would not be a Loyalist. A smiling, stout man opened it. "Come in and welcome," the cheerful fellow said, showing James into a long, low room warmed by a flickering fire, before which a couple of guests were sipping their ale.

"I am recently freed from prison through an exchange of prisoners," James explained, "and am on my way home to Boston. I have a letter telling of my freedom, should you wish to see it."

"A patriot, freed and on your way home? You are more than welcome to a night's lodging." The broad-bellied innkeeper wiped his hands, sooty from tending the fire, on his soiled apron, and shook James's hand. "I am Elias Hodgkin. These are dangerous times to travel, but you may arrive safely at home after all."

James thanked the innkeeper and nearly stumbled up the stairs to rest. He was worn out from the journey, his limbs sore and stiff after the exercise following months of confinement. Yet never had a night seemed so full of promise, of hope. He was halfway home, going back to his family and the chance to do some good for his country. Like a stone he sank into the lumpy bedding and slept without a twitch.

The next day, before he left, he asked Elias for pen and paper to write the brother of Captain Francis Proctor and tell him how Proctor was faring.

"You are welcome to paper, pen, and ink, and I will see to it that the letter will be delivered," kind Elias Hodgkin said.

James sat down at the broad table in front of the fire and began to write.

I left Captain Francis Proctor, your brother, on board the prison-ship Glascow, in New York harbor, the 3rd of this month. He is in good health, has some encouragement of being speedily exchanged, but hopes his friends will exert themselves to bring about that desirable event, as much as if he had not received any hints about it, for he fears

> *those hints are only to amuse him. I have been his fel-*
> *low prisoner for months at Halifax, where he had fared*
> *hardly, but greatly better than when under the control of*
> *Captain Montague, who seemed to aim at his life.*

He folded and addressed the letter to Thomas Proctor. Surely Francis Proctor would be freed soon; an exchange would be possible. The cruel treatment Francis had endured under Captain Montague, months in irons with poor food, made him certainly deserve a speedy end to his suffering. From James's own experience with barbaric usage, he knew Captain Proctor deserved release soon.

He checked that his letter of passage was in his pocket and said goodbye to Elias Hodgkin. "You're traveling to Boston," the innkeeper said, his gray eyebrows lifting in curiosity.

"Yes, I am," James said.

"Then," he said, motioning to a driver eating his biscuits and kidneys in the long room by the fire, "Samuel here can take you as far as he goes."

Samuel looked up from his meal and wiped his chin. "Isn't that right, Samuel?" Elias Hodgkin asked. "You'll take Master Lovell with you north, right? There's a good chap."

"I'm going to New Haven, Connecticut," Samuel said. "Does that help?"

"Yes, a great deal," James answered. "Thank you so much."

The cart bumped along the road, carrying its burden of furniture and personal belongings to a family who had moved. James found a seat by Samuel and the next days passed quickly. Before long they reached the inn at New Haven, where Samuel left James. "Have a good trip—Godspeed," the driver said, tipping his hat. "And here's a little something to help you get there," he added, putting a small purse in James's hand.

"Thank you, my friend," James said with deep gratitude. "Your generosity is most appreciated. If I can repay you, you may be sure I will."

Nearly home, he reflected, mounting the narrow stairway to his room at the inn in New Haven. *Such kindness I have lately received. I am most grateful. Indeed, I may make it home after all.*

A Hero's Welcome

NOVEMBER 30, 1776

James gripped the velvet seat as the polished carriage lurched to a halt.

"Whoa, boys," shouted the coachman to the matched team of blacks.

James stood shakily. The week's journey from New York—first on the driver's cart and then in this fine lacquered coach provided for him by Congress for the last part of his journey—had left him weary and sore. Yet the exhilaration of traveling freely, despite the constant motion, thrilled him after months of captivity. The sun sparkled on snowy fields as the coach journeyed northward, and hope sang in his heart at the prospect of being reunited with his family.

"The Congress wants to assist you in your journey," the gnarled coachman had said, bowing to him at the inn in Hartford. "I am to make sure you arrive safely."

It was hard to believe, as the carriage mounted the last hill and descended down the road to Boston, that it was now November 30. Just two months ago he had been languishing in a Halifax jail, unsure of the future. His eyes opened wide to see the familiar harbor spread out before him, fields and hills blanketed in pristine snow. The spires of a few Boston churches stood high above snow-blanketed rooftops, while smoke rose from chimneys into the bright air.

The coach rumbled over the hills and down the cobblestone streets of Boston, crossing the Neck on Orange Street, then rolling down Newbury and Marlborough Streets before reaching the State House. Buildings still bore broken windows and battered siding from the siege and cannonading, yet many people strolled about tending to daily business, shopping, shoveling show, visiting with friends. James stared at all the sights, hungry for the familiar places. It was so good to be home. The carriage bumped to a stop in front of the gilded dome of the State House. He noticed the roof was bare of the lion and unicorn, those carved symbols of royal authority that had been pulled down by exuberant crowds following the public reading of the Declaration of Independence in July. *So much the better,* he thought.

"Huzzah! Welcome!" Shouts greeted him. James stepped out of the dusty coach to see a large crowd of people clapping and cheering. He recognized faces: Robert Treat Paine, his white, ruffled shirt framing his serious face; John Adams, ruddy cheeks flushed with excitement. James was about to greet the nearest well-wisher, when from the midst of the throng a familiar figure stepped out. His heart leaped to see the wool-cloaked figure of Mary, a little boy cradled in her arms. She cautiously approached him, smiling confidently. Though her face was tired and worn, she put out her hand and grasped his shoulder. James stretched his arms around her and wrapped her tightly in a warm embrace.

"It is a blessing to see you, my dear," he said at length, his voice choking. At last, he was with Mary again. He held her out at arms' length, seeing all the pain, despair, and hard work of the last eighteen months. Her lips trembled and she looked seriously at him, searching his face for reassurance. Yes, her red curls were streaked with gray under her bonnet, and lines of worry had furrowed her forehead. But she was Mary and here at his side, at last. He enclosed her in another embrace.

"And this is little George, whom you really don't know. He should be baptized before long." Mary stood back and looked down at the baby, who hid his face shyly against her coat. She motioned to seven other children, all staring with big eyes at James. "Children, greet your father."

"How are you, Father?" they chorused. James bent to embrace each. "Mary, how big you are getting! Jemmy and Johnny, my boys, it is a delight to see you. You are looking well indeed. Joseph and William, you have grown so! I trust you are taking care of Thomas and Charles." Indeed, all his children had grown. Jemmy now, at fourteen, was nearly as tall as James himself, while Johnny, a year younger, stood almost at the height of his older brother. The children exchanged delighted, if shy hugs with their father.

But where was James Jr.? he wondered. "James Jr., is he still with the militia?" he asked Mary.

"He is studying at Harvard. It was his grandparents Hastings' request to provide the tuition for him, and he agreed. His studies are progressing nicely, and he is nearly finished." Mary nodded confidently.

James smiled his pleasure. James Jr. would do well, apply himself and gain the knowledge he needed for whatever his future would bring.

The crowd clapped and cheered. A fife piped a festive tune to the beat of a snare drum. James turned from his family to wave at the townspeople. John Adams, wrapped in a black muffler against the cold, stepped forward and extended his hand.

"James, it is a good sight to see you after so many months. A most sincere welcome to you." The lawyer and town leader shook James's hand enthusiastically, his round face pleased.

"I trust you can make your own way home at this time, sir," the coachman said, leaning down from his seat and tipping his hat to James.

"Thank you, yes. Your services have been most appreciated," James said with a smile. The coachman picked up the reins, clicked to his team, and pulled away, the horses' hooves clattering on the cobblestones.

James looked about the square at the cheering, clapping crowd, and at his family. A tremendous sense of happiness and expectation filled him. He had survived a nearly insurmountable circumstance and many physical dangers. At last he might find some way to serve his country. Congress had sent a coach. What kindness, what consideration. That Congress was thinking of him and aware of his situation could only mean the group thought of him favorably. What might result from that? But before he might find out, he must return home with his family.

He stood with Mary as dozens of well-wishers filed by, shaking hands, while pipes played the popular song "Free America" and spectators joined in singing. James recognized the words composed by his friend Dr. Joseph Warren, and for a moment his vision clouded as he remembered the brave young leader who had died fighting with militia at the Battle of Bunker Hill.

Torn from a world of tyrants, beneath this western sky
We formed a new dominion, a land of liberty:
The world shall own we're freemen here, and such
will ever be.
Huzza! Huzza! Huzza! Huzza for love and liberty!

Then clouds lifted and the sun broke through in a blaze on the gilded dome of the State House, favoring the happy occasion. James's heart filled with gratitude for all that had brought him to this day.

After shaking many hands with those in the throng who had come to bid him welcome, James began to feel tired and unsteady. It was time that he and his family left so he could get some rest. "Come, Mary," he said. "We should go now."

Mary nodded in agreement. At his side James saw not the lovely young lady he had married, but a strong and independent woman, her face betraying care and weariness, yet her red curls still bouncing bravely under her bonnet. "Yes," she said. "Come along, children." The family waved farewell to the crowd and turned to walk home.

"It is so good to be with you, my dear," he said to Mary, taking her arm. Despite his fatigue, he felt as though a huge weight had slid off his back. He smiled back at baby George, who peeked at James shyly.

"I've moved back in to the house at Chapman Place," said Mary, falling into step beside him. "The British troops broke in and took some silver, but otherwise the house remained undamaged. Even the goods you had stored for Oliver Wendell and Nathaniel Appleton have been returned mostly intact."

"That is wonderful news," James said gratefully. "And I am sure the children are glad to be back home. Have you continued your housekeeping and cooking for Dr. Joseph Gardner?" he asked.

"Yes, though I am there at his house less frequently these days," Mary answered, shifting the weight of little George from one arm to another. Her blue eyes regarded James thoughtfully, seeming to size up his gaunt, pale appearance. "However, as he is unmarried, he appreciates my services, especially the cooking, and certainly has been most helpful to us. His generosity has made it possible for me to buy supplies and food."

"I am most proud of you, my dear," James said. "You found a way when there was no help at hand, and for that I am truly grateful. Here, let me hold George." He reached for the little boy, who allowed himself to be passed to his father. James blew lightly on George's cheek, causing him to break into a giggle. George reached up and gripped his father's nose with two tiny fingers. James laughed and shook his nose free.

"You kept the children cared for in an extremely difficult time, while I was clearly helpless to give you any relief." Many times he had wondered how his family had fared, yet they had managed well. For that he must thank heaven.

Mary laughed. "I didn't have much choice." An edge of bitterness tinged her words, yet she smiled gaily.

"And," James continued, "you and the children have thrived. George must be about nine months old now." He returned little George's stare.

"Yes," Mary said. "The older children and I were inoculated against smallpox, which made us sick for a short while. But we recovered and so will be safe should the epidemic break out again. You should ask Dr. Gardner to inoculate you as well, soon." She pulled open the gate to their home. "Here we are," she announced, motioning James through the gate.

"I so admire your constancy and dedication. It has been invaluable." James felt again all the worry and pain of the last months. He broke out into a long series of coughs as he followed her up the path and into the house. The children trailed behind, looking at their father in awe, quiet and respectful.

He entered the door thoughtfully. The weight of months in prison was still with him, not so easily cast off. How fine the home looked. Pewter plates glowed on shelves by the hearth, brass candlesticks shone on the mantel, Mary's favorite china setting sparkled in its cupboard. He was about to sink into his chair by the fire when Mary took a firm hold on his arm. Startled, he looked at her.

"You've lost weight," she said, evaluating his size. "Quite a bit of weight, as a matter of fact." Her voice held a note of concern.

James sighed. "I have been near the point of starvation more often than I can tell. Yes, I have lost weight. But give me some time here with you and I'll make up for it." He sat down, relieved and weary.

"Here, you need some tea. Bohea, now. We have some in trade from France." Mary poured water into the kettle and set it on the fire. "Jemmy, fetch some wood in. Johnny, you and Joseph get the tea things and fresh bread. Mary, please come sit here with George and give him a cracker."

The boys left to do the chores needed, while little Mary picked up baby George and settled with him in her lap on the rug near James. She pulled off George's coat and offered him a cracker. George examined the cracker seriously and then bit into it, his bright dark eyes watching his father. Little Mary must be seven, James realized, fondly passing his hand over her blond curls. A shy, cheerful smile lit up her face.

"When James Jr. completes his studies at Harvard," Mary continued, "he plans to join the Continental Army."

"I am so glad he put his studies first," James said. "He has a fine mind and should use it. I am proud of him for his choice."

He put his feet up on a stool and felt the warmth of the crackling fire. "And is the Boston Latin School open? Are Jemmy and Johnny nearly finished?" he asked. He smiled as Jemmy came in with an armload of split logs for the fire. He set them in the brass basket by the hearth, chose a couple of pieces and laid them on the fire, then settled himself in the wooden chair nearby, listening expectantly.

"The school has been open since June, with Samuel Hunt, whom you will remember, as the master. Both have completed their studies and moved on to other work," said their mother.

"Ah yes, Samuel Hunt." James nodded. "He was my father's pupil and graduated from Harvard about four years after me. But what are the boys doing now?" He looked across the hearth at Jemmy, who politely waited for his mother to speak.

Mary glanced fondly at her son and spoke for him. "Jemmy may become a policeman, as he is assisting one of the police now and likes the occupation." James glanced at the tall young man sitting patiently at his side and nodded his head approvingly.

"Johnny has yet to determine a vocation, though he is talking about working for a merchant," Mary added, glancing up at Johnny, who walked in bearing the family's best silver tea tray laden with cups, saucers, and sliced bread. "But come, here is your tea. Set the tray here, Johnny," she said, motioning to the nearby table. "That will be fine." She lifted the simmering kettle from its hook, her hand protected by a thick pad, and poured steaming water into the fragrant leaves resting in the teapot.

"Thank you, Johnny," James said. Johnny sank into a chair next to his brother, his eyes glued on his father. Joseph, shorter and heavier than his older brothers, set a pitcher of cream and a bowl of sugar on the table by the tea things, then sat on the floor by his brothers. "Have you heard anything about my father, mother, and the girls—Mary, Elizabeth, and Rebecca?" James asked Mary, taking a long sip of the steaming tea.

"No, no news about them," Mary said, "but we do hear that the Loyalists in Halifax struggle with lack of food. Disease is another problem in that settlement, particularly smallpox. I hope they are all right."

"The girls will be fine," James said thoughtfully. "It's Mother and Father I worry about. They are none too healthy, and Father in particular is given to gout and rheumatism. But we must let them be. Whether or not we can see them, they have made their decision." He looked stonily into the fire for a few minutes, then took another swallow of the hot tea.

"But I am home, and it is so good to see you, my dear." He smiled with relief and pleasure, his eyes bright. Mary nodded and reached for the potato sack. She kept an eye on him as she peeled the potatoes, set the bread to baking, and sliced the beef. The warmth of the fire soon stole over James, and he shut his eyes and fell fast asleep, more at peace than he had been in a long time.

Chapter 52

Off to Congress

January 8, 1777

To James's surprise, after a few days a letter arrived from Congress. Enclosed in a crisp, ivory envelope bearing a red waxen seal, the flowing script extended an invitation for him to become a member of the Second Continental Congress as a representative from Massachusetts. Congress, he knew, had moved from Philadelphia to Baltimore, for safety from the British. He read the invitation, his heart beating. A tumult of contradictory emotions arose within him.

At first James wondered how he could possibly consider serving Congress. Though honored to be asked to serve his country, at the same time he had just come home from a terrible ordeal. Not only did he need to see that his family was well, he needed time to recover his strength. Then the thought came to him that he did need employment. It was time for him to help provide for his family. By serving in Congress, he might be able to meet that need.

James thought carefully over the matter for a week, saying nothing of it, while he enjoyed Mary's delicious cooking, played games and took walks with his children, and bounced the baby on his knee. A stream of visitors continually arrived at the house at Chapman Place to inquire about his well-being, and he relished visiting with them all, sharing the news of his confinement and hearing about the progress of the Continental Army.

Yet the consideration of Congress's invitation was never far from his mind. The way was open for the first time in many months for him to provide service to his country. He was wanted and needed, and the thought struck him that doing the honorable thing, serving in Congress, was exactly what he would most like to do. But doing so would mean leaving his family, probably for long periods of time. He felt torn between the two loyalties.

A lengthy week later, he talked the matter over with Mary.

"I am so honored to be asked to join Congress. I truly want to serve the country. Being part of the Second Continental Congress, coordinating needs for the war effort, it would not be so hard to be parted from you and the children. Not only that, but my pay would help support you," he said. He looked at her face carefully to see her reaction.

Mary cleared her throat. "Yes, James. I know that the Congress needs you. You have unique skills in speaking, writing, working with others. You would be a great benefit to that group at a time they need capable individuals very much."

She continued, an edge to her voice. "We will manage. For good or ill, I have become accustomed to caring for the children on my own. I do intend to continue to cook and care for Dr. Gardner, since he has been so kind to us. But we will miss you, my dear." She stifled a sob and looked at him, her eyes brimming. Then she quickly wiped away the tears and turned back to the shirt she had been mending. She kept her eyes down and refused to look at him, struggling for self-control.

"I will be gone just a year, most likely," James said, searching for words to reassure her. "In this way I am able to provide for you and assist my country as well."

"The children and I will make the best of it. We should be honored to have you serve Congress. I know in these times stability and competency is greatly needed. General Washington and the forces struggle to keep an upper hand on the conflict, if reports be true. However, I must say we have seen precious little of you in the last two years and now will lose you once again. Yet it will clearly be a good position for you. So apparently we must manage." Mary stabbed firmly at her needlework, her voice low and strained.

She has changed, James thought. All those months, those hardships, have caused her to realize the separation that must stand between us. Even so, she will care for the family well. My loyal, loving wife will play her part to help the family. And this is my chance, surely, to help my country.

"Thank you, my dear," James said. "Your understanding means more than I can say." He wished she would look up, to show her bright smile again. But for now, the pain of the time to come must be hard for her to imagine. *Yet to some extent she does understand,* he thought. *In any case, leaving to join Congress is the best decision, though it may grieve both of us in some way.*

On the day before Christmas, James sat down to compose a letter to Congress. At his desk, he picked up his pen.

> *After maturely deliberating the consequences of my pub-*
> *lic and private relations, I have concluded it to be my duty*
> *not to decline that honor to which, as you have informed*
> *me on the 5th of this month, I am appointed by the joint*
> *ballot of both houses of Assembly of this State.*

Another chapter begins, he thought. *Mary will be all right with the children. I will accept the honor bestowed on me by my country.*

On January 8, 1777, James rode out of Boston accompanied by John Adams. Samuel Adams, John Hancock, Elbridge Gerry, and Francis Dana would be the other delegates from Massachusetts. Glittering with new snow, the road was a long four hundred miles to Baltimore, but James looked forward to the journey. He knew he was ready to serve the cause. The trials and difficulties he had been through had sharpened his will to do his best to help his country through the hard times to come. Though he must again leave his family, possibly for quite some time, he had no intention of looking back.

Afterword

James Lovell did not return home to his wife and family for five years while he served his country in the Second Continental Congress, acting as its Secretary to the Committee for Foreign Affairs in a tumultuous time in the country's history.

My grandmother, Frances Josephine Loring Coffin, wife of a chemistry professor at Lake Forest College in Illinois, had a respect and appreciation for history shown in her care of the many antique pieces of furniture, china, and paintings in her home in Andover, Massachusetts. My three sisters and I often visited the house while growing up, exploring the peaked attic and secret room under the stairs. A historic plaque on the front of the house explains that the Marquis de Lafayette, French officer so encouraging to the Revolutionary forces, delivered a speech from its front steps to the citizens of Andover in 1781. Little did I realize the connection one of my ancestors had with Lafayette as I viewed the brass plaque with awe. As Secretary to the Committee for Foreign Affairs while in the Second Continental Congress, James Lovell interviewed the Marquis de Lafayette when he first arrived in Philadelphia, and informed Congress of his interest in serving in General Washington's forces.

My grandmother carefully copied by hand a journal that her grandfather had composed in 1892. She did so knowing the old journal was falling apart, realizing we might someday be interested in the stories it contained. In time I acquired a copy of that journal. Reading it, I was fascinated by the stories of the Lovells: John Lovell, the master of the Boston Latin School; and his son James, the usher or teacher at the School. The journal indicated that we were distantly related to James Lovell, a great-great-grandfather (four greats), but even more fascinating was James Lovell's role in the American Revolution. The master of the Boston Latin School and his teacher son stood at opposite sides of the widening split in beliefs for those in the colonies. John sided with the British, holding Tory beliefs, and James agreed with the patriots, choosing to actively help his country.

James did, in fact, make a huge personal sacrifice to support his beliefs. After the eighteen months he spent in jails for helping the patriot cause, spying for the Americans while Boston was under siege, he served his country for five years in the Second Continental Congress, longer than any other participant in that gathering. Evidence for his spying is scanty, but according to an article in the *Virginia Gazette* of August 11, 1775, which contains an excerpt from a letter of July 12, 1775, written from Josiah Quincy, Sr., to Samuel Adams, letters found in the pocket of Doctor Joseph Warren after his death at the Battle of Bunker Hill implicated James in spying and led to his imprisonment.

His father, Master John Lovell, gave up his comfortable home and secure position in Boston to go with the exodus of Loyalists to Halifax, Nova Scotia, when the British evacuated Boston. Master John Lovell was never to return to Massachusetts. These individuals were not alone in those days; giving up family, home, and belongings, many—both patriots and Loyalists—chose to endure hardship for the sake of advancing the vision of freedom and hope they believed to be most important. That conflicting vision turns out to be the story of the Revolutionary War.

Page from *Loring Family Journal*, 1892. Photograph of Jean C. O'Connor

When an opportunity for a sabbatical from teaching English became a reality, I decided to research the story; traveling to Boston, Halifax, Washington, D.C., and Ithaca, New York; focusing on the story of the Lovells, their conflicts and hopes. I could not have followed this story without the help of those whose generosity inspired and enlightened me, and for the assistance of librarians, researchers, friends, and family, I am forever grateful.

A NOTE ABOUT EXCERPTS OF OLD WRITINGS INCLUDED IN THE TEXT

When early writings are included as excerpts in the text, set aside in italics, the original spelling, punctuation, capitalization, and grammar are kept. However, when early works are included in the body, as words spoken by characters, these elements are standardized to make for easier reading. Original writings are given in italics for clarification.

In images of old writing, both print and hand-written, the letter that looks like an "f" where an "s" should be is an archaic form of the "s," called the "long s." It was used to replace the single "s" or the first "s" in a word with a double "s." Read these just as you would an "s."

HOW TRUE IS THE STORY OF *THE REMARKABLE CAUSE: A NOVEL OF JAMES LOVELL AND THE CRUCIBLE OF THE REVOLUTION?*

Of course, *The Remarkable Cause: A Novel of James Lovell and the Crucible of the Revolution* is historical fiction. That said, it is intended to bring to life what really happened—the sights, sounds, and experiences of Revolutionary Boston. Yet every effort has been made to convey real events. Major characters are all based on actual people. In cases when one can only imagine how something occurred, such as the ways James spied on the British in the weeks following the Battle of Bunker Hill, a character such as Zach comes to life, based on possible events.

WHAT HAPPENED TO SOME OF THE
KEY PLAYERS IN THE STORY?

James Lovell joined the Second Continental Congress in February, 1777, and served for five unbroken years to January, 1782, without returning to visit his wife and children during that time. John Adams described him in late 1776 as "A Man of Spirit, Fortitude, and Patience, three Virtues the most useful of any in these times. And besides these he has Taste, Sense, and Learning." He was head of the committee responsible for publishing the journals of Congress, and served as clerk and Secretary of the Congressional Committee for Foreign Affairs, corresponding with diplomats. He interviewed all the foreigners who offered their services and wrote reports on them, including the Marquis de Lafayette. While James Lovell at times differed with his fellow members of Congress, championing General Horatio Gates, of whom Washington disapproved, he served faithfully and with distinction. He was passionately fond of cryptography, creating ciphers for encoding official messages from Congress, and has been referred to as the "Father of American Cryptanalysis."

He signed the Articles of the Confederation in 1781. Unsure of his welcome at home, James made a visit to his wife and children in January, 1782, but as his visit was successful, he left Congress finally in April of 1782. In 1784 Mr. Lovell was appointed receiver of Continental taxes, and during the confederacy of 1788 and in 1789 he served as the collector for the port of Boston. He was the naval officer of Boston from 1790 until his death at Windham, Maine, July 14, 1814.

John Lovell, master of the Boston Latin School, never left Halifax after arriving with the Loyalists in March of 1776. He is probably the John Lovell referred to in *Carleton's Loyalist Index*, a refugee receiving rations along with three women in August of 1778. According to the "List of Persons who removed from Boston to Halifax with his Majesty's troops in the month of March 1776 with the numbers of their respective families," General Howe's record of the Loyalists evacuated from Boston, John Lovell left with four other family members. His time in Halifax was more than likely a difficult and disappointing anticlimax, since while he bravely left his home in Boston a respected scholar and academic, he must have found life in the rough, crowded fortress town of Halifax extremely difficult and arduous. At the age of sixty-eight he may have succumbed to typhoid or smallpox; in any event, he died in 1778.

Abigail Lovell, devoted mother and wife, made her will on November 4, 1792, giving to her daughter Rebecca Lovell "for her great and unselfish attention and affection to me through life" all her goods and chattels. Attached to the will is an inventory from the late John Lovell's estate listing the family's major possessions. The inventory is illuminating since it shows the family's reduced circumstances. Among the items are the following:

> A small mahogany desk
> A tea table
> A looking glass
> A pair of iron dogs, shovel, and tongs
> A carpet
> A bedstead and curtains
> 4 pewter dishes
> 2 kettles
> 2 feather beds
> 1 pair blankets
> 6 pairs of sheets
> 4 pillowcases
> 2 china bowls, 12 china plates
> 1 small copper tea kettle

Rebecca Lovell, the oldest of the three sisters who abandoned Boston for Halifax with their parents, never married, but cared for her parents in Halifax, as Abigail Lovell's will shows.

Elizabeth Lovell, though proof is elusive, is likely the temptress who distracted Colonel Cleveland, Commander of Ordnance at the Battle of Bunker Hill. She traveled to Halifax with her parents, where she married a Hessian Baron, Major Ludwig Van de Schallern, of the Regiment de Seitz, on January 11, 1781. The ceremony more than likely occurred in Halifax, as the *Nova Scotia Gazette and Weekly Chronicle* reported a marriage ceremony between a Miss Lovell and the Hessian Baron on January 16, 1781.

Mary Lovell, youngest sister of James, also left Boston for Halifax with her parents. She married Elias Burbidge in Nova Scotia.

John Lovell, older brother of James, joined the Loyal American Associators, a group of volunteers who offered their services to the commander-in-chief General Howe before the evacuation of Boston. He was arrested by the rebels about the time of the evacuation and spent the next three years in a Boston jail. Released from jail in 1779, he petitioned the British government for reimbursement for his service and loss of health.

Benjamin Lovell, youngest brother of James, was educated to become an Anglican minister but instead first joined the Royal Artillery, then left Boston for England in August of 1775, where he served as a tutor before obtaining a position as a minister.

James Lovell Jr., James's first son, received his B.A. from Harvard in 1776, then served the Continental Army with distinction from 1777 to 1783, becoming a Major. Among other positions, he served with Lt. Col. Henry "Light Horse Harry" Lee's battalion of light dragoons. A note in the journal left by my grandmother, written by her grandfather, indicates he brought up reinforcements and ammunition from Cambridge too late for use; later, returning to the site of Bunker Hill as an old man, he remembered it as "running with blood."

James Smith Lovell, James and Mary Middleton's first son, became a policeman in Boston and then a Customs House officer. His second wife was Helen Sheaffe. Their daughter was Mary Middleton Lovell, who was my grandmother's great-grandmother.

Acknowledgments

I first would like to thank Helena School District #1 for giving me a sabbatical of a semester, during which time I traveled, researched, and wrote. Helena School District in the capital of Montana sets a standard for other districts in the state as well as region. I am grateful for many aspects of its leadership, including the sabbatical opportunity.

The amazing thing I discovered as I began research was that libraries and archival institutions are fabulously helpful. Over and over I've posed questions to libraries, historical societies, universities, and museums. Every time someone has taken the time to answer me specifically, often sending me links to on-line publications, PDF files, and specific titles.

Some of the places and people I thank are the Massachusetts Historical Society, particularly Anna Cook and Katie Leach; the Boston Public Library, Jessy Wheeler; the Harvard Houghton Library, Frederic Burchsted; the New England Historic Genealogical Society, David Allen Lambert and David Dearborn; the Massachusetts Archives, Jennifer Fauxsmith; the New York Public Library, Susan Malsbury; the Concord Museum, Shane Clarke; the Harriet Irving Library in Fredericton, New Brunswick, Leah Grandy and Christine Jack; the Nova Scotia Archives in Halifax, Garry Shutlak; the Citadel, Halifax, Miriam Walls and Kevin Robins; the Halifax Central Library, Norma and Audrey; the Maritime Museum of the Atlantic, Halifax, Lynda Silver; the Division of Rare and Manuscript Collections, Cornell University; the Manuscript Reading Room at the James Madison Memorial Building, the Library of Congress, Bruce Kirby; and the Clements Library, the University of Michigan, Janet Bloom.

In addition I am indebted to my friend and colleague Dr. Beverly Ann Chin, Director of the English Teaching Program at the University of Montana, Chair of the English Department, and Past President of the National Council of Teachers of English, for her close reading of the manuscript and keen observations. Special thanks go to Malcolm Flynn, historian and assistant headmaster of the Boston Latin School, for his reading of the manuscript, encouragement, and comments. Many other readers shared insights or suggestions, including my dear father, Rev. Lewis E. Coffin, and my sisters Elizabeth Schuur, Margaret Hughston, and Barbara Talbot. Margaret was able to accompany me in traveling to Halifax, Nova Scotia, where she assisted me in research. My nephew Jared Talbot's skillful fingers provided final formatting on many images, for which I thank him. I am appreciative of writer and researcher Dorothea Susag for her careful editing comments, and thank my teaching colleague Colleen Hansen for her suggestions and advice. The talented editor Kate Monahan of Post Hill Press guided the manuscript through its final steps with care and consideration. I also greatly appreciate Heather Steadham, copy editor, for her perceptive and insightful comments on the work, as well as her kind observations. Especially, I am most grateful to my publisher Roger Williams of Knox Press, for his encouragement and guidance, as well as his belief in the power of this narrative.

Finally, I thank my husband Michael O'Connor, for his unflinching support and patience as I wrote this story.

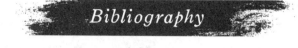
Bibliography

Archival Material Depositories

Boston Public Library, Boston, MA

Harvard Houghton Library, Cambridge, MA

Harvard Archives, Cambridge, MA

Harriet Irving Library, University of New Brunswick, Fredericton, New Brunswick

Kroch Library, Rare and Manuscript Collection, Cornell University, Ithaca, NY

Library Of Congress, James Madison Memorial Building, Manuscript Reading Room, Washington, DC

Massachusetts Historical Society, Boston, MA

New England Historic Genealogical Society, Boston, MA

Nova Scotia Archives, Halifax, Nova Scotia

William L. Clements Library, University of Michigan, Ann Arbor, MI

Books and Pamphlets

Primary Source Material

Acts and Resolves Passed by the General Court of Massachusetts, 1775–1776, Vol. XIX. Boston: Secretary of the Commonwealth, State Library of Massachusetts, Chapter 160, p. 69; Chapter 707, p. 140; Chapter 676, p. 723, archive.org/details/actsresolvespass7576mass.

Allen, Ethan. *A Narrative of Col. Ethan Allen's Captivity.* Burlington: Chauncey Goodrich, 1846, Google eBook.

Blatchford, John. *The Narrative of John Blatchford.* Intro. Charles L. Bushnell, 1865, Collection of Boston Public Library, The Internet Archive, archive.org/details/narrativeofjohnb00blat.

Boardman, Samuel Lane, ed. *Peter Edes, pioneer printer in Maine : a biography : his diary while a prisoner by the British at Boston in 1775, with the journal of John Leach, who was a prisoner at the same time.* Bangor: The De Burians, 1901, Google e-book.

Carleton's Loyalist Index: A Select Index to Names of Loyalists and their Associates Contained in the British Headquarters Papers, New York City 1774–1783, The Carleton Papers. Sir Guy Carleton Branch, UELAC, p. 2006–2008 of 2441, uelac.org/Carletonuel/kingname.htm.

"'Joy to America!' Colonists Respond to the Repeal of the Stamp Act, 1766." Making the Revolution: America, 1763–1791. *America in Class, from the National Humanities Center,* pp. 3-4. http://americainclass. org/sources/makingrevolution/crisis/text3/stampactrepealresponse1766.pdf

Dexter, John Haven and Robert J. Dunkle, et. al. *Dexter's Memoranda of the Town of Boston in the 18th and 19th Centuries,* New England Historic Genealogical Society, 1997.

Gelles, Edith Belle. *Portia: The World of Abigail Adams,* Indiana University Press, 1992, Google eBook.

Hewes, George R. T. *Traits of the Tea Party: A Memoir of George R. T. Hewes.* New York, Harper & Brothers, 1835, The Internet Archive, archive. org/stream/traitsofteaparty00that#page/n11/mode/2up.

A Journal Kept by John Leach, During his Confinement by the British, in Boston Gaol, in 1775. The New England Historical and Genealogical Register, 1865, p. 255–263, Massachusetts Historical Society.

"Joy to America, Colonists Respond to the Repeal of the Stamp Act, 1766." *America In Class, The National Humanities Center Resource Toolbox, Making the Revolution: America, 1763–1791,* americainclass. org/sources/makingrevolution/crisis/text3/stampactrepealresponse 1766.pdf.

Letters written at the time of the occupation of Boston by the British, 1775–6. Communicated by Wm. P. Upham, from the Historical Collections of the Essex Institute, Vol. XIII, July, 1876; Upham, William Phineas, ed. 1836–1905, Salem, Mass., Salem press, 1876, HathiTrust, catalog. hathitrust.org/Record/000581754.

Lovell, James. *An Oration Delivered April 2, 1771.* Boston, Edes & Gill, 1771. *Early American Imprints,* Harvard Archives. From NewsBank, Inc. and the American Antiquarian Society. All Rights Reserved.

---. *Sketches of Man "As He Is" Connected with Past and Present Modes of Education.* Boston, 1808. Early American Imprints, Harvard Archives. From NewsBank, Inc. and the American Antiquarian Society. All Rights Reserved.

The Oldest School in America: An Oration by Phillips Brooks, D.D., and a Poem by Robert Grant. At the 250th Anniversary of the Founding of the Boston Latin School, April 23, 1885. Boston and New York: Houghton Mifflin, 1885, worldcat.org/title/oldest-school-in-america/oclc/1921203.

Proceedings of the Bostonian Society Annual Meeting. Vol. II, 1898–1902. Boston: Old State House, published by the Society. The Internet Archive, archive.org/details/proceedingsofbo189195bost.

Proceedings of the Massachusetts Historical Society. Vol. 5 (1860–1862), p. 1–30. Letters by and to James Lovell, 1777–1778. HathiTrust, catalog. hathitrust.org/Record/008882540.

Proceedings of the Massachusetts Historical Society. Vol. 12 (1871–1873), p. 174–182. "Letter of Peter Edes; Letter of Harry H. Edes." HathiTrust, catalog.hathitrust.org/Record/008882540.

Proceedings of the Massachusetts Historical Society, Third Series, Vol. 50 (Oct. 1916–Jun, 1917). p. 413–503. Quincy's London Journal, 1774–1775; Letters to Josiah Quincy, Jr. HathiTrust, catalog.hathitrust.org/Record/008882540.

Publications of the Colonial Society of Massachusetts. Vol. VI. Transactions, 1899–1900. Boston: The Society, 1904, Google e-book.

"The Trial of Captain Preston: Key Evidence." *Famous American Trials: Boston Massacre Trials, 1770.* Famous Trials, by Douglas O. Linder. University of Missouri—Kansas City School of Law. 2016, law2. umkc.edu/faculty/projects/ftrials/bostonmassacre/prestontrialexcerpts.html.

Winsor, Justin. *The Memorial History of Boston 1630–1880*. Vol. 1—The Early and Colonial Periods. Boston: James R. Osgood and Company, 1880, Google e-book.

---. *The Memorial History of Boston 1630–1880*. Vol. II—The Provincial Period. Boston: James R. Osgood and Company, 1880, Google e-book.

---. *The Memorial History of Boston*. Vol. III—The Revolutionary Period. The Last Hundred Years, Pt. I. Boston, James R. Osgood and Co., 1882, Google e-book.

York, Neil L. *The Boston Massacre, a History with Documents*. New York: Routledge, 2010.

Secondary Source Material

"The American Revolution's One Man National Security Agency," Approved for Release by NSA 12-1-2011, Transparency Case # 63852, nsa.gov/news-features/declassified-documents/crypto-alma-nac-50th/assets/files/the-american-revolution.pdf.

Allison, Robert J. *The Boston Tea Party*. Commonwealth Editions, 2007, Google eBook.

Bakeless, John. *Turncoats, Traitors, and Heroes*. Philadelphia and New York: J.B. Lippincott Company, 1859.

Biographical Directory of the United States Congress, 1774 to Present. "Lovell, James, 1737–1814." bioguide.congress.gov/scripts/biodisplay.pl?index=L000463.

Brebner, John. *The Neutral Yankees of Nova Scotia, a Marginal Colony during the Revolutionary Years*. New York: Columbia University Press, 1937.

Crawford, Mary Caroline. *Old Boston Days & Ways, From the Dawn of the Revolution Until the Town Became a City*. Little, Brown & Co., 1910, Google eBook.

Drake, Samuel Adams. *Old Landmarks and Historic Personages of Boston*. Boston: James R. Osgood and Co., 1873, Google eBook.

Engelman, F. L. "Cadwallader Colden and the New York Stamp Act Riots." *The William and Mary Quarterly*, vol. 10, no. 4, 1953, p. 560–578. *JSTOR*, jstor.org/stable/1923595.

Fingard, Judith, et. al. *Halifax, the First Two Hundred and Fifty Years.* Halifax: Formac, 1999.

Forman, Samuel A. *Dr. Joseph Warren: The Boston Tea Party, Bunker Hill, and the Birth of American Liberty.* Gretna: Pelican Publishing Company, 2012.

Frothingham, Richard. *History of the Siege of Boston, and of the Battles of Lexington, Concord, and Bunker Hill.* Boston: Little, Brown, and Company, 1903, Google eBook.

Holbrook, Stewart. *Ethan Allen.* New York: Macmillan, 1940.

Holmes, Pauline. *A Tercentenary History of the Boston Public Latin School, 1635–1935.* Cambridge: Harvard University Press, 1935.

Jenks, Henry F. *Catalogue of the Boston Public Latin School, Established in 1635.* Boston: The Boston Latin School Association, 1886. Internet Archive, Courtesy the Boston Public Library, archive.org/details/catalogueofbosto00bost.

Jones, Helen. *James Lovell in the Continental Congress 1777 - 1782.* University Microfilms: Ann Arbor, Michigan, 1969. Courtesy Boston Public Library.

Loring, James Spear. *The Hundred Boston Orators, from 1770 to 1852.* Boston, John P. Jewett and Co., 1852. Internet Archive, Courtesy the Boston Public Library, archive.org/details/hundredbostonora00lorin.

Lyon, David. *The Sailing Navy List: All the Ships of the Royal Navy, Built, Purchased, and Captured, 1688–1860.* London: Conway Maritime Press, 1993.

MacKinnon, Neil. *This Unfriendly Soil: The Loyalist Experience in Nova Scotia, 1783–1791.* Montreal: McGill-Queen's University Press, 1986.

Maier, Pauline. *From Resistance to Revolution: Colonial Radicals and the Development of American Opposition to Britain, 1765–1776.* 1991, 1972. New York: W.W. Norton & Co.

Marble, Allen. *Surgeons, Smallpox and the Poor.* Montreal: McGill-Queen's University Press, 1993.

Marshall, James B. *The United States Manual of Biography and History: Lives of the Presidents, the Framers, the Signers, the Justices.* Philadelphia, James B. Smith and Co., 1856, Google e-book.

McCullough, David. *1776.* New York: Simon & Schuster, 2005.

New England Historic and Genealogical Register. Vol. 52, 1898, New England Historic Genealogical Society, (1898), reprint, index, illus., Google eBook.

The Oldest School in America. An Oration by Phillips Brooks, D.D. and a Poem by Robert Grant. Boston: the Boston Latin School Association, 1886. Internet Archive, Courtesy Boston Public Latin School, archive.org/details/oldestschoolinam00bostiala.

Raddall, Thomas. *Halifax, Warden of the North.* Toronto: McClellan and Stewart, Limited, 1974.

---. *His Majesty's Yankees.* Toronto: McClellan and Stewart, Limited, 1942.

Raphael, Ray. *A People's History of the American Revolution: How Common People Shaped the Fight for Independence.* New York: The New Press, 2001.

"Revolution 1773—The 'Body of the People' at Old South Meeting House." *The Dial,* Summer 2012. The Old South Meeting House, Boston, osmh.org.

Sabine, Lorenzo. *The American Loyalists: Or, Biographical Sketches of Adherents to the British Crown in the War of the Revolution.* Boston: Charles Little and James Brown, 1847.

---. *Biographical Sketches of Loyalists of the American Revolution,* Vol. II. Boston: Little, Brown, and Company, 1864.

Schouler, James. *Americans of 1776: Daily Life in Revolutionary America.* Maryland: Heritage Books, 1906.

Shaara, Jeff. *Rise to Rebellion.* New York: Ballantine Books, 2001.

Shipton, Clifford K. *Sibley's Harvard Graduates, Vol. VIII. Biographical Sketches of Those Who Attended Harvard College, 1726–1730.* "John Lovell, 1728." Massachusetts Historical Society, Boston, Massachusetts, 1968, HathiTrust Digital Library.

---. *Sibley's Harvard Graduates, Vol. XIV. Biographical Sketches of Those Who Attended Harvard College, 1756–1760.* "James Lovell, 1756." Massachusetts Historical Society, Boston, Massachusetts, 1968, HathiTrust Digital Library.

Stark, James Henry. *Stark's Antiqve Views of Ye Towne of Boston.* Boston, 1901, Google eBook.

Thwing, Annie Haven. *The Crooked and Narrow Streets of the Town of Boston – 1630–1822*. Boston: Marshall Jones Co., 1920.

Winsor, Justin, ed. *Narrative and Critical History of America*. Vol. VI, Pt. I. Boston and New York: Houghton Mifflin and Co., 1887, Google eBook.

ONLINE SOURCES

American Archives, Northern Illinois University

The Avalon Project: Documents in Law, History and Diplomacy, Yale Law School, Lillian Goldman Law Library

Bartleby.com, Great Books Online

Blog of J. L. Bell

Boston Massacre Historical Society

Crispus Attucks

Founders Online, National Archives

Google eBooks and Google Play

HathiTrust Digital Library

The Internet Archive

Library of Congress

Massachusetts Historical Society: *The Coming of the American Revolution;* and *The Siege of Boston: Eyewitness Accounts from the Collections of the Massachusetts Historical Society*

New England Historic Genealogical Society

SOURCE NOTES

Chapter 3. July 9, 1760. Wedding Plans

"At length happy old man, composed in pleasing peace…." Partial transcript of "A Funeral Oration," from James Lovell's *Oration for Tutor Flynt,* 1760, Harvard Houghton Library, used with permission.

Chapter 5. August 10, 1765. The Argument Heats Up

"Obedience to the civil magistrate is a Christian duty." Mayhew, Jonathan A.M., D.D. and Royster, Paul , Editor & Depositor, "A Discourse concerning Unlimited Submission and Non-Resistance to the Higher Powers: With some Reflections on the Resistance made to King Charles I. And on the Anniversary of his Death: In which the Mysterious Doctrine of that Prince's Saintship and Martyrdom is Unriddled (1750). An Online Electronic Text Edition." (1750). Electronic Texts in American Studies, 44. Preface. digitalcommons. unl.edu/etas/44.

---."no rational hope of redress...." Mayhew, Jonathan A.M., D.D., 1750.

---."to preserve the nation from slavery...." Mayhew, Jonathan A.M., D.D., 150.

"...the malice of men in power has less scope." Gordon, Thomas, qtd. in Maier, Pauline. *From Resistance to Revolution: Colonial Radicals and the Development of American Opposition to Britain, 1765–1776,* p.30, 1991, 1972. New York: W.W. Norton & Co.

Chapter 8. November 11, 1765. Chewing on the Stamp Act

"First man that either distributes or makes use of Stamped Paper...." Engelman, F. L. "Cadwallader Colden and the New York Stamp Act Riots." *The William and Mary Quarterly,* vol. 10, no. 4, 1953, p. 560–578. *JSTOR,* jstor.org/stable/1923595.

"*Whereas the just Rights of His Majesty's Subjects of this Province, denied to them from the British Constitution....*" Transcription from "Resolutions from Massachusetts," Boston Gazette, November 4, 1765. *Early American Imprints,* Boston Public Library. From NewsBank, Inc. and the American Antiquarian Society. All Rights Reserved.

Chapter 9. December 17, 1765. Under the Liberty Tree: Andrew Oliver Forced to Resign

"The True-born Sons of Liberty, are desired to meet under LIBERTY-TREE...." Transcription from Broadside, "Sons of Liberty Meet Under Liberty Tree," 1768, *Early American Imprints,* Boston Public Library. From NewsBank, Inc. and the American Antiquarian Society. All Rights Reserved.

Chapter 10. May 19, 1766. Stamp Act Celebration

"Our FAITH approved, our LIBERTY Restor'd...." "The Obelisk." "A view of the obelisk erected under Liberty-tree in Boston on the rejoicings for the repeal of the ---- Stamp Act, 1766," Prints & Photographs Online Catalog, *Library of Congress Prints and Photographs Division,* Washington, D.C., Library of Congress Online Images, loc.gov/pictures/resource/ppmsca.05479/.

Chapter 11. October 28, 1767. Merchants' Agreement, Faneuil Hall

"the King's majesty...with...parliament assembled...." "Great Britain: Parliament—The Declaratory Act; March 18, 1766," *The Avalon Project: Documents in Law, History and Diplomacy,* Yale Law School, Lillian Goldman Law Library, 2008, avalon.law.yale.edu/18th_century/declaratory_act_1766.asp.

"...the clandestine running of goods in the colonies and plantations..." "Great Britain: Parliament—The Townshend Act, November 20, 1767," *The Avalon Project: Documents in Law, History and Diplomacy,* Yale Law School, Lillian Goldman Law Library, 2008, avalon.law.yale.edu/18th_century/townsend_act_1767.asp.

"Join or Die." Franklin, Benjamin, 1706-1790, [1754 May 9] 1 print : woodcut. Benjamin Franklin's warning to the British colonies in America, "join or die," exhorting them to unite against the French and the Natives, shows a segmented snake. Prints & Photographs Online Catalog, *Library of Congress Prints and Photographs Division,* Washington, D.C., Library of Congress Online Images, hdl.loc.gov/loc.pnp/cph.3a12149.

Chapter 12. October 1, 1768. Troops Come to Boston

"*Deponite libros.*" Shipton, Clifford K. *Sibley's Harvard Graduates, Vol. VIII, 1726–1730. Biographical Sketches of those who Attended Harvard College in the Classes 1726–1730,* Massachusetts Historical Society, 1951, p. 445. HathiTrust Digital Library, Permalink: hdl.handle.net/2027/uc1.31970025342293.

Chapter 14. November 18, 1769. Non-Importation: Tea, Glass

"Throw aside your Bohea and your Green Hyson Tea..." The Boston Post Boy. Address to the Ladies, Verse from page 3 of *The Boston Post-Boy & Advertiser*, Number 535, 16 November 1767, *The Coming of the American Revolution*. Massachusetts Historical Society, masshist.org/database/viewer.php?old=1&item_id=413.

Chapter 16. Feb. 26, 1770. Burial of Christopher Seider

"Thou shalt take no satisfaction for the life...." "The Remains of young Snider, the unfortunate Boy who was barbarously Murdered the 22d of February last..." Article from page 2 of *The Boston-Gazette, and Country Journal*, Number 778, 5 March 1770, *The Coming of the American Revolution*. Massachusetts Historical Society, masshist.org/revolution/doc-viewer.php?old=1&mode=nav&item_id=349.

---."Though Hand join in Hand, the Wicked...." *The Boston-Gazette, and Country Journal*, 5 March 1770, p. 2.

---."*Innocentia Nusquam tuta.*" *The Boston-Gazette, and Country Journal*, 5 March 1770, p. 2.

---."*Latet Anguis in Herba.*" *The Boston-Gazette, and Country Journal*, 5 March 1770, p. 2.

Chapter 17. March 12, 1770. The Boston Massacre

"The Town of Boston affords a recent and melancholy demonstration..." "Yes, by God, root and branch." *The Boston Gazette*, March 12, 1770. York, Neil L. *The Boston Massacre: A History with Documents*. New York: Routledge, 2010. p. 88–89.

"Permit me through the channel of your paper...." "Boston-Goal (Jail), Monday, 12th March, 1770, Messeurs Edes & Gill, Permit me thro' the Channel of your Paper...." *Early American Imprints*, Boston Public Library. From NewsBank, Inc. and the American Antiquarian Society. All Rights Reserved.

Chapter 18. Boston Discusses the Massacre: A Short Narrative

"While the town was surrounded by a considerable number of his Majesty's ships of war…." York, Neil L. *The Boston Massacre: A History with Documents.* New York: Routledge, 2010, p. 132.

---."Thus were we, in aggravation of our other embarrassments…." York, Neil L. *The Boston Massacre: A History with Documents.* New York: Routledge, 2010, p. 132.

---."… *keeping a standing army within the kingdom in time of peace….*" York, Neil L. *The Boston Massacre: A History with Documents,* p. 132.

---."*Benjamin Frizell, on the evening of the 5th of March….*" York, Neil L. *The Boston Massacre: A History with Documents,* p. 132.

---."*Daniel Calfe declares, that on Saturday evening the 3d of March….*" York, Neil L. *The Boston Massacre: A History with Documents,* p. 137.

Chapter 20. October 24, 1770. Boston Massacre Trial Begins: Captain Preston

"His Majesty's Superior Court of Judicature begun and held at Boston within and for the County of Suffolk…." *Crispus Attucks.* 1 Oct. 2012, crispusattucks.org

Trial participant statements shortened and paraphrased from "A Short Narrative," York, Neil L. *The Boston Massacre: A History with Documents.* New York: Routledge, 2010. pp. 145–157, 176–186.

Trial participant statements, from Hinkley, Cunningham, Woodall, Hill, Whitehouse, shortened and paraphrased from *What Was the Boston Massacre?* Boston Massacre Historical Society, Boston, boston-massacre.net.

Chapter 21. November 27, 1770. Boston Massacre Trial: The Soldiers

Trial participant statements shortened and paraphrased from "A Short Narrative," York, Neil L. *The Boston Massacre: A History with Documents,* pp. 145–157, 176–186.

Chapter 23. April 2, 1771. Oration for the Boston Massacre

"Oration, 1771, James Lovell," "An Oration Delivered April 2nd, 1771. Boston, Edes & Gill, 1771." *Early American Imprints,* Courtesy of the Harvard University Archives. From NewsBank, Inc. and the American Antiquarian Society. All Rights Reserved.

---."The horrid bloody scene...." "Oration, 1771, James Lovell," p. 6.

---."...the pious will adore the conduct of that being...." Lovell, James. "Oration, 1771, James Lovell," p. 6.

---. "Our fathers left their native land, risked all the dangers of the sea...." "Oration, 1771, James Lovell," p. 7.

---."We have seen and felt the ill effects of placing standing forces in the midst of populous communities," "Oration, 1771, James Lovell," p. 7.

---."One article of the Bill of Rights is that the raising or keeping a standing army...." "Oration, 1771, James Lovell," p. 8

---."England has a right to exercise every power over us...." "Oration, 1771, James Lovell," p. 12.

---."We are rebels against Parliament—we adore the King." "Oration, 1771, James Lovell," p. 11.

---."...not only illegal in itself, but a down-right usurpation of his prerogative as King of America." "Oration, 1771, James Lovell," p. 16.

---."The design of this ceremony was decent, wise, and honorable." "Oration, 1771, James Lovell," p. 12.

---."May the all wise and beneficent Ruler of the Universe preserve our lives and health...." "Oration, 1771, James Lovell," p. 19.

Chapter 24. December 17, 1773. Boston Tea Party

"Salt Water would make as good...." Allison, Robert J. *The Boston Tea Party.* Commonwealth Editions, 2007, Google eBook, p. 28.

Chapter 26. April 17, 1775. Rising Tensions in the Schoolroom

"impossible to beat the notion of Liberty out of the people, as it was rooted in them from their childhood." Crawford, Mary Caroline. *Old Boston*

Days & Ways, From the Dawn of the Revolution Until the Town Became a City. Little, Brown & Co., 1910, Google eBook, p. 98.

"May this Hall be ever sacred to the interests of Truth...." Stark, James Henry. *Stark's Antiqve Views of Ye Towne of Boston.* Boston, 1901, Google eBook, p. 108.

Chapter 27. April 19, 1775. War Begins: *Deponite Libros*

"War's Begun and School's Done:" *Deponite Libros.* Shipton, Clifford K. *Sibley's Harvard Graduates, Vol. VIII, 1726–1730. Biographical Sketches of those who Attended Harvard College in the Classes 1726 –1730,* Massachusetts Historical Society, 1951, p. 445.

"Father and I went down to camp, Along with Captain Gooding...." "Yanke Doodle." New York, New York, Charles Magnus Hand-colored Song Sheets, hc00037b, Rare Book and Special Collections Division, *Library of Congress, Performing Arts Encyclopedia,* memory.loc.gov/diglib/ihas/loc.rbc.hc.00037b.

Chapter 35. June 26, 1775. Brother Benjamin

"Our conductor, he got broke For his conduct, sure, sir...." Loring, James Spear. *The Hundred Boston Orators. From 1750–1852.* John P. Jewett and Co., 1852, Google eBook, p. 31–32.

Chapter 40. August 23, 1775. Provost Prison: The Second Month

"And now, Dear Sir, as to the most important Point...." Letter to Oliver Wendell. Upham, William P. 1836–1905. *Letters Written At the Time of the Occupation of Boston by the British, 1775–6.* Salem, Mass: Salem Press, 1876, Hathi-Trust, p. 189, catalog.hathitrust.org/Record/000581754/Home.

"Mrs. Leach has the General's permission to visit her husband...." Letter from General Gage to Mrs. John Leach. *A Journal kept by John Leach, During his Confinement by the British, in Boston Gaol, in 1775,* Boston, 1865, p. 258, Reprinted from the New England Historical

and Genealogical Register, 1865, Collection of Massachusetts Historical Society.

Chapter 41. October 4, 1775. Provost Prison: Third Month

"*In Council, August 23, 1775. The Committee are of opinion....*" Samuel Adams, Massachusetts House of Representatives, 23 Aug. 1775. *Massachusetts Archives Acts and Resolves,* Report from the Governor's Council, Journals of the House of Representatives, August 24, 1775. *American Archives,* Northern Illinois University Libraries, Digital Collections and Collaborative Projects, amarch.lib.niu.edu/islandora/object/niu-amarch%3A92105.

"*I charge you to reflect continually upon that one easy rule for your behavior....*" Letter from James Lovell to his sons, written in the Boston Stone Jail, September 21, 1775, the original in the collection of the author.

"As Alexander Pope said,'*Teach me to feel another's Woe, To hide the fault I see....*'" *A Journal kept by John Leach, During his Confinement by the British, in Boston Gaol, in 1775, Boston,* 1865, p. 263, Reprinted from the New England Historical and Genealogical Register, 1865, Collection of Massachusetts Historical Society.

Chapter 42. March 9, 1776. Provost Prison: Winter

Provost's Prison, Boston, November 19, 1775. MAY IT PLEASE YOUR EXCELLENCY: Letter to General Washington from James Lovell. "To George Washington from James Lovell, 19 November 1775," *Founders Online, National Archives,* last modified July 12, 2016. founders.archives.gov/documents/Washington/03-02-02-0368. [Original source: *The Papers of George Washington,* Revolutionary War Series, vol. 2, *16 September 1775–31 December 1775,* ed. Philander D. Chase. Charlottesville: University Press of Virginia, 1987, p. 400–402.]

Boston Prison, December 6, 1775. SIR: I address your Excellency.... James Lovell to George Washington, December 6, 1775. *Peter Force's American Archives—*Fourth Series, Vol. 4 (Vol. 4 of 9), p. 158. The

Internet Archive, archive.org/stream/AmericanArchives-Fourth SeriesVolume4peterForce/AaSeries4VolumeIv#page/n157/mode/2up.

"The wantonness of the exertions of military power against me...." Letter to Oliver Wendell, Dec. 9, 1775" Letter to Oliver Wendell. Upham, William P. 1836–1905. *Letters Written At the Time of the Occupation of Boston by the British, 1775–6.* Salem, Mass.: Salem Press, 1876, Hathi-Trust, p. 201, catalog.hathitrust.org/Record/000581754/Home.

Boston, February 2, 1776. SIR: In answer to your letter of the 30th ultimo.... Letter from General Howe to George Washington. *George Washington Papers, Series 4, General Correspondence: William Howe to George Washington, February 2, 1776.* Manuscript/Mixed Material, The Library of Congress, loc.gov/item/mgw444447/.

Chapter 46. August 5, 1776. New Arrivals in Halifax

"In the name of the Great Jehovah, and the Continental Congress." Allen, Ethan. *Narrative of Col. Ethan Allen's Captivity, Written by Himself.* 4th Edition, Chauncey Goodrich, 1846, *p. 14–15.* Google eBook, play. google.com/books/reader?printsec=frontcover&outpu....

Chapter 47. August 6, 1776. Unexpected Help in Jail

When in the Course of human events.... "The Declaration of Independence," *Primary Documents in American History*, Library of Congress, loc.gov/ rr/program/bib/ourdocs/DeclarInd.html.

Chapter 49. September 30, 1776. Scurvy, Fleas, and Letters in Jail

"The *treatment of prisoners here is not only scandalous....*" Letter to the Selectmen of Boston criticizing harsh treatment of American prisoners at Halifax [manuscript], Lovell, James, 1737–1814; Boston (Mass.). Selectmen; Boston Public Library, American Revolutionary War Manuscripts Collection, 14 Aug. 1776, The Internet Archive.

Note: The date of this letter is August 14, 1776; I have taken the liberty of putting it in a chapter dated September 30, 1776.

"*A parent and head of a large family in Boston....*" James Lovell writing while in Boston Jail. [MS Am811.1.] Houghton Library, Harvard University. (68) [Lovell, James, 1737–1814] [Account of imprisonment by the British] A.MS. (unsigned); [n.p., 1776]. 1s.(4p.) in 1 folder.

---. "*In August I even expressed...*" Houghton Library, Harvard University. (68)

---. "*Tis not as a rebel that I am here.*" Houghton Library, Harvard University. (68)

---. "*I had broken no law civil....*" Houghton Library, Harvard University. (68)

Chapter 50. November 5, 1776. Freedom: Going Home

"*We hold these truths to be self-evident....*" "The Declaration of Independence," *Primary Documents in American History*, Library of Congress, loc.gov/rr/program/bib/ourdocs/DeclarInd.html.

"*I left Captain Francis Proctor, your brother....*" Letter to Thomas Proctor, brother of Francis Proctor, from James Lovell, Nov 5, 1776. *Publications of the Colonial Society of Massachusetts, Volume 6*, p. 75, Google eBook.

Chapter 51. January 8, 1777. A Hero's Welcome

"*Torn from a world of tyrants, beneath this western sky....*" Warren, Joseph, 1741–1745, "Free America." *Bartleby.com, Great Books Online.* Stedman and Hutchinson, comps. *A Library of American Literature: An Anthology in Eleven Volumes. 1891. Vol. III: Literature of the Revolutionary Period, 1765–1787,* bartleby.com/400/poem/466.html.

Chapter 52. January 8, 1777. Off to Congress

"*After maturely deliberating the consequences of my public and private relations....*" Letter from James Lovell to Congress, Dec. 24, 1776. *American Archives: Consisting of a Collection of Authentick Records, State Papers, Debates, and Letters and Other Notices of Publick Affairs, the Whole Forming a Documentary History of the Origin and Progress of the North American Colonies; of the Causes and Accomplishment of the American Revolution; and of the Constitution of Government for the United States, to the Final Ratification Thereof.* "Correspondence, Proceedings, etc., December, 1776," p. 1412, Google eBook.

Afterword: Key Players

James Lovell: "A Man of Spirit, Fortitude, and Patience...." Gelles, Edith Belle. *Portia: The World of Abigail Adams*, Indiana University Press, 1992, Google eBook, p. 187.

James Lovell: "Father of American Cryptanalysis." "A Look Back...Intelligence and the Committee of Secret Correspondence." News and Information, Central Intelligence Agency. Featured Story Archive, 27 Oct. 2011, Accessed 1 March 2017, cia.gov/news-information/featured-story-archive/2011-featured-story-archive/intelligence-and-the-committee-of-secret-correspondence.html.

John Lovell: "List of Persons who removed from Boston...." *Carleton's Loyalist Index: A Select Index to Names of Loyalists and their Associates Contained in the British Headquarters Papers, New York City 1774–1783, The Carleton Papers.* Sir Guy Carleton Branch, UELAC, p. 2006–2008 of 2441, uelac.org/Carletonuel/kingname.htm.

Abigail Lovell: "for her great and unselfish attention...." and list of items in will. Microfilm 19412, Halifax County Court of Probate, Estate File L77, Nova Scotia Archives.

IMAGES

Chapter 1. August 4, 1752. The Boston Latin School

"First School House on South Side of School Street." Boston Latin School (Mass.), and Henry Fitch Jenks. *Catalogue of the Boston Public Latin School, Established In 1635: With an Historical Sketch.* Boston: Boston Latin School Association, 1886. HathiTrust Digital Library, unnumbered page before 89, babel.hathitrust.org.

Chapter 3. July 9, 1760. Wedding Plans

Lovell, James. "A Funeral Oration." From first page of James Lovell's *Oration for Tutor Flynt, 1760.* Courtesy of Harvard University Archives. 2 April 2012.

Chapter 5. August 10, 1765. The Argument Heats Up

"John Lovell (1710--1778)." Nathaniel Smibert. Harvard University Portrait Collection, H46. Imaging Department © President and Fellows of Harvard College.

Chapter 6. August 14, 1765. Burned in Effigy: Andrew Oliver, Stamp Commissioner

"This is the place to affix the stamp." Bradford, William. 24 October 1765. Woodcut. Prints & Photographs Online Catalog, *Library of Congress Prints and Photographs Division*, Washington, D.C., Library of Congress Online Images, hdl.loc.gov/loc.pnp/cph.3a52298.

Chapter 8. November 11, 1765. Chewing on the Stamp Act

"Resolutions from Massachusetts." *Boston Gazette,* 4 November 1765. *Early American Imprints*, Boston Public Library, 29 March 2012. From NewsBank, Inc. and the American Antiquarian Society. All Rights Reserved.

Chapter 10. May 19, 1766. Stamp Act Celebration

"Glorious News." From the *London Gazette*, March 18, 1766. *Early American Imprints*, Courtesy of the Harvard Archives, 3 April 2012. From NewsBank, Inc. and the American Antiquarian Society. All Rights Reserved.

A view of the obelisk erected under Liberty-tree in Boston on the rejoicings for the repeal of the ---- Stamp Act 1766." Revere, Paul. Boston. Prints & Photographs Online Catalog, *Library of Congress Prints and*

Photographs Division, Washington, D.C., Library of Congress Online Images, loc.gov/pictures/item/2003690787/.

Chapter 11. October 28, 1767. Merchants' Agreement, Faneuil Hall

"Join or Die." Franklin, Benjamin. Woodcut, 9 May 1754, Prints & Photographs Online Catalog, *Library of Congress Prints and Photographs Division*, Washington, D.C., Library of Congress Online Images, www.loc.gov/pictures/item/2002695523/.

Chapter 12. October 1, 1768. Troops Come to Boston

The Miriam and Ira D. Wallach Division of Art, Prints and Photographs: Print Collection, The New York Public Library. "A view of part of the town of Boston in New England and Brittish [sic] ships of war landing their troops 1768." *The New York Public Library Digital Collections.* 1778–1890, digitalcollections.nypl.org/items/510d47da-2dd4-a3d9-e040-e00a18064a99.

Chapter 13. October 2, 1768. Non-Importation: The Shop of Abigail Whitney

"The True Sons of Liberty." Broadside, Boston, 1768, *Early American Imprints*, Boston Public Library, 29 March 2012. From NewsBank, Inc. and the American Antiquarian Society. All Rights Reserved.
"Imported from London by Abigail Whitney." *Supplement to the Massachusetts Gazette*, 24 March 1768, *Early American Imprints*, Boston Public Library, 29 March 2012. From NewsBank, Inc. and the American Antiquarian Society. All Rights Reserved.

Chapter 17. March 12, 1770. The Boston Massacre

Revere, Paul, Engraver. "Four coffins of men killed in the Boston Massacre." *Boston Gazette*, 12 March 1770, *Early American Imprints*, Boston Public Library, 29 March 2012. From NewsBank, Inc. and the American Antiquarian Society. All Rights Reserved.

"Permit Me Through the Channel of Your Paper." *Supplement to the Boston Gazette*, 12 March 1770, *Early American Imprints*, Boston Public Library, 29 March 2012. From NewsBank, Inc. and the American Antiquarian Society. All Rights Reserved.

Chapter 19. June 30 1770. Spinning and Tea

"Boston, June 8: At a Meeting of the Merchants." *The Massachusetts Gazette and Boston Weekly*, 28 June 1770, *Early American Imprints*, Boston Public Library, 29 March 2012. From NewsBank, Inc., and the American Antiquarian Society. All Rights Reserved.

Chapter 20. October 24, 1770. Boston Massacre Trial Begins: Captain Preston

The Miriam and Ira D. Wallach Division of Art, Prints and Photographs: Picture Collection, The New York Public Library. "The bloody massacre perpetrated in King Street, Boston on March 5th, 1770 by a party of the 29th Regt.," *The New York Public Library Digital Collections*, digitalcollections.nypl.org/items/510d47e0-f4d5-a3d9-e040-e00a18064a99.

Chapter 24. December 17, 1773. Boston Tea Party

"Boston, December 1, 1773, Committee of Correspondence." Boston Tea Committee Correspondence, Broadside, 1 December 1773, *Early American Imprints*, Courtesy of the Harvard University Archives, 2 April 2012. From NewsBank, Inc. and the American Antiquarian Society. All Rights Reserved.

Chapter 25. January 25, 1774. The Tar and Feathering of Malcolm

"The Bostons paying the excise-man or tarring & feathering." Johnston, David Claypoole, 1799–1865, lithographer. Boston: Pendleton, 1830, Retrieved from the Library of Congress, 2 February 2020, loc.gov/pictures/item/2006691557/.

Chapter 28. April 20, 1775. What Happened at Lexington and Concord

The Miriam and Ira D. Wallach Division of Art, Prints and Photographs: Photography Collection, The New York Public Library. "Battle of Lexington (painting), Lexington, Mass." *The New York Public Library Digital Collections*, 1898–193, digitalcollections.nypl.org/items/510d47d9-a440-a3d9-e040-e00a18064a99.

Chapter 32. June 14, 1775. A Message

Burgoyne, John, and Robert Sayer And John Bennett. "A Plan of the battle, on Bunkers Hill fought on the 17th of June." London, Printed for R. Sayer & J. Bennett, 1775. Map. Prints & Photographs Online Catalog, *Library of Congress Prints and Photographs Division*, Washington, D.C., Library of Congress Online Images. Lower portion, "The following description of the Action near Boston, on the 17th of June, is taken from a Letter written by General Burgoyne to his nephew, Lord Stanley," cut out, loc.gov/item/gm71002452/.

Chapter 33. June 17, 1775. Bunker Hill

The Miriam and Ira D. Wallach Division of Art, Prints and Photographs: Print Collection, The New York Public Library. "Battle of Bunker's Hill." *The New York Public Library Digital Collections*, digitalcollections.nypl.org/items/510d47da-2f01-a3d9-e040-e00a18064a99.

Chapter 38. July 2, 1775. Provost Prison, Boston

"Master Lovell taken up and put in jail." Virginia Gazette. 11 August 1775, extract of a letter from Cambridge, July 12. Permission granted by the Omohundro Institute of Early American History and Culture, Request ID 1088.

Chapter 49. September 30, 1776. Scurvy, Fleas, and Letters in Jail

"A Parent and Head of a Large Family." Excerpt from letter. [MS Am811.1.] Houghton Library, Harvard University. (68) [Lovell , James , 1737– 1814] [Account of imprisonment by the British] A.MS. (unsigned); [n.p., 1776]. 1s.(4p.) in 1 folder.

Chapter 50. November 5, 1776. Freedom: Going Home

"Sailing from Halifax to N. York." Spencer Collection, The New York Public Library. "12th June 1776. Sailing from Halifax to N. York." *The New York Public Library Digital Collections*, 1776, digitalcollections. nypl.org/items/be0f6d75-d1e1-1529-e040-e00a18065909.

"A map of the provinces of New-York and New-Yersey, with a part of Pennsylvania and the Province of Quebec." Sauthier, Claude Joseph, and Matthäus Albrecht Lotter, *A map of the provinces of New-York and New-Yersey, with a part of Pennsylvania and the Province of Quebec*, Augsburg, 1777, Retrieved from the Library of Congress, loc.gov/ item/74692644/.

Afterword.

Page from *Loring Family Journal*, by James Lovell Loring and Emma Gephart Loring, 1892, hand copied circa 1978 by Frances Loring Coffin. Photograph by Jean O'Connor.

Materials and images used or cited are either in the public domain or else specific permission has been requested and received for their use. In the case of materials and images in the public domain institutions providing them can neither offer nor deny permission for their use. Every effort has been made to ascertain correct and lawful use of materials and images.

Thinking / Discussion Questions

Use these Thinking and Discussion questions to explore further the ideas presented in *The Remarkable Cause: A Novel of James Lovell and the Crucible of the Revolution*. At the author's website, jeanoconnor.com, find a **Study Guide**, including questions, suggestions for further research, writing ideas, images, and sites for exploration and primary source research on the era before and during the Revolutionary War, as well as contact information.

1. What factors prompted those first shots in the conflict that becomes the Revolutionary War? What did you think were the factors before reading *The Remarkable Cause*? After?

2. Like young James before he leaves for Harvard, have you ever wondered about changes, difficulties in society, but had no one to talk about them with?

3. America is a "melting pot," a blend of peoples and cultures. Just as Mary knew of Scottish traditions and practices from her Scottish parents, does your family treasure any unique traditions from your heritage? Does your community?

4. (After Chapter 12) James has a number of conversations with his father about taxation. What are Master Lovell's reasons to support the British policy on taxation? What do you think of his reasons?

5. (After Chapter 15) Consider the sit-down strikes of the Civil Rights movement of the 1960s. Consider marches and other forms of protest held today, both in the United States and in other countries throughout the world. How are these similar to some of the actions of protest in Boston in the years prior to the American Revolution? How are they different?

6. (After Chapter 23) Have you ever had to defend your right to participate in something others disagreed with? How did you handle it?

7. (After Chapter 25) What are some of the clashes in *The Remarkable Cause* between authority and society? Would you characterize these as peaceful or violent?

8. Is violence justified when peaceful actions do not achieve the desired results?

9. In *The Remarkable Cause*, newspapers create vital communication in society. How important is a free press to a free society?

10. Mary Middleton Lovell typifies in many ways Revolutionary War-era women. What are some of those ways? How is she different from many women of today? How is she like women today?

11. What would have happened if those in Boston had not felt so strongly about their rights?

12. Have you ever had a serious conflict with someone you love? How do you think James is handling his differences with his father?

13. Is it possible to peacefully co-exist with someone with whom you completely disagree? Explain.

14. Would the ways James carries on his relationship with his father work for you in a relationship with someone with whom you disagree? Explain.

15. *The Remarkable Cause: A Novel of James Lovell and the Crucible of the Revolution* is a story written based on extensive primary source research. The author identified questions about James Lovell and the world of pre-Revolutionary Boston after reading her grandmother's journal. Do you have a story you would like to tell, or a nagging question you would resolve through inquiry or research? Explain.

About the Author

Photo by Audrey's Fine Portrait Studio

Growing up in New England, Jean C. O'Connor developed a fascination with the American history evident in so many landmarks there. Her grandmother's house in Andover, Massachusetts, has a historic plaque by the front door; the Marquis de Lafayette made a speech from its steps when he came to visit the new United States following the Revolutionary War. Her enjoyment of history as well as literature led to a teaching career of thirty-seven years in Montana, particularly in Helena, the capital. She is passionate about meaningful learning experiences for students, and about working with teachers. Her work with the state teachers' association led to her receiving the Montana Association of Teachers of English Language Arts Distinguished Educator Award. As an educator, she received the NCTE High School Teacher of Excellence Award 2018, one of only fourteen teachers in the country. A few lines in her grandmother's journal inspired her interest in the story that forms the basis for *The Remarkable Cause: A Novel of James Lovell and the Crucible of the Revolution.*